THE AMBITIOUS M̶ ̶ ̶AME
BON̶ ̶

THE AMBITIOUS MADAME
BONAPARTE

a novel by

RUTH HULL
CHATLIEN

The Ambitious Madame Bonaparte © Copyright 2013, Ruth Hull Chatlien
All rights reserved. No part of this book may be used or reproduced in any manner whatsoever without written permission from the publisher, except in the case of brief quotations in critical articles and reviews. This book is a work of fiction. Names, characters, places and incidents either are products of the author's imagination or are used fictitiously. Any resemblance to actual events or locales or persons, living or dead, is entirely coincidental.
First Edition   ISBN 13: 978-1-937484-16-3
AMIKA PRESS   53 W Jackson BLVD 660 Chicago IL 60604   847 920 8084
info@amikapress.com   Available for purchase on amikapress.com
Edited by John Manos. Cover illustration by Ruth Hull Chatlien; framing by H. Marion Framing. Author photograph by Mike Krasowski. Designed & typeset by Sarah Koz. Set in Ronaldson, designed by Alexander Kay in 1884, digitized by Rebecca Alaccari & Patrick Griffin of Canada Type in 2006–2008. Thanks to Nathan Matteson.

 FOR MICHAEL

CONTENTS

THE FAMILIES

THE PATTERSONS

William Patterson
b. 11-1-1752

married Dorcas Spear
b. 9-15-1761

William Jr.
b. 3-21-1780

Robert
b. 7-16-1781

John
b. 3-24-1783

Elizabeth "Betsy"
b. 2-6-1785

Joseph
b. 12-6-1786

Edward
b. 7-14-1789

Augusta Sophia
b. 11-27-1791

Margaret
b. 3-20-1793

George
b. 8-19-1796

Caroline
b. 6-30-1798

Henry
b. 11-6-1800

Octavius
b. 8-28-1802

Mary Ann Jeromia
b. 10-3-1804

THE BONAPARTES

Carlo Bonaparte
b. 3-27?-1746/d. 2-24-1785

married Letizia Ramolino
b. 8-24-1750

Joseph
b. 1-7-1768

Napoleon
b. 8-15-1769

Lucien
b. 3-21-1775

Elisa
b. 1-3-1777

Louis
b. 9-2-1778

Pauline
b. 10-20-1780

Caroline
b. 3-25-1782

Jerome
b. 11-15-1784

THE AMBITIOUS MADAME
BONAPARTE

TAKING the footman's hand, eighty-five-year-old Betsy Bonaparte gingerly alighted from the carriage and readjusted her voluminous skirts. How she hated the current bustled fashions, so much more cumbersome than the slim empire gowns of her youth.

As Betsy labored up the marble steps of her son's mansion, her daughter-in-law opened the door. Susan May's round face was lined with worry, and her dark eyes were sorrowful. She stepped back to allow Betsy to enter and then bent to kiss the tiny older woman's cheek. "Mother Bonaparte." Her tone was respectful but cool, which was all that Betsy expected. Their mutual antipathy was too long established to be overcome by shared anxiety for the man who linked them.

"How is Bo?" Betsy asked, using the family nickname for her son.

"No better. The doctor is upstairs now, so I am afraid you will have to wait a bit to see him. Maisie can serve you tea in the parlor."

"No, thank you. I will wait in the Bonaparte room."

Irritation flashed across Susan May's face, but her demeanor remained polite. "As you prefer. I am sorry to desert you, but I must return upstairs."

Betsy slowly crossed the hall to the reception room that Bo had turned into a museum dedicated to his Bonaparte heritage. Around the room's perimeter, damask-upholstered chairs alternated with pedestals displaying marble busts of Bo's paternal grandparents, Carlo and Letizia Bonaparte, and his uncle Napoleon. Against the red brocade wallpaper hung family portraits, including three of a younger Betsy.

Gazing at her favorite portrait, painted when she was a nineteen-year-old newlywed, Betsy remembered how her husband held her hand the whole time she posed. How happy she had been just to sit with Jerome, a contentment that lit up her face and enabled the painter to capture a supremely joyful expression. In Betsy's opinion, it was the only portrait that had ever done justice to the classic beauty that once made her famous on two continents.

Betsy sighed for her lost youth. Then she crossed to the center table and picked up a miniature of her husband as a dashing young naval officer, wearing one of the braid-encrusted uniforms he had loved so much.

She closed her eyes and recalled standing at the railing of the French frigate *Didon* as it lay at anchor in New York's upper harbor. Betsy had stared past other ships toward the strait they would take to reach the Atlantic. Somewhere out there, British warships were patrolling with the intent of capturing her husband. It was vital for her and Jerome to travel to France to obtain the emperor's approval of their marriage, yet the prospect of waging a battle to break free terrified her. She and Jerome had already overcome so many obstacles just to wed.

As Betsy stood at the rail brooding, Jerome had called her name. She turned to see him approach her across the open deck. The sun picked out highlights in his curly black hair, and his face wore an expression of love and pride as he gazed at her. When he drew near, he said, "Captain Brouard wishes to see us. The pilot boat has returned from scouting the lower harbor."

She laid a hand on his arm. "Is it bad news?"

He glanced swiftly around to make sure no crew members were near and kissed the top of her head. "I don't know, *ma chérie,* but do not distress yourself. We will find a way to reach France, and when we arrive at Napoleon's court, he will be delighted to welcome such a charming sister-in-law. Trust me."

Betsy stared up into his dark eyes. "I do trust you, and I love you."

"Then all will be well. With you at my side, I can accomplish any-thing."

Betsy sighed again and wrenched herself free of the seductive whirl-pool of memory. She ran her finger across the surface of the miniature as though she were caressing her late husband's face. "Oh, Jerome. Our son is dying. How I wish I did not have to face this alone."

IGHT-YEAR-OLD Betsy Patterson glanced up from her sampler and watched her mother lean back against her banister-back wooden chair and close her eyes against the mid-July heat. Even though the sashes of the two narrow front windows were raised, not a whiff of breeze found its way into the drawing room. The sheer white curtains sagged, as limp as wilted lettuce.

Normally at this time of year, the family would have retreated to Springfield, their country estate 30 miles west of Baltimore, to escape the risk of summer fevers. This year, however, Betsy's father, William, thought it prudent to stay in town because of the Saint-Domingue crisis. For the past week, dozens of French merchant ships—mostly small double-masted schooners and brigs and single-masted sloops—had arrived in port carrying terrified people fleeing from the burning of Cape François. For years, the coffee and sugar plantations of the French colony had produced fabulous wealth, but now much of the island was a charred ruin because of a slave rebellion discussed only in whispers around children. Even though Betsy was not supposed to know about the troubles, she was proud because she had overheard that her father was one of the merchants donating funds to help the refugees.

Betsy believed it was only right that William Patterson should play a leading role in important events. After all, he was a friend of both

Thomas Jefferson and President George Washington. Patterson had emigrated from Ireland in 1766 when he was fourteen. Later, during the Revolutionary War, he earned the beginnings of his fortune by running cargoes of gunpowder and weapons past the British blockade and supplying them to a Continental army on the verge of collapse. Now he was one of the wealthiest men in America. Given his worldly success, Betsy thought, he should be one of Baltimore's most prominent citizens.

Betsy's mother Dorcas was sitting by the side of the hearth, and Betsy glanced at the fireplace with approval. It was one of the finest features in the pale yellow room and demonstrated her family's status without ostentation, something her father abhorred. The wooden mantel, painted dark teal, had fluted pilasters at each side and egg-and-dart molding running beneath the top shelf. Grey marble made up the surround. In the wingback chair on the opposite side of the fireplace, Betsy's father sat reading his Bible, as he did every Sunday afternoon after dinner.

Betsy felt clammy with perspiration beneath her many layers of clothing. Taking advantage of her parents' inattention, she stuck her needle into the linen stretched taut on the standing embroidery frame and committed the unladylike act of wiping her sweaty palms on her pink cotton skirt. She did not want to risk soiling her sampler. It displayed ten rows of text carefully embroidered in cross-stitch using red, blue, and green floss. The top six rows consisted of three different styles of alphabet, each running two lines. Beneath the alphabets ran a fancy border, and below that was a verse, which Betsy had chosen in defiance of the usual custom of using a pious motto:

We should manage fortune like our health,
enjoy it when it is good, be patient when it is bad,
and never resort to strong remedies but in an extremity.

The lines came from La Rochefoucauld's *Maxims,* a book of sayings about human nature published in France in the 1600s. Betsy, who was halfway through memorizing all 504 maxims, loved to astonish adult visitors to her Baltimore home by reeling off a string of the mottos.

Currently, she was stitching the last word of the verse. All that remained to be done after that was the bottom line, which would read "Elizabeth Spear Patterson, Her Own Work. Anno Domini 1793."

As Betsy bent to her embroidery again, two of her three older brothers bounded into the drawing room. Robert and John wore matching green cotton suits with long pants and loose jackets over open-collared, ruffled shirts. "Father, may we walk to the harbor?" twelve-year-old Robert asked. On the northern shore of the squarish tidal estuary of the Patapsco River their father had built his warehouse near the commercial wharves owned by their mother's relatives, the Spears, Buchanans, and Smiths. The wharves were only four blocks from the Patterson home on South Street.

Patterson gave his two sons an appraising stare. "What business do you have at the waterfront on the Lord's Day?"

"Josiah told us after church that more refugee ships are arriving."

Patterson closed his Bible and set it on the marble-topped table next to his chair. "Son, we have had more than 30 shiploads of refugees. What is so compelling about these?"

John's head drooped and he stepped backwards, but Robert said, "Sir, if we go on a Sunday, we will not get in the way of tradesmen."

To Betsy's surprise, their mother spoke up. "Let them get some air, Mr. Patterson. This is such a stifling day. Mayhap the breezes will be stirring by the water."

"Mayhap." Rising, Patterson smoothed down his coat. "I shall accompany them."

Betsy stuck her needle in the sampler and stood. "May I come too?"

"No. Stay with your mother. Right now the harbor is no place for you."

"But, sir, I have been there many times."

"Elizabeth, you heard me." After giving her a quelling look, he left the room with the boys.

With a flounce of her skirts, Betsy sat back on her stool but did not voice the complaint that screamed inside her head. Even so, Betsy's mother sighed.

"You misapprehend his motives. The planters and merchants fleeing Saint-Domingue have witnessed terrible cruelties. Your father is only protecting you."

"What kinds of things?" Betsy demanded, knowing that she could push her mother in ways her father would never tolerate.

"Child, you do not want to know." Dorcas rose from her chair and went upstairs to check on her younger children, napping in the second-floor nursery.

THE NEXT MORNING as Betsy dressed, she saw Robert pass the nursery door on his way down to breakfast from his third-floor bedroom. "Bobby, wait!"

She dropped the shoe she was holding and hurried to the doorway. Robert, just steps behind William Jr., mumbled to their oldest brother and turned back.

"What was it like?" she whispered eagerly.

"What was what like?" Idly, he grabbed one of the leading strings customarily attached to the shoulders of little girls' gowns and flipped it so it fell down Betsy's back.

She glanced behind her and saw Mammy Sue buttoning the back of Gussie's frock. "The refugee ship. Was it very horrible?"

"No, Goose. Just a shipload of miserable people who escaped the island with only the clothes they were wearing."

"Mother said cruel things are happening on Saint-Domingue."

Robert frowned. "Yes, but I did not see anything like that yesterday."

"But you know about it. I can tell." Betsy smiled in her most coaxing manner.

Robert shook his head and said quietly, "Father made me promise not to talk about it at home. He says that it is a man's duty to shield women from ugliness."

"Oh, fudge. You know that I have as stout a heart as you do. Johnny is the one who cries if we find a dead sparrow."

Bending down, he gazed at her with a serious expression that reminded her of their father. "Both the blacks and whites are killing each other in unspeakable ways. The things Josiah said kept me wakeful all night. Do not ask me anymore."

Betsy darted another glance at the family's enslaved wet nurse and whispered, "Such a revolt could not happen here, could it?"

Robert shook his head, but his eyes still looked anxious. "No, Goose. Now go put your shoe on and I will tie the lace."

ONE NIGHT IN November, the crying of the baby dragged Betsy from heavy sleep. "Mammy Sue?" she murmured and waited for a deep, calming voice to answer.

When no reply came, Betsy reluctantly opened her eyes. The chilly nursery was dark except for a glimmer of light around the edge of the door. That in itself was unusual. Betsy's father was always the last person in the household to retire, and he not only made sure the outside doors were locked but also checked that the nursery door was tightly shut. Betsy strained her ears for the sound of Mammy Sue in the hall, but she could not hear anything except her sister's bawling. Turning on her side and pulling the covers over her ears, Betsy felt surprised to find herself alone in the bed she shared with two-year-old Augusta Sophia. Then she remembered that Gussie was sleeping in their parents' room next door because she was sick with a sore throat and strangling cough.

Baby Margaret wailed on, her tone building to outrage at being ignored. After another minute of ineffectually trying to block the noise, Betsy sat up, causing her bed to creak. Her little brother Joe whispered from across the room, "Do something, Betsy. Make her stop."

With a sigh, Betsy flung off the bedclothes, stepped onto the cold wooden floor, and half hopped, half scurried to the cradle. As the oldest daughter, she was always the one who had to tend her siblings when Mother and Mammy Sue were too busy, and in a family of eight children, more problems occurred than the adults could handle: quarrels, scraped knees, runny noses, lost toys. Betsy envied her three older brothers, removed from the turmoil of the nursery—especially William Jr., who had a small bedroom of his own.

Someday when I am older, I will have a room to myself, she thought as she slipped a practiced hand into the cradle to see if Margaret had wet herself. Finding the diaper dry, Betsy decided to carry the baby to her own bed.

As she placed a protective palm under Margaret's head and carefully lifted the baby to her shoulder, she heard a muffled shriek followed by the sound of a door being flung open in the hall. Her mother shouted, "No! Leave her with me."

Pulled by dread and irresistible curiosity, Betsy crept to the nursery door and opened it a few inches more. Instinctively, she put her thumb in Margaret's mouth to give her something to suckle, and the baby quieted. Then Betsy looked into the hall.

Mammy Sue stood by the opposite wall holding a bundle wrapped in a sheet; she cradled it as if it were Margaret, while Betsy's mother wept and clutched the wet nurse's arm. Dorcas's beautiful face was pinched and white. Betsy had never seen her mother in such disarray; her wrapper was unfastened, and her light reddish hair hung tangled on her shoulders.

Patterson stepped from the master bedroom and gripped his wife's shoulders. "That is enough. You must not question God's will."

"God's will?" Dorcas pawed the bundle in Mammy Sue's arms. "How can it be God's will to take my pretty girl?"

Betsy gasped. Then she squeezed the increasingly heavy Margaret as she fixed her gaze on the sheet-wrapped figure. Her father said, "Do not commit blasphemy, Dorcas. You know that such ills are the result of man's sin, not from any evil in the divine nature."

Betsy's mother slumped and hid her face against his chest. Stroking his wife's hair, Patterson made a shushing sound. "Remember that our Lord said, 'Suffer the little children to come unto me.' Gussie is with Him now."

As he led Dorcas back into their room, he nodded at Mammy Sue. Betsy saw the slave begin to come her way, so she stepped back into the darkness of the nursery. She did not want the adults to know she had witnessed the scene.

For the next few months, Betsy found herself remembering Gussie's dimpled face at odd moments and wishing she could feel her sister's arms around her neck. She kept those feelings to herself, however, because her mother remained too sad to discuss Augusta Sophia's death. Gradually, as baby Margaret began to display her own personality, Betsy stopped thinking of the sister she had lost.

In late February, two weeks after Betsy's ninth birthday, a blizzard struck Baltimore. The sight of thick-falling snow outside the front windows proved to be too much for Betsy to resist, especially since her mother was talking to the housekeeper in the back building, which housed the kitchen, pantry, and servants' quarters. Betsy hurried into the front entryway, donned her cardinal-red winter cloak, pulled up the lined hood, and crept outside.

When her father first came to Baltimore as a wealthy trader in 1778, he built three-story, red brick houses side-by-side on South Street, one to serve as his residence and the other as his place of business. Each had a front building approximately thirty feet wide and fifty feet deep, connected by a passage to a narrower back building that was not visible from the street. Because of the way the façades were constructed, the two buildings looked like one very wide mansion with two center doors beneath a classical portico. The first floor was raised slightly above street level, so a stoop of five steps—made of the local white marble so characteristic of Baltimore—climbed to the entrance. Betsy crouched by the side of those steps, concealed from her brothers as they returned home from school. As she waited, she formed a snowball and packed it tightly.

Soon she heard the shouts of boys coming toward her. She lifted her head just enough to peer through the iron railing at the side of the stoop and saw Robert approaching the counting house next door.

Rushing from her hiding place, Betsy flung the snowball, which missed her brother widely. He spotted her and shouted, "You little minx!"

Betsy shrieked as an unexpected snowball hit her left ear. Her hood had fallen back, so icy snow slithered down her neck. She whirled in the direction of the missile and saw Johnny slip in the snow as he ran, while William Jr. stood yelling for them to stop.

All four children fell silent as their father opened the black-painted door of his counting house. "Boys! Come inside." Patterson stepped backwards. "You too, Betsy."

He led them into the large front room where his clerks sat on stools before high slant-top desks, and the dusty ledger books of years past lined the shelves above their heads. Patterson set the boys to doing their daily bookkeeping exercises under the supervision of his senior clerk. Then he motioned for Betsy to follow him into his private office, which was furnished with a glass-fronted bookcase and a wide Sheraton writing desk that had raised cubbyholes along either side edge. A pair of framed etchings of company ships hung above the plain brick fireplace.

After closing the door, Patterson stood before his desk and gazed down at his daughter in silence. Betsy felt miserable. Her cheeks grew hot beneath his severe stare, while her feet were cold and clammy because she had run into the snow wearing flimsy shoes.

After a long moment, he said, "You know that I do not approve of my children running wild in the streets. Especially you, Betsy. You are getting to be a young lady."

"Yes, Father. I am sorry."

Patterson walked behind his desk and, from a side drawer, took out the slate he used when he wanted to test Betsy in arithmetic. "Your aunt Nancy says you are making such good progress at multiplication that she has started you on simple percentages. Can you do a problem for me?"

Betsy bit her lip and nodded. She still felt unsure of her skill with percentages, but if she could do the problem correctly, perhaps her father would smile and forget her roughhousing.

He handed her the slate and a pencil. "Listen carefully. You invest a thousand dollars in a security that pays out an income of five percent per annum. How much money will you have after three years?"

As Betsy took the writing implements, her mind raced. The question seemed too easy; even without doing a calculation, she knew that five percent of a thousand would be $50. After three years, the investment would gain $150. What was the trick? Her father never set her such an obvious task, preferring to see if he could catch her in mistaken thinking.

Betsy shed her cloak and sat cross-legged on the wooden floor. Bending over the slate, she carefully did the multiplication for the first year. As she had suspected, the answer was $50. Dutifully, she added that amount to the original $1,000, and as she formed the last zero, she realized the flaw in her thinking. For the second year, she had to take five percent of the new total of $1,050, so the interest would be larger that year and still larger in the third.

She worked with mounting excitement, and after a few minutes, handed her father the slate with her careful calculations and a final total of $1,157.625. Betsy could not keep the triumphant grin off her face as he nodded his way through her figures. "This is almost correct," he said, raising his eyes from the slate.

Betsy's smile faded. "What did I do wrong?"

Patterson's expression softened, and he beckoned for her to lean against his arm. Gesturing to the slate, he said, "You did your calculations correctly. If the money remains invested in the security, the interest will grow each year as this shows. Where you failed was in listening carefully as I instructed. I said that the annuity was to be paid out. That means that you would receive an income of $50 each year, and the principle would hold steady at $1,000 no matter how long it was invested."

"Oh," she said in a small voice, crushed by disappointment that even though she had expected a trick, she failed to detect it.

Her father squeezed her shoulder. "Never mind, lass. You did better than Johnny. The first time I set this problem for him, he thought the investment would earn $50 every year even if it accumulated." Patterson laughed indulgently and put the slate and pencil back in his desk.

"You have an unusual head for figures for a girl, which may keep you from trouble one day. Life does not always turn out the way we plan, Betsy. Many a widow has ended in the poor house because she did not know the first thing about investments."

"Yes sir," Betsy said, but she frowned at the thought of someday being poor and alone. Surely that would never happen to her, whom everyone said was so pretty and clever.

Patterson removed his arm from her shoulder and opened a ledger book on his desk. "Go back home now like a good girl and help your mother."

OVER THE NEXT year and a half, Betsy worked hard at the lessons her mother and Aunt Nancy set her. Her parents gave her books for every birthday, so when she did not have to look after the younger children or do schoolwork, she curled up in the drawing room to read.

One Sunday in September 1795, her mother's older sister Margaret Smith and her family came for an afternoon visit. Ten-year-old Betsy sat on the double-chair-backed settee near the front windows with her older cousin Elizabeth, who was showing off her latest drawings. Betsy gazed at the pencil sketches with only partial attention because she was listening to the conversation between their mothers at the nearby drawing room table.

"Dorcas, you look unwell," Aunt Margaret said. "You are as white as my linen shift."

"I am quite all right."

Betsy saw her aunt glance toward her husband and brother-in-law, who sat on the teal damask sofa facing the fireplace at the center of the room. She lowered her voice. "Are you with child again?"

Instead of answering, Dorcas shook her head, and Betsy thought she saw tears in her eyes.

Biting her lip, Betsy murmured half-hearted words of approval about her cousin's artwork as she wondered why her mother was so pale and listless. Was she ill or still plagued with melancholy?

The arrival of the housekeeper, a thin, thirty-year-old widow named Mrs. Ford, cut short the women's conversation. After Mrs. Ford set down the tray with the tea service and departed, Dorcas picked up her English china teapot, formed in the classical style with a fluted barrel decorated with gilt edges and painted garlands. Betsy rose. "May I help you, Mother?"

Dorcas smiled and nodded at the cup she was filling. "Take this to your uncle."

Betsy carried the cup and saucer carefully as she made her way around the younger children playing on the floor. Then she stood before the sofa.

Uncle Smith and Betsy's father were deep in conversation, so Betsy waited before interrupting them. Standing there, she noticed how differently the two men dressed. Her father was wearing a dark brown broadcloth tailcoat cut in the new short-waisted fashion with matching breeches, a tan waistcoat, and white stockings, but instead of shoes, he wore comfortable red leather mules. His dark, unpowdered queue was pulled back plainly. Her uncle Samuel Smith—a Revolutionary War officer now serving in Congress—wore a powdered hairstyle with a top puff and side curls. His old-fashioned long blue frock coat had embossed brass buttons, his waistcoat was embroidered, and silver buckles ornamented his shoes.

Uncle Smith said, "I do not think the newspapers have caught wind of the Treaty of Greenville. I just received word of it this morning."

"I suppose more people than ever will be packing up for Ohio now that the war with the Indians is won."

"I hope they will. We need to end British influence in the Northwest Territory. I do not trust their intentions." Uncle Smith stretched out his legs and spotted Betsy. "Why, there is my pretty niece."

"Your tea, Uncle," she said, handing him the cup and saucer.

"And what have you been memorizing lately, child?"

"Parts of Edward Young's poem *Night Thoughts.*"

"Be damned if you are. Your aunt Margaret tried to make me read that when we were courting, but it was too long and does not even rhyme."

Betsy laughed at the thought of such a blunt man trying to plow through the meandering poem. "Procrastination is the thief of time," she intoned, quoting the most famous line.

"Impertinent chit," he burst out but then joined her gleeful laughter.

Glancing at her father, Betsy saw that he did not share their amusement. "I will get your tea, sir," she said before he could rebuke her for teasing her elders.

As she walked away, she heard Uncle Smith say something that made her slow her steps to listen. "You might consider putting Betsy in school. Have you heard of Madame Lacomb? She is an émigré who has opened a boarding school for girls right here on South Street. My sister, Mrs. Hollin, has enrolled her daughters. I believe the Caton girls will attend as well."

"The Catons?" Betsy's father asked. He sounded impressed that the Frenchwoman's students included the granddaughters of Charles Carroll, a signer of the Declaration of Independence and the only man in Maryland wealthier than he was. "Then I shall look into it."

To Betsy's delight, her father did enroll her in school. Madame Lacomb and her husband had been low-ranking nobles who fled to Saint-Domingue during the French Revolution. Monsieur Lacomb died not long afterward, and Madame Lacomb came to Baltimore with other refugees from the slave revolt of 1793. She moved into a small, blue wooden house that was as much a survivor of a different era as she was—it had been built in the 1750s and remained standing as more imposing brick townhomes replaced the wooden houses around it. It had two bedrooms upstairs and a parlor and a kitchen on the ground floor. Madame Lacomb had furnished the parlor as a classroom with straight-backed wooden chairs and a few plain tables. Under her tutelage, Betsy studied French, history, geography, composition, drawing, fine needlework—and dancing once a week, taught by a French émigré named Moreau whom Monsieur Lacomb had known in Paris.

One Friday afternoon in late autumn, after Monsieur Moreau had spent an hour berating the girls for their clumsiness and then departed following a torrent of French complaint to his countrywoman, Madame Lacomb directed the girls to replace the furniture that had been shoved against the walls. Then the schoolmistress rang the bell. Odette, the slave she had acquired during her brief stay in Saint-Domingue, carried in tea. As the tall West African set down the tray on a small mahogany table, her gaze settled on Betsy with an intensity that made the girl shiver. Then Odette left the room.

Sitting in the sole upholstered armchair, Madame Lacomb poured tea into pewter mugs and passed out slices of buttered bread to her students, who ranged in age from six to fifteen. Contrary to Uncle Smith's prediction, the Caton girls were not among them.

As the girls started to eat, Madame Lacomb poured her own tea into a china cup. *"Mes petites,* perhaps you are saying to yourselves that Monsieur Moreau is too harsh with you. You think that dancing has its place at parties but is not a serious accomplishment?"

Betsy raised her head in surprise because her father had made just such a complaint.

Pausing for effect, Madame Lacomb fingered the edge of the fichu covering her bosom. She had a thin face with sagging cheeks and dark, mournful eyes. "When I was at the court of France, everyone remarked on how beautifully Marie Antoinette walked. She had the graceful, elegant carriage of a goddess. Do you know how she learned to carry herself that way? By taking dancing lessons as a young girl in Austria."

Sarah, the oldest girl in school and one of the few who boarded there, asked, "Madame Lacomb, what was the queen like? Was she as bad a woman as people say?"

"No, no." Madame Lacomb raised a hand to readjust her cap. "She was very young when she went to France, younger than you are now, Sarah. She was foolish at times, as when she appointed a friend to be the royal governess for *les Enfants de France* rather than choosing a woman of high birth as was the custom." The teacher shrugged. "We French do not like to see our cherished traditions tossed aside, especially by a foreigner. The nobles whom she had snubbed spread malicious lies.

"And she liked to play at living the simple life by building a little farm and dressing *à la paysanne.* To spend money on such *frivolités* when the treasury is bankrupt and people want bread seemed like a mockery. By the time I escaped to Saint-Domingue in 1791, she was the most hated person in France."

"Did you ever see her?" Betsy asked. "Was she beautiful?"

"*Naturellement,* I saw her both at court and in the Queen's box at the opera. She was—" Madame shrugged again. "Not a classic beauty. Her face was long and her lower lip too fat. But she had a lovely complexion and radiant blue eyes. When she was in court dress, her silk skirts as wide as the sea and trimmed in expensive ribbon and lace, with her hair piled high on her head, she looked every inch the queen."

Betsy sighed, imagining a figure in gleaming blue satin but with reddish-brown hair like hers, dancing lightly across the parquet floor of Versailles. She thought such a life must be glorious and wondered why the French had done away with it. "Do you think France will ever have a king again?"

"*Mon dieu,* I do not know." The teacher shuddered. "After the violence waged by Robespierre and his minions, I think the people are tired of turmoil. No one seems to like the Directory, but they will endure it to keep the peace." She sighed, and then straightened her posture and clapped her hands. "Enough of this, girls. It is time for our geography lesson."

AFTER THE LAST class, Betsy walked out to the street with the Hollin girls. As they passed the building next to Madame Lacomb's small house, Betsy heard a sharp hiss from a figure standing in the shadowy arched passage that led to the back yard.

"Mademoiselle Betsy!" A heavily wrapped woman stepped into the open, and when she lowered the shawl from her head, Betsy saw that it was Odette, Madame Lacomb's slave.

As the other girls murmured in surprise, Betsy said, "Go on. I will see you next week."

"But Betsy!" Ann Hollin exclaimed, her voice tight with concern.

"Do not fret. Madame Lacomb must have sent her with a message."

The Hollin girls walked away, glancing back over their shoulders. Betsy took a step toward Odette. The African woman searched her face and then said in a low voice, "I have been having dreams of great import about you."

"Why would you dream about me?"

"They contain a message that I must give you."

A chill of suspense raced down Betsy's spine.

Odette stared at the space above Betsy's head as if an image floated there. "I saw you as a woman grown, in France or some other place across the sea. You wore a silk gown with a crown on your head, and when you entered a room full of people, they bowed like you were a princess."

Betsy caught her breath. "Me? How could I be a princess?"

"Child, that is the wrong question. Seek not how to be high and mighty, seek how to have wisdom."

"I don't understand."

Odette frowned. "I fear for you because I sense in you a hunger for high station, so I consulted the sacred palm nuts on your behalf. If you pursue the life you desire, it will come with great obstacles and a powerful enemy."

Betsy pressed her lips together and then, deciding that she was willing to face anything to become a princess, resolutely raised her head. "Is there more?"

Odette started to speak and then seemed to change her mind. "No."

"What is it? You saw something else."

"*Ça suffit.* You are still a child, and I have said enough." She pulled up her shawl and walked back to Madame Lacomb's house.

Betsy gazed after the woman without really seeing her. She was going to be a princess someday in a country far from Baltimore. Glancing

at the solid brick houses on South Street, she pictured a radically different scene: a gilt-trimmed carriage pulled by white horses rolled up
to a turreted chateau, and she stepped out wearing a beautiful purple
velvet cloak. Someday she would leave this boring town for such an
elegant life. She knew it.

After checking to make sure that no one was near, she said the
words *Princess Betsy* aloud to see how they sounded. Then she shook
her head. "No, I shall be the Princess Elizabeth." Betsy raised her
chin and drew back her shoulders to stand taller. *I will be royalty,* she
thought, *but I shall not be as foolish as Marie Antoinette. I shall not
lose my head.* Then she walked down the street trying to move as
gracefully as a queen.

II

B ETSY glanced through the drawing room window at the grey sky
and wondered if spring would ever arrive. The March morning
was chilly, and her impatience to break free of winter's grasp
was exceeded only by her desire to escape the drudgery of her never-
ending daily chores.

Beside Betsy on the teal damask sofa, her three-year-old sister Caroline struggled with chubby fingers to pull a calico dress off her doll—
a lumpy, stuffed cotton figure with yarn hair and embroidered features.
Before them, five-year-old George sat cross-legged on the rug in front of
the fire. He bent over a slate copying the alphabet from the colonial-
era hornbook their mother had used as a little girl.

Caroline tugged the fringe of Betsy's shawl. "Look." She held up her
doll to show that the skirt of the dress was tearing away from the bodice.

Betsy took the doll and examined the garment. The edges of the
fabric had not begun to fray, so she said, "I can mend this."

"Can you?" The little girl wore such a woebegone expression that
Betsy felt a surge of pleasure at being able to relieve her distress.

"Of course, I can, Caro." Betsy stroked her sister's golden, floss-
fine hair. "If you like, I will sew her something new too. I have some
scraps of material and lace that will make a lovely ball gown. Now
run upstairs and fetch my workbasket."

Before running from the room, Caroline hugged her oldest sister's neck, suddenly reminding Betsy of poor Gussie, dead and buried for more than a decade.

Betsy exhaled slowly to dispel the ache of that old loss, and then she checked on George's progress. He was not ready to show her his alphabet, so she opened her well-worn copy of La Rochefoucauld's *Maxims.* Knowing exactly which maxim would suit her mood, Betsy turned to number 41: "Those who apply themselves too closely to little things often become incapable of great things."

The observation pithily summarized Betsy's deepest fear. As the oldest daughter in a family of ten surviving children, she had as full a schedule of domestic duties as many a married woman, and she worried that her mind and talents were growing dull from such pursuits. Her father often reminded her that she was more fortunate than most young women because he had given her an education. Once Betsy left school a year ago, at age sixteen, however, he expected her to put aside intellectual interests and devote herself to women's duties: "Elizabeth, you have had more than enough schooling to run a household and teach your children to read and cipher."

Life offered more stimulation to her three older brothers, who all worked in their father's shipping business. Betsy envied their ability to go out and mingle with people daily while she spent hours trapped at home. She was far more sociable than William Jr., a better writer than Robert, and more skilled at arithmetic than John, yet her father denigrated her wish to employ her talents more productively. From childhood, Betsy had been allowed, even encouraged, to read widely, and now William Patterson regretted it, complaining that books like *A Vindication of the Rights of Woman* had given his daughter unsuitable ambitions.

To be fair, Betsy had to admit that her father held the whip hand over each of his children with equal severity—even her two oldest brothers, who were both over twenty-one. Patterson monitored all his children closely and required them to be home and in bed early each night unless they had an engagement he had previously approved.

Pressing her lips together to stifle a sigh, Betsy set aside the *Maxims* and glanced at her mother, who sat at the table near the front of the room. Although Dorcas was supposed to be working on her household accounts, she was staring through the mullioned windows that overlooked South Street. Her head drooped as she leaned her chin upon her palm. Strands of faded hair escaped her cap, soot stained her bodice, and the lace edging on the sleeve hung limply. All those details told Betsy that her mother was suffering from melancholy again, a condition that had plagued her since Gussie's death.

Her low spirits always seemed to worsen with pregnancy, and that morning at breakfast, Dorcas had confirmed Betsy's suspicion that she was expecting her twelfth child. Betsy said little about the news, not wanting to wound her beloved mother, yet she feared her determined silence had eloquently conveyed her disgust.

To make amends for that earlier coldness, Betsy said, "Is there any way I can help you?"

"What?" Dorcas turned, revealing a weary countenance. The skin below her eyes was shadowed purple. Betsy glanced at the gilt-framed portrait that hung over the fireplace, the one that showed Dorcas holding her as a one-year-old child. In that painting, both faces displayed a delicate roselike beauty. At age forty-one Dorcas was still a lovely woman, but to her daughter's eyes, her bloom seemed to be fading, not blossoming.

"I asked if I could help you with anything."

Her mother smoothed the bent corner of the page she was working on in her ledger. "Your father wants me to have these accounts ready for him by the time he comes home tonight, but I cannot make them balance."

"Allow me to look at them." Betsy walked to her mother's side and swiftly checked her figures. "Here is the problem. In this column, you forget to carry the tens."

"Oh, I see." Dorcas crossed out the mistake and wrote in the correct number so that it would be in her handwriting, not Betsy's. "I fear I shall never have your skill with numbers."

"You are overly tired. That is reason enough for the error." Betsy kissed her forehead and then returned to the sofa. Picking up her book again, she extracted a folded letter from its pages. It had come from her cousin Elizabeth Smith, but Betsy had little interest in rereading

Elizabeth's message. Instead, she skipped straight to the postscript added at the bottom by another cousin, Smith Nicholas. Smith had described in detail how he had been distracted by "ten thousand inexpressible sensations" simply from seeing Betsy's name on the address.

Betsy smiled with satisfaction that he had fallen under her spell, even though she did not intend to encourage him. Ever since receiving Odette's prophecy, she had believed she was destined for something greater than a life as a Maryland housewife. To achieve that aim, she needed to attract suitors. Sometimes she worried that her small stature—she was only four feet, eleven inches tall—might cause men to overlook her, but she consoled herself with the reflection that it was probably better to be too short than too tall like her unmarried aunt Nancy.

As Betsy pensively refolded the letter, Caroline rushed back into the room with Betsy's workbasket. Betsy threaded a needle and began to mend the doll's garment. Moments later, George rose and handed her his smudged slate.

Checking the alphabet he had copied, Betsy saw that his B, R, and S were reversed. She reached down to pick up the hornbook, abandoned on their father's prized Turkish carpet, which displayed magenta and blue flower sprays against a gold-beige ground. "Look, Georgie, can you see any differences between what you wrote and what is printed here?"

The little boy squirmed and twisted his neck as though he were wearing a too-tight collar. "No," he said without glancing at his work.

"You have these letters backwards." She pointed to them with the pencil. "I want you to wipe the slate and then write each of these three letters ten times."

"But you said I could play with my soldiers."

"I said you had to do your alphabet correctly first." Betsy handed him the slate, trying not to smile at his pout. "When you do, I will fetch you a piece of gingerbread."

As George settled to his task, Betsy finished stitching the short seam of the doll's dress. She was just knotting her thread when she heard the knocker rap on the front door. Too restless to wait for a servant, she jumped up. "I will answer it."

The visitor was her friend Henriette Pascault, the oldest daughter of the émigré Marquis de Poleon. Henriette, who was several years older than Betsy, had red-gold hair, a lightly freckled complexion, and a pretty heart-shaped face. Today she was wearing a scarlet pelisse and a yellow bonnet with a white lace veil. After the two young women exchanged greetings, Henriette said, "Papa allowed me to take the carriage so I could drive to the milliner's shop. Would you like to accompany me?"

Betsy bit her lip, glanced over her shoulder at the open doorway to the drawing room, and whispered, "I would love to go, but I cannot leave my mother. She is very low this afternoon."

"Perhaps she could come with us?"

As Betsy shook her head, her mother came out to the hall. "Hello, Henriette."

Henriette curtsied. "Madame Patterson. I came to see if Betsy could come with me to the milliner's shop."

"How kind. I am sure she would be delighted."

"But, Mother, I am still in the middle of George's lesson."

"Nonsense." Dorcas displayed the first smile of genuine pleasure that Betsy had seen from her in days. "I presume that he will not object to having his lesson cut short."

"Thank you." Betsy kissed her and inwardly resolved to bring back some ribbon and a silk flower to refresh the trimming on one of her mother's bonnets. Then she put on a hooded cape and gloves.

The two friends went outside and descended the marble steps to where the Pascault carriage waited. It was a handsome coach—cream with gilt swags framing the family crest painted on the door—a conveyance more appropriate to the noble status the marquis had held in pre-revolutionary France than to his current occupation as a Baltimore merchant.

As soon as the two young women were seated within, Henriette laughed. "Oh, I am so glad that you decided to accompany me. I have the most delicious news."

Betsy pushed back her hood. "What is it?"

"Do you remember Nathan Montgomery, the young Bostonian we met at Justice Chase's house last week? He was overheard to say that you were so lovely he could not look at anyone else once you entered the room."

"What a charming deceit."

Henriette arched one eyebrow. "You know very well it was no lie."

Betsy glanced instinctively toward the window to check her reflection, but it was impossible to see anything in the glass during daytime. It did not matter. She knew her appearance well enough. She had inherited her mother's Grecian nose, hazel eyes, and auburn hair, although Betsy's curls were darker than Dorcas's and her chin was rounded rather than pointed so that her face was an almost perfect oval. Betsy accepted that she was beautiful the way she accepted that she was female, as a simple fact of birth. For the past two years, she had been known throughout town as the Belle of Baltimore.

Turning back to Henriette, she waved a hand in the air and answered, "What good is it to be attractive if we never meet anyone but merchants' sons?"

"Is that what bothers you today? You begin to doubt your future?"

"How can I have a future in a city such as this? Baltimore has no culture to speak of. All anyone here cares about is making pots of money and raising hordes of obedient children. I feel that I am suffocating." Betsy removed her gloves and flung them on the royal blue velvet seat. Thinking of all the tantalizing stories Madame Lacomb had told during lessons, she exclaimed, "I wish I could go to Paris!"

"They say that Britain and Napoleon are on the verge of peace. Perhaps—"

Betsy rolled her eyes. "Oh, of course. I am *sure* my father would be delighted to send me to Europe on a pleasure trip."

Henriette patted her arm. "There are many French émigrés here in Baltimore. Perhaps you will meet someone dashing at my father's house."

"The Europeans I have met so far have all been your father's age, and I am not yet so desperate to escape as to marry a middle-aged widower." Betsy bit her lip. "So far, my suitors have been merchants' sons, planters' sons, and one tongue-tied schoolteacher. Marriage to any one of them would sentence me to a life like my mother's, bearing child after child until my mind is rusted from disuse."

The carriage halted before the shop. Henriette touched her hair to make sure it was in place and then handed Betsy back her gloves. "You do not need a score of suitors to fulfill the prophecy. Only the right man. Be patient, my friend. Your destiny will find you."

On August 28, 1802, Dorcas Patterson bore her eighth son and accordingly named him Octavius. She recovered slowly from his birth, and the melancholy to which she was prone deepened into pervasive gloom. Betsy tried to cheer her with unexpected cups of tea or little presents of fruit or marzipan from the market. Dorcas would smile gratefully at the gestures, but the improvement they produced in her spirits was ephemeral.

With a new infant in the family, Mammy Sue had less time for baby Henry, who had begun to walk that summer. Often, it fell to Betsy to make sure he did not tumble into a fireplace or down stairs. At the same time, Betsy began to teach Caroline the alphabet. The winsome child trailed her everywhere, prattling constantly, so Betsy had little time alone even though she finally had her own bedroom, the small front chamber next to her parents' room on the second floor.

One responsibility was taken off her hands that fall as George joined Edward and Joseph at school. Nine-year-old Margaret was going to Madame Lacomb's, where she showed promise as an artist and little interest in other subjects. In the evenings, Betsy had to badger her to read and do her needlework instead of drawing constantly.

Only social engagements relieved the tedium. During long afternoons of sewing and tending children, Betsy dreamed about the next party she would attend. Would it be the night she finally met the man who could offer her a way to escape her dull hometown and take her place among witty, intellectual people? Since women could not attend college and only lower-class women worked, she had little else to hope for but to marry well. In the meantime, she read as much as possible and pored over the newspapers for reports about fashion and culture in Europe.

As Betsy dreamed of making a brilliant match, her male relatives kept an anxious eye on foreign events. Two and a half years earlier,

Napoleon Bonaparte had overthrown the Directory, the corrupt government that succeeded the violent reign of Robespierre. A new executive of three consuls was established with Bonaparte as First Consul. At first, he concentrated on improving government and defeating Austria. Then, after having broken apart the Second Coalition that was arrayed against him, Bonaparte was finally able to force Britain to make peace in early 1802.

In response to Uncle Smith, who had brought that last bit of news, Betsy's father said, "I, for one, welcome that humiliation to our former colonial masters."

Uncle Smith shook his head. "Do not be so quick to applaud Bonaparte. Rumor is that he plans to create an American empire out of the Caribbean islands and the lands west of the Mississippi. And once he accomplishes that grand design, what will stop him from swallowing the United States as little more than a tasty sweet at the end of an enormous meal?"

"I admire Bonaparte!" Betsy exclaimed as she approached the sofa where the two men sat drinking tea. She handed each a plate of fruit-cake. "He is the only person who has managed to bring stability to France since the Revolution."

"Betsy, mind your manners and do not express opinions you are not qualified to hold."

"Yes, Father," she said with apparent meekness, but her cheeks burned from the sting of the reprimand.

In the months that followed, to Betsy's disappointment, events seemed to prove the alarmists correct. Shortly after negotiating peace with Britain, Bonaparte sent an expedition to reconquer Saint-Domingue. Then in October 1802, Spain ceded the vast Louisiana Territory back to France. Immediately afterward, French officials closed the port of New Orleans to American shipping, leaving those Americans who lived upriver in territories along the Mississippi without a way to transport goods. To the farmers of the Northwest and merchants such as the Pattersons, that act was an outrage.

Then fate turned against Bonaparte. Yellow fever killed thousands of French soldiers on Saint-Domingue, including their commander— Napoleon's brother-in-law General Charles Leclerc. The resulting failure to reestablish a Caribbean base fatally compromised Bonaparte's plan for an American empire. Hostilities with Britain broke out again in May 1803. It soon became an open secret that President Jefferson had sent ministers to offer to buy New Orleans from France, which needed money for its army. Many of the Americans who had called for war when New Orleans was closed adopted a wait-and-see attitude.

In June 1803, the Pattersons retreated, as was their custom, to their Springfield estate 30 miles west of Baltimore. It was a sprawling, white, 175-foot-wide country house with pillared porches on each of the two stories. To Betsy, the best thing about being there was that the family had room to spread out and the children spent most of each day outdoors, freeing her from the need to give lessons.

Their Smith cousins came to visit in July, and Uncle Smith, who was now a U.S. senator, brought astonishing news. On Independence Day, President Jefferson publicly announced that he had purchased not just the port of New Orleans but also the entire Louisiana Territory, a move that instantly doubled the size of the United States.

Of all the listening family, only William Jr. frowned at the report. He frequently displayed a priggish turn of mind that annoyed Betsy. "But sir, does the president have the constitutional authority to make such a purchase?"

"Perhaps not. I believe even Mr. Jefferson doubts its legality. But we in Congress will pass an act to regularize it. This acquisition is too important to the future of this country."

With the threat of French empire-building eliminated, the Pattersons could relax and enjoy the benefits of country living. Dorcas shook off her lethargy and spent time working in her flower garden, and her increased participation in family life allowed eighteen-year-old Betsy more freedom to go walking or riding through fields and woods. As a result, both women were in better spirits when they moved back to their town house in August.

The following week, Betsy convinced her parents to let Robert escort her to the races, one of the most popular events in Baltimore. The day after Betsy's arrival home from Springfield, Henriette had paid a call to share the incredible news that Jerome Bonaparte, Napoleon's youngest brother, was visiting their city. "I met Lieutenant Bonaparte at a soirée last night, and he asked about you! He had already heard that you are the most beautiful girl in Baltimore, and of course, I confirmed the report."

"You are too kind," Betsy had replied with a slight dip of the head. "Why would you praise me to such a distinguished visitor instead of trying to charm him yourself?"

The older girl waved the question away with an airy gesture. "Lieutenant Bonaparte does not interest me. I prefer one of his companions." Henriette had gone on to say that Bonaparte traveled with an entourage of a physician, a secretary, and two aides—a ridiculously large retinue for someone of his rank. "He carries himself more like a prince than a naval lieutenant."

"Perhaps the First Consul is preparing him for great office."

Now as Betsy dressed for her outing, she recalled that Henriette also described Lieutenant Bonaparte as loving amusement. Perhaps, he would be at the races. Betsy felt restless with anticipation as she chose her attire, a buff silk gown that set off her auburn hair and a lightweight brown spencer. Topping off the outfit was her new leghorn hat, trimmed with pink tulle that flattered her fair complexion and a curling black ostrich feather that gave her a saucy look.

Every sort of conveyance—from small one-horse gigs and chaises to ornate coaches drawn by matched teams of four—crowded the road from town, so it took twice as long to reach the racetrack as Betsy expected. She bit her lip and fretted that they would arrive too late to enjoy the pre-race socializing, but Robert was a more experienced racegoer than she and had made certain they left in time.

When they finally arrived at the grounds, Robert and Betsy alighted from their carriage and gave the coachman orders to come back at the end of the day. Since the Revolutionary War, the sport of horse racing had grown in popularity so that, in America at least, it was no longer the "sport of kings" but was a democratic amusement enjoyed by everyone who could pay the price of admission. Robert glanced around at the mixed crowd and rubbed his chin. "Stay close by my side, Goose."

"Do not call me that in public," Betsy whispered.

Before finding a seat in the whitewashed wooden stands, they made their way to where Uncle Smith was talking to Commander Joshua Barney, a naval officer in his forties who had collar-length hair and dark eyes that drooped at the outer corners. Barney was famous for having captured a British ship during the Revolutionary War. He had recently returned to Baltimore from a period of service in the French navy, and today he wore a dark blue French uniform with red collar and gold epaulets. Betsy's heart beat faster when she saw him because she had heard that Barney was Jerome Bonaparte's host in Baltimore. However, as she scanned the people milling about the commander, she could see no sign that the officer had brought his guests.

Uncle Smith saw the two Pattersons approaching and called out, "Robert, how did you talk your father into letting you leave work?"

"Betsy wanted to attend the races, and Mother persuaded him that we both deserved a holiday." Robert shook Commander Barney's hand. "Good to see you again, sir."

"And you, Robert. I hear tell that your brother John has gone to live with the Wilson Cary Nicholas family. Is that so?"

"Yes, sir. He and Senator Nicholas's oldest daughter have an understanding." Robert glanced toward the track. "What animals do you expect to make a good showing today?"

The men became engrossed in analyzing the horses that would run and the odds of each one winning. Bored by the talk of wagering, Betsy opened her parasol to protect her skin from the bright September sun. The Caton family was standing against the whitewashed wooden railing that enclosed the track, and fifteen-year-old Marianne was tossing her head and flirting outrageously with sixteen-year-old Lloyd Rogers as though they were old enough to be courting. Betsy clucked her disapproval. Although she hardly knew the Caton sisters, she had no liking for them. In her opinion, they were entirely too proud of their status as Charles Carroll's granddaughters, as if they had been the ones to sign the Declaration of Independence and not he.

A gust of wind blew dust from the track. Betsy shifted her parasol and glanced to her left and then caught her breath. Walking toward her from the stables were two uniformed men she had never seen before. One was a tall man in his late twenties with brown hair and a serious expression. He wore a French army uniform of white trousers and blue jacket with red cuffs and collar, topped by a bicorn hat with the tri-color cockade. The other, much younger man was of medium height, and he wore a naval uniform embellished with so much gold braid that it bordered upon bad taste. He carried his hat under his arm, and the sun glinted off his black hair.

The two men were talking intently. Seizing the chance to look close-ly at the younger man, Betsy decided he must be Napoleon's broth-er. He had the same deep-set eyes, long nose, and firm chin she had seen in engraved portraits of Bonaparte published in the newspapers. Yet he had a more romantic appearance than his stern older brother, perhaps because of his tousled curls or the merry look on his face. As she tried to estimate his age, he glanced in her direction.

Not wanting to be caught staring, Betsy stepped near her broth-er and pretended to listen to him. She strove, however, to catch the conversation between the two young men as they came up behind her. They were speaking in French and, apparently assuming that Amer-icans could not understand the language, spoke at full volume even though their comments were far from discreet. Betsy, who had learned French from Madame Lacomb, heard one of them say, "Bonaparte, I think the young lady before us is the one whom Mlle. Pascault de-scribed, the girl called the Belle of Baltimore. Certainly, I have not seen anyone else who fits the description."

"You must be right. My God, she is a beauty."

Betsy raised her chin slightly and turned her head a bit to show off her profile. An instant later, she was shocked to hear, "Holy Mother, I have decided. That woman, she is my wife."

"For the love of God, Bonaparte. You have not even met her."

"I do not care. I shall declare to everyone I meet that she is mine and no one else's."

Outraged that she was being claimed like a trinket in a shop win-dow, Betsy stiffened. As if to punctuate her humiliation, a burst of rau-cous laughter came from a group of working men passing on her right.

Moving her parasol to shield her face, she leaned in close to Rob-ert and tugged his sleeve. "The crowd is becoming unruly. May we please take our place in the stands?"

He shot her a glance of concern, and Betsy let her head droop to simulate fatigue. "Of course," Robert said instantly and turned to their uncle and Commodore Barney. "Excuse us, gentlemen. My sister wishes to find a seat."

He took Betsy's right arm and led her toward the stands. They had taken only a few steps when Lieutenant Bonaparte approached them. *"Mademoiselle."*

Betsy's cheeks flamed, and she kept her gaze lowered as Robert said, "Sir, I do not know who you are or where you learned your manners, but in Baltimore, we do not accost women to whom we have not been introduced."

"Pardonnez moi." Jerome bowed, sweeping his arm elegantly to one side.

"Pompous little jackanapes," Robert muttered as he guided Betsy through the knots of people loitering before the stands. "Did you see that uniform? It looks like a costume from a comic play."

Startled, Betsy shot her brother a sideways glance. Plays had been performed regularly in Baltimore since just after the Revolution, but such amusement was not something their Presbyterian parents condoned. "Bobby, when did you go to the theater?"

He grinned sheepishly. "When Father sent me to New York last spring. Do not tell him I did anything so frivolous."

"Of course not." She laughed, her spirits momentarily improved by his minor defiance.

Once she was settled in her seat, however, Betsy thought back over the encounter and squirmed beneath the hot sting of mortification. Robert was more right than he knew. Jerome Bonaparte *was* pompous and arrogant in thinking he could pluck her for his own as though she were a ripe pear hanging on the nearest tree, yet what else could she expect from someone whose station in life was so far above hers? He was, after all, related to the first man in France. Napoleon Bonaparte might be one of three consuls that headed the French government, but everyone knew that he ruled virtually alone.

You are never going to make a brilliant marriage if you act like a Puritan schoolgirl when you meet a great man, she told herself. *Why could you not charm him?* She scanned the crowd for Jerome Bonaparte's curly head but saw no sign of it.

THE NEXT MORNING, Betsy awoke with a headache and the certainty that something was wrong. The sound of her father slamming the front door just below her room had broken her sleep, and as she rose, she could hear Octavius screaming down the hall. She wondered what the trouble was as she dressed.

Before going downstairs, Betsy stopped by the nursery. "He is cutting more teeth," Mammy Sue said as she walked Octavius up and down.

As Betsy turned back into the hall, Caroline rushed to her side and clutched her skirts. "You are not going away again today, are you, Betsy?"

"No," Betsy answered, stroking the child's hair as they descended the stairs. On the first floor, they turned down the main passage. She sighed. "I am not going anywhere."

Betsy and Caroline entered the dining room, which was furnished with a long oval table and ten mahogany chairs that had urn-shaped splat backs and bottle-green silk cushions. Dorcas was at the foot of the table, leaning her head on one hand as she gazed down at Henry, who sat on the green crumb cloth that protected the Brussels carpet. He was hiccupping and rubbing a fist on his tear-streaked cheek, which displayed an angry red mark. Betsy noticed that Henry's white gown—the garment that children of both sexes wore for their first three or four years of life—was spattered with splotches of ink.

"What is wrong?"

Dorcas smiled wanly at her. "While I was talking to Mammy Sue about Octavius, Henry slipped out of the nursery and ran downstairs. He climbed onto your father's desk and overturned the inkwell onto some important papers."

"And Father blamed you."

"He was right to be angry, Betsy. The child has cost him additional work."

"I see." Betsy went to the sideboard, poured herself a cup of tea, and sat at the table. "No doubt he thinks Henry's accident is my fault because I did not rise early."

"He did not say that."

That may be, Betsy said to herself, *but I will wager he thought it.*

Later that morning when the post arrived, Betsy received a momentous letter—a note from Henriette saying that her father, the Marquis de Poleon, was going to invite the Pattersons to a formal supper. The gathering's purpose was to introduce leading members of Baltimore society to Lieutenant Jerome Bonaparte.

Betsy folded up the note and tapped it against her chin as she contemplated the news. Jerome Bonaparte might not be a prince, but he certainly was a handsome young man whose brother was a ruler. Most importantly, he could take her to France. For a moment, Betsy's confidence faltered as she realized that Lieutenant Bonaparte would compare her to the sophisticated women he had known in Paris. How could she compete against such a standard? She bit her lower lip and then lifted her head in determination. *Somehow, you will have to show him that you are just as charming as they are. You will never have another chance like this again.*

III

For the next two days, Betsy fretted over what to wear when she was formally presented to Lieutenant Bonaparte. She wanted to demonstrate that even though Baltimore might be a staid community obsessed with commerce, she was a woman of culture. Recalling one of her favorite La Rochefoucauld maxims, she told herself, "To establish ourselves in the world, we do everything to appear as if we were already established." Yet, despite her resolve to appear sophisticated, she knew that Americans invariably lagged far behind France in fashion.

Betsy finally decided on a gown that her dressmaker had sewn using a recent French pattern. Made of white muslin in the empire style, it had cap sleeves edged with bands embroidered with the Greek key design in lavender silk. The low-cut round neckline showed off Betsy's figure to advantage. Her bosom, which had been the envy of many of her schoolmates, was full enough to attract the male eye but not so large as to spoil the graceful line of her gowns.

Saturday evening, the largest of the Patterson carriages conveyed Betsy, her parents, and her two oldest brothers to the house of Jean-Charles-Marie-Louis-Felix Pascault, the Marquis de Poleon. Like Madame Lacomb, Pascault had been born in France but came to Baltimore after a time in Saint-Domingue. His estate was on the outskirts of the city, several miles northwest of the Patterson home. Their carriage entered the grounds through magnificent French iron gates and then proceeded down a lengthy drive lined with Lombardy poplars. The approach always made Betsy feel as though she had been whisked away from Baltimore to a grand European estate.

The elegance of the drive was echoed by the two-story Pascault house, built upon a raised basement, about seventy feet wide with six windows across the upper story. The middle section of the house projected slightly to form a central block with double doors topped by a pediment that had a semicircular window. As Betsy entered the wide hall, she saw Henriette standing in the doorway of the library to the right of the entrance.

Betsy thought her friend looked splendid in a gown of primrose yellow embroidered with white flowers. With an expression of breathless anticipation, she beckoned to Betsy. Once they were alone in the library, Henriette said, "The French officers are not here yet." She crossed to the front windows, where Betsy joined her. As they gazed outside, Henriette smoothed back her hair with a light, fidgety gesture.

The Caton coach arrived. Mary Carroll Caton alighted, followed by her husband, who had lately become a pitiable figure in Baltimore. Married into the planter elite, Richard Caton had tried to make a fortune of his own with mercantile investments, but his speculations were so risky that they led him to the verge of bankruptcy, threatening his wife's fortune and their four daughters' future. Only the intervention of his father-in-law had saved Caton from debtor's prison. Now he worked as a manager on Charles Carroll's estates. Betsy, whose father followed the cautious principle of investing half his money in real estate and risking only half on commerce, felt little sympathy for the imprudent Mr. Caton.

As the Catons entered the house, Henriette grabbed Betsy's arm. "Look."

A coach with distinctive yellow wheels came up the graveled drive. It stopped at the front steps and the young officers Betsy first saw at the races descended. "Who is the taller gentleman?"

"Jean-Jacques Reubell. His father was one of the five executives who ruled during the first Directory."

"Yet he is friendly with Napoleon's brother?"

Henriette shrugged. "His father retired from public life after the Directory was overthrown and bears no grudge against the First Consul." Then she glanced sideways at Betsy. "May I tell you something in confidence?"

"Of course," Betsy said, her attention fixed on the two officers as they paused to survey the grounds. Again, she was struck by the laughter on Jerome Bonaparte's face.

"Commandant Reubell is going to be my husband. Papa has given his permission."

Betsy's head whipped around. "Why, Henriette, you just met! I had no presentiment that things had moved so quickly. Do you love him?"

Henriette nodded.

Overcome by the conflicting emotions of joy and envy, Betsy leaned forward to kiss her friend's cheek. She swallowed back the tightness in her throat and said in what she hoped was a gay tone, "If you are going to marry Reubell, then I shall have to marry his companion."

Henriette squeezed her hand. "Oh, Betsy, if you could, that would be perfect."

Betsy glanced out the window. Noticing the grace with which Jerome Bonaparte mounted the steps to the house, she murmured, "We shall see."

WHEN THE MARQUIS de Poleon introduced his guests of honor to the Pattersons, Jerome Bonaparte bent over Betsy's gloved hand. Then he stood and swept her figure with a bold glance. "Mademoiselle Patterson, I cannot express the pleasure it gives me to be introduced to you at last. Your fame as a beauty precedes you—which is the only excuse I can offer for my presumption at the race. However, now that I have the privilege of speaking to you, I must swear that the praise I heard does not do you justice."

"And you, sir, live up to the reputation of Frenchmen as consummate flatterers," she answered, not wanting him to suspect the delight she took in his words.

He smiled, undismayed by her tart rejoinder. Then he and Commandant Reubell moved on to meet the Yardleys, a prominent Baltimore family. Within a few minutes, Henriette's father called the party in to supper.

The men dominated the conversation during the meal by asking the officers about events in Saint-Domingue. Even though the French had captured the revolutionary leader Toussaint L'Ouverture that spring, the rebellion continued unabated and the disease-ravaged French troops seemed unlikely to fight on much longer. When asked why he was on furlough with the outcome of the war uncertain, Jerome Bonaparte laughed. "There were reasons that made it expeditious for me to leave. I can say no more."

He must be on a mission, Betsy thought as Monsieur Pascault asked Jerome about his older brother's intentions now that he had been award-ed the title First Consul for life. "Are we to assume that this is the end of the French republic?"

"Not at all," Jerome exclaimed in his strongly accented English. "Na-poleon has no ambition for himself. His only desire in this world is to preserve the good that the Revolution accomplished."

"And what good would that be?" Betsy's brother William Jr. asked, dropping his fork noisily onto his plate. "We have read about the atroc-ities committed in the name of revolution."

Jerome thrust out his chin. "My brother was not responsible for the Terror, sir. It was he who brought order back to France, and it is he who stands between France and the return of absolutism."

"By becoming a dictator himself?"

Commandant Reubell leaned forward to forestall Jerome from an-swering. "The title the First Consul bears is one that the citizens awarded him by plebiscite, and he exercises his power with the sole purpose of defending France. Even now, Great Britain—which I must remind you, sir, is our mutual enemy—seeks to return the Bourbons to the throne and overrule the desire of the French people to live in a republic."

Betsy could see from the tight muscles along her brother's jaw that he remained unconvinced. He retorted, "Then your people have a very different idea from ours of what constitutes a republic."

During the tense silence that followed, Betsy felt humiliated by William's rudeness. Impulsively, she said, "Please excuse my brother, gentlemen. He fancies himself a great patriot, although I can assure you that his guiding motto is not *Liberté, Égalité, Fraternité* as you might suppose, but rather *Security, Annuity, Commodity.*"

Most of the dinner party erupted in laughter, but Betsy's father glared and her mother shot her a look of astonished hurt. Betsy's face flamed. Too often, she made what she meant to be a clever rejoinder, only to wish seconds later that she had remained silent. She glanced at Lieutenant Bonaparte, fearing to see disapproval on his handsome face.

Instead, he smiled at her and then said to the table at large, "Perhaps a story from my childhood will help you understand my brother better. Our family has a long history of fighting for Corsica, but when France took over our country, we accepted the inevitable. My three oldest brothers were educated in France, where they came to believe in the ideals of the Revolution. In 1793, the Corsican patriot Paoli launched an insurrection against revolutionary rule. He had been a great friend to our family. Our parents even fought with him against the Genoese during the 1760s. But because Paoli became a royalist, Napoleon opposed him. For this, the Bonapartes were denounced as traitors, and we had to flee Corsica leaving everything behind. This is why I assert that Napoleon seeks nothing for himself. He lives only to serve the glory of France."

"How old were you then?" Dorcas Patterson asked.

"I was eight years old, Madame. Never will I forget looking back as we climbed a hillside in the night and seeing flames consume my home."

Betsy felt unexpected tenderness as she imagined a terrified, curly-haired lad not much older than her brother George. Until that moment, her encounter with Jerome Bonaparte had been simply an exciting flirtation with a man who symbolized the realization of her dreams. Now, she glimpsed the possibility of deep emotions hidden beneath the charm, and she longed to talk together and compare experiences. If she read him correctly, he would know that a person who led a life of privilege could possess secret disappointments. He might understand why she was desperate to leave Baltimore where the cords of familial and societal tradition wrapped her in a net of expectation she feared she would never escape.

Lifting her eyes from her reverie, she saw Bonaparte raise his wineglass to her and then take a sip.

THE FOLLOWING MONDAY, Betsy returned from a fitting with her dress-maker to find her mother and favorite aunt in the drawing room. Dor-cas's younger sister Anne Spear, familiarly known as Nancy, had nev-er married despite having the auburn hair and elegant beauty of the Spear women. Gossips claimed that she was too tall and awkward to entice men. Instead of bemoaning her unmarried state, she relished her independence to travel and control the money she had received from her father—a financial responsibility the law did not allow wives to exercise.

As Betsy entered the room, Dorcas rose. "I will ask Mrs. Ford to prepare tea." She left without greeting her daughter.

Betsy tried to mask her hurt at the snub by bending to kiss her aunt's cheek. Then she untied the ribbons to her bonnet. "It is love-ly to see you, Aunt. I heard that you are going to Washington earlier than expected this year," she said, referring to Aunt Nancy's habit of living with the Smith family whenever they resided in the capital so that she could sit in the congressional gallery during legislative ses-sions and watch the representatives at work.

"Oh, yes. Samuel says that the president has asked Congress to con-vene early because of this Louisiana business."

"Is it true that there is to be an expedition to explore the territory?"

Aunt Nancy shot her a shrewd look. "Do not try to distract me. Sit down so we can talk before your mother returns. What is this I hear about you humiliating your brother?"

Although Betsy sat on the sofa as her aunt requested, she jutted out her chin. "He deserved it. He was insulting Monsieur Poleon's guests."

"Do you imagine that the First Consul of France needs your feeble defense? Or were you, perhaps, desirous that the First Consul's broth-er should witness your cleverness?"

Her aunt's sharp question made Betsy feel a prickling of shame. Gazing at the bonnet in her lap and smoothing its ribbons, she asked, "Is it wrong to want Lieutenant Bonaparte to think well of me?"

"It is if you are willing to mock your family to acquire that esteem."

"But Aunt, William was intolerably rude. Why has not anyone chas-tised him?"

"Do you know for a certainty that your parents have not?"

Betsy blinked. "No. I—"

Aunt Nancy laid a hand upon her arm. "Listen to me. Your brother is a grown man, and if occasionally his dour nature causes him to act the fool, then people will decide for themselves how to evaluate his worth. Since he is a man, they will likely overlook any minor defects so long as he remains successful in business. You, on the other hand, are a woman and held to a different standard."

Indignation swept away whatever remorse Betsy felt. To hear such counsel from the aunt who had urged her to read *A Vindication of the Rights of Woman* was shocking. "I cannot believe that you of all people would warn me to be more ladylike. When have you ever cared what people think of your interest in politics?"

"My dear niece, I am content to remain unmarried, and so I can afford not to care. You, however, have different desires. You want to make an important marriage."

"Yes, I do. Are you saying that you think me wrong?"

Aunt Nancy pressed her lips together. "No," she finally said, drawing out the word in a way that expressed reservation despite her denial. "I am simply cautioning you to behave in a way that will help you achieve your aim. If you want to marry a man of high station, you must not give him reason to suspect that you will embarrass him in society."

Betsy settled back against the cushions and gave her aunt a troubled look. "You are saying that even if I do marry a European nobleman, my life will have as many constraints as if I remained in Baltimore."

Aunt Nancy smiled wryly. "I have never yet met a man of any nationality who regarded his wife as an equal. The only way to achieve freedom as a woman is to be financially independent and single."

Betsy frowned. She loved her aunt dearly—admiring the older woman's independence and enjoying her eccentricities—but Betsy did not want such a life for herself.

Exhaling deeply, she marshaled her thoughts. Ever since her time at Madame Lacomb's school, she had set her heart on living in Europe. The United States was such a young country that it had very little music, literature, or art. Not only was Europe far ahead of America in culture, but Betsy had also heard that in France, clever women could participate in intellectual life by hosting salons where learned people debated ideas. "I think," she said at last, "that if I must accept constraint no matter which path I choose, I would still prefer a life of rank in Europe."

"I thought that would be your choice."

As her mother re-entered the room, Betsy reflected on how different the three Spear sisters were in character no matter how similar their looks. Her mother was gentle, compliant, and easily wounded. Nancy was astute and independent, yet often nervous. And Margaret Smith was elegant, strong-willed, and opinionated, often stating how much she hated living in the new, still-raw city of Washington, which looked more like a muddy wilderness than a national capital.

Aunt Margaret certainly has not allowed matrimony to stifle her, Betsy thought. Perhaps a spinster like Aunt Nancy was not the best source of advice about marriage.

Betsy noticed that her mother was avoiding her gaze, so she crossed the room and kissed her. "I am sorry I embarrassed the family. I will be more circumspect in the future."

Dorcas laid a soft hand on her cheek. "Thank you, my dear."

A FEW DAYS LATER the Pattersons were invited to a ball being given for the visiting French officers. The host was Samuel Chase, one of Maryland's four signers of the Declaration of Independence and currently a Supreme Court justice. Chase's daughter had married Commodore Barney's son, so no one in Baltimore was surprised that Chase would honor Barney's guests.

This time, Betsy knew exactly what to wear. The gown of sheer white cotton mull her dressmaker was finishing would be perfect. Both the square-necked bodice and cap sleeves were loosely gathered, with the bottom edge of the puffed sleeve accented by a ruffle. The hem of the narrow skirt and rounded train featured a wide border of geometric shapes and flower sprays embroidered in heavy white floss. Under the nearly transparent dress, Betsy would wear both a chemise and an underdress to preserve modesty. To further convey a demure appearance, she would don a delicate seed-pearl cross on a fine gold chain.

When the Pattersons arrived at the Chase mansion, they found their host greeting guests in the reception hall. Sixty-two-year-old Justice

Chase was a tall, corpulent man with long white hair worn in the manner Benjamin Franklin had favored. Infamous for his abrasive personality, Chase had made an enemy of President Jefferson by supporting his opponent, John Adams, during the last presidential campaign
and, more recently, by injecting political opinions into his judicial decisions. Uncle Smith had told Betsy's parents that the president was
trying to convince the House of Representatives to impeach the justice.

As the Pattersons approached their host, Betsy glanced around to
see if Lieutenant Bonaparte had arrived. Then she saw Chase glare
at her father. "Ah, Patterson, I wondered if you would show your face.
I imagine you approve of your friend's campaign to force me off the
bench."

William Patterson stiffened. "My business is shipping, sir. I do not
meddle in affairs of state."

"Of course not." Chase smirked. "All the same, you may tell your
brother-in-law to deliver a message for me. Old red-headed Tom may
think he has me by the balls, but I am a slippery old devil and will escape his clutches yet."

Betsy felt her cheeks flame. Chase had a reputation as a profane
man, but she had not expected him to display such vulgarity in front
of ladies. Patterson took his wife's arm and walked away without re-
plying, and Betsy and her brothers followed.

A few feet away, John Eager Howard, the former senator whose seat
Uncle Smith now filled, stood talking to Mrs. Chase. Howard was a
stout man in his early fifties who for the occasion had squeezed himself into his Revolutionary War colonel's uniform. The red lapels of
the blue coat were separated by a bulging mound of buff waistcoat
that threatened to pop its buttons. Betsy smiled at Howard's vanity
but did not think less of him for it. He was a principled man who devoted himself to philanthropy and public service, and everyone in Baltimore admired him.

Scanning the rapidly filling reception hall, Betsy saw that the Buchanans, Catons, and Carrolls had all arrived before them. Within
moments, Charles Carnan Ridgely Jr. approached and asked for the
honor of dancing with her. His father owned Hampton Hall, one of
the most extensive country estates in Maryland. After allowing him

to claim a cotillion, Betsy excused herself and walked toward the Pascaults on the other side of the room. As she threaded her way through the crowd, a Spear cousin, James Buchanan, and Robert Gilmor Jr. all requested dances. Gilmor was a family friend rather than a beau; he was eleven years older than Betsy and rumored to be plagued by the beginnings of lung disease, but he was an intelligent man who loved art, so she found him one of the few tolerable men in Baltimore.

As Betsy reached Henriette's side, the noise of conversation and laughter in the hall dropped so suddenly that she could hear the musicians warming up in the next room. Betsy turned and saw that Jerome Bonaparte and his friend Reubell had arrived. Reubell was dressed as before, but Bonaparte had on an entirely different uniform. His short waist-length tunic was made of light blue wool and decorated across the chest with at least a dozen rows of silver braid, each punctuated by three silver buttons. The tight-fitting light blue pants had a stripe down the outside of each leg. Around his slender waist he wore a red-and-white striped sash.

After greeting his host, Jerome Bonaparte came straight to Betsy. He bent over her gloved hand and said, "Mademoiselle Patterson, how lovely you look tonight. I hope that I have arrived in time to commandeer all of your dances."

All around them, people were moving toward the back hall, which was being used as the ballroom, and Betsy noticed that the musicians had progressed from tuning their instruments to playing fragments of melody. She shook her ringlets at Lieutenant Bonaparte. "Sir, I regret to say that you have not. Several of my dances have been claimed by others before you."

For the briefest of moments, Jerome's face betrayed surprise, making Betsy glad that she could teach him that he had rivals.

He quickly adopted an expression of acute disappointment and placed his hand over his heart. "Then please may I beg the honor of being your first partner of the night?"

She hesitated a moment before giving him her arm.

As they entered the ballroom, Betsy was pleased to see that many people broke off their conversations to watch them. The first dance of the evening was to be a contradanse, which would have the advantage of pairing them for at least ten minutes and of having periods when they could converse because they were not required to take part in the moves. The first time they were an inactive couple, Betsy said, "Lieutenant Bonaparte, I have never seen a uniform like yours. Is it a naval dress uniform?"

Jerome laughed. "No, it is a hussar's uniform."

"But, hussars are cavalry. I thought you were in the navy."

"I am." He shrugged. "But I like the way this one looks. It is debonair, is it not?"

Before Betsy could answer, it was their turn to take part in the next movement, and by the time they could speak again, she decided not to pursue the subject. She suspected that it was a tremendous breach of protocol for a military officer to wear the uniform of a different branch of service. Clearly, being Napoleon's brother came with unusual privileges, liberties that the youngest Bonaparte did not hesitate to enjoy.

As she pondered these things, Jerome complimented her on her elegant gown. "It is—*très à la mode,*" he said after a moment of searching for an equivalent English phrase.

"*Merci, monsieur,*" Betsy answered, gratified that he considered her stylish.

"*Ah, parlez-vous français?*" he exclaimed, sounding like a boy in his excitement that she spoke his language.

Betsy nodded, and he gave her gloved hand a quick squeeze of approval. Then returning to the previous subject, he said, "Your taste in clothing reminds me of *ma belle-soeur* Josephine. She truly knows how to set Paris on its ear."

"Oh, please tell me about her."

He chuckled and said in French, "A while back, she started a new fashion of wearing sheer gowns such as yours but with nothing underneath."

Betsy's cheeks burned as Jerome continued, "Napoleon considered the style too immodest. One day, finding Josephine and her ladies sitting in the drawing room in such flimsy attire, he gave orders for the servants to pile wood on the fire. When Josephine complained that she was roasting alive, he said, 'My dear, I was afraid you might catch cold sitting here naked.'"

In spite of her discomfort with the indiscreet topic, Betsy found herself joining in Jerome's laughter. Then, after her first wave of self-consciousness passed, she felt a delicious sense of freedom in being able to talk so openly of things forbidden in Baltimore society.

The last move of the dance required Jerome to grasp her hands and swing her through several revolutions. After the last twirl, he flirtatiously pulled her closer to his body than was proper before releasing her. As they pulled apart, Betsy found herself halted. Her gold chain had caught on one of his buttons.

She dared not look up at him. With the rapidity of lightning, she felt as embarrassed as if she had found herself publicly wearing one of Josephine's revealing gowns.

"Permit me." Jerome used his index finger to unhook her necklace. Instead of releasing the chain, however, he kept it on the crook of his finger and whispered, "Do you see, *chère mademoiselle?* Fate has brought us together, and we are destined never to part."

Betsy caught her breath at the romantic perfection of the moment, but then her natural skepticism reasserted itself. She perceived that this man to whom she was temporarily joined—handsome, warm-hearted, and fun loving though he might be—lacked the steely resolve of his famous older brother. He seemed content to glide through life feasting on whatever privileges fell to him in Napoleon's wake.

"Fate seems to have forgotten that I promised my next dance to someone else."

Jerome released her gold chain. "If that is your wish."

"My wish, sir, is for a partner who understands that I am a kingdom that must be won rather than claimed as a birthright."

For a moment, he seemed perplexed and she feared the sentiment was too complex for him to understand it in English, but then laughter returned to his eyes. "Truly, Mademoiselle, that is a challenge worthy of a Bonaparte." He bowed and watched her walk away.

IV

THAT night, Betsy lay awake reliving every moment she had spent with Jerome Bonaparte. They had danced twice more, but he kept his banter light and did not return to the tantalizing subject of their destiny. At the time, disturbed by the heat she saw in his eyes, Betsy was glad that she had challenged his assumption that she was his for the asking. Now, however, she worried that she had been too aloof.

She sat up in bed, wrapped her arms around her knees, and smiled at the memory of a story he told during their last dance. When Jerome was fifteen, Napoleon had taken him to live in the Tuileries in the hope of imparting discipline to the baby of the Bonaparte clan. Napoleon, however, was often away on government business, and during his absences, Jerome discovered the delights of shopping in Paris. After one such trip, the First Consul found that his youngest brother had purchased an elaborate shaving set whose articles were made of gold, silver, mother of pearl, and ivory—and ordered that the bill of 10,000 francs be sent to the palace. "This is ridiculous! You do not even have a beard!"

The boy looked longingly at the objects his brother had confiscated. "I know. But I just love beautiful things."

Jerome laughed at himself while telling the tale, and Betsy had laughed with him. She appreciated his ability to mock his foibles, yet she wondered if he was still so extravagant. Surely, now that he was subject to naval discipline, he had learned more practicality. If not, perhaps if she became his wife, she could provide the strength of character he lacked.

But she was racing too far ahead of events. As Betsy lay down, she noticed that her stomach still churned from the evening's emotions, and she feared that it would keep her awake. She decided to go down to the kitchen in search of some leftover cornbread, so she slipped on her wrapper and mules.

Betsy left her room and crept past the closed door of the master bedroom to the head of the staircase, which was across from the closed nursery door. After descending to the first floor, she felt her way without a candle past the drawing room and dining room. Then she entered the passageway linking the main house to the back building. As she passed the housekeeper's chamber and reached the junction where the main hall met the passage to the back staircase, she heard a thud behind the housekeeper's door, followed by muffled laughter. Betsy halted, wondering what Mrs. Ford could be doing at this early-morning hour. To her consternation, the housekeeper's door began to open.

Betsy ducked into the dark kitchen but remained near the doorway. Mrs. Ford, however, did not appear. Instead, William Patterson stepped into the hall holding a candle whose light revealed him to be wearing a white nightshirt over bare legs.

"Good night, my dear." Patterson closed the door and started up the back stairs.

For an instant, Betsy fought against the meaning of what she had seen, but then she had to admit that such a nocturnal visit had only one explanation. The pain in her stomach grew more acute, and tears filled her eyes. Her first thought was for her mother—that gentle woman sleeping upstairs, who had exhausted her strength bearing a dozen children for this man who did not even have the decency to respect the sanctity of her home.

How in God's name could he do it? To Betsy, her father had always seemed the model of probity, and even when she chafed against his uncompromising views, she had admired his integrity. Now her faith in him shattered.

To think, only a few hours earlier she had been shocked at Jerome
Bonaparte for referring to nudity. How painfully naïve her reaction
seemed now. She who prided herself on her sophistication knew nothing of the world. "Oh, Father," Betsy whispered and, doubling over in
distress, began to cry.

Tʜᴇ ɴᴇxᴛ ᴡᴇᴇᴋ, Betsy attended the Pascault-Reubell wedding at St.
Peter's Church in Baltimore, a simple red brick building that looked
more like a school than the seat of the first Catholic diocese in the
United States. During the Roman Catholic rite, which Betsy could
not follow because it was in Latin, she called to mind the vows she
had heard during Protestant weddings. Remembering the phrase *keep
thee only unto her,* Betsy brooded about her father's flouting of that
promise. In the days since her discovery, she had debated whether
to tell her brothers what she saw, but so far, she had been unable to
broach so painful a subject.

After the morning ceremony, the guests traveled to the Pascault
home for a wedding feast. Jerome sat next to Betsy at the table and
insisted that she accept portions of all the dishes the servants offered,
even though she protested that she had no appetite. Her stomach ached
as it had ever since the night of the ball.

Finally, Jerome lowered his voice to ask, *"Mademoiselle, vous êtes
si pensive. Est-ce qu'il y a un probléme?"*

"Ce n'est rien. Je vous en prie, ne vous préoccupez pas au sujet de moi,"
Betsy answered to deflect his concern about her low spirits.

Once the meal was over, Jerome begged her to take a turn in the
garden. Betsy pressed her lips together as she debated what to answer.
Flirtation was the last thing she wanted to engage in at the moment,
but neither was she ready to go home and discuss a wedding with
her unsuspecting mother. At least, walking was active and might give
Betsy a chance to forget her unhappiness for a while, so she agreed
to Jerome's suggestion.

They were silent as they strolled down one of the gravel paths that
divided the garden into quadrants featuring shrubbery pruned into
geometric shapes. When they reached the far end of the formal beds,
Jerome turned into a small grove, and Betsy followed. After a moment,

he said, "Mademoiselle Patterson, a wedding should be a joyous occasion, but your face is so *triste.* I am certain that something troubles you."

Tears sprang to Betsy's eyes. "Yes, but I cannot divulge the problem to anyone outside my family."

"Is there no way I can help?"

Leave me alone, she thought but would not be so cruel as to say it. "Distract me. Tell me about your homeland. I know nothing about Corsica."

"I come from Ajaccio, a harbor on the west coast. The town is surrounded by shrubbery-covered hills. Oh, how I miss the smells of the maquis—the juniper, sage, and myrtle." He snapped a small branch off a nearby pine, crushed the needles between his fingers and sniffed them, then threw the branch away. "Thinking of it makes me homesick."

"Then we are opposites. You long for your birthplace, while I hate mine."

Jerome looked at her in astonishment. "Why?"

She waved her hand dismissively. "The United States is such a young country, and its people care only for commerce. That is particularly true of Baltimore. I find our society crass and uninspiring."

"But you are American, and you are neither of those things." He seized her gloved hands. "Mademoiselle Patterson, forgive my haste, but I must declare that I adore you. I would give anything to win your love. Please allow me to hope that someday you and I will repeat the vows we heard our friends exchange this morning."

Startled, Betsy glanced around to make sure that the surrounding trees shielded them from sight of the house. She turned back to Jerome. "This is happening too quickly, Lieutenant Bonaparte. You and I still know little of each other's character."

He smiled at her. "That is not true. I know that you are clever, honest, and prudent. I can see that you are beautiful and have excellent taste." Pulling her closer, he lowered his voice. "And I sense that beneath your proper manners, you are a tender-hearted woman who feels deeply. What more do I need to know?"

As Betsy stared into his dark eyes, she felt flustered. Jerome was close enough that she could smell a tang of perspiration beneath the mingled lavender and citrus scents of his *Eau de Cologne.* "But I know so little about you."

Jerome lightly grasped her arms just below her sleeves. "I do not demand an answer now. I ask only to be allowed to court you so that we can become better acquainted."

Mesmerized by the touch of his hands on her bare skin, Betsy gazed at him a full two seconds before recalling the answer propriety demanded. "You must speak to my father." As she spoke, the bitter memory of William Patterson leaving Mrs. Ford's room flickered in her mind and then faded as Jerome placed two fingers under her chin and tilted up her head.

"I will ask him as soon as possible," he whispered and bent to kiss her.

As soon as their lips touched, Betsy felt a rush of emotion that swept away her doubts. She had never suspected she could feel such physical hunger. The desire to let Jerome take full possession of her body shocked her, yet she had no wish to resist.

When he pulled back after a long kiss, she waited to see if he would attempt further liberties. To her surprise, Jerome tweaked her nose. "You see? I was right about your passionate nature. But one kiss is enough for now, Elisa."

"Elisa?" she murmured.

"It is a French form of Elizabeth, and I think it suits you better than Betsy. May I call you that?"

"Yes," she answered, pleased that he would christen her with a name all his own.

Jerome caressed the line of her jaw. "Your eyes are so bright. When you look at me like that, I find you irresistible."

"Then kiss me again."

"No." He lifted her hand to his lips. "This will have to do. I want to be truthful when I tell your father that my intentions are honorable. I want you for my wife, Elisa, nothing less."

Betsy ached with desire, but she knew that Jerome was right. By guarding her honor, he was demonstrating that she could trust him, not only today but in the future. To a heart still sore from the discovery of a father's betrayal, such restraint was a balm.

She sighed. "Then let us return to the house before people begin to talk."

As the family carriage conveyed her home, Betsy wondered, *What has happened to me?* One kiss from Jerome Bonaparte, and she had grown wanton in thought if not in deed.

When Jerome took her in his arms, she had expected to feel instinctive resistance to his passion. Instead, Jerome's kiss had awakened her as if she were the sleeping princess in a tower she had read about as a child. Betsy still felt the vestiges of that newborn desire coursing through her body, transforming her from a mere coquette into a woman possessed by forbidden longing for her lover.

She laid her fingertips on her lower lip and pressed it lightly, wondering why Jerome's touch felt so different from all others. Then, because she had more privacy in the carriage than she would ever have at home, she cupped her hand around her breast and tried to imagine him caressing her there. Betsy's face grew hot, and discontentment stirred within her. The private recesses of her body felt uncomfortably swollen, yet empty too, and she feared they would remain that way until Jerome took her to bed.

Until today, she had always assumed that carnal appetites were the province of men and low women like Mrs. Ford, not proper young ladies like herself. Was she wrong? Was it possible that even a mild, devout woman like Dorcas Patterson—who after all had married at the age of seventeen—once felt this raging in her blood?

Or, frightening thought, had Betsy inherited this aspect of her nature from her father?

It is not the same, she thought indignantly. *He is old and has a wife. He has no need for another woman. It is disgusting.*

By contrast, she and Jerome were young and free to marry. If perchance, their passions led them astray while they were unwed, they might create a mild scandal as others had before, but they would have broken no vows of fidelity. Reaching this conclusion, Betsy settled in her seat and wondered how long it would be before Jerome kissed her again.

Betsy rose early the next morning and went down to the dining room to find that Robert was just finishing his breakfast. Dorcas sat at the long oval table too, but Betsy had finally made up her mind and would not be deterred by her mother's presence.

Standing close by Robert's chair, she said quietly, "May I talk to you privately before you leave for the counting house?"

"I am going to the harbor this morning, Goose. Can it wait until evening?"

Betsy scrunched up her nose at the nickname. "It is important," she whispered.

Robert's teasing expression faded. Darting a glance at their mother, he laid his napkin on the table. "Will you walk with me?"

Nodding, Betsy turned away to get her spencer and bonnet before going out. Her mother called to her, "You have not had breakfast."

"I will eat when I return."

The brother and sister exited the front door, descended the marble steps, and turned right. The first building they passed on their way to the harbor was their father's counting house. South Street was lined with wall-to-wall town houses like their family home. Since the end of the Revolutionary War, property in downtown Baltimore had grown increasingly valuable, so the small, brightly painted wooden houses of the last century were being replaced by tall homes on narrow lots, allowing a denser population to live in the thriving port.

Neither sibling spoke at first, and the clopping of passing horses punctuated their steps. "What is it?" Robert finally asked after they had gone a block.

"I need to tell you about something upsetting that occurred the night of the ball."

He faced her and his eyebrows came together just as their father's did when he was angry. "Did someone take liberties with you?"

"No, it happened afterward. At home." Betsy twisted her hands together. "I could not sleep, so I went downstairs to get something to settle my stomach. And I saw Father come out of Mrs. Ford's room. He was wearing his nightshirt."

Robert turned away and gazed down the street. They had come far enough to glimpse the top of a two-masted ship at one of the docks and to smell the odors of fish and seaweed. Robert said, "Perhaps he was giving her orders. You did not actually see them—"

"No," Betsy interrupted. "But I am sure. It was far after midnight.

They were behind closed doors, and when he came out, he called her by an endearment."

Robert winced. "I shall have to tell William, but without more certain proof, he may not believe it."

"You mean he will not believe me."

"I do not think he has forgiven you, Betsy. He was very embarrassed."

She nodded to acknowledge her wrong but kept to the subject at hand. "What are we to do?"

"No matter what course we take, we cannot allow Mother to hear of this. I suppose I shall have to keep watch and see what I can discover."

"You mean spy on Father in his own house?"

"I do not see any alternative."

Betsy sighed. As they turned left on Pratt Street, which ran along the manmade waterfront, she glanced across the water to Federal Hill, a rise of land on the south shore of the basin where public celebrations were often held. "Was I right to tell you?"

"Of course." Robert paused as a squawking gull flew overhead. "Just before John went to live with the Nicholas family, I heard him arguing with Father in the office. John would not tell me the reason for their quarrel, but he said he intended never to come back."

"Do you think he knows?"

"I think it likely, but it is not the kind of thing I can ask in a letter. His engagement to Polly gave him a good reason to relocate without causing a family scene."

"He too wanted to protect Mother," Betsy whispered, staring at the cobblestone pavement so Robert would not see the tears in her eyes. Of her three older brothers, she respected John the least because she considered him weak and sly, but in this instance, she could not fault his decision to keep quiet.

Robert put his arm around her shoulder. "Do not be so downcast, Goose. If what you suspect is true, our father has committed a very grave error, but he is a good man in most other respects. Try to remember that."

Unable to speak because of the tightness in her throat, Betsy nodded. Robert squeezed her arm lightly and then continued on toward the docks.

One of few aspects of her domestic duties that Betsy enjoyed was using her skills at needlework to create presents for the people she loved. That evening she sat on one of the shield-back chairs by the drawing room table, embroidering flowers and birds on a white satin reticule she planned to give Henriette. To Betsy's surprise, her father arrived home an hour before his usual time. Patterson entered the drawing room and curtly told the younger children, who were regaling Dorcas with tales about school, to go upstairs. "Your mother and I need to talk to Elizabeth."

The use of her full name and the unusual circumstance of his leaving business early told Betsy that the occasion was serious. She laid her embroidery on the table next to a pile of brightly colored skeins of floss and then folded her hands demurely in her lap. Then she looked up expectantly.

As soon as the room had cleared, William Patterson stood on the Turkish carpet at a spot where he could see both his wife and daughter. "I was astonished to receive a visit from Lieutenant Bonaparte today."

"Yes, sir?" Betsy asked, surprising herself with her calm. Knowing her father's guilty secret made her feel almost as though she had hidden power over him.

Patterson's heavy black eyebrows came together in a sharp v. "Elizabeth, you have met this man only three times in the space of a fortnight. How could you so forget yourself as to receive his attentions?"

"I have done nothing improper." Betsy congratulated herself on not blushing at the lie. "When he spoke of his wish to court me, I told him to address his request to you."

"He seems to have formed the impression that you welcome his suit."

Betsy glanced at her mother and saw that she looked amazed but not displeased by Jerome's interest. Taking courage from that, Betsy said, "Sir, I give you my word that I have done no more than indicate I would receive his calls with an open mind. Yet, I must remind you that I have always made it known that I dream of making a European alliance."

"Nonsense! Those were the whims of your childhood. Surely, you have learned better than to be governed by such girlish fancies."

Betsy lifted her chin and gave her father as steady a look as she could manage. "On the contrary, now that Napoleon Bonaparte has returned stability to France, my interest in living in Europe has increased rather than diminished. Even if it were not so, I would have no reason to scorn Lieutenant Bonaparte. His brother is the First Consul. We are not of such great estate that we can look down on his claims."

"But Betsy," Dorcas exclaimed. "If you were to marry Lieutenant Bonaparte, you would live overseas. Your father and I might never see you again."

"Madam, you speak in haste. There is no question of marriage here."

Dorcas raised a hand to her lips as if in apology, but Betsy refused to be stifled. "No question of marriage as yet. Unless you were so indifferent to my interests as to refuse Lieutenant Bonaparte's request."

"Indifferent to your—" Patterson struck the mantelpiece. "You forget yourself, Elizabeth. This man is a complete stranger to Baltimore society. Why is he absent from the navy and in no haste to return to his post? Those are not the actions of a responsible person."

"Unless he is on a secret mission for the First Consul."

"What manner of mission would require him to dance attendance upon a young woman such as yourself? No, for all we know, Jerome Bonaparte could be a rake. If I were to blithely consign my daughter's welfare to such a cipher, then truly could I be accused of indifference."

Deciding that it would be prudent to appear more yielding, Betsy lowered her gaze. "Yes, Father. But are those not reasons to get to know him better, rather than to reject him?"

A moment of silence followed, and when she dared to look up again, she saw that her father's fury was spent. Patterson drew close and placed a hand on her shoulder. "Betsy, are you so very taken with this man that you would defy my judgment and plead for him?"

She bit her lip, then decided to be truthful. "You are right in saying that we still do not know his full character—although he is a friend of Commodore Barney's and thus not a total stranger. But yes, I have found Lieutenant Bonaparte to be a most delightful companion, and I was hoping for the chance to deepen our acquaintance."

"She makes an excellent point, Mr. Patterson," Dorcas said. When her husband glared at her, she added in a rush, "Lieutenant Bonaparte is an amiable young man connected to the ruler of France. You would not wish to create tension between our two countries by insulting him."

"You have not the least conception of what you are saying, madam. We are not discussing a political alliance, but rather a young man's infatuation. If anything, the First Consul would thank me for preventing his brother from forming a too-hasty attachment."

Betsy pressed her hands together before her chest. "But we have not been guilty of haste. I am merely requesting time to know Lieutenant Bonaparte better. Have you irrevocably decided against him?"

William Patterson shook his head. "I did not refuse his request. I asked him to call again tomorrow to receive my answer."

Betsy caught her breath. After a moment, during which her father obstinately remained silent, she asked, "What will you tell him?"

"That he may call upon you here at the house. I do not want you to go walking or riding with him alone until I feel more certain of his character. Will you agree to that?"

"Yes, Father," she answered and tried not to let him hear her sigh of relief.

V

J EROME lost no time in commencing his courtship. He rented lodgings on South Street for himself and his retinue, and he proceeded to call upon the Pattersons every day.

After the first week, Betsy asked him, "Do you mean to wear my
family down with your persistence?"

He grinned. "No, Elisa, I visit at every opportunity because I do not
know how much longer I may be in the United States. The French
chargé d'affaires, Monsieur Pichon, continually urges me to return to
the navy. I have forestalled him by saying that I have my orders and
by sending my aide to France to receive confirmation from my brother, but nearly a month has passed since Lieutenant Meyronnet sailed,
and I am not certain when he might return."

Betsy's happiness contracted at the thought that duty might separate them before they decided their future. "In the right conditions, a
fast ship could make the eastbound crossing in three to four weeks.
But a bulkier ship would surely take longer."

"That leaves us only a few months at most to win your father's consent."

"Lieutenant Bonaparte, do you forget that *I* have not yet accepted
your proposal?" She smiled to take the sting from her rebuke.

"No, my lovely Elisa, I do not forget, but I possess a nature that
lives on hope." He kissed her hand. "You look like you belong in the

Bonaparte family, you know. You greatly resemble Pauline."

"Really? You never told me that," Betsy said, far from pleased. To be told by a suitor that she resembled his sister was hardly romantic.

Seeing her expression, Jerome added, "But you are prettier. Your lively disposition gives you a more vivacious air."

"Why, thank you, sir," she said and bowed her head in acknowledgment.

Although Betsy worried that Jerome's impulsive nature might offend her family, she was relieved to see that he behaved impeccably whenever he stepped foot inside the Patterson home. On his first visit, he brought wooden soldiers for Betsy's younger brothers, sugarplums for her sisters, French lace for her mother, brandy for her father, and for Betsy herself, the properly impersonal gift of a book of nature poetry called *Les Jardins* by Jacques Delille. Jerome spoke only English in her family's presence so that no one could accuse him of deviousness, and he avoided the risqué subjects with which he had amused Betsy at the ball.

The family did not know quite what to make of the gregarious young Corsican. The younger children burst into giggles whenever they heard him called their sister *Elisa*. Privately, Betsy's older brothers mocked Jerome's penchant for fancy clothes, and her father expressed astonishment that any man could so enjoy idleness. Little by little, these criticisms eased as they saw the extent to which Jerome exerted himself to be agreeable. He expressed interest in their concerns, even ignoring Betsy at times to ask after business. Jerome further endeared himself by teaching the little boys Napoleon's battle tactics and performing errands for Dorcas. He recounted amusing descriptions of life in France yet was also an attentive listener—even managing to draw from Dorcas stories of her girlhood that her children had never heard.

One Sunday as Jerome took tea with the family, Betsy's father crossed the drawing room and sat at his desk, which stood against the wall opposite the front windows. After calling his two eldest sons to his side, he began to read a letter he had received the day before, speaking loudly to be heard over the clamor of children playing about the room. In the letter, Mr. James McIlhiny, Patterson's London agent, reported that he suspected the company's agent in Holland was cheating them by inflating the amount he claimed to have paid in tariffs.

Glancing toward her mother, Betsy saw Dorcas frown in disapproval of business being conducted on Sunday. Betsy rolled her eyes at Jerome to convey her own exasperation and then picked up a book she had just finished reading, a novel he had given her called *Atala* by the French writer Chateaubriand. The tale was a tragic love story between Indians in the American South, as told to a young Frenchman who had married into the tribe. As soon as her father finished reading his letter, Betsy said, "Robert, come look at this book. I think you might enjoy it."

Half leaning over his father's desk, Robert glanced back at her and shook his head. "Not now. Can you not see that we have something important to discuss?"

Dorcas stabbed her needle into her embroidery. "It is also imperative to take a day of rest."

Patterson shoved back his chair and stood. "Madam, do you dare to question my conduct? In my own home before my adult sons?"

His wife blanched. "No, Mr. Patterson. I only wished to remind you that this is the Lord's Day. Can you not deal with this correspondence on the morrow?"

"No, madam, I cannot. We have other pressing obligations."

Reaching for the letter, he said to William Jr., "Let us go next door to discuss this since the sound of honest labor is so upsetting to your mother's religious sensibilities."

"Please, do not go," Dorcas pleaded, but her husband ignored her. He stalked out, followed by William and Robert, who threw a regretful glance in his mother's direction. Dorcas dropped her embroidery and hurried upstairs. At a nod from Betsy, Margaret went after her. In the uneasy silence that followed, Caroline climbed onto the sofa to lean against her oldest sister's arm, and the young boys played more quietly.

Betsy sighed, and Jerome asked her, "Your family, do they ever discuss anything but business?"

"Never."

He gently stroked her cheek with the back of his hand. "No literature? No philosophy? No art?"

"Only the fine art of making money."

"Ma pauvre Elisa," Jerome murmured. "You belong in Paris. I wish

I could transport you there to participate in the salons. With your wit and vivacity, you would add much to the debates. And you would be celebrated for your beauty. If only I could commission Jacques-Louis David to paint your portrait, your lovely face would be preserved for posterity."

Putting an arm around Caroline, Betsy sighed. "Sometimes, I fear that I would be as out of place in Paris as if I were a savage Indian."

"Nonsense. Every day, you impress me with your natural gentility." Jerome lowered his voice. *"Je rêve du jour quand je te présenterai à Napoléon. Il verra que j'ai choisi un femme aussi élégante que Josephine."*

Although Betsy felt gratified that Jerome would compare her favorably to Josephine, she could not allow him to assume their marriage was a certain thing. "Lieutenant Bonaparte, I—"

"Shhh," he said, surreptitiously squeezing her hand. "I know you cannot give me an answer yet. I will wait."

ALTHOUGH BETSY ENJOYED the hours she spent with Jerome, one aspect of their courtship frustrated her. Having experienced the pleasure of her first kiss, she longed for the chance to be alone so they could embrace once more. Jerome remained circumspect, never hinting that he shared Betsy's hunger, but she could not believe that he was any more satisfied with their chaste interactions than she was.

Three weeks passed, and Betsy received a note asking her to visit Henriette Reubell, just returned from her wedding trip. After gaining permission to be driven there in the family's small calash, Betsy sent word to Jerome not to call that day.

A footman showed Betsy into the Pascault parlor, a handsome room with tall mullioned windows, acanthus leaves on the cornice and plaster ceiling medallion, and imported French furnishings. When Henriette rose to greet her friend, Betsy saw that her eyes glowed with happiness. "You look wonderful. Commandant Reubell must be good to you."

"He is a kind man." Henriette resumed her seat on the scroll-arm sofa, upholstered in a dark green silk figured with gold peacocks. Betsy sat beside her. "But I hear that you have news of your own. Papa says all of Baltimore is gossiping that you are to marry Lieutenant Bonaparte."

"You know how idle tongues exaggerate. Father allows him to call on me in the presence of my family, that is all."

"Oh." Henriette looked nonplussed. "Perhaps I have made a grave error."

"What do you mean?"

"Lieutenant Bonaparte arrived here half an hour ago and begged me to allow a private audience with you. He is waiting in Papa's library to see if you will receive him. I would never have agreed if I had known it violated the understanding with your father."

In her excitement, Betsy clapped her hands like a little girl. "What an unexpected boon. I cannot tell you how I have longed for us to meet alone."

Giving her a sharp look, Henriette said, "Have you fallen in love with him?"

"I have scarcely admitted it to myself, but I think I have. The day of your wedding, I allowed him to kiss me in the garden, and since then, I can hardly think of anything else. The more I see him, the more essential he seems to my happiness."

Henriette shook her head. "I am not sure such immoderate feelings ever lead to true happiness. Marriage should be approached more dispassionately."

"But you married for love!"

"Yes, but I did not commit myself until after I ascertained that Papa approved of him."

Feeling rebuked, Betsy scooted farther from Henriette. "If it troubles your conscience for us to have an assignation here, then ask Lieutenant Bonaparte to leave."

"Don't be so tetchy. I am thinking only of your welfare. Bonaparte is so young that I fear he lacks the maturity required for marriage."

Betsy waved her friend's words away. "He is old enough to be a naval officer."

"Shall I send him to you then?" Henriette asked, smiling with the air of a tolerant older sister.

"Please."

As her friend left the parlor, Betsy hurried to the gold-framed mirror on the wall and checked her hair. She arranged her lace fichu more becomingly and then saw in the mirror the reflection of Jerome entering the room. Betsy turned to face him.

He closed the door but, to her surprise, did not cross to her. His face wore an uncharacteristic gravity that made her wonder if he had received orders to rejoin the navy. Forgetting all restraint, she rushed to him and threw her arms around his neck.

Instead of kissing her, Jerome gently pushed her away. "No, Elisa. We must talk."

Betsy's stomach cramped with dread as she returned to the sofa and sat down. Jerome came to stand before her with his hands behind his back.

"Your father remains troubled by the speed of our courtship and has asked Commodore Barney to assist him in effecting a separation. Barney called on me this morning to say that he thinks it prudent for me to accompany him on a tour of other American cities."

"Who cares what Commodore Barney thinks? He is nothing to do with us. Besides, you yourself have pointed out how little time we have."

Lowering his head, Jerome said, "I am sorry, but I find myself compelled to comply with his request."

Betsy pressed a hand to her forehead. "I do not understand. What power does Barney have over you?"

Jerome drew a deep breath as if preparing to say something difficult. Then he met Betsy's eyes and shrugged her question away. "For one thing, I must see Monsieur Pichon and ask him to advance me funds."

"Is that all? Washington is only a day's journey from Baltimore. Surely, you need not be gone more than three days."

He rubbed his upper lip before saying, "I am sorry, Elisa, but our separation must be longer than that. Your father insists."

Recalling the ardor with which Jerome had recently promised to wait for her, Betsy wondered why he had agreed to this separation so tamely. Could it be that his love for her had withered as quickly as it had bloomed?

Distressed, she rose and crossed to the front windows, which were swagged with lengths of green and gold silk. Looking out on the front lawn, she remembered seeing Jerome come up the drive the night they first met—so dashing that Betsy had been certain Odette's long-ago prophecy was about to come true. Now the hope that had flared so brightly that evening burned to ashes and fell around her feet.

"Are you angry?" Jerome asked, coming up behind her.

"No, but I wonder if you have ceased to care for me. If you have, I wish you would tell me so at once."

"Oh, Elisa, how can you think such a thing?" Betsy felt him gently lift her cascading curls and move them to rest upon her right shoulder. Then he ran his fingertips down the left side of her neck and across her collarbone to her shoulder. She sighed and tilted her head in response. The image of him putting his hands upon her breasts seized Betsy's imagination and made her weak with longing.

Jerome took her in his arms and kissed her, much more passionately than before. Although Betsy knew she should push him away, her body cried out for him and her emotions greeted the embrace as proof of his love, even though her skeptical mind knew that it was not necessarily so.

When he finally released her, Betsy was breathless. She took a step backward and found herself against the windowsill. "How long will you be gone?"

"A month, perhaps a little more."

"A month! But we have known each other only a month, and in that brief time, you have repeatedly declared your desire to marry quickly. Now you speak of a month's parting as though it were of no import. How can I know that you will even return? Is not Pichon likely to force you back to your post?"

Grasping her hand, Jerome raised it to his lips. *"Ne t'inquiètes pas, ma chérie.* I have orders from my brother that supersede any authority the *chargé d'affaires* may have."

"Then you leave on a mission for your brother and not because of what Barney said."

Jerome tilted his head to one side as though weighing his next statement. "Not entirely. We must win your father's consent, and if a time apart can do that, it is well worth the pain of separation. This proposed excursion is but a temporary absence meant to test our ardor. Let us yield to their demands. Then when I return, your father will see that I am worthy of you."

Betsy gazed deeply into his eyes, fearing that he was hiding something. How could she be sure that this was not just a ruse to break his promises to her? On the other hand, if he did have to accomplish a mission for Napoleon, surely he would have to keep the details secret. If only she could know the true reason for this journey.

"Of course, you should go if you feel you must," she said in as cool a voice as she could manage. "If you return, then we will determine if there is a reason to continue our acquaintance."

Jerome winced. "Have no fear that I will forget you, Elisa, or ever cease to love you. Perhaps when I return, you will be willing at last to entrust me with your happiness."

"Perhaps."

"Will you allow me to write to you?"

"Yes, if you gain permission from my father."

Jerome kissed her hand one last time. "Thank you."

He departed then, leaving Betsy dazed and wondering if she would ever see him again.

Two days later, Jerome left for Philadelphia. Betsy found that the ease with which he had agreed to the trip made her doubt his affection, so she warned herself not to assume that his offer of marriage still stood. Instead, she resolved to look for another path to happiness.

The afternoon following his departure, Betsy sat sewing with her mother and pondering how to protect herself if Jerome should prove fickle. Perhaps there was a way to convince her father to let her tour Europe despite the war between England and France, so she could meet other highborn suitors. As she considered the problem, two women from church came to call. Sixty-four-year-old Frances Purviance had stooped posture and arthritis-ruined fingers. Her companion, Janet Johnston Inglis, was a round-faced, bashful nineteen-year-old who had recently married their pastor. Betsy marveled that anyone her age could sacrifice her youth to a life of church work and studiously proper conversation.

Dorcas greeted the pair warmly, and the women began to describe a new charitable endeavor to help the widows of Baltimore seamen. Listening to them, Betsy kept her eyes on her sewing so they could not see her boredom. Later over tea, Mrs. Purviance recommended that

Dorcas try a new medication—Samuel Lee's Bilious Pills—and Betsy pressed her lips together to keep from saying something sarcastic. If the conversation followed its usual course, it would soon move on to talk of babies and colic remedies. God forbid that women should discuss a book or a political idea. How she hated the infinite tedium of Baltimore's domestic life.

THE FIRST LETTER from Jerome arrived within a week. He had addressed it formally to *Ma chère mademoiselle Patterson* and then described his journey by stagecoach in detail. He had decided to use the trip as an opportunity to educate himself about her country, so he asked Commodore Barney to show him sites like Independence and Congress halls.

> *I wish that Napoleon, who is such an ardent disciple of republicanism, could see these sacred buildings where your country was born. The chance to visit such shrines to liberty is the one thing that makes our separation tolerable. The memory of your exquisite beauty and admirable character fills my every waking hour. I beg that when I see you again, you will finally accept my hand in marriage.*

Betsy raced through the letter and then reread it slowly to analyze each nuance. As much as she wanted to be persuaded by Jerome's words, their eloquence felt false. Her own emotions were in such turmoil that she knew she would be incapable of writing anything so glib.

You dare not trust him, warned the skeptic in her, nurtured since childhood on La Rochefoucauld's cynical writings. *It is time to put this episode behind you and pursue a new course.* Perhaps she had been too hasty in disparaging every potential suitor in America. Surely Maryland, Virginia, or New York contained at least one young man sophisticated enough to offer the cultured life she dreamed of living.

She refolded the letter, stored it in a casket that she kept in her bedroom, and forbade herself from running upstairs to reread it more than once a day.

AWARE THAT BALTIMORE was gossiping about the absence of her suitor, Betsy determined to act as though nothing was amiss. When the Pattersons were invited to a ball at Belvidere, the fashionable mansion of Colonel John Howard Eager, Betsy put on her second-best gown—unable to endure the white gown that had elicited Jerome's admiration—carefully styled her hair, and put on rouge borrowed surreptitiously from Henriette.

As the carriage drew up to the columned portico of the mansion, Betsy admonished herself to affect a liveliness she did not feel. She greeted her hosts in the front reception hall, noting silently that Colonel Howard had dressed more comfortably this evening in a suit that fit his present girth. Then, as she strolled through the hall, she went out of her way to greet even casual acquaintances, and she dropped witticisms at every opportunity. When asked about Jerome, Betsy shrugged with feigned nonchalance. "I believe he is touring the Atlantic seaboard. Perhaps he is on a mission for the First Consul."

To those who pressed the issue, she laughed. "My, how people love to make matches where none exist. Lieutenant Bonaparte was invited frequently to our home because my parents knew that he must miss his own large family."

She danced that night with more than a dozen partners, and while the whirl of activity may have dispelled the rumors that she was pining for Jerome, it did little to dull the pain in her breast. Not a man in the ballroom had an appearance as pleasing as Jerome's tousled black curls and laughing eyes. When her partners appeared before her in fashionably cut suits of dark green and brown, she pictured the elaborately braided uniforms that hugged Jerome's broad shoulders and narrow waist. While the young men of Baltimore talked about commerce and hunting, she recalled stories of evenings at the Paris opera followed by gay midnight suppers. And with the slurred accent of Maryland in her ears, she longed for the melodious sounds of Jerome's voice in their French conversations.

By the time she arrived home, Betsy was exhausted by the pretense that she was still the lively Belle of Baltimore. Throwing herself onto her bed, she wept over the arid desert in which she felt herself trapped.

JEROME WROTE BETSY every day, continuing to swear that he loved her and was eager to see her again. He also described the people he and Barney met and the places they visited; Jerome believed that a person should always see the major sights of interest when visiting a new country. As she read each missive, Betsy could hear his voice in her mind, and she found herself sniffing the paper for a hint of his cologne. Every new letter eroded her resolve to end the relationship.

After two weeks in Philadelphia, Commodore Barney took Jerome to Washington, D.C., where he met the Smiths and Nancy Spear. "Their kindness and warmth—and the beauty of your aunts—has made me miss you even more."

While in the capital, Jerome also saw Monsieur Pichon, who urged him to return to duty. Jerome described the meeting as a joke, yet Betsy worried that the diplomat would have his way and part her from Jerome. As uncertain as she was about their future, she did not want the impersonal forces of the French government to make such a decision for her.

ONE MORNING AFTER Betsy had sat up far into the night rereading Jerome's letters, she woke from a dream in which Jerome had crept into her room and begun kissing her, first on her mouth, then down the length of her body, drawing down her chemise as he progressed.

Waking to find herself alone, Betsy pounded the mattress and curled up on her side. Her body felt so swollen with desire that she thought she would go mad. No other gentleman had ever excited such feelings within her. She longed for Jerome to come take possession of her quickly and, if necessary, with masterful persuasion if that was what was required to banish her terrible indecision.

Betsy brought her fist to her mouth and bit the knuckle of her index finger until the pain diminished her arousal. Then she sat up and gazed at the letters strewn across the nightstand. Jerome's repeated declarations of love echoed in her mind.

On top of the letters was the red leather volume of La Rochefoucauld's *Maxims*. The night before, she had looked through it to settle her mind and found the saying, "In great matters we should not try so much to create opportunities as to utilize those that offer themselves." At the time, she had taken it as a sign that she should marry Jerome despite her father's objections. Now she snatched up the book and threw it across the room so it hit the far wall.

A minute later, a knock on the door was followed by her mother's entrance. Dorcas was still in her wrapper but her hair was already tucked in a cap. "Are you all right?"

"Yes, Mother, I am fine."

Dorcas's glance flicked from the copy of the *Maxims* on the floor to the correspondence scattered on the bedside table to Betsy's woe-ful expression. She picked up the book and sat on the edge of the bed. "I am worried about you. You hardly eat, and your temper is fitful. Do you miss Lieutenant Bonaparte so very much?"

Feeling like a child caught with a telltale smear of jam across her cheek, Betsy nodded.

"But he has written you every day. Have his letters grown cold? Do you fear that his attachment has waned?"

"No, his letters express as much devoted affection as I could wish. I worry—" Betsy fell silent as emotion constricted her throat. Taking a deep breath, she calmed herself enough to say, "I have known him such a short time. I wonder if I can really be certain of his character."

Her mother reached over to smooth the sleep-tangled curls from her daughter's forehead. "It is impossible to know your husband com-pletely before you enter into marriage. Even the best of men have fail-ings that they hide from public view."

Looking up swiftly, Betsy wondered if that was an oblique refer-ence to her father's infidelities. "Please be frank. What do you think of Lieutenant Bonaparte?"

Dorcas smiled. "He is a warm-hearted, generous young man who perhaps lacks the uncompromising discipline you are accustomed to in your father. Yet I think his character and station in life make him a more congenial prospect for you than a sober businessman would be."

Impulsively, Betsy hugged her mother and spoke softly into her ear, "He has led such a worldly life. I am afraid the very qualities that make him so attractive to me also make him, well, perhaps not steady enough to marry."

Dorcas pulled back and cupped a hand under Betsy's chin. "Lieu-tenant Bonaparte loves you deeply, I am certain, and that might be enough to mature his character. But I think you may be correct in judging that he is weaker than you in some respects. You must decide whether your love for him is strong enough to try to help him overcome his weaknesses and forgive him when he fails. None of us is perfect, Betsy. You will do better if you understand that from the start."

"Mother, I do love him. I want to marry him more than I have ever wanted anything."

"I thought as much." Rising, Dorcas kissed the top of Betsy's head. "I will tell your father that you have decided on this match."

After her mother left the room, Betsy dressed with a lighter heart than she had known in weeks. As soon as she ate breakfast, she would write to Jerome in Washington and assure him that she eagerly awaited his return.

VI

A FEW days later Betsy sat in the nursery teaching Caroline embroidery when a maid came to find her. "Miss, you have a visitor in the drawing room."

"All right." Bending over her sister, Betsy said, "Caro, keep working on this until I return. I want to see how much you can accomplish."

"I will." Caroline frowned and tried to insert her needle at exactly the right spot in the linen.

Betsy stopped in her room to check her appearance. Then, as she descended the stairs, she heard the rare sound of her mother laughing below. Entering the drawing room, Betsy stopped short at the sight of Jerome sitting beside Dorcas on the sofa.

"Lieutenant Bonaparte! When did you return?"

He rose, and for a moment they gazed at each other with the sofa forming a barrier between them. Then Jerome said, "Last night. When I received your letter, I wanted to come right away, but Monsieur Pichon insisted that I wait until we had met with President Jefferson." He laughed. "Not wanting to cause a diplomatic incident, I dined with him on Wednesday and traveled all day yesterday."

Dorcas Patterson stood. "I think you two must want to be alone."

She left the room and closed the door behind her. Then Jerome asked, "Elisa, is it true, what you wrote in your letter? That you are

70

eager to see me again?"

"Yes," Betsy answered simply.

Jerome hurried around the sofa to stand before her but made no move to embrace. "Dare I hope that this means you have decided to accept me?"

"Yes."

He kissed her with surprising gentleness, then held her close. "My beloved Elisa, I was beginning to fear that I would never know this happiness. Do you truly still care for me?"

The irrepressible laughter of unexpected joy bubbled out of her, and she allowed herself to defy maidenly decorum by declaring, "I love you."

Jerome led Betsy to the sofa, pulled her onto his lap and kissed her again and again. After several minutes, he slipped his hand beneath her fichu and caressed her left breast. His touch awakened the memory of her passionate dreams. Although Betsy wanted to give herself to him then and there, she gripped his lapels and said, "Jerome, we dare not."

"Forgive me, my love." He inclined his head until their foreheads touched. "You are the most captivating woman I have ever met, and I find it difficult to control myself."

Feeling the same frustration, Betsy moaned and nearly gave in to her desire, but Jerome kissed her lightly and took her hands in his. "Be patient. I will speak with your father this afternoon. If he consents, then I shall apply for a license tomorrow and we will be married as soon as possible."

Betsy felt far from certain that her father would agree. Leaning her head on Jerome's shoulder, she asked, "What shall we do if he says no?"

"I think your mother favors us. Between the three of us, we will convince him."

His characteristic optimism made Betsy laugh again, and she settled comfortably beside him on the sofa. "You are possessed of such a rosy outlook, more so than I can ever muster."

"Then I am good for you, my love, as you are good for me."

ONCE AGAIN WILLIAM Patterson came home early from the counting house and called his wife and daughter into the drawing room. Betsy sat on the sofa, while Dorcas sat in her usual place, the banister-back wooden chair to the left of the fireplace.

Patterson stood on the hearth at an angle to face them both. Now in his fifties, he could no longer pass for a young man. His figure had grown thick around the waist, and his once-dark hair, cropped to collar length, was threaded with grey. His complexion, however, still retained the high ruddy color of his youth in Ireland.

"Betsy, I wish that your young man would not persist in encroaching upon my business hours. What possesses him to be in such a hurry?"

"He expects to receive orders from the First Consul any day now, sir, and he wants to resolve this business before that happens."

Shaking his head, Patterson crossed to his desk. He took some letters from a drawer and returned to stand in the same spot. "I have not been idle this last month. I used the time to make inquiries."

"Inquiries, sir?"

"Yes, inquiries." He slapped the papers against his left palm. "I realized that Lieutenant Bonaparte has never told us his age, so I asked your uncle Smith to question him while he was in Washington. Bonaparte told him that by French law, a man must be twenty-one before becoming a lieutenant, so at least he meets our age requirement for marriage. But I intend to write my lawyer and ask him to investigate French marriage law."

Betsy gripped the edge of the sofa cushions. "Is that necessary? We are planning to marry in the United States."

"Normally, nations honor the matrimonial bonds contracted in other lands, but in this case, the eminence of Lieutenant Bonaparte's brother makes it prudent to comply with French laws as well as our own. In fact, I think it advisable for you to delay marrying until Lieutenant Bonaparte has received the First Consul's blessing."

"But sir, there is no time for that."

"No time? What can you mean?" He glanced at his wife in alarm and then at Betsy. "Tell me the truth. Is there something that you have kept from your mother and me?"

Betsy realized that he feared her honor might be compromised, so she shook her head. "No, Father. I meant only that Lieutenant Bonaparte may soon be ordered back to the navy, and with France at war, who knows when he will return to Baltimore again?"

"Is that not reason enough to delay this marriage? Do you want to risk becoming a widow a few scant weeks after becoming a wife?"

Betsy lifted her head proudly. "Sir, I would rather be the wife of Jerome Bonaparte for an hour than married to any other man for a lifetime."

Patterson again looked to his wife. "Have you nothing to say to this headstrong girl? Surely, this is not how you were taught to conduct yourself when you were her age."

Dorcas shook her head. "As you well know, I was already a mother at her age. Times have changed. Young people now have more say in deciding their marriages than I did as a girl."

Patterson's cheeks turned red as he took in the unflattering implication behind her words. Before he could respond, Betsy pulled his attention back to the matter at hand. "Have you any reason to feel uneasy about Lieutenant Bonaparte apart from our haste, Father?"

He scowled at her and sat in his teal wingback chair. "Commodore Barney wrote to me last week." As he unfolded a letter, Betsy's heart sank, but she strove to keep her face blank. "He says that Lieutenant Bonaparte behaved correctly during their trip and showed not the slightest interest in making the acquaintance of other young women. Ah, here is the passage I want. 'His persistence in declaring his affection for your daughter was, in fact, fatiguing to all who heard him, and I retain no doubt that he is sincerely attached to her.'"

After folding up the page, Patterson asked, "Betsy, are you absolutely determined to accept this man?"

"Yes, Father."

"Very well. When he calls on me this evening, I will give him my consent."

THE NEXT DAY, Jerome came to dine with the Pattersons. As soon as the soup was served, he announced, "I have good news. This morning, I obtained a marriage license."

"You waste no time," William Jr. said in a tone that made it clear he was not paying a compliment.

Jerome took a biscuit from the bread basket. "No, not in a matter as important as this. I also mailed invitations to Monsieur Pichon and the Spanish ambassador Yrujo to attend the wedding. I set the date for November 3."

As William Patterson looked up, his heavy eyebrows came together in a way that Betsy knew meant trouble. "You presume too much, sir. Mrs. Patterson and I have not agreed to a date, and the third is out of the question. That is only five days hence."

"But why wait? We want to have time together before duty calls me back to the navy."

Ignoring him, Patterson glared at his eldest daughter. "Did you know of this plan?"

Betsy glanced regretfully at Jerome. "No, I did not."

Jerome put down his biscuit and shifted in his seat to face her. "But I thought we agreed that we would marry as soon as possible."

"We did, but five days is not enough time. I need to prepare to leave my home."

"Oh, I see." He sounded chastened. "Forgive me, I should have consulted you."

"You should have consulted our parents," William Jr. interjected. "Unless, of course, you have a secret reason for marrying in such unseemly haste."

Jerome pushed back his chair violently and stood. "How dare you malign my honor, sir! And to besmirch the reputation of your sister is even more unforgivable. If you were not about to be my brother, I would challenge you."

"Enough!" Patterson rose and frowned at his eldest son. "William, kindly remember that I am the head of this family and will deal with the matter of your sister's marriage."

Then he shifted his disapproving scowl to Jerome and Betsy, who shrank back in shame even though she had done nothing wrong. She glanced at her mother for sympathy, but Dorcas sat with her lips pressed tightly together and her eyes downcast.

After a long pause, Patterson said, "Lieutenant Bonaparte, although my son speaks out of turn, he merely gives voice to the suspicion all Baltimore will harbor if you and my daughter marry too speedily."

Flushing, Jerome resumed his seat. "Forgive me. I am too used to France, where people have lived with the exigencies of war for a long time and do not find hasty marriages such a scandal as they seem to be in this more placid society."

Leaning forward, Betsy said, "Father, as you know, Lieutenant Bonaparte could be recalled to duty any day. How long an engagement do you require?"

Patterson looked to his wife, who nodded silently. He sighed. "You may marry at the end of November."

A FEW EVENINGS LATER, Betsy was sitting on the sofa in the drawing room reading aloud to Jerome from the book of French verse he had given her. As she paused to ask the meaning of an unfamiliar word, her father entered the room.

"I have received a letter from my lawyer that concerns you."

Betsy set her book aside. "What can Mr. Dallas have to say that concerns us, Father?"

He stood before the hearth, clutching a folded-up letter in his hand. "It is about French marriage law. Under the new civil code that went into effect last year, no one under the age of twenty-five may marry without parental permission."

The smile vanished from Jerome's face. "Where did he hear such a thing?"

"From Monsieur Pichon, who further informed Dallas that he told you of the law when you were in Washington."

"Did he?" Jerome shrugged. "I have no memory of such a conversation."

Patterson brandished the letter. "Lieutenant Bonaparte, affecting such a cavalier attitude will not improve your standing with me. Might I remind you that I can withdraw my permission for Betsy to marry, as she is only eighteen? Now, did you know of this law or not?"

Jerome turned red and was about to respond angrily when Betsy laid a hand upon his arm. Glancing at her, he mastered himself. "Yes, he did mention the change, but I did not think it of any import as we will be marrying under the laws of the United States."

"Why did you not tell us this before?"

"Father, he just explained that he did not think it mattered."

As Patterson looked from one to the other, he rubbed his forehead.

"Do neither of you comprehend the seriousness of making a marriage contract? It must be undertaken in full conformity with the law."

Betsy scooted forward to the edge of the sofa. "But, sir, you told me yourself that it is customary for nations to honor each other's matrimonial laws. We are not at war with the French, so they would have no reason to dispute a marriage conducted in this country. Has Mr. Dallas said anything in his letter to contradict that interpretation?"

"No." Patterson sank into his armchair. "In fact, he makes the same point, although I must hasten to add that he believes as I do that you should err on the side of caution."

"But that would mean waiting four years before we could marry!"

Betsy's horrified expression drew a smile from her father. "Not at all. It means that Lieutenant Bonaparte should do as I suggested before and write the First Consul for his consent."

"Permission is not his to give!" Jerome exclaimed.

"What do you mean?"

Jerome lifted his chin in a mannerism that Betsy had learned indicated stubbornness and a certain haughty pride. "Napoleon may be the chief executive of France, but he is neither my father nor my eldest brother. If I must apply to anyone for permission, it would be my mother."

"That is even better!" Betsy grasped Jerome's arm. "You have told me that she has never denied you anything. If you write and ask her consent, surely she will say yes."

Instead of agreeing readily, Jerome glowered at her. "I am not a child. I find it offensive that I must ask permission of anyone."

Bewildered by his coldness, Betsy pulled back. "But if it is the law?"

"It is not the law here." Jerome turned back to William Patterson. "I do not see why we must change what is already decided. To wait for my mother's consent would delay our wedding by months. Our marriage will be perfectly valid in this country."

"That would be enough if your intention was to settle here, but since it is not—"

"But of course, I will write to her." Jerome placed his hand on his heart. "I love my family too much not to inform them of such a momentous change in my life. As Elisa says, my mother is certain to agree. So why must we wait upon such a foregone eventuality? We can marry as planned and make certain that we obtain my mother's consent before going to France."

"I do not deem this a prudent course, but if neither of you will listen to reason—" Falling silent, William Patterson sat back in his chair and regarded them wearily. "I cannot allow Betsy's standing as a married woman to come under question. Will you promise not to take my daughter to France until you hear from your mother?"

"Yes, sir, gladly, if that will satisfy you."

Patterson rubbed the side of his jaw. "I suppose it must."

For an instant, Betsy felt a spasm of guilt at causing her father so much distress, but any remorse was quickly swallowed up by joy at the prospect of being Jerome's wife.

She jumped up and kissed her father's cheek. "All will be well. I feel certain that Lieutenant Bonaparte and I are destined to be together."

Two days later as the family sat at dinner, the post arrived, and William Patterson opened a letter marked URGENT. Within seconds, his face grew as stormy as Betsy had ever seen it. He stowed the letter in his inside pocket.

For nearly a minute, he glared down the oval table to where Jerome and Betsy sat side by side. Finally, he said, "Lieutenant Bonaparte, I have just learned of a family matter requiring some delicacy, and I must ask you to leave as soon as our meal is finished."

Jerome looked up from his whispered conversation with fourteen-year-old Edward. "Is there no way I could be of service?"

"No, that is impossible. We require the utmost privacy."

In response to Jerome's inquiring glance, Betsy shook her head to indicate that she had no idea what was wrong. Glancing around the table, she saw that William Jr. and Robert looked equally flummoxed, while Edward, Joseph, and Margaret displayed open curiosity. Mercifully, the four youngest children were upstairs in the nursery, so no one filled the air with impertinent questions.

The rest of the meal passed in silence. As soon as the servants had cleared the dishes, Jerome rose and bowed to Dorcas. To Betsy he said, "I will see you tomorrow. Do not hesitate to send for me if I can be of assistance to your family." He kissed her hand and left.

As William Jr. pushed back his chair, his father said, "No, wait. I want you, Robert, and Elizabeth to stay. The younger children may be excused."

Frowning, Betsy wondered if her brother John had landed in a scrape in Virginia. That was the only thing she could think of to provoke an adults-only family council.

As soon as the younger children had left, Patterson removed the letter from his pocket and unfolded it again. His hand was trembling so that the paper shook as he read.

> *Is it possible, sir, you can so far forget yourself, and the happiness of your child, as to consent to her marrying Mr. Bonaparte? If you knew him, you never would, as misery must be her portion—he who but a few months ago destroyed the peace and happiness of a respectable family in Nantz by promising marriage, then ruined, leaving her to misery and shame. What has been his conduct in the West Indies? There ruined a lovely young woman who had only been married for a few weeks! He parted her from her husband, and destroyed that family! And here, what is his conduct? At the very moment he was demanding your daughter in marriage he ruined a young French girl, whom he now leaves also in misery!*

Betsy interrupted by demanding, "Who wrote that?"

Her father looked up, frowning at her importunate tone. "The letter is unsigned."

"Then I do not believe it. It contains nothing but lies written by someone who envies Lieutenant Bonaparte and wants to do him harm."

"That is hardly likely," Robert said. "The writer could do him far more harm by complaining to his superiors or the First Consul. The motive behind this letter is clearly to warn us of his false nature."

"He is not false! He is warm and open. How can you place more trust in a scurrilous letter writer who was too cowardly to sign his name than in someone you know?"

"Oh, my poor child," Dorcas said, coming around the table to embrace Betsy. "I know you must be upset to learn that your fears about Lieutenant Bonaparte's character are justified."

William Patterson jerked in surprise. "Madam, to what fears do you refer?"

Betsy wanted to pull away from her mother, but she managed to conceal her fury over the betrayal of her confidence. "Mother misunderstood me. I once said that I feared Lieutenant Bonaparte was too impulsive to make a suitable husband. But I never meant to imply that I thought him capable of such calculated debauchery. I do not believe it."

"Elizabeth! You astonish me. Do you mean to say that you accepted this man even though you had qualms about his character?"

"I do not have qualms, Father. I only remarked that he is a less disciplined man than you might wish. I have no fear that Lieutenant Bonaparte means to abandon me. Why would he trouble to obtain a license and plan a wedding if marriage were not his object?"

"You foolish girl. Do you think a marriage vow in a foreign country will hold a man like that? Listen to what else this letter says: 'He now wishes to secure himself a home at your expense until things can be arranged for his return to France, when rest assured he will be the first to turn your daughter off and laugh at your credulity.' Betsy, can you not admit the possibility that Lieutenant Bonaparte has deceived you?"

As her father asked that question, Betsy had the strange feeling that her character, not Jerome's, was on trial and she must testify well to save her life. "No, Father, I cannot. I know Lieutenant Bonaparte loves me and I swear to you that he has treated me honorably. Even if he has made past errors of judgment, does not any Christian deserve the chance to redeem himself?"

Patterson shook his head. "Not at the risk of my daughter's happiness."

"But Father, I love him. My happiness depends on him."

"My child, I know you believe that now, but you will recover from this blow. You are young and know little of the world. A man like that cannot be trusted."

Betsy's temper snapped. "How can you look me in the eye and say that? Do you think me blind to what goes on in this very house?"

Dorcas cried out and pulled away from Betsy, while William Patterson's face turned purple. After a moment, he rose, stood behind his chair, and gripped the top of it with white-knuckled hands. "The only question under discussion is Lieutenant Bonaparte's conduct, which I find completely unacceptable. You will write to him immediately and end your engagement."

"I will not."

"Yes, Elizabeth, you will. You have one hour to produce an appropriate letter. If you do not, I will, and I assure you I will express myself in more brutal terms than you would like."

He moved toward the door, paused, and turned back. "As of tomorrow, you leave this house. I am sending you to relatives, where Bonaparte will be unlikely to find you."

"Where?"

"You will find out during the journey. Your eldest brother will accompany you. William, come with me. We have much to discuss before your departure."

Betsy sat on her bed with a portable writing desk on her lap, staring through tear-blurred eyes at a blank page on the green baize surface. She had already written and rejected three drafts of a letter. What she wanted was to word the message in such a way that would satisfy her father while still giving Jerome hope, but such a task was beyond her skill.

She had just written, "Dear Sir," for the fourth time when a knock sounded on her door.

"What is it?" she called irritably, certain that her mother had been sent to hurry her.

Instead, it was her brother Edward. A sensitive boy, as given to passionate outbursts and willful independence as Betsy, he slipped into the room, checked to make sure no one had seen him, and shut the door. "Is it true? Is Father making you give up Lieutenant Bonaparte?"

"Yes."

"But why?" Edward strode toward her. "I like Jerome."

"I like him too, but—" She fell silent as her tears started to flow. After wiping her eyes with an already damp handkerchief, she said, "Someone accused him anonymously of wrongdoing, so Father has withdrawn his consent for the match."

"That is very mean of him. Do you want me to ask him to give Jerome another chance?"

"No, Edward. You would only make Father angrier and get your-self in trouble."

"I don't care. I want to help."

"You cannot." With a sense of doom that she thought must rival the feelings of a noblewoman being sent to the guillotine, Betsy picked up her quill. As she again tried to compose the perfect farewell, her brother's restless pacing distracted her. Then an idea struck.

"Edward, if I keep Father and Mother occupied in the drawing room, do you think you can slip out of the house without anyone seeing you?"

He nodded vehemently. "I think so. Why?"

"I need you to take a secret message to Lieutenant Bonaparte's house. No one else must ever know. Do you promise?"

"Oh, yes," he said, filled with youthful ardor over being given a mission.

Quickly, Betsy crossed out the formal greeting and scrawled a mes-sage below it:

Dearest Lieutenant Bonaparte. My father has received an anony-mous letter making the vilest of accusations against you. I believe them to be lies, but all my pleading has been in vain, and he has re-voked his consent to our marriage. Shortly you will receive a formal communication from me to that effect. Know that I am forced to take this step and that my heart is unchanged. Tomorrow Father sends me from Baltimore, I know not where. If you love me, make every ef-fort to repair this breach so we can be reunited. I remain yours. E.P.

❧ VII ❧

Tʜᴇ next morning Betsy's father woke her before sunrise. He allowed her only a quick breakfast of bread and tea before he bundled her and William into the family coach, which waited in front of their house. Peter, the family's enslaved coachman, lifted Betsy's trunk onto the luggage shelf in back and then climbed onto the high driver's seat.

Patterson leaned through the window next to Betsy's seat. "I know yesterday's events came as a shock, Elizabeth. I hope you will use this opportunity to put Bonaparte out of your heart and recover the good sense I know you to possess."

Glancing past him to the upstairs windows of her home, Betsy felt unhappy that she had not been given time to tell her mother good-bye. "How long before I may return?"

"That depends entirely upon you." Patterson turned to his oldest son, who sat in the opposite seat, his arms crossed before him and a resentful scowl upon his face. "William, remember all that we discussed yesterday evening."

"Yes, Father."

Even though the sun had fully risen by then, the grey November sky threatened rain, so William pulled down and fastened the curtains on the carriage doors and either side of his seat. Likewise, Betsy

pulled down the curtain between her and the street, but not the nearest one. She did not want to feel completely shut in with her disapproving oldest brother.

Unfolding a newspaper, William began to read. Betsy gazed at passing
buildings as the coach moved slowly, clattering on the cobbles. Within
moments, they passed the narrow brick town house Jerome had rented, but she saw no sign of activity in the windows. What would happen if she leaped out and pounded his brass doorknocker? Would he
open the door in time to admit her before her brother forced her back
into the coach? Was Jerome even awake at this early hour? Before she
could act on her impulse, they turned west onto Market Street. To
Betsy's ears, the clopping of hooves on the stones counted out the increasing distance from her love.

When they turned south onto Bladensburg Road, Betsy deduced that
she was being sent to one of three locations: to Washington, where the
Smiths were in residence; to Richmond, where her cousin Mary Spear
was married to Philip Norborne Nicholas; or to Wilson Cary Nicholas's plantation, Mount Warren, where her brother John was living.

As the coach drove through the Maryland countryside, Betsy noticed a young man dressed in rough homespun clothes picking late ap-
ples in an orchard. When he caught sight of her, he took off his ragged
straw hat and made a clumsy bow. The gesture, though awkward, reminded her of Jerome and brought tears to her eyes.

Not long afterward, a light rain began to fall and mist blew into her
face, so Betsy fastened the last curtain.

William snapped his paper in irritation and set it aside. "It is too
damned dark to read."

Half rising, he removed a snuffbox from his greatcoat pocket, took
out a pinch of powdered tobacco, inhaled it, and then sneezed into a
handkerchief. Betsy suspected he was trying to provoke her into a
quarrel; it was rude to take snuff in the presence of a lady, but she
chose not to complain. William settled back into his seat. "I hope this
unfortunate episode will teach you to give up your foolish dreams of
a noble alliance. The proper ambition for a woman is to marry a reliable man and raise children of good character who will grow up to
be responsible citizens."

Betsy clenched her teeth and swallowed back a retort disparaging the popular ideal that a woman's primary duty was to train her children to be good patriots. "William, I am not so bad as you think. I do not grieve for lost trips to Europe or the chance to be presented to Napoleon. It is Lieutenant Bonaparte alone that I miss."

"I fail to see why you took such a fancy to the man. A sillier coxcomb I never met."

The insulting words brought an angry flush to Betsy's face. "He has a warm heart and many good qualities."

William again folded his arms across his chest. "You astound me. Although I know you to be vain, I have never had reason to doubt your intelligence. How can you defend the man after the letter that Father received?"

"Because I do not believe it." She slid over to sit directly across from him and leaned forward. "I do not claim that Lieutenant Bonaparte is without fault. He can be too rash and lighthearted. Perhaps he indulged in flirtations that went too far and caused misapprehensions. But he is not wicked. I would stake my life upon that."

"Then how do you explain the letter? What would it profit anyone to fabricate such lies?"

Betsy clasped her hands beneath her chin and spoke hurriedly, "I lay awake all last night thinking about that, and I think it must come from Monsieur Pichon. He has been very upset about Lieutenant Bonaparte's refusal to rejoin the navy. I believe that the minister fears the First Consul will hold him accountable, so he wrote the letter to sever the tie he blames for Lieutenant Bonaparte's sojourn in the United States."

William rubbed his temple. "I suppose there could be something in that."

She crossed to sit beside him and placed her hand on his arm. "I know I have little right to ask your help, William. I behaved rudely on the occasion of your first meeting Lieutenant Bonaparte, but I beg you not to hold that against me now that I am in such desperate straits. All my hopes lie in ruins, and I entreat you to be my ally, not my jailer."

He turned away, and Betsy felt humiliation wash over her. A moment later, however, her brother faced her again. "I admit that at first I believed only your vanity had suffered a blow. I now see that these events have wounded your heart. But Betsy, even though your arguments have merit, I still cannot accept that Lieutenant Bonaparte would be a worthy husband."

Exhausted by the appeal she had just made, Betsy leaned against his shoulder and whispered, "Will, when I think I may never see him again, I despair of living."

"Have courage, sister. Time will make this bearable."

THAT EVENING, THEY took a suite of rooms in an inn and ordered supper to be sent up to them. As they waited, William spread business correspondence on the scratched surface of the gateleg table in the parlor and began to work. Pacing before the rough brick fireplace, Betsy saw that his papers included a letter addressed in their father's hand to John, so she slipped into her bedroom and wrote a hasty note.

> *Henriette, I write from northern Virginia. On Saturday, my family received an anonymous letter accusing Lt. Bonaparte of dissipation, so my father ended our engagement and sent me into exile. I believe my destination to be Mount Warren, a plantation on the James River. My family's indignation burns so hot that I dare not write Bonaparte. I fear that any attempt on our part to meet would cause my father to take even more drastic action. My only hope is that Lt. Bonaparte may find a way to refute the charges and appease my father's wrath. Forgive me, dear Henriette, for not taking leave of you. Please be so good as to write to me, my sweet and loving friend.*

When the maidservant arrived with the food, William stacked his papers and carried them to his bedroom. Through the open door, Betsy saw him remove his coat and roll up his shirtsleeves to wash. She asked the maid quietly, "Could the innkeeper mail a letter for me?"

"Yes, miss."

"Thank you." Betsy slipped the woman a coin and the letter addressed to Henriette.

THE LAND BELONGING to the Mount Warren plantation had been in the Nicholas family since 1729. In the 1790s, a small town called Warren sprang up nearby at the mouth of Ballenger's Creek to accommodate the business generated by the estate. As his fellow Virginian George Washington had before him, Wilson Cary Nicholas believed in using crop rotation to increase agricultural yields, so he grew both wheat and tobacco—although by November, both crops had been harvested and the fields were nothing but stubble.

The Nicholas house was a wide Palladian structure whose two stories featured tall arched windows. A pillared porch topped by a pediment fronted the whole. Because the Senate was in session, Wilson Cary Nicholas was not at home, but his wife Margaret—Samuel Smith's sister—met Betsy and William in the wide front hall, which had a black-and-white marble floor and sweeping walnut staircase. As Mrs. Nicholas greeted her guests with warmth but some surprise, John Patterson stood silently behind her.

After the formalities of the initial welcome, John's fiancée Polly stepped forward and offered to lead Betsy up to the guest room. Polly was a pale, blue-eyed girl with the bland prettiness of a porcelain figurine. Betsy glanced back as she followed Polly up the staircase and saw her brothers and Mrs. Nicholas retire to the library. Presumably, they were about to hold a conference about the reason for the unexpected visit. Betsy's cheeks burned.

"I have not seen you in so long," Polly gushed as she opened the door to a front bedroom, which had a high four-poster bed with bright floral chintz bed curtains. "From what John has shared of his letters from home, I was certain that next time we met, you would be a married woman."

Betsy stopped short, feeling as though the other girl had stabbed her. "If only that were so!" She pulled off her hat and threw it onto the bed. Then she crossed to the window and stared down the driveway, wondering if she could find a way to escape back to Baltimore. Could she ride a horse so far, or would she need to steal a carriage?

Polly stepped close beside her. "Betsy, whatever can be wrong? Has Lieutenant Bonaparte cooled in his feelings toward you?"

Betsy shook her head violently. When she felt the unwelcome touch of Polly's hand on her shoulder, she jerked away and faced the other girl. "No, we remain devoted to each other. But recent events have caused my family to doubt his character, so Father sent me away."

"Oh." Polly's face clouded over. "But surely, you would not want to marry a man of questionable character. Is it not better to find out such things before you have taken an irrevocable step?"

Looking at her future sister-in-law, Betsy sighed. Polly was the kind of young woman most men would consider a perfect wife—firm with children and servants, gracious to guests, conventional in manners, and possessed of a limited imagination. Having to explain herself to such a person was unbearably wearisome. "I believe that Lieutenant Bonaparte has been accused unjustly and the decision to separate us made in haste."

"Oh, if that is the case, I am sure the truth will out and you will be reunited shortly," Polly answered with irritating ease. Hearing a noise in the hall, she went to the doorway. "Miss Patterson's trunk comes in here, Jonah." A slave wearing the neat clothes of a house servant carried in Betsy's trunk and set it at the foot of the bed.

Watching Jonah exit, Betsy felt a burst of unfamiliar empathy for him. Never before had she considered how it must feel to be ordered where to live and what to do while under the constant threat of being sold away from the people you love.

Polly broke into her reverie. "I will leave you to unpack. Call me if you need anything."

"Thank you." As Polly shut the door, Betsy felt thankful to be alone.

THAT NIGHT AFTER the family retired, Betsy sat at her dressing table writing to Jerome. As her quill raced across the page, Mrs. Nicholas entered her room. The older woman approached, holding a candlestick in her right hand. She peered at the papers before Betsy.

"You might as well throw that missive away, Elizabeth. The servants and children all have strict instructions not to mail any letters you give them."

"You cannot deprive me of my rights, madam."

"Do not talk like a fool. Your father has placed you into my keeping and authorized me to lock you in your chamber if you prove willful. And if you do not find our company amenable, you will be sent to an even more remote location."

Betsy rose and went to the window, wishing she could see whether anyone moved upon the dark lawn. Was it possible that Jerome might come for her by using the information she had sent Henriette? Over her shoulder, she said, "So I am made a prisoner for the crime of love."

"No, you have been placed in protective custody to save you from your own imprudence."

Turning, Betsy stared at her hostess. Margaret Smith Nicholas had her brother Samuel's blue eyes, but they displayed none of the warmth with which Betsy's uncle habitually regarded her. "Madam, I am fatigued from my long journey. Good night."

"Think on what I have told you. We are happy to have you stay with us, but you must endeavor to put this error in judgment behind you." With that, Mrs. Nicholas picked up the letter Betsy had been writing and carried it from the room.

Tears sprang to Betsy's eyes, not because she had lost the letter, but because this icy woman would read its sentiments. She felt as mortified as if someone had stripped her naked in the public square. Turning back to the dark glass, she rested her forehead on its surface. *I will play the obedient daughter for now. Just long enough to give Jerome time to come for me.*

The NEXT DAY, William left early to return home. In the afternoon, as Polly took drawing lessons from a local master, Betsy went alone into the Prussian blue drawing room. She chose a needlepoint-cushioned, mahogany corner chair by the windows because it afforded a view that extended nearly to the main road. After gazing down the driveway, she took out a man's pocketbook she had recently begun as a gift for Jerome. Her length of wool measured about seven by sixteen inches. The first step was to cover one side with embroidered Irish stitch, which produced rows of flamelike designs in graduated colors. Because Jerome was French, Betsy had chosen shades of red and blue. Once she finished the embroidery, she would line the piece with linen, bind the edges with tape, and fold the two ends toward the center to make pockets.

Betsy had seen her father's acquaintances using wallets like this and, knowing Jerome's love of finery, thought it would make the perfect present to give him when they married. Now, working on it helped sustain her belief that they would see each other again.

The mental absorption required by the pattern served to distract

Betsy from her misery. The repetitive nature of forming row upon row of tiny stitches reminded her of a Catholic prayer called the Rosary that Jerome had described as a favorite of his mother's. Although Betsy was not especially pious, she came to regard her work as a prayer in which, instead of counting beads, she counted stitches, with each one marking a repetition of the plea that God would restore Jerome to her.

The more Betsy worked on the pocketbook, the more eager she became to complete it. However, she was afraid that her brother would confiscate the project if he discovered she was making it for Jerome, so she worked on it only in the daytime when estate business kept John from the house. After several days at Mount Warren, Betsy learned that John was supping at the tavern, so she decided to use the opportunity to embroider that evening.

After supper, Betsy chose a chair close to the center of the drawing room where the lamps were lit. Mrs. Nicholas and Polly sat on the midnight blue cabriole sofa sewing, and a younger daughter, Charlotte, practiced minuets on the pianoforte. The women worked in silence for more than an hour. Then Polly asked, "Betsy, what are you making?"

"A man's pocketbook."

"I have never seen anything like it."

"It will fold like this, do you see?" Betsy turned the two ends to the inside and folded it in half again to wallet shape to hide the inner edge where she had embroidered Jerome's name. Then she held it up so that Polly could see the outer stitched design.

"How clever." Before Betsy could object, Polly took the pocketbook from her. She examined the embroidery and then unfolded the fabric. Shock registered on her face. "Betsy, why have you marked this with Lieutenant Bonaparte's name?"

"Because I hope to give it to him one day."

Mrs. Nicholas put down the boy's shirt she was mending. "Elizabeth, have you been in contact with him since you arrived?"

"No, ma'am, but I find it impossible to believe I will never see him again. I feel certain that our lives are destined to be joined together."

The sound of clapping came from the doorway, and they turned to see John enter. Charlotte's playing ceased. John walked with deliberate care to a sack-back Windsor chair that faced the sofa and sat heavily upon it. "Spoken like the sister I remember from childhood," he said and belched. Betsy, who sat nearest to him, could smell whiskey.

"Mother Nicholas, did you know that when Betsy was ten, she claimed that a prophecy had foretold she would marry a European prince? It was a curious thing to grow up with a younger sister who thought herself my superior and even more curious that our parents rarely troubled to curb her airs. They were proud to have her known as the 'Belle of Baltimore.' No doubt we landed in this predicament because the family was flattered by Bonaparte's attentions. It goes without saying that Betsy thought them only her due." He laughed nastily. "What a comeuppance it must be, sister, to learn that you are not so irresistible as you had supposed."

"John, you have not met Lieutenant Bonaparte, so I hardly think you qualified to judge his regard for me. Particularly not when you are the worse for drink."

Stretching out his legs before him, John laughed again. "Oh, I still have enough wits about me to know that you will never see your Jerome again. He saw that your ambition made you an easy victim for his schemes."

Betsy rose with as much dignity as her tiny frame could convey. "Whiskey has made you insufferable."

John lifted his head and squinted at her. "What is insufferable is your ingratitude toward the family that attempts to save you from folly. They should let you learn for yourself what happens to women who cannot govern their passions."

Polly gasped, and Mrs. Nicholas exclaimed, "John, you go too far!"

"Sorry, Mother Nicholas." He passed his hand over his eyes. "Perhaps I have had a drop too much. If you will excuse me, I shall retire."

As he walked unsteadily from the room, Betsy remained standing by her chair. She had no desire to remain with these women, but she feared to encounter John on the stairs.

"Please, dear, do not take his words to heart. John sometimes worries that he lives in the shadow of your brothers, which causes him to imagine slights that do not exist."

Betsy looked at Mrs. Nicholas with raised eyebrows. "You, no doubt, understand my brother better than his own family does."

"Perhaps I do. He is a dear young man who simply wants more confidence."

"He will not find it in a bottle."

"No, but he may gain it from being shown patience and loving-kindness."

Folding her arms below her bosom, Betsy said, "How tolerant of you. I find it passing strange that when I declare Lieutenant Bonaparte to be deserving of patience and loving-kindness, my family calls me obstinate. I know that he has faults, but I love him as deeply as you and Polly love my brother, and since no one else will advocate for Bonaparte, I must."

Betsy took the pocketbook from Polly and stowed it in her workbasket, which she carried with her as she went upstairs.

The NEXT MORNING when Betsy entered the breakfast room where the family was assembled, John had the grace to look shamefaced. "Forgive me. I understand that I was rude last night."

Betsy did not believe he had forgotten their conversation. "You most certainly were, but I am willing to overlook it this once for the sake of family harmony."

As she took her seat, John handed her a letter. Betsy turned the folded-up paper over so she could break the seal, only to discover that it was open.

"You read it?"

He turned red. "Under Father's orders."

"This is intolerable." She pushed back from the table and ran from the room.

Once she reached the privacy of her bedroom, she read the letter, which was from Henriette. It reported that the Reubells had seen Jerome, who swore that the anonymous letter was full of falsehood.

Bonaparte informed us that when he attempted to see your father, he was peremptorily turned away. He is quite in a lather and declared his intention to travel to New York to prove his love for you. Reubell and I are at a loss to know what he means.

Stricken, Betsy allowed the page to flutter to the bed as she gazed out her window. *New York? Why had Jerome gone to New York?*

Although Betsy had never been there, Robert had described it to her. It was the largest city in the United States, more than twice the size of Baltimore and easily five times more cosmopolitan. Jerome would find every possible luxury there, a dizzying variety of entertainments, and more than enough beautiful women to make him forget Betsy. How could traveling to New York advance their cause? As far as she could see, all it did was make it impossible for her to run away to him.

Betsy snatched up Henriette's letter, reread it, and took comfort in the description of Jerome's agitation. She felt grateful to her friend for her tact in not sending a direct message from Jerome, which would have caused the letter to be kept from Betsy. Instead, Henriette provided just enough information to show that he had not given up but rather was acting out a plan. What that plan might be, Betsy could not imagine, but she would try to trust him.

Despite her intention to remain resolute, Betsy's hope faded. The stomach pain she had experienced during their prior separation returned, and her appetite failed. In the evenings, she reread the letters she had received while Jerome was traveling with Barney and tried to reassure herself that he would never forget her. However, whenever she sat still, whether reading or sewing, she imagined him at a string of parties dancing with women who wore the latest fashions and flirted charmingly.

Vexed by the growing fear that she would never see him again, Betsy paced before the drawing room windows by the hour, twisting a handkerchief until it was reduced to a frayed rag. On the third day of this behavior, Mrs. Nicholas entered the room and demanded, "Can you not find some employment? You will drive us all mad."

Polly, who was kneeling on the sofa, gazing at Betsy over its curved back as she tried to engage her in conversation, said, "Let us go riding. I am sure the air and exertion will do you good."

Within an hour, the two young women were on horseback trotting down a country road that led between barren fields bordered by split-rail fences. The land rolled gently to the horizon, and in the distance, Betsy could just make out the misty blue silhouette of hills. The temperature was crisp and the sky clear. Although she would not admit it to her companion, it felt good to be out of the house and in the open air.

After glancing sideways at Betsy several times, Polly said, "I thought we could ride to the river and back if that is agreeable."

"I don't care. It matters little where I am."

They passed a grove of bare oaks where squirrels raced through the undergrowth gathering acorns from beneath crackling brown leaves. Moments later, Polly tried again. "Betsy, I know that you greatly regret your separation from Lieutenant Bonaparte, but is it not best to put him out of your mind? From what John said, he seems to be a man of questionable character."

"A pretty instance of the pot calling the kettle black. John's drunkenness hardly qualifies him as a model of rectitude. And if I were to tell of the other hypocrisies in my family—"

Polly raised her left hand to shield the side of her face. "I do not want to hear. I don't think it very kind of you to use people's weaknesses as weapons in your campaign to achieve what you desire."

Betsy pulled up her horse. "It is very easy for you and John to deride my efforts to obtain what I want. No one is throwing obstacles in the way of your happiness."

Seeing that Betsy had halted, Polly pulled her horse around and came back. "No one wishes to make you unhappy."

"Then why can you not understand? I love Bonaparte, and every day we are separated is a torment. It is all that I can do to keep myself from running to New York in search of him."

"Betsy!" Polly's agitation was so pronounced that it unsettled her horse, and she had to calm him by rubbing his withers. "If you have made such threats to your family, it is no wonder that they despair of you. No decent woman says such things."

"Polly, we are nearly the same age. Do you truly have no conception of what I mean? You say you want to marry my brother and yet you propose to wait for years. Do you never lie awake at night and burn for him?"

The other girl blushed. "I will not discuss such things."

"Then we have nothing whatever to say to one another." Jerking the reigns, Betsy turned her horse around, lashed it with her crop, and galloped back to the house.

Polly reported the conversation to her mother, who wrote her displeasure to the Pattersons that very night. Within four days came the reply that John should bring Betsy home. He was so furious with her for having upset Polly and disrupted the Nicholas household that he barely spoke during the two-day journey—a silence Betsy viewed as a godsend rather than the rebuff he intended.

They arrived home late at night, and Betsy went straight to her room. Her mother brought her some soup and bread on a tray.

"Child, you cannot go on like this," Dorcas said as she stood watching her daughter eat.

Betsy set down her spoon. "Mother, what have I done that is so terrible? I fell in love with a man who stands accused of wrongdoing, but nothing is proved. Yet when I beg for him to be allowed to defend himself, everyone treats me as though I were a strumpet."

"You told Polly you wanted to run away to New York in search of him."

"Polly is a ninny with no depth of feeling."

Dorcas pushed a few strands of hair back into her cap. "You know that I like Lieutenant Bonaparte. He is very amiable, but ease of manner is not everything. We cannot allow you to marry a rake."

Folding her arms across her chest, Betsy glared at her mother. "You condemn him on the basis of gossip. I know that he tried to speak to Father about the accusations and was turned away. Without investigating, how can Father be so sure that the letter is truthful? There could be other explanations."

Dorcas sighed. "William told us of your belief. But Lieutenant Bonaparte has left Baltimore and evidently given up his design of marrying you. For the sake of your happiness, you must accept that this is over."

"I can never be happy without him, Mother. And I do not believe that all is lost. If Father were to ask Reubell, I am sure that he could reach Bonaparte and ask him to return."

Dorcas shook her head. "Your father believes it best to end the acquaintance."

Betsy pushed away her half-eaten soup. "You can take this back downstairs."

"You have to eat."

"No, Mother. I cannot."

As soon as she was alone, Betsy began to pace. There had to be a way to convince her father to let her contact Jerome. Perhaps if she agreed to a long engagement to give her parents time to test his character, her father might relent.

Inspired by the idea, Betsy left her room and descended the stairs quietly, uncertain what manner of reception might await her. As she neared the drawing room doorway, she heard her father say, "I am at my wit's end. I do not know what else to do with her."

John broke in, "Father, if she is so determined, let her marry the man. If he proves, as we suspect, to be a libertine, then she will have to live with his infidelities."

"You are talking about your own sister. And that possibility is not the worst of my fears. The letter warned that Lieutenant Bonaparte intended to marry her and then cast her off as soon as he felt it safe to return to France. I do not want her to end up as an abandoned wife."

"Mr. Patterson, I fear a much worse possibility," Betsy's mother said, her voice breaking. "What if he leaves without marrying her and we find out later that she is carrying his child?"

"Do you really believe that things have gone so far?"

"I don't know. We made every effort to prevent such intimacies, but who can be sure with young people? Their passion for each other is so very great that it has changed her."

"Changed her? How?"

To Betsy's surprise, William Jr. answered, "I think I know what Mother means. At first, I thought these tantrums were a calculated move on Betsy's part to achieve the highborn match she desires. I do not think so now. Her emotions have an intensity that took me by surprise."

"And you attribute this change to the possibility that they have been intimate?"

"I do not think any of us know the answer to that question."

"Dear God," Patterson cried, and Betsy heard him pound the furniture. For a moment, she hesitated, torn between the indignant desire to defend herself and the shamefaced realization that letting her family believe the worst might turn the tide in the direction she wanted. Finally, pragmatism won and she quietly slipped back upstairs.

VIII

WHEN Betsy entered the dining room the next morning, she saw an unfamiliar, stout, grey-haired woman setting the coffeepot on the table between her mother and William Jr. "Who is this?"

Betsy's mother answered, "Meet our new housekeeper. Mrs. Mc-Dougal, this is our eldest daughter Elizabeth."

"Miss." The woman bobbed her head in Betsy's direction, folded up the towel she had used to hold the coffeepot, and left the room.

Betsy sat in one of the splat-back chairs and shot Robert a questioning look. He answered with a shake of his head and continued eating porridge.

"What do you want for breakfast?" Dorcas asked.

"I am not hungry. All I require is bread and tea."

As Betsy reached for the cornbread, her mother filled her teacup. William looked up from his paper. "Are you ill? Did you catch something from one of the Nicholas children?"

"No, my appetite has failed the last few days, that is all." Seeing her mother and William exchange a quick glance, Betsy wondered if they feared her queasiness was a confirmation of pregnancy. Here in the cold light of morning she realized she could not carry out her plan to deceive them because it would grieve her mother. She rose to fetch the honey pot from the sideboard. "My stomach always turns tetchy when I am distressed."

"Are you certain that is the problem?"

Betsy faced her mother. "Yes, it could not be anything else."

"I am glad. I would not want anyone in the Nicholas family to be ill."

Resuming her seat, Betsy said, "May I inform Henriette of my return?"

Robert pushed his empty bowl to the side. "Do you think that wise?"

"Am I a prisoner being held incognito?"

"Of course not," William said. "What Robert means is—"

"I know what he means. You fear the Reubells will tell Lieutenant Bonaparte where I am. But if you mean to cut me off from my friends, why did you allow me to come home?"

William laid down his paper. "Betsy, do not think me unsympathetic to your plight. I know the last two weeks have been a severe trial to you. We are doing everything we can to determine the best course to take, and until we do, I counsel you to exercise patience."

"What is there to determine? I thought Father has decreed that I am never to see Lieutenant Bonaparte again."

"That was his initial position, but I spoke to him after my return and endeavored to make him see that a man may make mistakes and, if he changes his ways, be forgiven. Father is lately more inclined to adopt that view." William darted a glance at the coffeepot as a way, Betsy thought, of referring to the change in housekeeper. "He may yet be persuaded to give Lieutenant Bonaparte an audience."

Although William's words offered only a tiny ray of hope, it was as glorious to Betsy as if he had thrown open the door freeing her from an inky-dark prison. "All I ask is for Lieutenant Bonaparte to be allowed to answer the charges."

"I know. Give me a little more time to persuade Father. If you display defiance, you risk undoing all that I have accomplished."

Betsy nodded, picked up her teacup, and sipped the aromatic liquid. Waiting passively for her father to change his mind was the hardest task she could imagine, but she could not deny the wisdom of her brother's advice.

Days passed, and Betsy began to think that William's efforts on her behalf would never bear fruit. Life seemed even drearier than at Mount Warren, and her stomach pains persisted. She reread Jerome's letters so many times that they lost the power to conjure his voice or recall his image. Instead she saw him in nightmares in which he danced with other women, then hurried away down corridors to disappear behind locked doors.

At odd times, she recalled hateful phrases from the anonymous letter, and she began to fear that the charges were true. Even if they were exaggerated, Jerome must bear some guilt for the misunderstandings. How improper had his behavior been? Did she really know his character well enough to entrust him with her future?

Yet, what was the alternative? Betsy could not imagine feeling the same devouring passion for anyone else, so she would have to marry for practical considerations—which would mean enduring the embraces of a man to whom she was indifferent. How could she stand that after the giddy joy of Jerome's kisses?

And what would she gain from such a sacrifice? A wearisome life like her mother's, bearing a dozen children and raising them to be proper Americans, pursuing commerce and possessing scant knowledge of the wider world. Betsy longed for more than that.

If she had any hope of receiving a financial settlement from her father such as Grandfather Spear had given his daughters, she could live independently as Aunt Nancy did. But William Patterson displayed no inclination to relinquish his money. Even if he were willing to settle part of his fortune on his children, Betsy felt certain that only her brothers would benefit.

Few women supported themselves. Madame Lacomb and others like her survived by running schools or giving lessons, but such occupations entailed a loss of social prestige. One Baltimore woman was professionally successful and widely admired—the newspaper publisher and former postmistress Mary Katherine Goddard—but her achievements were so exceptional as to be irrelevant to Betsy's prospects. If Betsy were to live independently, she would most likely have to eke out a genteel but meager living doing needlework.

As she tried to decide whether to marry a man of fortune or seek to earn her own money, she felt like a blind woman groping her way down a strange corridor that opened on many unmarked passages. Betsy could find no clear indication of which one to choose. Then an unexpected whiff of lavender sachet or the sound of Joseph humming dance tunes would remind her of Jerome and cause a pang of intense longing. It maddened Betsy that her passion for him was impervious to logic. No matter how often reason told her to give Jerome up, she felt that she would pay any price to see him again.

A WEEK AFTER HER return home, Betsy sat on the double-chair-backed settee before the front windows in the drawing room. She was reading the volume of verse Jerome had given her. In truth, she did not particularly like the poet, who wrote in a highly artificial manner, but she thought it was important to keep her French in practice.

However, her depressed spirits made concentrating difficult. After bogging down in an abstract passage, she set the book aside and wondered what Jerome was doing. Perhaps he was riding in a park with a young lady or being dined by a fat matron who wanted him to marry her daughter. He was almost certainly not sitting alone trying to improve himself with literature.

Betsy's imagination conjured up a sudden, clear image of Jerome gazing at her from across the room. The vision was so strong that it produced a powerful sense of his presence. Betsy had such an overwhelming feeling that someone was staring at her that she hurried to the door to see if anyone was in the hall. The passage was empty. Returning to the settee, she knelt upon it to look out the window. In the street below, her father was approaching the house for midday dinner. A few yards away, another man walked away toward the harbor. Betsy gasped when she saw him. Above his dark blue cape was a head of curly black hair, and his gait was similar to Jerome's. Yet, she knew Jerome to be far from Baltimore, and the cruelty of her disappointment made her grasp the settee back, lean her head upon her hands, and sob.

Then a man spoke her name.

Betsy lifted her head to see her father. Flustered at being found in such anguish, she stammered, "F-forgive me. I thought myself alone." Hastily wiping her eyes, she rose to leave.

"Wait. I want to talk to you."

"Please, sir, allow me to go to my room and compose myself."

"You are fine as you are. Sit down." Patterson nodded at the settee and then moved a chair from the nearby table to sit facing her. "You have had more command of yourself these last few days, and I hoped you were beginning to recover from your unhappiness. Was I wrong?"

Betsy gazed at her lap and did not answer.

"My dear child, are you not able to free yourself from this attachment?"

"I have tried, Father. Since returning from Mount Warren, I have endeavored to resign myself to life without Lieutenant Bonaparte. I find the prospect most distressing."

"I wish that you were better able to govern your heart, Elizabeth. After all that has happened, how can you still wish to accept this man?"

She looked up. "Father, I have not absolutely decided to accept him. How could I? We do not know any more about his answer to the charges than we did three weeks ago. The deeds he stands accused of might be lies. Or they might be the rash impulses of youth that he regrets. Or he might indeed be a man so flawed that he would make an untrustworthy husband. Until we hear what he has to say, how can we know which is true?"

Her father scowled. "You speak like a child. Why should we believe his excuses? Will he not say whatever he thinks we wish to hear?"

Betsy's head started to throb, so she rubbed her temples. "Father, we could debate this all day and come no nearer to reaching an agreement. Each of us is firmly convinced that our belief about Lieutenant Bonaparte is true, and we are unlikely to persuade the other. Since he has withdrawn to New York, it is pointless to discuss this any further." Fighting tears again, she added, "You may congratulate yourself on your success in driving him away from me."

As she rose, William Patterson held out his hand. "Wait." He hesitated, gripped the arms of his chair, and then said, "Bonaparte has returned. He wrote to me yesterday requesting an audience, and I have spent the morning closeted with him."

Betsy glanced at the window, certain now that Jerome had been the man she saw walking down South Street. She sank back to her seat, struggling to control her breathing. "What did he say?"

"It was a difficult conversation. He admits to some guilt but swears that the charges are exaggerated. He seems to have hoped that if he could make me appreciate the intensity of his affection, I would understand that it renders him incapable of repeating such errors. However, I fear that when his first infatuation wears off, he will return to the bad habits he contracted in youth and you will suffer the acutest misery." He drummed the arm of his chair. "Some women can endure living with a husband's errors, but you have not the temperament to overlook such failings for the sake of marital harmony."

In other words, I am not as complacent as Mother, Betsy thought bitterly. "Do you think it impossible that a man could sincerely desire to reform?"

"Not impossible but more difficult than you imagine. Bonaparte has not yet displayed the strength of character to make me think him one of the few who are capable of change."

Patterson rose and crossed to the fireplace, where he studied the portrait of his wife and daughter. Then he turned back to Betsy. "I abhor the power that he has over you, and I fear that you are making a foolish choice."

"I love him. And I believe that I can influence him for good."

Drawing closer, Patterson leaned both hands upon the table and searched his daughter's face. "Is there nothing I can say to dissuade you?"

Betsy shook her head.

"Very well. I gave him permission to call this afternoon, but I have not yet renewed my consent to the marriage. Betsy, I beg you to listen carefully to what he has to say and to look for the motive behind his words. Do not commit yourself if you harbor any doubts."

"Yes, Father," she said even as her heart rejoiced that she would soon see Jerome. Betsy's relief was so great that she felt as if she might float away, so she hugged herself tightly until her father left the room. Then she jumped up, flung out her arms, and twirled in delight. Jerome still loved her and would be here within hours.

Betsy stopped spinning with a jerk. She hurried across the drawing room to the mirror that hung opposite the front windows. It was a large mirror, flanked by gilded columns and topped with an American eagle, and the glass reflected three-quarters of her figure.

I look pale. She turned her head from side to side. *Perhaps I should put on a bit of Henriette's rouge.*

Then Betsy changed her mind. She would style her hair prettily and don one of her most attractive afternoon gowns, but she would not put on artificial color for Jerome Bonaparte. Better that he should see how much gloom and anxiety he had caused her.

A maid entered the drawing room and said, "Miss Betsy, your mother asks you to come to dinner."

Betsy turned from the mirror. "What?"

"Dinner," the maid repeated.

"Oh, of course. Tell her I will be there directly."

Glancing back at the mirror, Betsy wondered whether she was really so sure that she wanted to marry Jerome. How could she ever be certain of him after the things the letter said? She hoped to God that when she saw him again, her heart would know the answer.

W̲ʜᴇɴ D̲ᴏʀᴄᴀs sʜᴏᴡᴇᴅ Jerome into the drawing room, Betsy stood but offered no greeting. He was uncharacteristically grave and hesitant, and his manner constrained her.

As soon as they were alone, Jerome burst out, "Elisa, you are so thin and white. I fear this contretemps has caused you to neglect your health."

Betsy gestured for him to sit on the sofa, while she chose the safety of her mother's banister-back chair. "I have been very unhappy. Can you possibly be surprised?"

"No, *moi aussi,* I have been in misery. It drove me mad to think that your father might not let me see you again."

"He was doing what he thought best. The letter that he received was vile."

"It was full of falsehood."

His answer came too quickly and contradicted what he had earlier admitted to her father. Fixing him with a piercing look, Betsy said, "It was not entirely false. Was it?"

Jerome flushed. "No."

Silence fell between them and Betsy found herself once again imagining him in the arms of another woman. She shut her eyes and tried to banish the thought, but the harder she fought it, the more jealous she felt. Looking at him again, she decided there was only one way to discover if she could live with his past. "Have you had many mistresses, Jerome?"

His dark eyes widened in shock. "Elisa! A man does not discuss such things with the woman he is going to marry."

"*If* we are to marry—and that is still an open question—then we *must* have this out," Betsy said, surprising herself with her own firmness. "I cannot live with the possibility that at any moment, more accusations will arrive to disturb our peace. Therefore, I must know at least the general extent of your dissipations."

For an instant, Jerome glared at her, but then his shoulders slumped. "I cannot give you a number. I was young, I thought only of my own pleasure and told myself it was the woman's duty to resist if she cared for her honor. Had I foreseen what pain my actions would cause my future wife, I would have been more circumspect. But it has never been my habit to look ahead."

As Betsy considered his confession, she unconsciously pressed her hands together in an attitude of prayer. "You have been very irresponsible to members of my sex."

Jerome sighed. "Yes, I see that now. But my father died soon after I was born, and I had no one to teach me how wrong I was. In the upper circles of French society, such casual affairs are very common. More so than here."

His words stung Betsy in a way he could not guess. "They are more common here than you suppose. Just not so openly accepted. I warn you, Jerome, that I will not tolerate a repetition of such behavior. I will not be made a laughingstock."

He stiffened. "Is it only your pride and reputation that concerns you?"

Betsy shook her head. "No. When I think of you with another woman, I feel ill. I would fight to my last breath for you, but I cannot command your fidelity. Only you can do that, and I do not feel certain that you possess the firmness of character for a lifetime of self-control."

"Elisa, how can I convince you of my sincerity except to tell you again that I will never betray you? I swear that since the day we met, there have been no other women."

"Not even in New York?"

"What do you mean? Has someone accused me?"

"No. I ask the question." Betsy placed a hand over her heart. "Why, instead of remaining here to persuade my father, did you travel to New York? Was it in search of society to help you forget me?"

"*Mon dieu, non!*" Jerome held out his hands, palms upward. "Do I look like a man who has forgotten you? I was seeking a way to prove to your father how much I adore you."

"Then why go away?"

"I went to New York so I could buy you a dowry of clothing and jewelry."

His answer so completely astonished Betsy that she stared at him open-mouthed. "You bought me presents? You thought that would persuade my father?"

"He refused to meet with me. I had to do something."

Betsy began to laugh, covering her mouth when she saw that it offended him, yet unable to dam the wild surge of levity. Only Jerome, whose love of buying beautiful things had so angered Napoleon, could imagine that he might solve their problems by shopping. After a few minutes, she mastered herself. "That possibility never occurred to me."

Jerome stiffened and spoke in a tight voice, "You believed I was going to parties and making love to other women? Have you so little faith in me?"

"Forgive me. You must understand that my family exiled me to the country, and the people with whom I was staying were at me day and night to forget you."

"What did you tell them?"

His beseeching tone stripped away Betsy's last reserve. "I told them I love you and that when I thought I might never see you again, I despaired of living."

He bowed his head for a moment and then looked up with tear-filled eyes. "I do not deserve you. But if you can forgive me, I will spend the rest of my life trying to be worthy."

"Jerome, I do not ask you to be a penitent. All I want is your oath that this will never happen again."

"I swear it," he said, crossing the room to pull her into his arms. As Betsy relaxed into his embrace, she felt convinced of the rightness of their being together.

Unable to weaken Betsy's resolve, William Patterson agreed to let her marry Jerome on the condition that they wait until the family lawyer could draw up a marriage contract. Still fearing the letter writer's prediction that Jerome would desert Betsy, Patterson wanted to provide her as much legal protection as possible.

The contract written by Mr. Dallas stipulated that if anyone cast doubt on the validity of their union, Jerome would do whatever was necessary in either the United States or France to ensure that the marriage was legal. William Patterson promised that Betsy would inherit a share of his estate equal to the legacies of his other children. Further, she was to inherit one-third of Jerome's property upon his death while retaining control of any property of her own—and those terms were to hold if the marriage ended for any reason.

Betsy considered the contract unduly pessimistic in guarding against such possibilities, but she was so happily absorbed in preparing for her marriage that she left it to her father and Jerome to agree on the final details.

The wedding took place on Christmas Eve in the drawing room of the Patterson home, which was brilliantly lit by dozens of candles. The room held Betsy's family and eighteen guests including the Reubells, the Smiths, Aunt Nancy, Commodore Barney, Jerome's secretary, the mayor, and the new French vice-consul for Baltimore. Minister Pichon refused to attend, as did Jerome's personal physical Dr. Garnier, who begged off due to a suspiciously sudden illness. Betsy's parents chose not to invite many friends—they claimed they did not want to intrude on the holiday—but Betsy suspected that her father still resented her decision. She told herself she did not care. This night would set her on the path to achieving everything she had ever wanted.

For the ceremony, Betsy decided on the embroidered white gown she had worn the first night she danced with Jerome but with one major difference. This time beneath the gown, she wore only one thin chemise so the outline of her figure was visible in the French manner. Jerome lived up to his reputation for fashion by wearing powder in his hair, a long-tailed purple velvet coat lined with white satin, and shoes with diamond-studded buckles.

Because Jerome was Catholic, Betsy had agreed to be married under the Catholic rite, so the bishop of Baltimore—Charles Carroll's brother John—performed the ceremony. Betsy loved the extra pomp provided by the heavy gold cross the bishop wore and his embroidered cope and miter, so much richer than the sober vestments of her own Presbyterian minister.

This time, when Betsy heard the bishop speaking in Latin, her heart filled with pride because for centuries this liturgy had been used to marry European kings. The bishop had instructed her beforehand, so when he asked in Latin if she accepted Jerome as her husband according to the rites of the Church, she answered without hesitation, *"Volo."*

Moments later, Bishop Carroll pronounced them husband and wife. After receiving the congratulations of their guests, Betsy and Jerome led the way to the wedding supper.

HOURS LATER, WHEN they were alone together in the bedroom of Jerome's rented house, he tenderly kissed Betsy. "Are you happy?"

"Yes," she whispered.

He kissed her again, then began to undress her. "I want tonight to be perfect for you."

"It already is," she answered as her gown fell to the floor.

She stepped out of it, and Jerome pulled her chemise over her head. Betsy blushed self-consciously, yet when she dared to look at her husband, her embarrassment faded away. The expression of delight on Jerome's face proved that he found her desirable.

Jerome stripped off his own clothing, carried Betsy to bed, and placed her on the covers. When he knelt beside her, Betsy noticed a raised scar on his breast and, reaching out to touch it, felt something hard lodged beneath his skin. "What caused this?"

"A foolish duel with pistols when I was in the Consular Guard. Napoleon was very angry with me for risking my life."

"As well he should have been." Betsy lay back on the bed. Jerome kissed her, beginning sweetly and then with increasing insistence. The longing Betsy had fought for the last several weeks stirred to life, and her lower body throbbed with anticipation. Jerome cupped his hand around her left breast and squeezed it gently. Betsy gasped.

He lifted his head. "Did I hurt you?"

"No. No, I—liked it."

Jerome chuckled and slid down her body. His tongue explored her nipples with rapid licking strokes that caused her breasts to tingle. Betsy's face grew hot as she realized that she wanted Jerome inside her, pushing against the restless, hungry place she had never known existed until she met him.

Her kissed her on each breast and then slowly planted kisses in a line down the length of her stomach to her lower abdomen. Betsy had not expected that—it had never occurred to her that a man might put his mouth down *there* where she felt so unclean—and she tensed. Jerome must have sensed her unease because he moved up to kiss her lips again.

Then he ran his hand down her hip, slipped it between her legs, and caressed her inner thigh until she moaned. Jerome gently inserted one finger inside her and stroked the exact spot that was the locus of her desire. Betsy gripped his back and cried out, and Jerome responded by caressing her more urgently. After several minutes, he finally entered her. Betsy felt a sharp pain followed by a wave of hot pleasure as he moved back and forth inside her. Then he gave one powerful thrust and relaxed on top of Betsy. All her tension and frustration drained from her body like an outrushing tide. A moment later, Jerome whispered, "Have I pleased you?"

"Yes." Putting her hands on each side of his head, she lifted it and kissed him. *"Je t'adore, mon mari."*

"Moi aussi, Elisa." He moved off her to stretch out on the bed.

Lying beside him, Betsy basked in a moment of perfect happiness. Then, as she gazed at Jerome's face, an unwelcome thought forced itself into her mind: *He knew how to please you only because he is so practiced a lover.*

She sat up and covered her breasts with her arms.

"What is it?" he asked, half rising to kiss her shoulder.

"Oh, Jerome, I wish we were the only two people in the world."

"Tonight we are." He drew her back down again and kissed her lips, and Betsy allowed her swelling desire to banish all thought.

✎ IX ✎

BETSY awoke reluctantly, filled with a languorous calm she was loath to disturb. Keeping her eyes closed, she rolled onto her back. A moment later, she felt chill air hit her chest as the bed-covers were drawn away. She opened her eyes and saw Jerome sitting beside her in the enclosure formed by partially closed bed curtains.

"Merry Christmas, Madame Bonaparte."

"Merry Christmas, husband."

Jerome laid his head between her breasts. "Did you sleep well?"

"I did until someone forced me awake." Betsy pulled one of his curls as a rebuke.

"I could not wait any longer. Do you want your presents?"

"What presents?"

"I told you that I bought you clothing and jewelry in New York."

"Oh, yes," she said, glad that she had the embroidered pocketbook to give him.

With a proud grin, Jerome rose and pushed back the bed curtains. Draped over the furniture around the bedroom were everyday gowns in printed cotton and formal gowns in a variety of styles that Jerome said were the latest imports from Paris. Betsy climbed down the bed steps, pulled on her wrapper, and walked around the room gazing at gowns of satin, barred muslin, crisp lightweight silk, and even one of black lace. The one that most surprised her was made of sheer sarcenet and crepe, with tiny cap sleeves, a round neckline cut lower than anything she owned, and a back that scooped more than halfway to the waist. Fingering the delicate material, she said, "I don't have a chemise cut to fit such a revealing gown."

Jerome laughed. "These gowns are not worn with a chemise."

Feeling herself blush, Betsy said, "But this fabric would display everything. Surely, you expect me to preserve some modesty."

"Of course, Elisa. Did you not see the pantaloons?" He pointed to a stack of folded, flesh-colored garments that looked like men's breeches.

Betsy pressed her lips together. The story about Josephine's revealing fashions had been amusing, but she could not imagine wearing such gowns herself. "I fear you do not understand my country. A woman who dressed like this would be shunned as a trollop."

Jerome slipped his arms around her waist. "Your respectability is unquestioned, Elisa. I chose these gowns to show the world what a charming wife I have. When we go to France, you will outshine even Josephine."

Betsy sighed. "Of course, I will dress as you prefer when we go to Paris. My only concern is wearing such gowns here."

"You will set the style. Before long, ladies will compete to imitate you." When she hesitated, Jerome bent to kiss her neck. "Please, try on the gown. I will go tell the servants to prepare breakfast and then return to see how you look."

"All right." After he left, Betsy pulled on a pair of pantaloons, which fitted smoothly from her waist to just above her knees, and then the gown, fastening it as best she could without help. Gazing in the mirror, she felt like crying. Because the pantaloons were flesh-colored, she appeared to have on nothing at all beneath her skirt. The bodice, at least, was gathered so that folds rather than a single thickness of fabric covered her bosom, but her nipples were still visible.

Jerome entered the bedroom and gazed over her shoulder into the glass. "Exquisite. You look like the statue of a Greek goddess come to life."

Lifting her eyes, Betsy stared at her husband in the mirror. Jerome's face shone with admiration, and she felt an upwelling of joy at being able to inspire such love. Setting her embarrassment aside, she turned to kiss him.

THEY HONEYMOONED AT Cold Spring, one of her father's country houses, and then returned to Baltimore. During that first month of marriage, Betsy felt like a rural cousin being tutored in a more cosmopolitan way of living. Not only did Jerome replace her wardrobe, but
he also taught her far more ways of making love than just a man lying
atop his wife in bed. Some of his suggestions embarrassed her, but
most of the time, Betsy complied without demur—not only to ensure
that Jerome would remain a contented husband but also because she
came to enjoy being daring. To further please Jerome, she kept herself fresh for lovemaking by washing daily in a French bidet, a silver
basin made by Napoleon's own silversmith and set in a wooden stand.

Jerome encouraged her to enhance her charms with cosmetics and
violet-scented power. He schooled her in the French etiquette of exchanging kisses on both cheeks, and one lazy afternoon, he picked up
a fan and taught her the gestures French women used to flirt with their
lovers. Among the jewelry he gave her were a double-stranded pearl
bracelet and necklace and a pair of teardrop-shaped earrings; he said
the pearls' glow drew attention to her beautiful white throat and arms.

By the time they started attending parties again, Betsy felt secure
in her ability to fascinate any man—even the jaded sophisticates of
continental Europe.

AT THE END of January, Jerome decided to take Betsy to Washington,
where they would stay with the Smiths. He wanted to visit President
Jefferson again and to ask Pichon for more funds. To make the journey, they borrowed a coach-and-six from Joshua Barney.

Betsy looked forward to her first visit to the capital and to spending time away from her family, whose tolerance for Jerome was wearing thin. After an incident in which he offered a $500 reward for the
capture of some urchins who hit Betsy with a snowball, her brothers
mocked his prickly pride. And her father became angry after receiving a second anonymous warning that Jerome planned to abandon his
wife. When Patterson privately showed Betsy the letter, she laughed
it off. "I assure you, Father, that Jerome could no more imagine living without me than I could without him."

The family's concerns intensified when Jerome's aide Lieutenant

Meyronnet failed to return from France and no reply came to Jerome's letters. Patterson feared that the First Consul meant to snub his daughter, so he decided to send Robert to Paris to make inquiries—after first obtaining letters of reference from his friends President Thomas Jefferson and Secretary of State James Madison. To Betsy, Patterson grumbled about the time and money he was expending to secure her recognition as Jerome's wife.

Only Dorcas still displayed warm, uncomplicated affection for her son-in-law. As Betsy kissed her mother good-bye the evening before the Washington trip, she whispered in her mother's ear, "Do not heed what Father says. I am happy with my husband."

Dorcas hugged her tightly and whispered, "Be well."

THE FORTY-FIVE-MILE TRIP from Baltimore to Washington was an all-day journey through much undeveloped country. Because it was winter, darkness fell long before they reached the city, and Betsy was disappointed that she could see little of the capital on their way to the Smith home.

The next day, however, Aunt Nancy took them on a carriage tour. After Congress had decided in 1790 to build the nation's capital in a newly created federal district, President Washington commissioned civil engineer Pierre Charles L'Enfant to devise a plan. Originally from France, L'Enfant wanted to construct a city in the European style with important buildings set far apart to allow for public gardens and plazas. At the time of Betsy and Jerome's visit, the wide spaces between public buildings were occupied by a mix of uncleared land, small plots with cabins, and recently built houses—giving the city of Washington the disconcerting appearance of a sparsely settled wilderness with a few grandiose structures set down at random. Stories abounded of Congressmen going squirrel hunting within the city or getting mired in a swamp as they drove to their quarters at night. Uncle Smith was one of the few legislators who rented a home for his family each year rather than living in a boarding house with other senators.

As the Smith carriage drove down Pennsylvania Avenue, Aunt Nancy pointed out the imposing stone Presidential Mansion. Betsy saw that it still had temporary wooden steps and overgrown grounds. At the Capitol, only the Senate wing was occupied as construction on the Representatives' wing had barely begun. Indeed, they could hear the clang of hammer hitting stone as they passed. Aunt Nancy boasted of the city's progress, but Jerome disparaged it to Betsy in French, contrasting all they saw with the cathedrals, palaces, and monuments of Paris.

Samuel Smith's brother, Secretary of the Navy Robert Smith, invited the Bonapartes to their first party in Washington. Despite Jerome's reassurance that she looked beautiful, Betsy felt qualms about the daring gown he asked her to wear, so she donned her cloak while still in their bedroom to prevent her aunts from seeing her attire before they left.

In the reception hall of the Robert Smith home, Betsy handed her cloak to a servant and turned to greet her hosts. Secretary Smith, a portly man with a heavily jowled face, blinked in surprise when he saw her. "Betsy, my dear. It has been much too long."

"It has indeed, sir. May I present my husband, Jerome Bonaparte."

As the men shook hands, Betsy moved to Mrs. Robert Smith, who said, "Elizabeth, you must be cold. Allow me to send upstairs for a shawl."

Betsy raised her chin. "No, madam, I assure you that I am quite comfortable." She introduced Jerome, and then they excused themselves and crossed the hall.

When they entered the drawing room, Betsy noticed with chagrin that people turned to gape at her. Several women moved away before the Bonapartes reached them, and some even exited the room. Then two young men who were distant cousins approached them. As Betsy introduced Jerome, she saw one of the men stare at her bosom for several moments and blush.

She glanced at Jerome, who smirked and asked the embarrassed young man if he enjoyed attending the races. A minute later, three more men joined them. The newcomers all inspected Betsy's figure a bit too long before raising their eyes to her face. Jerome stood by her side, speaking without the slightest appearance of jealousy.

Betsy's discomfort soon gave way to amusement that men could be such children, peeking surreptitiously at something they considered forbidden. Many of those who flocked around her that evening were

married men, who presumably had seen their wives in a state of undress, and those who were single had surely seen nude statues. Yet
nearly all acted as if this were their one chance in life to view the female
form. Jerome remained unperturbed by the ogling, and as Betsy grew
used to the attention, she began to enjoy it.

When they returned to the Samuel Smith home after the party, Aunt
Margaret and Aunt Nancy insisted on speaking to Betsy alone. "I will
be up in a minute," she told Jerome and followed her aunts into the
sitting room.

Aunt Nancy gestured toward a seat, but Betsy shook her head and
remained standing. Aunt Margaret said, "While you are in my home,
I must act in the place of my sister Dorcas. You offended every woman
at the reception tonight. Several warned me that unless you consent to
wear more clothes, they will not attend any future functions to which
you have been invited."

"Such a dictate is absurd. These fashions have been accepted in
France for years."

"We are not in Paris. In your eagerness to please your husband, you
flout what you know of American conventions. You do yourself no favors by such behavior."

Betsy pressed her lips together and gazed at her aunts in silence. In
each face, she could trace a resemblance to her beloved mother, which
made it difficult to respond defiantly. "I will consider what you have
said," she finally answered.

Climbing the stairs to the second floor, Betsy wondered how Jerome
would react to her aunts' ultimatum. As she entered the guest room
and shut the door, she saw that he had undressed down to his shirt.
He swept her up into his arms. "I was so proud of you. You were the
most beautiful woman in the room, and I am certain that I was the
envy of every man."

He deposited her on the checked linen coverlet, knelt beside her,
and caressed her breast. "They will all dream of you tonight, Elisa,
but only I have the right to possess you."

Smiling at him, she whispered, "Then take me, Monsieur Bonaparte."

THEIR SOCIAL CALENDAR remained full with a card party at the Pichons' home, supper with Secretary of the Treasury Albert Gallatin, and a ball given by the two Smith families. Betsy continued to wear her French fashions, but mindful of her aunts' admonitions, she draped a gauzy scarf over her shoulders to make her attire seem more modest.

They were also invited to dinner at the President's Mansion. Beforehand, Uncle Smith told Betsy that in a perverse display of neutrality, President Jefferson had invited both the French minister and the new British ambassador, despite the war between their two countries.

For the occasion, which would begin at 3:00 in the afternoon and last until late evening, Betsy wore a sheer gown bedecked with gold embroidery that would sparkle in the candlelight. This would be her first visit to the home of a head of state, and she wanted to demonstrate to Jerome that she knew how to dress for such occasions.

As the Smith carriage drove up to the north entrance, Betsy stared avidly at the details of the building and wondered how it compared to the palaces she would someday live in with Jerome. The President's Mansion was an imposing light-grey stone structure, wide enough that eleven windows stretched across its upper story. The center block of the mansion was decorated with four Doric columns crowned by a triangular pediment. A small pediment also topped each window, but Betsy was surprised to see that they were not all the same. Rather, triangles alternated with rounded arches.

Following the Smiths, Betsy and Jerome climbed the stone steps and walked through the front door into the entrance hall, a marble-floored space that was wider than it was long. On the far side of the room, four Doric columns marked the boundary between the entryway and the central cross hall.

Servants came to take their outer garments, and after Betsy handed over her cloak, she noticed that the entrance hall was cold despite having facing fireplaces on the east and west walls. She hoped that she would not be covered in goose skin by the time she made it through the receiving line into the oval drawing room where the president stood greeting his guests. As they stepped through the central columns into the cross hall, she glanced left to see if she could catch a glimpse of the East Room—infamous as the vast unfinished space where Abigail Adams had once dried laundry. Betsy had heard that, even though it was intended to be a public reception room, the East Room was still unplastered. Just last year, Aunt Margaret had written that the first attempt at installing a ceiling in the room had collapsed. Now a piece of canvas stretched across the doorway, so Betsy could not see a thing.

When she and Jerome were presented to President Jefferson, Betsy was amused to see him in the characteristically plain dress he wore on republican principle: an old blue coat, dark corduroy breeches, dingy white hose, and run-down backless slippers. "Madame Bonaparte, allow me to welcome you to Washington. I hope your father was well when you left him."

"He was, Mr. President, and he particularly charged me with thanking you for the very kind letter of reference that you wrote."

"It gave me great pleasure to do whatever I could to further an alliance that will cement relations between the United States and France. As you know, I spent several years as ambassador to France and I retain great fondness for our sister republic."

From the corner of her eye, Betsy saw a distinguished-looking man in formal diplomatic dress shoot the president a frosty glare. After Mr. Jefferson moved to another guest, Uncle Smith introduced Jerome and Betsy to the irate gentleman, who was the British ambassador Mr. Anthony Merry.

"Citizen Bonaparte." Mr. Merry gave a curt nod. "I greet you as a fellow guest of Mr. Jefferson and not as the enemy of my country."

Betsy answered before Jerome could, "Sir, how wise you are to know that for tonight, we must draw blades against the roast and not the person opposite."

Merry smiled grudgingly. He then introduced them to his wife, Elizabeth Death Merry, a fiftyish woman with heavy eyebrows and a long nose in a horsy face. Despite her plain looks, Mrs. Merry was dressed as a beauty with rouge on her cheeks and a chandelier necklace of sapphires around her throat. Her blue velvet gown was cut so low that her enormous bosom, restrained only by a film of lace, threatened to pop free. As soon as they were out of earshot of the Merrys, Betsy whispered to Jerome, "Law, she displays those melons as though she were a market."

When it came time for the meal, President Jefferson further offended his English guests by leading Betsy from the drawing room into the dining room instead of following protocol and honoring Mrs. Merry. Betsy could not resist glancing back over her shoulder to grin trium-phantly at Jerome.

Unlike his two predecessors, Jefferson did not believe in seating dig-nitaries by rank. Instead, he left his guests free to choose their places at a round table. Betsy ended up between Monsieur Pichon and Un-cle Smith, while Jerome sat opposite between Mr. Jefferson and at-tractive, dark-haired Dolley Madison, who acted as hostess for the widowed president.

As they ate a first course of rice soup, Betsy heard Jerome tell the president about conditions in the West Indies. Betsy amused herself first by observing that an angry flush had rendered Mrs. Merry's rouge superfluous and second by practicing her French as she told Monsieur Pichon of her admiration for Napoleon.

Toward the end of the meat course, Betsy overheard Jerome recount the story of his buying the expensive shaving set shortly after going to live in the Tuileries. "My brother was furious with me because I was still too young to shave. I was only fifteen."

Both Dolley Madison and President Jefferson laughed, but Betsy frowned. She knew more of Napoleon's history than she had when Jerome first told her the tale, and one aspect of the narrative seemed wrong. She tried to catch Jerome's eye, but he was too busy compliment-ing the president on his excellent French wine. As Monsieur Pichon asked her a question, Betsy decided to quiz Jerome about the discrep-ancy later.

She remained quiet during the ride back to the Smith home, not wishing to start a quarrel in front of her aunt and uncle. Besides, she was not sure of her complaint. Because France and the United States used different calendars, she might have misunderstood the details of Jerome's story. They went up to the guest room, where Jerome took off his cloak and then helped Betsy out of hers. When he tried to kiss her, she turned her head away.

"What is wrong?"

"I must talk to you." Betsy put a hand over her stomach, which was starting to ache with dread, and sat in a chair in the far corner. Following her, Jerome stopped next to the bed, took off his coat, and then leaned casually against the corner post as he unbuttoned his waistcoat.

"In what year did Napoleon become First Consul?"

Jerome tilted his head as he considered her question. "In the year VIII according to our Republican calendar. That would have been 1799 here."

A rising tide of panic threatened to engulf Betsy. "And you were fifteen?"

"Yes." He removed his waistcoat, laying it on a chair.

"Then how old are you now?"

Jerome lifted his head warily, like an animal scenting danger.

"Do not claim to be twenty-two because I will not believe you."

He thrust out his chin. "Nineteen. My birthday was in November."

How odd that such a simple statement could ring down disaster. Betsy shut her eyes and pressed both hands against her stomach. "Then we are not married. It was a sham."

"Elisa, do not say that." Jerome squatted before her and clasped her thighs.

"But you deceived me. You are under age and did not have consent, so the marriage is invalid. You lied to my father to get what you want."

At the thought of her father, Betsy covered her face with her hands. Everyone would hear that she had been tricked into a mock marriage, and she would return to Baltimore with her reputation in tatters. Her father would never let her forget that he had warned her against Jerome, and she would spend the rest of her life enduring his rebukes. No one else would marry her now.

She lowered her hands and stared at Jerome as tears coursed down her face. "The person who wrote the anonymous letter was right. You have ruined me. I have been living with a man who is not my husband, and now I am disgraced."

"But we are married." He grasped her hands. "The bishop pronounced us husband and wife. No one can undo that."

"Yes, they can! Our marriage has no standing under the law." As she remembered more of the letter writer's accusations, her eyes grew wide. "You did this on purpose. Now you can go back to France a free man whenever you tire of me."

As the enormity of what he had done became clear, Betsy yanked her hands free. She pushed past him, threw herself on the bed, and sobbed, keeping her grief muffled by the bedclothes so her aunt and uncle could not hear. When Jerome laid an arm across her back, she rose up in fury. "Do not touch me. You have no right. Don't ever touch me again."

"But Elisa—"

"You lied!" She raised her curled hands to claw his face, then just as swiftly lowered them. Attacking him would accomplish nothing except to alert the household to their quarrel. "Why did you do it? What could you hope to gain from a sham marriage?"

A toxic brew of rage, disgust, and shame choked her, and she threw herself back down. As Jerome backed away, Betsy clutched her pillow to her chest and cried herself to sleep.

The next morning she awoke with dry, scratchy eyes and a pounding headache. Her neck was stiff from the way she had lain. Stretching gingerly, Betsy rubbed her shoulder as she sat up. Then she saw Jerome asleep in the chair where she had been sitting the night before, slouching with his head resting on the back and his legs stretched out before him.

The obvious discomfort of his position roused her concern for him, and Betsy swallowed back the angry words that had sprung to her lips. He looked so young and innocent. Why had she never realized that he was still a boy?

Pressing a palm to her throbbing forehead, she berated herself for not having listened to her father. What had possessed her to insist on marrying Jerome no matter what anyone said? Surely, she could have found another way to get to France. The answer came swiftly. She loved him, and she had allowed her physical passion for him to overrule all rational judgment. *I was foolish and obstinate,* she told herself, *and for those faults I must pay, but that is nothing to the fact that he lied outright.*

"Jerome, wake up." He grunted and stirred. "What are you doing there?"

He pulled himself up to a sitting position, rubbed his eyes, and shook his head. "How could I leave when you were so distraught?"

"So you slept in that chair all night?"

"I had to watch over you to make sure you were safe."

His anxiety for her produced an upwelling of tenderness in Betsy that threatened to undermine her indignation. She scooted back to sit against the headboard and hugged her pillow before her chest. "How can you have the effrontery to pretend that you care for me?"

"I love you. That has not changed."

"If you loved me, you never would have seduced me under false pretenses."

"I wanted you for my wife, Elisa."

"Do not call me that. My name is Betsy."

Jerome flinched and leaned forward, resting his forearms on his thighs. "I did not mean to hurt you. I could not bear to wait two years to marry. I thought that you felt the same."

His forlorn tone pained her. A moment earlier Betsy had thought herself cried out, but now the tears started again. "I wanted a real marriage, to be your wife for the rest of our lives."

"But you will be."

"Jerome Bonaparte, how can you say that? We are not married now."

"In the eyes of God, you are my wife, and I will not allow anyone to cast aspersions on your reputation. As soon as we receive my mother's consent, everything will be in order."

Betsy shook her head. "You cannot promise that your mother will give her consent. If she chooses not to, then I am your whore and not your wife."

"Never say that," Jerome said sternly. "Never."

"You deceived me into a sham marriage. You knew it was the only way into my bed."

"That is not true. If all I wanted was to bed you, don't you suppose I would have made the attempt before asking you to marry me? On the contrary, you know that I took great care not to seduce you before the wedding."

Although Betsy wanted to retort angrily, she could not deny that Jerome spoke the truth. She lowered the pillow she held like a shield. "Then why did you do it?"

"Because from the moment I saw you, I wanted you more than anything else on earth. As my partner in life, not my mistress. And I was willing to do anything to bring about our marriage before orders from my brother forced me to leave you, my beautiful Betsy."

"Elisa," she whispered.

Jerome walked to the end of the bed. "Does that mean you forgive me?"

Betsy sighed. "What choice do I have? You are the only man on earth who can now make an honest woman out of me."

"My darling Elisa, you are the finest, most honest woman who lives." He placed one knee on the edge of the bed and looked inquiringly at her.

Smiling wanly, she nodded, and Jerome climbed onto the bed and took her in his arms.

"I do not know why I let you talk me out of my anger," she said.

"Because you love me as much as I love you."

She pushed back his curls. "Yes, I love you. But I am not sure that I trust you."

"Do not say that," he murmured and, after laying her down, began to kiss her breasts. "Fate brought us together, and from now on, I live only for you."

Jerome eased up the skirt of her sleep-crumpled, gold-embroidered gown, and as his hand ran along her legs, Betsy felt the return of her urgent hunger for him. Her body seemed not to care that they had no right to be lovers. She groaned with pleasure as he entered her and started to move in rhythm. Moments later, Jerome shuddered and lay heavily on top of her. Stroking his hair once more, Betsy thought, *My God, what if I have a child?*

As February slipped into March, signs of spring began to appear in the capital, and Betsy tried to find hope in the trill of returning songbirds and the thrust of green spears rising from newly thawed ground. On mild afternoons, she walked alone in the brick-paved courtyard garden behind her uncle's Washington home so she could analyze her situation.

Jerome's deceit had left her deeply shaken and vulnerable to moments of suffocating panic. Betsy knew that gossip claimed that ambition alone had motivated her marriage to Napoleon's brother, so few people would excuse her for making such a questionable alliance. But although rank had played a part in her decision, she truly loved Jerome. Now, as she paced the garden paths attempting to find cheer in the blooming crocuses—whose purple hue reminded her of Jerome's wedding coat—Betsy mused on her husband's character and concluded that he was neither malicious nor intentionally dishonorable. Rather, he was a spoiled boy who thought that, if he felt something strongly, it must be so. She had known he was impulsive when she decided to marry him. She simply had not realized how far afield of propriety his rash nature would lead them.

After that terrible night, Betsy refused to dwell upon what might happen to her if the truth about Jerome's age became known. Instead, whenever fear assailed her, she reminded herself of the way fate had brought them together and took comfort in thinking that this marriage was her destiny.

If only his mother gives her consent, all will be well. We will go to France, he will return to the navy, and with duty to perform and a regular income, he will become more responsible. Someday we will look back upon this uncertain time and laugh.

She smiled at the vision of the two of them as white-haired elders, telling their grandchildren how their great passion had led them to make what many considered a hasty, imprudent marriage, but they had been proved right in the end.

Pulling her merino shawl more tightly around her, Betsy returned to the house and went through the garden door. As she walked down the passage leading to the front staircase, she glanced into her uncle's library and was surprised to see Jerome seated at the tall secretary. Entering the room, she said, "What are you doing?"

He looked up. "I am writing another letter to my mother."

Betsy stood beside his chair and glanced at the paper on the secretary's drop-down writing surface. The message was in French, so rather than translate it herself, she asked, "What are you saying?"

"I told her that I was drawn to our marriage as to a destiny that could not be avoided, and I emphasized how dear you are to me." Jerome lifted Betsy's hand and kissed it. "And I said that I await her approval of my marriage, without which I cannot be happy."

Tears filled Betsy's eyes. "Then you fear, after all, that she might withhold her consent."

"No. Because we have not heard from her, I fear that my first letter home might have been lost. When *Maman* learns how essential you are to my happiness and how respected your family is in this country, she will eagerly give her blessing."

"But you don't know that the letter was lost. Your family may be withholding communication because they disapprove of your choice."

Moving back his chair, Jerome pulled her onto his lap. "Promise me not to fret about this. If the worst should happen and they withhold their consent, I will stay in America and we will build our life here."

"But what if your true age becomes known?"

"Who could discover such a thing? And if they did, they could never force me to give you up. I would go away with you, Elisa, into the wilderness rather than be parted."

Putting her arms around his neck, Betsy rested her head against his for a moment. Then, kissing his cheek, she stood. "If we are caught in this attitude, we will scandalize the household."

He laughed. "I have nearly finished my letter. Wait for me in our bedchamber, and I will join you there in a few minutes."

A FEW DAYS LATER at breakfast, Jerome said, "Elisa, we have an important engagement this morning, so I want you to put on your most beautiful gown."

"Where are we going?"

"It is a surprise."

"Then how can I know what to wear? None of my best gowns is suitable for morning."

"Put on the white crepe. You can wear a cloak out on the street."

Aunt Margaret set down her cup of cocoa with a sharp click. "Jerome, Betsy cannot go out in the morning in a sheer, low-cut gown, even if she does wear a cloak over it."

With a smile playing about his lips, Jerome went around the table to whisper in Aunt Margaret's ear. An expression of delight replaced her frown. "Oh, I see. That is quite different." Picking up her cup, she told Betsy, "Do as your husband asks."

Betsy pushed her half-eaten muffin away. "You two have spoiled my appetite with your air of mystery. I will go complete my toilette. When do we have to leave?"

"Not for another hour. Our appointment is at ten."

Borrowing Uncle Smith's carriage, Jerome drove Betsy to a small one-story building just north of Pennsylvania Avenue, about halfway between the President's Mansion and the unfinished Capitol. When he led her into what she took to be a shop, Betsy was intrigued to discover the room filled with paintings on easels, including several copies of the same portrait of George Washington. She looked at Jerome quizzically.

Just then a man of about fifty with receding hair and a jutting nose came from the back room. He wore a paint-stained apron. "Ah, Monsieur Bonaparte, you are punctual. As I told you, I do not know if I can accept your commission. I can scarcely complete those I have."

"I understand, but before you refuse us, allow me to introduce my wife, Madame Bonaparte. Elisa, this is the great Gilbert Stuart." After helping Betsy remove her cloak, Jerome nudged her toward the painter, who gazed at her with a look of greedy wonder.

Stuart peered into Betsy's face and then slowly circled her. "By gad, Monsieur Bonaparte, you did not exaggerate."

Stopping in front of Betsy, he reached two fingers toward her chin and said, "May I?" Without waiting for permission, he tilted her head up and stared at her features. Betsy held her breath, hardly able to believe that this famous artist was considering her.

Stuart went to a table several feet away and, picking up a small frame, held it at arm's length and gazed through it at Betsy. Moving back and forth, he checked the front and side views. "By gad, I cannot decide which pose best captures her beauty. She has the true classic profile, but her eyes are so expressive that it would be a shame not to show them fully."

After dropping the frame on the table, he frowned for a long moment, softly beating one fist against his thigh. Then he said, "I remember seeing a style of portrait in England that I have never dared attempt, but now I see that I must. I am going to do a triple portrait of Madame, which will feature her profile, a three-quarters view, and a front view of her face."

"Bravo!" Jerome exclaimed. "When do you want us to come for our first sitting?"

"Right now. This is one portrait I cannot wait to start."

For several days, Betsy and Jerome went to sit in Stuart's studio. Betsy was fascinated by the artist's workroom, which was more chaotic than she had expected. Ornate chairs, rich cloths, Greek and Chinese vases, mahogany canes, classical statues, and pedestals displaying busts were scattered about the studio. Attached to one wall was a pole from which hung several draperies that allowed the painter to choose the background color he required. Paint-splashed worktables held knives, palettes, mortars and pestles, earthenware pots of brushes, and corked bottles of liquid in varying shades of gold. Several easels stood on the floor, some empty and some with partially completed paintings. The room was full of the sharp piney smell of turpentine, and Betsy discovered that being there for more than an hour gave her a headache.

Each was having a portrait painted, so they took turns sitting for the artist. Whenever it was Betsy's turn to pose, Jerome sat by her side holding her hand.

He nearly ruined their relationship with the artist the first day by exclaiming in surprise when Stuart used a paintbrush dipped in turpentine-thinned burnt umber paint to record the first outlines of Betsy's head on his canvas. "The painters I have observed on the continent always make a preliminary sketch using charcoal."

The artist tossed down his brush. "Sir, I know my own powers, and I do not need to resort to the methods of lesser talents. I would not presume to tell you how to fight a battle."

Hearing Jerome's sharp intake of breath, Betsy intervened. "Mr. Stuart, he meant no offense. Having seen examples of your work, we know what a master you are. My husband was merely expressing his astonished delight that we are in the hands of someone even more expert than the artists he has known at Napoleon's palace."

She smiled as winsomely as her anxiety would allow, and the painter picked up his brush.

They were not allowed to see either portrait until Stuart had captured their likenesses to his own satisfaction. Finally, one Friday afternoon, he let them view the works in progress. The faces on Betsy's portrait were subtly executed and looked finished, but the throats and shoulders remained rough. Surrounding the three busts was a background of swirling masses painted in shades of burnt umber. Next to the faces, Stuart had begun to add a top layer of pale blue highlighted with lavender to give the appearance of sky. Betsy was delighted, judging that not only was the portrait an excellent likeness, but it also captured her lively personality. Jerome, however, frowned. "Her shoulders are bare. You should put clothes on each of the figures."

"You can find a picture like that in any shop in town!"

"But the three heads are rising from a bank of clouds."

Stuart's eyes glinted dangerously. "They serve to emphasize her angelic beauty."

"Then why use such dark turbulent forms?"

"To add depth to the painting, sir. When I finish the top layer, those dark values will show through as shadows in the cloudy mass."

Again Betsy spoke to avoid a conflict. "What a fascinating process. I had no idea that was how it is done. May we see my husband's portrait?"

"If you insist." Stuart took her arm and led her to the other easel.

In contrast to Betsy's portrait, Jerome's was a conventional three-quarter view from the waist up, with the face gazing right. Betsy saw that Stuart had perfectly captured the haughty look Jerome wore whenever he was insisting upon his honor. As with her portrait, the face appeared finished, but the background and clothing—a frill-fronted shirt and a black uniform coat with gold epaulets—were still rough.

Jerome made no comment on his likeness but instead asked, "Shall we come back Monday? I should like to have these finished as soon as possible."

"No, I have other appointments next week."

"But, sir, you have a prior commitment to us."

"And I have awarded you ample time. The paintings are far enough developed that I should be able to finish them at my leisure."

Jerome stiffened, and his expression so matched the arrogant face on the portrait that Betsy would have laughed if the situation were not so tense. "At your leisure, sir? I require you to finish these portraits before taking other commissions."

"You require?" Stuart put his hands on his hips. "You impudent little puppy. Who are you to place requirements on me? You have nothing to recommend you but your name, and that is a dubious enough calling card."

"Do you dare to insult my family, sir?"

"Gentleman, please!" Betsy cried. "I find this needless argument most upsetting."

Stuart made a stiff bow to Betsy. "Forgive me, Madame. I do not want to distress so charming a lady, but I must ask you both to leave." He glared over her shoulder at Jerome. "Your husband and I have nothing more to say to one another."

"Mr. Stuart, I beg you." Betsy boldly laid her hand upon his arm. "Let us resolve our differences, so you may complete the work you started so brilliantly."

Stuart glanced at Betsy's portrait, and regret flashed upon his face. Then his expression hardened. "No. I never finish a painting once the subject has insulted me."

"Say something," Betsy implored Jerome, thinking that if only he would apologize, they could salvage the situation.

"Let us depart," Jerome said and, taking her arm, led her from the studio. Once they were out on the street, he shrugged off his bad mood. "From all I hear, the man has trouble earning enough to support his family. I will give it a day or two and then send a friend with the message that I will pay extra if he finishes the commission quickly."

DURING THEIR STAY in Washington, Jerome visited the office of Minister Pichon several times to ask for additional funds and to see if he had received a dispatch from Napoleon. There he often encountered Admiral Jean-Baptiste Willaumez, who had been in charge of the French bases at Saint-Domingue while Jerome was serving in the Caribbean.

Since October, Willaumez's ship, the 42-gun frigate *Poursuivante,* had been docked in Baltimore, where it was being repaired from damage it had sustained in battle. All winter, both Willaumez and Pichon tried to convince Jerome that his duty required him to sail on the *Poursuivante* once its repairs were completed and it returned to France.

Betsy was not present for any of those conversations. Whenever Jerome came home, he recounted the arguments in detail and reassured her that he had reminded the officials that he was waiting for direct orders from the First Consul. Jerome grew more exasperated each time Pichon and Willaumez taxed him about the subject, and Betsy feared that his temper might cause him to cross the line of mutiny toward his superior. In her anxiety that he could be arrested, she forgot that French officials were too terrified to discipline any of Napoleon's relatives. At the end of March, Willaumez commanded Jerome to board the *Poursuivante,* to which Jerome retorted that he took orders from no one. Instead of being clapped in the brig for insubordination, he was allowed to leave Pichon's office with only a verbal reprimand. The admiral sailed without him.

AFTER NEARLY TWO months of social engagements and many unsuccessful appeals to Gilbert Stuart, Jerome and Betsy returned to Baltimore. They arrived at Jerome's rented town house late at night and went straight to bed. The next morning, as soon as she finished her breakfast, Betsy walked from their house down the street to her childhood home. She and her mother had never been separated for more than three weeks, and Betsy wanted desperately to see her.

Finding Dorcas in her banister-back chair in the drawing room, Betsy longed to kneel before her mother and embrace her, but she admonished herself that she was a married woman now who must act with decorum. She bent to kiss her mother's cheek and then sat on the sofa. "Aunt Margaret and Aunt Nancy send their love."

Dorcas smiled. "I miss them. I know that Samuel's service to the country is important, but it is hard that families must be separated for such a large part of the year."

Gazing at her mother's face, Betsy saw that she was pale with dark circles beneath her eyes. Perhaps she was overworked now that Betsy was no longer at home to assist her. "Mother, are you ill? You look very tired."

"I am not sick." Dorcas turned red. "I believe I am with child again."

"I see," Betsy whispered and gripped her hands tightly in her lap to keep from betraying the resentment she felt at the news. She could not help but think that as a three-month's bride, she should be the one to make such a blushing announcement, even if it was better for her not to conceive while her marriage was in doubt. "What did Father say?"

"Oh, he grumbled as he always does about how crowded the house is, but I pointed out that with you married, the number of people living here will remain the same."

Betsy longed to respond tartly that if her father was concerned about having too large a family, he should learn to control his carnal appetites. Then a distasteful idea occurred to her. If her brothers had not forced their father to give up his mistress, he might have taken his satisfaction with her and spared his wife this pregnancy.

Shocked by her thoughts, Betsy cleared her throat. "Is there anything I can do to help prepare for the child?"

ONE AFTERNOON AT the beginning of April, as Betsy sat sewing with her mother in the Patterson drawing room, Jerome came looking for her. "I have had a letter from France."

Betsy dropped her work in her lap. "From your family?"

"No, from Minister of the Navy Decrès. He says that Napoleon orders me to return to France on the first available frigate." Jerome sat beside her and handed her the letter.

Betsy scanned the page but could not find what she was looking for. "It says nothing about our marriage?"

"No, Elisa. Lieutenant Meyronnet, who delivered this, said that when he left France in January, my family still knew nothing of our nuptials."

"I see." She forced herself to read the letter from beginning to end. It suggested that Jerome return on the *Poursuivante,* which he could no longer do. "Do you think your brother is angry with you for staying in the United States so long?"

"No. Meyronnet said that Napoleon thinks I acted wisely in not traveling on a merchant vessel that could easily be boarded. But with war heating up, he wants me to return as soon as possible and resume my duty to France."

Handing back the letter, she asked, "What are we to do? You cannot ignore this directive."

"I swore a sacred oath to your father not to take you to France as long as our marriage is in question. We cannot go there until we receive my mother's consent."

"Then you will be guilty of desertion, and when you do return to France, you will be liable to imprisonment. Or even hanging."

Jerome laughed. "The admiralty would not dare to hang me. No, Napoleon will rage at me as he has done many times, but I will win him over in the end."

Dorcas said, "Jerome, my daughter is right. This is a more serious offense than any boyish prank you may have committed before. To defy the First Consul will not induce him to look with favor upon your wife, whom he will certainly blame for your defection."

Betsy looked up in surprise at her mother's astute observation, but then she realized that Dorcas was speaking from long experience as the wife of an authoritarian man. Telling herself not to give way to fear, Betsy raised her chin. Jerome was her husband now, and it was her duty to help his career. In the long run, winning Napoleon's favor would benefit them both. "Perhaps we should go to France no matter what you promised my father."

Jerome scanned the letter again. "Since they did not know of our marriage, there is nothing in these orders to prevent you from traveling with me."

"Will the captain allow me aboard a warship?"

His eyes flashed. "I will order him to do so as the First Consul's brother."

Glancing toward her mother, Betsy saw that Dorcas was worried, yet Betsy had made up her mind. "How long do you think it will be before another frigate docks in Baltimore Harbor?"

"There is no way to know. I think we would do better to travel to New York and see if any French ships have landed there." Jerome smiled impishly. "While we wait, I will show you the sights of that great city."

Betsy laughed, her anxiety eased. The news she found so troublesome had not dampened Jerome's irrepressible pursuit of amusement in the slightest. "All right, let us go to New York."

❧ XI ❧

B EFORE leaving Baltimore, Jerome wrote to Victor du Pont, an émigré businessman he had met on his previous trip to New York. Jerome announced their upcoming visit and asked du Pont to recommend a house that he and Betsy might rent during their stay.

Because they were in no special hurry, on their third day out Jerome and Betsy stopped in Philadelphia to visit some friends of the Pattersons. Then they set out across New Jersey. They were traveling in the new coach-and-six Jerome had purchased because he felt it was the only vehicle impressive enough to suit the Bonaparte dignity. Jerome's physician and secretary followed in a rented curricle—an open, two-wheeled chaise—while Lieutenant Meyronnet accompanied them on horseback, and the servants traveled by public coach. The Bonapartes arrived at the du Ponts' three-story town house the second week of April. Their companions took rooms in an inn.

The du Ponts lived in Greenwich Village, just north of New York. The city was growing increasingly crowded, causing epidemics of diseases like cholera to occur more frequently, so in recent years, wealthy families had begun moving to communities just beyond the city limits. Greenwich Village still had a rural character, but because of the exodus, more mansions and town houses were going up all the time.

The du Ponts, both of whom were in their mid-thirties, greeted

Jerome and Betsy in their front hall. Victor du Pont had a cleft chin, kindly eyes, and heavy eyebrows. He took both of Jerome's hands and welcomed him enthusiastically in French. Then du Pont and his wife greeted Betsy in English. *"Je suis enchantée de faire votre connaisance,"* she replied, earning a warm smile from her hostess. Madame du Pont had coppery ringlets piled on top of her head and blue eyes in a plump face.

After they exchanged a few more remarks, Madame du Pont turned to Jerome. "Your wife is charming, Monsieur Bonaparte. I can see why you were so distressed by your separation when last we met."

"Was he very upset?" Betsy asked.

Madame du Pont laughed. "Oh, Madame Bonaparte, I have never seen a young man so stricken. I thought that I was watching a tragedy by Racine."

"Ma chérie, I told you not to doubt me," Jerome said. To Madame du Pont, he added, "I am afraid that my wife was made a skeptic at a very tender age. When she was a girl, she memorized all of La Rochefoucauld's *Maxims."*

"Heavens, such a cynical man!" Placing one hand upon her bosom, Madame du Pont turned to Betsy. "What possessed your mama to allow you to undertake such an unsuitable project?"

"My mother had so many children to supervise that she was happy to allow anything that would occupy me."

"Come, why are we standing in the hall?" Du Pont ushered his guests into the parlor, which was furnished with pieces that Betsy was certain had been imported from France. The chairs and tables were carved in classical forms and embellished with gilt, and hieroglyphics inspired by Napoleon's Egyptian campaign decorated one chest.

"Bonaparte, tomorrow I will take you to view a house that I think will suit your purpose. It is quite nearby. When I told the owner, Monsieur Magnitot, that you were uncertain how long you would need it, he agreed to flexible terms."

"Thank you, Monsieur, for taking so much trouble on our behalf. When I return to Paris, I will make sure that my brother knows how much assistance you have provided."

Du Pont flushed, but Betsy could not tell if it were with pleasure or embarrassment. "At week's end, we are hosting a formal ball to honor you and your bride."

"That sounds delightful," Betsy said.

THE NEXT DAY Victor du Pont took them to see a narrow, three-story town house on Washington Street a block east of the river. The raised first floor had two mullioned windows and an off-center blue door flanked by ornamental columns. At street level, a plain wooden door allowed horses to be led directly to the back yard where the carriage house stood.

Jerome liked it, particularly because of the ease with which he could go riding. After he signed the lease, they moved in with their servants and Jerome's three companions. Betsy disliked the idea of living with such a large retinue when they were so newly married, but she made no protest. She told herself she would have to grow accustomed to having an entourage of royal proportions if they were to live at Napoleon's court.

Because the house was let completely furnished and their residence would be temporary, they made only one change to the décor. Jerome took down the gloomy portrait hanging over the fireplace in their private sitting room and hung a sword in its place. When he was fifteen, he had begged to take part in the Italy campaign, but Napoleon declined his request. When a victorious Napoleon returned to Paris, Jerome refused to speak to him until he agreed to give up the sword he had carried during his victory over the Austrians at Marengo. The narrow gold-encrusted saber, curved like the scimitars Napoleon had seen in Egypt, was Jerome's most cherished possession.

After they moved in, Jerome inquired whether any French frigates were in the harbor. Nothing was there at the moment, but he learned that members of the fleet often docked in New York for supplies or repairs. "We might as well enjoy ourselves while we wait," he told Betsy on his return to the house.

Their first week in New York, Jerome took her to see a musical drama at the New Theatre, a three-story building with a disappointingly plain exterior. The interior, however, was as splendid as Betsy could wish, with a crystal chandelier hanging from the center of a domed ceiling and three tiers of boxes decorated in blue and gold. Jerome obtained a box for them in the lowest tier.

The play, *The Wife of Two Husbands,* portrayed a countess who received word that her first husband—a rogue who had charmed her into eloping and then destroyed her love through abuse and criminality—was not dead as she had been told. He had recently escaped from prison and threatened to ruin her happy second marriage to the count.

At the first intermission, Betsy opened her fan and waved it languidly. "Are all dramas as contrived as this? Upon my word, I never heard so convoluted a story."

"Do not feign indifference, Elisa. I saw you wiping away tears."

She laughed that he had seen through her façade of jaded sophistication. "It was because of Eugenia's song about pining for her love. The lyrics reminded me of when I was exiled to Virginia and had no way of knowing if I would ever see you again. It was such a cruel time."

Jerome raised her hand and kissed it. *"Ma chère petite femme, je ne te quitterai jamais."*

She leaned close and whispered, "I know you would not leave me willingly. But it seems an odd circumstance that you would bring me to see a play about a woman who learns that her marriage is invalid."

"Elisa!" Jerome's tone was aggrieved. "This performance—" He gestured broadly to the stage. "Is meant to amuse you. If it causes you distress, then by all means let us go."

Betsy shut her fan and laid it across his chest. "No, I do not wish to leave. Forgive me for being out of temper." To change the subject, she leaned forward and surveyed the audience below. Pointing with her folded-up fan, she whispered, "Look at that woman in the pale blue gown with the pleated hem. I thought that style had gone out of fashion. I must say, I don't see a woman here whose clothes rival the wardrobe you gave me."

"More importantly, my love, none of them can rival you for beauty."

Her good humor restored, Betsy settled back in her seat. As the second act began, she imagined that she was already in Paris watching plays that were far more sophisticated than this production. How wonderful life would be when she and Jerome were established at court.

Saturday was the night of the du Ponts' ball. Because it was given in their honor, Betsy and Jerome stood for a long time in a hallway outside the reception room meeting émigrés, American businessmen, and New York dignitaries. The last two days, the weather had been hot, so Betsy fanned herself between introductions. Several of the French guests remarked on her resemblance to Pauline Bonaparte, and Betsy grew curious to meet her sister-in-law.

When they were finally able to enter the reception hall where the dancing was taking place, Betsy immediately noticed how warm it was. Even though the room was large and had three sets of double doors open at the far end, it was packed with a swarm of people. Candle smoke and human sweat tainted the atmosphere.

Jerome was impatient to dance. As they attached themselves to the end of two lines doing a contradanse, he said, "You are the most elegant woman here, Elisa. Did I tell you that Madame du Pont thinks you are as lovely as an angel?"

"No." Betsy grinned. "Do you wish I were an angel, Jerome?"

"*Mon dieu, non!* I prefer you as flesh and blood, my love."

As the guests of honor, they had to partner with other people after their first turn together. Betsy danced without ceasing for more than an hour, making small talk with a variety of men she had never met before that night. Even in her lightweight dress, she found herself perspiring and, at times, struggling to catch her breath. When the musicians finally took a break, Jerome came to find her. "Elisa, your face is so red. Are you well?"

Betsy fanned herself. "The air is very close. I had no idea the du Ponts were going to ask so many people."

"Come." He pulled her off the dance floor to a side gallery where several middle-aged women sat on delicate gilt chairs. Betsy was about to protest against joining such staid company when she realized that Jerome was still moving. Reaching their destination took several minutes because many people stopped them to speak. Finally, after politely breaking off their fourth conversation, they arrived at the open doors in the back.

Jerome escorted Betsy onto a deserted balcony overlooking a rear courtyard garden. Two torches extended from brackets in the wall, and flanking the three sets of doors were potted evergreens. Leading Betsy around the shrub at the far right, Jerome showed her to a small stone bench in a secluded corner. "Rest here. I will be back in a few moments with lemonade. Or would you prefer champagne?"

"I am very thirsty. Lemonade might be best."

She sat fanning herself. Stars twinkled in the dark sky overhead, and Betsy searched for a meteor so she could make a wish. *What a wonderful night we are having,* she thought. Being admired by so many émigrés gave her a taste of what life might be like when they reached Napoleon's court. She felt more certain than ever that she and Jerome were going to be the most brilliant young couple in Paris.

Hearing footsteps come onto the balcony, Betsy closed her fan, brushed back a wisp of hair, and prepared to greet her husband. Instead, she heard a strange man's voice, speaking English with an American accent, from the vicinity of the balustrade beyond the potted fir. "Have you ever seen such a crush? There must be a hundred people here."

"At least," answered a second man, a New Englander by his speech. Betsy smelled the leafy aroma of burning tobacco. "I wonder why the du Ponts are incurring so much expense for a scapegrace like young Bonaparte. I heard that Victor paid the couple's rent and even loaned Bonaparte several thousand dollars."

Stunned, Betsy remained very still as the other man replied, "There is no surprise in that. Du Pont makes his living supplying French troops. He must think that if he keeps the younger brother happy, the First Consul will favor his bids."

"Then he is a fool. From what my European friends tell me, Boney is an iron-hard man who will not be swayed by such fripperies." A pause occurred, which Betsy attributed to the men puffing their cigars. Then the New Englander said, "I tell you what, if Jerome Bonaparte is hard up for money, I would gladly pay a hundred dollars to dance with his pretty wife and take a long gander at those luscious bubbies."

The other man laughed coarsely. "No need to pay, Bill. She gives away the view."

A wave of burning shame swept over Betsy. Realizing with alarm that her husband had been gone long enough to fetch her drink, she rose. She had to stop this malicious talk before Jerome arrived, or he would be likely to issue the men a challenge. Although her legs were trembling, she forced herself to walk past the obstructing evergreen, where she found two merchants she had met earlier. "Gentlemen, I believe you wished to see me?"

The one nearest to Betsy, a portly middle-aged man in a cheap suit, whirled around and said, "Damn!"

The other man, about thirty and fashionably dressed, stammered, "Madame Bonaparte, I—I—Please forgive us. We had no idea that you were so near."

"Your comments would not be acceptable were I on the moon, sir."

"No, no, you are right. I do not know what to say."

She lifted her chin and gave him a cutting stare. "I suggest you rejoin the other guests before my husband returns, because I warn you that he does not suffer insults to his honor lightly. Especially when made by grubby tradesmen like yourselves."

The younger man tossed his cigar to the lawn below and hurried away, but the older one took a last leisurely puff. "Grubby tradesman, eh? You are nothing but a merchant's daughter yourself. But of course, you have since married a Bonaparte, and we all know how highly that family is esteemed." He made a mocking bow. Then he snuffed his cigar in a nearby pot and left.

As soon as Betsy was alone, her tremors increased and she grasped the balustrade for support. Gazing at the dark garden below, she tried to dismiss the men as odious nobodies. She did not know which was more upsetting, their comments about her appearance or their assumption that Jerome was sponging off their host. Surely, the remarks about money were merely speculative gossip.

Yet, as she recovered from the shock of the encounter, Betsy began to wonder if Jerome was deceiving her about his sources of income. She had to admit that he had a record of being financially reckless. Betsy also knew that few men would tolerate their wife's interference in money matters—and Jerome with his Corsican pride was not likely to be one of them. All she could do was to steer him gently to be more moderate in their outlays.

She sighed and then heard Jerome say her name. As he came onto the balcony and handed her a cup of lemonade, he said, "Why are you standing here? I thought you were going to rest."

"I was looking at the stars and wondering what they will be like during our voyage to France. Will they be much brighter than this?"

"Oh, yes, wait until you see the wonder of the night sky over the Atlantic."

"Something to look forward to," she murmured.

Jerome tilted up her chin. "I cannot wait to see the starlight reflected in that luminous gaze of yours." As she met his glance, Betsy felt tears pooling in her eyes. Jerome frowned. "Elisa, are you crying?"

"It is nothing. I am just happy to be with you."

He seized her hand, drew her back into the shadows, and kissed her.

A FEW WEEKS PASSED without the opportunity to sail. One morning, as Jerome and Betsy sat at breakfast in their private sitting room, Jerome's manservant came to announce a visitor. "Monsieur du Pont is downstairs, sir. He insists on seeing you."

"Show him up."

As soon as the servant left, Betsy stood and fastened her wrapper more tightly over her chemise. "I wish I were dressed."

Jerome shrugged. "You will not be the first woman he has seen in *déshabillé.*"

A minute later, the servant ushered Victor du Pont into the room. He bowed. "Forgive me for disturbing you at such an unseemly hour. I would not have presumed if it were not urgent."

"Please, have a seat," Betsy said.

"Thank you." He took a chair but perched on the edge. "I heard upsetting news from an associate just arrived on a merchant ship from France, and I did not want you to read it in the newspaper. In March, there was another plot to assassinate the First Consul."

"Another?"

"Elisa, hush," Jerome said in a tone of command unlike anything she had ever heard him use. "Du Pont, is my brother safe?"

"Yes. They discovered the scheme before the plotters were able to act."

"Thank God for that!"

"But there is more. The First Consul received information that the Duc d'Enghien was involved." Glancing at Betsy, du Pont explained,

"Enghien was a prince of the blood of the House of Bourbon."

"Was?" Jerome asked.

"Yes," du Pont said, nodding emphatically. "As I said, rumor implicated him in the plot, but there was little evidence. Even so, the First Consul sent dragoons into Baden to arrest him. They brought him back to France, where he was immediately tried and executed."

"Good!"

"That is not all, is it?" Betsy asked, seeing the anxiety on du Pont's face.

"No. All of Europe is in an uproar over the insult to Baden and the haste with which the execution was carried out. They are calling it judicial murder akin to the Reign of Terror."

"That is absurd. My brother did only what was necessary to protect himself."

Betsy and du Pont exchanged an uneasy glance, and she said, "No one is denying Napoleon's right to defend himself. The only question is the method. To invade another nation and extract one of its residents could be considered grounds for war."

"So can plots of assassination!" Jerome exclaimed, shoving his plate away.

"Yes, of course, but he should have found a way to take legal action against the plotters." Betsy thought of an example to help him understand. "You have heard my father complain of the way the British navy impresses our sailors into its service. It shows that Britain does not respect our sovereignty as a country. Napoleon's action demonstrates the same disrespect for Baden."

"Elisa, are you siding with my brother's enemies?"

"No, of course not," she answered, keeping her voice calm in the face of her husband's fury. "I was trying to explain why the other rulers of Europe are shocked. Has the First Consul never spoken of the need to understand how one's foes are thinking?"

Jerome was speechless a moment, and then he laughed without mirth. To du Pont, he said, "Do you see why I love her? Beneath that angelic face is a mind that seeks to emulate the greatest strategist in Europe." He stood and kissed the top of her head. "You are adorable."

Irritated by his condescension, Betsy remained silent.

Jerome crossed to a cabinet on the other side of the room and poured a brandy. "This news makes it even more imperative that we get to France. My brother will need the support of all his family."

"With luck, a frigate will arrive before long," du Pont said.

After tossing back his drink, Jerome said, "With luck. Thank you for coming. It was good of you to see that I did not learn the story from a hostile source."

"It was the least I could do." Rising, du Pont bowed to Betsy again. "Madame Bonaparte." Then he took his leave.

Once they were alone, Betsy asked Jerome, "What did he mean by saying this was 'another' plot to assassinate Napoleon?"

"On Christmas Eve three years ago, a group of conspirators exploded an infernal machine in the street, hoping to catch Napoleon on the way to the opera. My brother and Josephine narrowly escaped, but many bystanders died."

"How horrible! What do they hope to gain from such violence?"

"The overthrow of the Consulate, of course." Jerome poured another half measure of brandy and drank it.

"But could they not wait and oppose him at the next election—" Betsy fell silent as she realized the error in her thinking. The Constitution passed in 1802 had made Napoleon First Consul for life. For him, there would be no more elections. For an instant, Betsy recalled how scornfully her brother William had dismissed the idea that France could still call itself a republic. The French people had no recourse against abuse of power except to resort to violence. *But Napoleon is not a tyrant,* she reminded herself.

She saw that Jerome was frowning at her prolonged silence, so she said, "What you are telling me is that without your brother at the helm, the current government will founder and the Bourbons may return."

Jerome nodded. "Precisely. That, no doubt, is why Enghien was involved."

To Betsy, it was clear where her allegiance lay. She crossed to Jerome and hugged him. "I am so sorry. It must be vexing to be so far from your family when Napoleon is in danger."

Jerome stroked her hair. "We must go to Paris as soon as possible."

WEEKS PASSED WITHOUT a French warship arriving in New York.

Toward the end of May, as Betsy and Jerome sat at breakfast, they received an urgent letter from William Patterson: "Betsy, I have news from your brother Robert, but I dare not trust it to the mails. Come home at once."

They hastily packed, wrote the necessary letters to cancel their engagements, and set off for Maryland.

Even with a good carriage, the journey from New York to Baltimore took four days. The highway just outside New York was tolerable, but once they crossed into New Jersey, the roads were in notoriously poor repair—so bad that two years earlier a newspaper had declared them the worst on the eastern seaboard. The poor time they made the first two days irritated Jerome so much that he swore at every minor annoyance. Betsy kept silent in spite of sharing his vexation. She suspected that on his own, Jerome would have gone on through the night, but he would not subject her to the discomfort of continuous traveling.

South of Philadelphia, the roads improved again, and their carriage progressed more swiftly. Even so, Betsy chafed at the length of the trip. While she appreciated her father's discretion, given how frequently mail was opened and read in transit, she was desperate to know how the Bonapartes had reacted to her marriage. For the entirety of the journey, her curiosity was an itch akin to the torment she had suffered as a child whenever she got chigger bites from walking in wet summer grass on her family's country estates.

They reached Baltimore in the late evening of the fourth day and went straight to the Patterson house, where they found her parents in the drawing room. Betsy immediately asked her father, "What does Robert say?"

Patterson crossed to his desk, unlocked the top drawer, and pulled out a sheet of paper. "He wrote the day after arriving in France and seeing the American minister. Mr. Livingston has already spoken to the First Consul and your other brothers, Jerome, assuring them that you have made a respectable alliance, but the situation remains precarious." He handed his daughter the letter and pointed to a particular paragraph. "Read that aloud."

After biting her lip, Betsy complied. "Bonaparte is of a very irritable temper, and as he is at present highly incensed with his brother, he might, were Jerome here, take some violent measures with him."

Overcome by this pessimistic assessment, Betsy sank onto her father's wingback chair before continuing.

> *Still, Mr. Livingston thinks the First Consul will after awhile become better satisfied with the union; and as he has by his conduct hitherto uniformly endeavored to impress on the world the highest idea of his moral character, he will not lightly, in this present affair, do anything to impeach or bring that character into question.*

"See, Elisa! All will be well. We just have to be patient to allow the volcano of my brother's temper to stop erupting, and calm to be restored."

Despite her anxiety, Betsy smiled at his colorful metaphor before reading further.

> *When the account of Mr. Jerome Bonaparte's intentions first reached the consular ear, the First Consul had determined to recall him instantly. Since the marriage has taken place, I believe it is his intention Jerome should remain in America for some time. Mr. Joseph Bonaparte has consulted Mr. Livingston respecting the most eligible place for Jerome to reside.*

Betsy turned to her husband. "But we do not want to live in America. Why does your oldest brother try to order our lives without consulting us?"

William Patterson answered instead of Jerome. "I believe this scheme is proposed on the possibility that we will prove unable to reconcile the First Consul to your marriage. However, if you continue reading, you will see that Robert describes more than one contingency."

Returning to the letter, Betsy skimmed a long passage that discussed how much money would be required for Jerome to live in a style appropriate to his rank, and then she read aloud, "For the present, it will be much better the parties should remain in America; but should he be directed to return, I am of the opinion she ought to accompany him."

Betsy decided not to read the next sentence aloud because it expressed Robert's fear that Jerome's affections might diminish if he returned alone.

She handed the letter back to her father. "Jerome has already been ordered by Minister of the Navy Decrès to return to France as soon as possible, so I think this idea of settling in America is an impossibility."

"I am not certain I share that opinion. Jerome, you know your brother's temper. Is he likely to recover from his displeasure at your marriage?"

Watching her husband closely, Betsy could see a glib assurance rise to his lips, but he took one look at his father-in-law's grim expression and refrained from uttering it. "I cannot say. At times, Napoleon can be obdurate in demanding that the rest of us yield to his point of view, while at others, he punishes us for a while and then forgives. But I can be as unyielding as he, and I will never consent to give up Elisa. Once he sees my determination, he will have to receive us to preserve the family peace. And I feel certain that the moment he meets Elisa, her beauty and excellent character will overcome any reservations."

Patterson frowned. "I hope so. I pray God you do not both end up in a French prison."

✒ XII ✑.

ETSY and Jerome had been in Baltimore only three days when Lieutenant Meyronnet arrived, dust covered and weary, after traveling on horseback at breakneck pace from New York. He said that two 40-gun French frigates, the *Cybèle* and the *Didon,* had arrived shortly after the Bonapartes departed the city, and their captains had orders to take Jerome back to France.

Before leaving for New York, Jerome went to Washington to ask Minister Pichon for traveling money. When he returned three days later, his face was a storm of resentment. "Pichon has been forbidden to advance me more funds. He told me to borrow from your father."

Betsy made no answer since they both knew that petitioning William Patterson would be useless. Watching Jerome pace before the unlit fireplace in the parlor, she sensed that something more was bothering him. "What else did Pichon say?"

Jerome stopped pacing and shot her an anguished look. "Elisa, Napoleon has decreed that you must not come to France. In the dispatch Minister Dècres sent Pichon, he called you 'the young person to whom Citizen Jerome has connected himself' rather than my wife. If you try to land in Europe, you will be sent immediately back to the United States."

Betsy's stomach contracted with alarm. "Is the First Consul so powerful that he can control an entire continent?"

"Of course not. He means to frighten us with his bluster."

"But he clearly intends to effect our separation in the hope that you will forget me."

Jerome pounded his right fist into his other hand. "If he thinks I will meekly abandon my wife, then he little knows me. I am no longer a boy to be chastised by my brother. I am a man who must fulfill my sacred duty to you."

Hearing that impassioned speech, Betsy could not help but question whether it expressed his true character or simply what Jerome imagined himself to be. She had lately begun to wonder if he was secretly regretting their marriage. "What do you propose?"

"We will go to New York, and I will speak to this Captain Brouard who sent Meyronnet to fetch me. I will make him understand that he must take you or I will not go."

Betsy stared at the floor as she tried to foresee the difficult course ahead of them. "What if he forces you to leave me by holding you prisoner aboard the ship?"

"He would not dare."

She looked up at him. "But Napoleon would. When we reach France, how do you imagine your brother will respond? Is he not likely to imprison you for your defiance?"

"I would gladly suffer a brief imprisonment to demonstrate my resolve, Elisa, but I doubt it will come to that. As I told you before, it is not Napoleon's place to approve our marriage. All we need do is speak to my mother apart from my brother's influence."

Even though he had given the reassurance she sought, Betsy pushed him a little further. "So you have said many times, but why should your mother favor your wishes over Napoleon's? He is the one who has won prestige for your family."

Jerome smiled. "Because I am more like my father than any of my brothers, and she has always seen me as the compensation God gave her for that loss."

Betsy shivered in repugnance at his answer. "How can you be so unfeeling as to use your mother's sorrow against her?"

"Would you rather I allow my brother to inflict an equally bitter sorrow upon us?"

"No." Despite her efforts to remain calm, she began to weep. "Why does Napoleon bear such a grudge against me? Am I so inferior that it is an insult to have me as a sister-in-law?"

"Elisa, it is nothing to do with you." Jerome knelt before her to wipe away her tears. "He is angry because I did not play the good soldier but rather dared to choose my own fate."

"And do you regret that choice?"

"No, I will never regret you as long as I live."

WHILE JEROME MADE arrangements to give up the Baltimore house and return to New York, Betsy went to tell her parents of their plans. Her father's response surprised her: "If you have room in your carriage, I should like to accompany you."

"You are welcome to join us, Father, but why would you take time away from business?"

Patterson glowered at the question, yet his answer revealed a tender concern. "Jerome might be confident that his determination will carry the day, but I am not so sure. I foresee that he may be forced to sail to France without you, and I could not rest easy knowing that you might be abandoned in a strange city without a protector."

Betsy wanted to rush across the room to hug him, but such displays of affection had never been their custom. Instead, she said, "I thank you for your consideration, sir, and welcome your companionship."

THEY REACHED NEW York on June 12. After taking Betsy and her father to the Washington Street house, Jerome went immediately to report to the captains of the two frigates. When he returned home, he told Betsy, "You need to put on an evening gown, my love. I invited the captains to attend the theater with us tonight."

William Patterson, who sat at the desk in the drawing room writing to his wife, looked up. "Jerome, this is no time for frivolity!"

"Father, you misjudge him. The officers have been several weeks at sea and no doubt will appreciate the entertainment. Such a gesture may help win them to our side."

"I suppose you know best," Patterson answered and returned to his letter.

That evening at the theater, both officers behaved gallantly toward Betsy, and neither expressed qualms about her accompanying her husband. During the interval, they gave Jerome the latest information about the naval war. Then after the play, as the four sat over supper in the private room of a tavern, Captain Brouard told them astonishing news.

After the last assassination attempt, the public had demanded that Napoleon become emperor of France with the office becoming hereditary. Ensuring that his title could pass to his heirs was seen as the only way to preserve the government from royalist plots to overthrow it. The frigates had departed from Brest before the Senate made its official proclamation, but both captains felt sure the change of government had taken place while they were at sea.

If what the officers said was true, then Betsy immediately understood why Napoleon was displeased with his youngest brother's impetuous marriage to an unknown American. Jerome was in the imperial line of succession now.

At the end of the evening, the Bonapartes made arrangements to board the *Didon* the next day. Captain Brouard wanted to weigh anchor before the week was out.

Neither Betsy nor Jerome slept that night because they were so taken up with packing and discussing the prospect of becoming royalty. When Betsy expressed doubt that Napoleon would accept her in that role, Jerome said, "Do not esteem yourself so lightly. You have more charm and grace than any princess of the blood. Now that we know the reason for Napoleon's disapprobation, I am certain we will overcome it. Once he meets you, he must see what an ornament you will be at court."

Betsy, who had been gathering the personal items scattered about the sitting room, placed a stack of books, stationery, and loose embroidery floss on the table. Her arms, freed of their load, began to tremble, and she clasped her hands together so Jerome would not see her anxiety. "But I fear he objects for reasons of state. As an unmarried brother, you could be used to forge a political alliance. Fettered with an American wife, you have not the same utility."

"Do you think I have any interest in marrying a fat, homely princess?"

He took down the sword of Marengo and its scabbard. "Elisa, surely you know me better than that. If Napoleon could marry for love, why should I not do the same?"

Jerome carried the sword to the table where he wrapped it in a protective cloth. "*Sainte Mère,* that gives me an idea. We must enlist Josephine on our side. She and I have always got on very well, and if she pleads our cause, perhaps Napoleon will relent."

"Perhaps," Betsy said doubtfully. It seemed to her that if Josephine were disposed to intercede on their behalf, she would have already done so.

Then Betsy went into their bedroom, brushing Jerome's arm as she passed for the comfort of physical contact. As she checked that all her jewels were in their casket, she tried to lift her spirits by telling herself that Providence had smiled on them by making Captain Brouard amenable to her passage aboard his ship. Surely fate was still on their side. She reminded herself of Odette's words from so long ago: "When you entered a room full of people, they bowed like you were a princess." As a child, Betsy had wondered how a Baltimore girl could become royalty. Now she had the answer. Not only had she connected herself to the most powerful family in Europe, but her husband might soon attain the rank of prince.

PATTERSON ACCOMPANIED THEM to the harbor the next day. Because their decision to sail was so precipitous, he had agreed to remain in New York until he was certain of their safe departure and then close the house and return the keys to Monsieur Magnitot.

They stood on a dock on the Manhattan side of the East River, watching their trunks being rowed out to the *Didon,* a 160-foot frigate with three square-rigged masts. The ship was painted black except for the gun deck, which was mustard yellow. Jerome pointed out the windows across the broad stern. "Those belong to the captain's quarters." Then he shaded his eyes and walked further down the dock to watch the ship's boat return for them.

Betsy turned to her father. "It would seem there was little need for you to take this journey, but I confess that I am grateful to have you here so I can say farewell. Give Mother my best love. I do not know when I am likely to see either of you again."

Patterson bent down to speak in a voice only she could hear. "I hope that you have chosen well, Elizabeth. Jerome's devotion appears unquestioned, but I fear that he will find it hard going to defy his brother." He pressed a sealed document into her hand. "These are the names of my bankers in Europe. If you find yourself in trouble, contact one of these men. I have already sent them the authority to release funds should you need assistance to return home."

Tears pricked her eyes, and all she could do was nod. Jerome called that it was time to leave. Impulsively, Betsy hugged her father and was gratified to feel his arms enclose her. Then she crossed to the end of the dock, where Jerome helped her into a waiting rowboat.

ONCE THEY BOARDED the ship, Captain Brouard told them that they would be given the quarters that belonged to the ship's second-in-command. He ordered a seaman to lead them to their cabin and then turned away to speak to another officer.

The sailor went down the ship's ladder first, followed by Jerome, who stationed himself at the base to prevent any common seamen from catching a glimpse of his wife's limbs as she descended in her gown. When Betsy reached the bottom, she found herself in an open deck that had dozens of massive cannons pointing toward the gun ports on each side of the ship.

"*Venez.*" The sailor led them halfway down the central aisle to another ladder that they descended to the berth deck. This time Betsy found herself in a space filled with iron supports, which Jerome told her bore the weight of the cannons above them, and a web of hammocks strung so that they filled every available space. The smell of stale sweat was so overpowering that Betsy held a handkerchief to her nose.

They followed the sailor down a narrow path between hammocks, past a partition, and into a corridor that ran between cabins. "*Voilà,*" the sailor said, pointing to a door. Then, after touching his cap in a gesture of respect to Jerome and swiftly running his gaze over Betsy's figure, he hurried away.

As Jerome opened the door, he warned Betsy that it had a raised sill. She carefully stepped into a cramped closet of a room with a single bunk, small writing desk and chair, and washstand. A whale-oil lamp was mounted to a bracket on the wall. Although her father earned much of his fortune through shipping, Betsy had never been on a vessel before and was shocked by the tight spaces and the pervasive odors of pine tar, mildew, and worse.

Jerome ducked to enter the low door. Straightening again, he laughed when he saw Betsy's expression. "Oh, my poor Elisa. You did not expect anything so Spartan, did you?"

He took her into his arms and kissed her. "A frigate was never meant to house such a fine lady as you."

They ate supper in the wardroom that evening, and as they dined on beef, fresh bread, fruit, and cheese, the officers teased Betsy that she was lucky they had just victualed the ship. "If we had been at sea for many weeks, we would have had to serve you ship's biscuit riddled with weevil worms."

At the end of the meal, when the Bonapartes rose from the table, Captain Brouard told Jerome that he was sending a pilot boat out the next day to see if the coastal waters were clear.

"An excellent precaution." Jerome answered.

"What did the captain mean?" Betsy asked Jerome once they were alone in their cabin.

He knelt on the bunk to open their porthole and get some fresh air. "My sojourn in the United States is no secret, Elisa. For weeks the New York newspapers have been publishing accounts of our plans to sail."

"And the British would like nothing better than to capture Napoleon's brother," she said with a shudder.

Her frightened tone caused him to turn and peer at her. *"Sois tranquille.* You are in experienced hands. If we should be attacked during our journey, I will place you in the most protected part of the ship, and if the worst happens and we are forced to surrender, you will be sent to your family. Not even the British would use a woman as political hostage."

Betsy went into his arms. "That would be little comfort to me if you were made prisoner. I would rather share your fate."

"I would never allow that." He stroked her hair. "But have no fear. The *Didon* is our navy's fastest frigate."

The next afternoon as they waited for news, Jerome gave Betsy a tour of the main deck of the ship, showing her the enormous ship's wheel, the compass, the bell, the masts, and the rigging. As he explained the various sails and their uses, he noticed the pilot boat returning from its scouting mission. They waited impatiently as the boat's skipper made his report. Finally, the captain summoned them to his stateroom.

"The scout brought grave news," Brouard said. "Two British warships, a corvette and a frigate, are lying off Sandy Hook just south of the place where we must enter the lower bay."

"A corvette is not much threat. How many guns has the frigate?" Jerome asked.

"Forty-four."

"Then taken together, the *Cybèle* and the *Didon* outgun them."

"Yes, but our maneuverability will be limited. I take it you have not sailed the Narrows before. We will be in single file as we pass between Staten Island and Long Island, while they will have the advantage of being in open water. And our scout saw more ships on the horizon."

The news terrified Betsy, and she bit her lip. Jerome had a glint in his eyes that made her think he relished the idea of fighting their way free, but seeing her fear, he said, "Perhaps they have nothing to do with us. Let us wait a day or two and see what action they take."

The next day, the captain reported that the skipper of the pilot boat had sighted two more British ships, one of them a 32-gun frigate, anchored off Sandy Point. At that, Jerome shook his head. "I cannot risk my wife's safety on such a rash attempt at escape. We shall have to find other means of transport."

"But you are ordered to return on my ship, sir."

Jerome frowned. "Perhaps we can decoy the British into leaving. If Madame Bonaparte and I disembark and state publicly that we will take a merchant vessel from Baltimore, our enemy might sail south. Then we can board under cover of night and slip out of the harbor."

"I think it unlikely they will fall for such bait, but I suppose the ruse does no harm."

"Then are we getting off the ship?" Betsy asked.

Jerome laughed at her look of relief. "Yes, but it is only a temporary feint to deceive our enemies. Unless I miss my guess, the British have rowed scouts ashore to keep watch on us. So we will perform a little farce for their amusement."

After dispatching Lieutenant Meyronnet for their carriage, they had their trunks rowed to the dock. Then Jerome appeared on deck, gesticulating to Captain Brouard. "No, absolutely not. I care nothing for my brother's orders. I cannot expose my wife to such danger!"

Brouard shouted back, "I can have you arrested, sir. I am your superior officer."

"And I am your prince! You dare not lay hands upon my person."

Betsy hoped that no spyglass was trained upon her face because she found it very hard not to smile at their theatrics. Once she and Jerome had been rowed ashore and were closed in their carriage, she burst into giggles. "You have an unsuspected talent for drama, Jerome."

He made a little bow and joined in her laughter.

OVER THE NEXT few weeks, daily communications went back and forth from their Greenwich Village house to the French frigates. Although the British sent two small ships south, their main force remained stationed off Sandy Hook. Frustrated by the failure of his scheme, Jerome suggested sending the *Cybèle* through the Narrows alone to engage the British ships and disable as many as possible before the faster *Didon* tried to escape. The two captains, however, refused because they were certain the plan would result in the loss of both ships.

One morning as Betsy started downstairs, she heard Jerome and his Creole secretary Alexander Le Camus in the hallway below. "The only thing for it is to leave your wife with her family and go throw yourself on the emperor's mercy."

Assailed by panic, Betsy grasped the railing and held her breath until she heard Jerome answer, "How can you say such a thing? I will not desert her."

"It would be only a temporary expedient until you can convince Napoleon of the wisdom of your choice."

"No. I promised my father-in-law that I would never do such a thing. I cannot go back on my word."

Does that mean he would leave me if he had not made the promise? Betsy wondered. Then she admonished herself, *I must not think such things.* She took a deep breath, called out Jerome's name, and continued down the stairs.

Nearly three weeks passed. One morning Jerome opened a note to learn that Captain Brouard had received a dispatch from Minister of the Navy Dècres. The packet had been delayed because it was mistakenly sent to Pichon in Washington and then returned. Among the other papers was an ominous order to the French fleet:

> *By an act of the 11th Ventose, all the civil officers of the empire are prohibited from receiving on their registers the transcription of the act of celebration of a pretended marriage that Jerome Bonaparte has contracted in a foreign country, during the age of minority, without the consent of his mother and without previous publication in the place of his nativity.*

Betsy gasped at the pronouncement, then covered her mouth with her hand. Were all of her dreams of becoming royalty nothing more than a castle in the air, an insubstantial structure that could be demolished by a few strokes of Napoleon's pen? Was she still in danger of being disgraced as a woman who had never been legally married?

As Jerome lifted his eyes from the paper, Betsy could see by his open-mouthed expression that he felt as shocked as she did.

"Que devrions-nous faire?" she whispered, thinking that surely Jerome must have some insight into his older brother's character that would help him form a plan.

To her disappointment, he answered, *"Je ne sais pas."* Then he passed her a small sheet of notepaper. "Captain Brouard enclosed a message with the announcement. He has withdrawn permission for you to sail on the *Didon.*"

Betsy waited for Jerome to say more, but he began to read a newspaper article that Brouard had also sent. *"Mon dieu,"* he murmured but then said no more.

Watching Jerome read the lengthy article strained Betsy's already frayed nerves. To keep from losing her temper, she picked up the official pronouncement denying the validity of her marriage and read it for herself. Then she laid the paper down. Her husband was still frowning over the sheet of newspaper, so she said, "Jerome, we must talk.

We have to come up with a plan to get around this prohibition. Clearly, we cannot rely upon the French navy to take us to France. Do you think it would be safe for you to sail aboard a merchant ship?"

He pressed his hand to his temple. "Elisa, I cannot think about that now. This article contains a very distressing story, one that is detrimental to our cause."

"What could be worse than the emperor's proclamation?"

"Do you recall what I told you about the crucial role my brother Lucien played in Napoleon's career?"

"Of course, I remember." In 1799 when Napoleon overthrew the Directory, he had faced an angry mob that denounced him as a dictator. Lucien had defused their hostility by flourishing his own sword and swearing to run Napoleon through if he ever violated the revolutionary principles of liberty, equality, and brotherhood. By that dramatic act, Lucien assured his brother's election as First Consul. "What possible bearing does that have on our situation?"

"A few years back, Lucien fell in love with the widow of a Parisian stockbroker and made her his mistress. Last year, she bore him a son, so he married her. Napoleon did not approve the match because he wanted Lucien to make a political alliance, but Lucien refused to set Alexandrine aside. So Napoleon flew into one of his rages, forcing Lucien to flee to Italy with his wife and child."

Betsy shivered. "And Napoleon will not forgive him?"

Jerome shook his head. "Not according to the reports. If Napoleon can cast Lucien aside, what chance do we have to placate his displeasure?"

"Then what should we do?"

He tossed the letter on the table and began to pace. "I don't know. Perhaps nothing just yet. Perhaps—" Jerome rubbed his chin. "Perhaps the reason for the estrangement with Lucien is more than just his marriage. Lucien has antagonized Napoleon before this by accusing him of straying from republican ideals. And then there was the matter of Christine."

"Who is Christine?"

"Lucien's first wife. A very common woman. The illiterate daughter of his landlord." Jerome paused to pour a brandy and then walked back to Betsy with a surprisingly cheerful expression. "Now that I think of it, Lucien's case is much different from mine. I married a renowned beauty, the daughter of a wealthy and respected American who is the friend of President Jefferson. There is no doubt you are well suited to life at court. If only we can contrive to have Napoleon meet you, you will easily demonstrate your worth."

Betsy shook her head in bewilderment at how swiftly Jerome's mood had rebounded. "That brings me back to the same question. How do we travel to France?"

"I will go to the *Didon* tomorrow afternoon and make one more appeal to Brouard to let you sail."

"But if you go on board, the captain may not allow you to disembark."

After setting down his brandy, Jerome sat beside her on the sofa and took her hands. "Elisa, that farce we acted for the British contained the seeds of truth. I am a member of the imperial family now. No one but my brother would dare lay hands on me."

"Are you certain?" she asked, unable to keep a tremor from her voice.

"Entirely." He kissed her. "I do not like the idea of your sitting home worrying. Your father plans to meet with a business associate tomorrow, so you will be alone much of the day. Du Pont tells me that his wife would be delighted to see you again. I want you to call on her."

"No, Jerome, I would not be good company."

"But it will occupy your mind. Promise to obey my wishes."

Wondering at Jerome's uncharacteristic insistence, Betsy agreed to do as he asked.

GABRIELLE DU PONT received Betsy in her personal sitting room, which was furnished with a sofa upholstered in rose-striped fabric and chairs that had matching seat cushions and rams-head armrests. As the maid laid out an elaborately gilded, blue porcelain coffee service, Betsy told the older woman of all that had occurred since their last meeting.

After Betsy finished, Madame du Pont asked, "If the First Consul— or rather, the emperor—is so adamantly opposed to your marriage, would it not make sense to remain in the United States?"

Filled with revulsion for the idea, Betsy offered the first excuse that came to mind. "My husband has no profession but the navy, and as a French citizen, he would never be able to enlist in the U.S. service.

I do not know how we would contrive to live."

"Surely your father settled some money on you when you married."

Betsy shook her head as she reached for one of the delicate almond cakes on the serving plate. "No. He does not believe in disposing of his wealth during his lifetime."

Gabrielle du Pont blotted her lips with a napkin. "Such things are a matter of course in Europe. Your husband should have insisted on a marriage settlement. His failure to do so shows his youthful inexperience."

"Be that as it may, we have no certain source of income unless he returns to France and takes up a position there."

Madame du Pont refilled Betsy's cup. "Nonsense. Look at my husband. Look at your father. Both are immigrants who became masters of their own business. Surely, Jerome Bonaparte is an enterprising enough young man to find some means to earn a living."

Betsy poured cream in her coffee and stirred so vigorously that the spoon rang against the china. "Madame, that is not the life that either one of us desires. We want to be at court."

"My dear, we all want many things, but we do not always get them. Would life as a merchant's wife be so very terrible? It is, after all, the life in which you were raised."

"I can think of nothing worse."

Madame du Pont raised one eyebrow. "Nothing?"

Betsy sighed and conceded, "Losing my husband would be worse, of course."

"Then why do you wish to return him to a ruler who will assuredly send him to war?"

Remembering the fire in Jerome's eyes when he contemplated having to fight his way out of the harbor, Betsy answered, "Because it is what he desires. He admires Napoleon above all men, and I think he dreams of achieving military glory to match his brother's."

"A foolish dream for which women usually must pay."

"Perhaps so, but I cannot change him, Madame."

The older women smiled, but her eyes contained pity. "No, I suppose you are right. The world is ordered so that men have all the power, and women must adapt."

When Betsy returned to the Washington Street house, she noticed immediately how silent it was. Not only was Jerome still out, but his companions and the servants were gone as well.

Wearily, she climbed the stairs to the second-floor. She entered the sitting room and removed her hat and lightweight summer gloves. Flinging them onto the table, she glanced at the clock on the mantel and saw that the sword from Marengo, which was supposed to be hanging above it, was gone.

For an instant, she thought that her recollection of the sword's whereabouts must be mistaken. Yet she could clearly remember Jerome taking it from his trunk and hanging it back in its place of honor after they returned from the *Didon*.

Despite that certainty, she went into the bedroom and flung open her husband's trunk. The velvet in which he had wrapped the sword lay in a heap on top of his folded uniforms, the box holding a pair of pistols he had bought in Baltimore, and the leather case containing miniatures of his family.

"No!" Betsy bent over the trunk and clawed through the items it held even though she knew that Jerome would never risk harm to the sword by placing it beneath other objects.

After a few minutes of futile searching, she returned to the sitting room, where she looked under every piece of furniture and in every corner. Finding nothing, she ran downstairs and raced through the first floor.

By the time Betsy climbed back up the staircase to the sitting room, she was breathing heavily. Perspiration had soaked through her chemise, causing it to cling disagreeably to her skin—just as opprobrium would cling to her name if Jerome had abandoned her. *But that cannot be,* she thought desperately. *He loves me as I love him.* She stood in the center of the room and stared at the wall above the fireplace, willing the sword to reappear. In spite of her effort to tell herself otherwise, she knew that the weapon's absence could mean only one thing. If the sword was gone, then so was Jerome.

That then was the explanation for the empty house—and the reason her husband had insisted she go calling. He had taken Le Camus's advice and left without her.

Betsy howled and sank to her knees. She cried so hard that she lost her breath, so she pressed her hands against her stomach and tried to master herself. Yet the thought that Jerome had crept away without saying good-bye smote her as sharply as a saber blow. How could he have betrayed her this way? The idea that he had deceived her just to make the departure easier for himself was unendurable, and she gave way to grief.

Betsy had no idea how long she lay on the floor sobbing, but after what felt like hours, she heard someone say her name. Strong arms pulled her into an embrace.

"Elisa, what has happened? Why are you so distraught?"

Stunned, she tried to stop crying, but all she could do was wheeze.

Jerome held her tighter and barked an order, "Fetch Dr. Garnier." Then he began to rock her. "Please, Elisa, do not weep. Everything is all right."

"You were gone," she gasped.

"Of course, I was gone. You knew that I was going to the ship."

She pulled back and wiped her wet face. "The sword—"

"Here it is." Jerome touched the scabbard at his side, which was attached to his belt and stretched out behind him. "I wore it to give myself an air of authority when I met with Brouard."

Hysterical laughter boiled up inside Betsy, and while she was trying to bring herself under control, Dr. Garnier entered the room.

"Doctor, my wife is distraught, and I cannot determine why. Is there anything you can give for her relief?"

Jerome rose, and Garnier took his place before Betsy. "Go pour a strong measure of brandy," the doctor ordered and then took Betsy's hands. "Madame Bonaparte, take deep breaths and let them out slowly. Think of nothing but the necessity to breathe."

As Betsy complied, her turbulent emotions gradually subsided. Jerome fetched the glass and the doctor handed it to her. "Drink this, and do not speak until you have finished it."

Betsy was accustomed to wine but nothing stronger, and the brandy burned her throat as it went down. As she forced herself to swallow the last of it, she felt very childish. Handing the empty glass to Jerome, she found it difficult to meet his eyes.

"What happened? Why were you so upset?"

"Forgive me, but when I saw that you had taken Napoleon's sword, I thought you must be leaving today. That you had decided to sail on the *Didon* and leave me behind."

"But I swore I would never do that."

"I know, but I overheard your conversation with Le Camus, and I feared that you decided to take his advice and not tell me good-bye to avoid a scene."

"You foolish little girl." Jerome embraced her. "Do you love me so very much?"

"You know I do." She put her arms around his neck.

"Then how can you doubt the strength of my love for you?"

As she rested wearily against Jerome's chest, she heard Dr. Garnier say, "Do not blame her, Bonaparte. The strain of the last few weeks has been too much for her nerves. Put her to bed, feed her a light supper, and try to protect her from unnecessary agitation for a while."

Betsy snuggled closer to Jerome and laughed feebly. "Doctor, such a treatment is not possible. Have you not heard? The emperor views us as little better than traitors."

"Shhh, Elisa. Put that out of your mind." Jerome rose, pulled her to her feet, and steered her toward the bedroom. "You heard Dr. Garnier. You must rest."

✒ XIII ✒

ETSY awoke in a dim room, forced from sleep by a heavy pain in her head. She opened her eyes and saw yesterday's gown draped over a chair instead of sitting folded in the wardrobe where it belonged. The sight brought back the memory of Jerome tenderly undressing her, helping her into bed, and holding her hand until she fell asleep. As Betsy recalled the hysteria that had prompted his solicitude, a sense of shame as oppressive as her headache settled on her. Sitting up, she discovered that her throat was dry and her stomach queasy. She reached for the carafe of water on her nightstand and filled the nearby glass.

As she sipped the water, Jerome entered the room. "How do you feel?"

"A little ill and very thirsty."

He kissed her. "You are unaccustomed to brandy. The unsettled feeling will pass, all the more quickly if you can bring yourself to eat breakfast."

"I may take a bit."

"Good." He crossed the room to open the draperies, and Betsy squinted uncomfortably as light flooded the room. Jerome said, "I would like to ask your father to join us at breakfast."

"Has he not eaten? He is usually an early riser."

"He breakfasted an hour ago, but he can sit with us a while. I want to talk to you both."

Betsy rose and pulled on her wrapper, trying not to show that she felt apprehensive about Jerome's desire for a conference. "Let me wash my face and comb my hair before I join you."

The two men were at the table when Betsy entered the sitting room. Jerome was cracking the shell of a soft-boiled egg, while Patterson sat with a cup of coffee. "Good morning, Father." She took her seat.

"Good morning. Are you better? I understand you had an attack of hysteria."

Betsy selected a scone, split it, and buttered it. "I am quite well. I foolishly let my feelings run away with me yesterday."

"Elisa, you must not blame yourself. You heard Dr. Garnier's opinion." Turning to his father-in-law, Jerome said, "The doctor believes that recent strains have overtaxed her nerves."

"It might help if you would lessen your number of social engagements. It cannot be good for your constitution to be out late night after night."

"Perhaps," Betsy murmured, stung by the criticism.

"Well, I have devised a plan that will undoubtedly restore the roses to my Elisa's cheeks. I mean to take her on an excursion."

Patterson froze with his cup in mid-air. "You cannot be serious. How can you propose a pleasure trip now? You have not settled the question of whether you are sailing."

"Yes, I have. Yesterday, I informed Captain Brouard that I will neither subject Elisa to the danger of the British blockade nor depart without her. I left Meyronnet aboard ship."

Jerome's nonchalance bewildered Betsy. "But you still have orders to return to France. And the frigates are bottled up in New York Harbor without any way of escape. An excursion will not resolve either of these issues."

Scooping up the last bit of egg, Jerome said, "Listen to my plan before you judge it. Last night, I decided that we should travel to see the great falls at Niagara."

"Niagara!" Patterson exclaimed. "This is madness. The area is a wilderness. It will take weeks of rough traveling to reach the falls. What would possess you to plan such a needless excursion now, of all times? You have more vital things to attend to."

"I am attending to them. The trip will accomplish two purposes. First, it will get Elisa away from all this tumult and into the wholesome air of the country. Second, it will convince the British that we have decided to settle in the United States, so they will abandon New York Harbor, allowing the frigates to depart. Elisa and I can sail after our return."

Betsy sipped her coffee, hoping that it would ease her headache. "But how do we get to Niagara if the falls are in unsettled wilderness?"

"When we were in Washington, Vice-President Burr told me about a honeymoon journey that his daughter Theodosia took there. More people are settling the area all the time, and inns are to be found almost the whole way."

Patterson slapped the table. "Jerome, with the British seeking to capture you, you should avoid Niagara at all costs. It lies on the border with Canada."

"We will travel under an assumed name—Monsieur and Madame d'Albert—and we will not cross to the Canadian side."

Betsy placed her half-eaten scone on her plate. She had never considered doing anything so rugged as the proposed trip, but the enthusiasm she saw on Jerome's face and the memory of his seeming relish for battle made her wonder if, as a virile young man, he might require a more active life than she did. "All right, Jerome. We will go to Niagara."

Patterson pushed back his chair. "If you are determined to pursue this reckless endeavor, then I will return to Baltimore as soon as possible. I for one have serious business to attend to."

Despite reassuring his father-in-law that inns existed almost as far as Niagara, once William Patterson departed, Jerome told Betsy that he wanted to camp during the latter stage of their journey. "It will help preserve our secrecy."

"Is it safe?"

"I have been told that as long as we have a fire burning all night, that should be sufficient to keep danger at bay."

Betsy did not find Jerome's answer reassuring, but she acceded to his obvious excitement. With a nod she said, "With you as my protector, what do I have to fear?"

Under his direction, she packed simple cotton dresses, her riding habit, leather ankle boots, and an old leghorn hat with a veil for protection. Jerome packed his oldest clothes and assembled a travel kit of two bedrolls and a knapsack that held canteens, a hunting knife, a hatchet, a tinderbox, a spyglass, and some ointments prepared by Dr. Garnier. He also bought saddles and bridles, which they would need on the final portion of their trip.

To travel from New York to Albany, they boarded a sloop on the Hudson River. The lower half of the Hudson was an estuary, so for two six-hour periods each day the incoming tides of the Atlantic Ocean pushed saltwater up the Hudson River channel past the capital, flowing at a considerable rate and reversing the river's current. In the summer, the prevailing winds blew from the south, which gave an additional push to sailboats on their journey upstream.

The sloop had a single mast that was rigged with a jib sail forward and both a topsail and a gaff-rigged mainsail aft. Accommodations for a dozen people took up nearly the entire quarterdeck, but each cabin was tiny with only room for a bunk and a washstand.

Betsy quickly perceived that despite their incognito, Jerome was not discreet enough to keep others from guessing his identity. The first morning she steered her irritated husband away from accosting a clump of businessmen—some Federalist, others Republican—who were arguing about whether President Jefferson was a "damn fool" for his pro-French opinions.

The other passengers included the twenty-year-old son of a New York state legislator, two men who made their living poling rafts, a wizened Revolutionary War colonel, and a half-soused schoolteacher. Betsy was the only woman aboard. To keep Jerome from spilling their secret, she told him she did not want to associate with such vulgar companions.

The first day, they sailed past the Palisades, a stretch of towering reddish cliffs scored by deep vertical notches. Mounds of shrubbery grew between the cliff base and riverbank. The steep, craggy walls astonished Betsy. After lunch, she sat on a bench on the open deck sketching the landscape while Jerome sat at her side teasing her that she rivaled Gilbert Stuart.

The next day, they entered the Highlands, where rounded green mountains rose on each side of the river. "Can you believe the stark landscape of yesterday gave way to this undulating country?" Betsy asked.

She turned to Jerome, who stood beside her at the railing, admiring the scenery and sniffing the fragrant air. "I am so happy to be in hilly country again. This puts me in mind of Corsica."

He pointed to a shallow tidal pool along a stretch of sandy beach hugged by a curving cliff. Betsy saw two young boys wading at the edge of the water. One of them poked a stick into a clump of aquatic plants and then reached in to pull out a blue crab, which he grasped at the back away from the snapping claws. After waving the crab overhead triumphantly, he carried it to a cloth-covered wooden bucket on the beach.

"My friends and I used to go crabbing when I was a boy," Jerome murmured and then walked to a bench near the bow. Betsy followed and sat beside him.

He took her hand and gently pulled her fingers. "That scene reminded me of my boyhood. We did not always have enough money, but to me life seemed simple and easy. Finding a crab for supper felt like a victory as great as any of Napoleon's conquests."

"Oh, Jerome. I think you grow weary of your prolonged idleness."

He stopped playing with her hand and enclosed it between both of his. "I begin to feel that my brother is right and that I am not acting the part of a man. I should be defending France instead of dawdling in America with you."

Betsy yanked her hand free. "Then why did you not sail back on the *Didon?*"

"It would have been foolhardy." Jerome rubbed his upper lip. "I know your brothers think me an idle fool, but I am not so feckless as they believe. I have two duties. One is to you, Elisa, and the other is to France, and I have not yet devised a way to fulfill both with honor. Unless we can change my brother's mind, I shall have to break faith with my family and my country, and how then will I ever achieve anything worth remembering? What is more, I miss my mama and my brothers and sisters, and I feel like an exile in this alien country of yours."

"If you dislike the United States so much, why did you come here?"

Staring at a thick, oily rope coiled upon the deck, Jerome sighed. "While I was cruising in the West Indies, I fired a warning shot at an unidentified merchant ship that refused our signal to heave to. I sent a boat alongside, and when the crew discovered she was a British ship, I made my apologies and thought that would suffice since the Peace of Amiens was still in effect. My admiral, however, feared the incident might provoke war, so he ordered me to return to France and make my report to Napoleon. We agreed that coming to the United States to seek passage in a neutral vessel was the best plan, and once here, I called upon my friend Joshua Barney."

Betsy felt a crack rupture the edifice of her belief in Jerome. All this time, she had assumed that he came to the United States on a mission when he had been merely fleeing the consequences of a rash mistake. For the first time, she understood why Napoleon dismissed their marriage as a youthful error best set aside and forgotten. History had taught him to expect little else from Jerome. The realization did not bolster Betsy's hope of winning the emperor's favor.

"Madame du Pont made a suggestion last week. She thinks you should take up a profession in this country so that we can live free of the threat of Napoleon's vengeance."

Jerome frowned. "I thought that your dearest desire is to leave Baltimore."

"It is, but if we cannot enter France as man and wife, we shall have to live somewhere else. In America, at least, we have a wide acquaintance. Do you think we could contrive to be happy if we lived here?"

"Here?" He gestured at the scenery. "Do you mean for us to settle among these hills?"

She smiled. "Perhaps, or close to the shore. You can be a Corsican fisherman, and I will be a fisherman's wife, selling your catch to passing travelers."

"They would be so dazzled by your beauty that they would buy more than they need, and we would grow as rich as kings." Then Jerome shrugged. "Such a life is possible, I suppose. It would be gratifying to be answerable to no one but ourselves."

Betsy heard doubt in his voice. "But you would miss the society of Paris."

"Not as much as I would miss you, Elisa, should Napoleon have his way."

"Which brings us back to the question of what to do."

Jerome put a consoling arm around her. "You should not fret. The reason I planned this excursion was to relieve your anxiety. Do not worry, my love. I will find a way to work everything out."

Betsy leaned against his shoulder and murmured, "I hope so."

At the state capital, they left the sloop and took seats on a stage-coach to Utica, which was a two-day journey away, heading west-north-west. As the coach drove from the river to the western edge of Albany, Betsy gazed out the window. She marveled at how different the architecture was from that of Baltimore. Several buildings had step-gable roofs that gave the skyline a saw-tooth appearance. Some houses even had upper-story doors but no stairs leading up to them. "What is the purpose of those?" she asked the Revolutionary War colonel, who was also taking the coach.

"Oh, that's a feature often found in Dutch houses. They haul up heavy furniture using block and tackle and take it into the house through those doors rather than struggling to carry it up the inside stairs. See the pulley near the apex of the roof?"

"A very ingenious idea," Jerome said.

By the time they left the city and were out in open country, Betsy realized this stage of the journey was going to be less comfortable than she had hoped. The coach was old and in poor repair, with threadbare upholstery and springs that no longer cushioned the shocks of bumpy roads. The colonel and the schoolteacher who accompanied them were both disagreeable men. The colonel complained of his rheumatism and swore at each jolt. The teacher started each day pleasantly enough, but he tippled constantly and by mid-morning was maudlin.

"I am meant for finer things than exile to the wilderness. Look at these hands." He held out his pudgy, milk-white extremities. "Madam, are these the hands of a rustic buffoon?"

"No, sir, they are *very* fine," Betsy answered, hoping her sarcastic tone would squelch further confidences.

"I am the victim of vicious gossip. It was my custom to call upon my students' families of a Sabbath afternoon. One Sunday last spring, I awoke late, so I took no food before setting out. It was a fearsome hot day, and each family I visited pressed me to take a little wine for refreshment. By the supper hour, I was tipsy from the unaccustomed quantities of drink. This gave rise to the rumor that I was an inveterate sot, which I assure you, madam, I am not. But they sacked me without ceremony, so I must journey west." Tears ran down his red cheeks. "I will probably die by the hand of a savage Indian."

"Don't be a goddamned fool," shouted the colonel, who sat beside him. "The tribes of western New York have been peaceful for many a year. You are more likely to die tripping over your piss pot and breaking your neck."

Jerome stirred. Betsy feared he was about to remonstrate with the men for their vulgarity, but instead he asked, "Is that true, sir, that the savages of western New York are subdued?"

The old man squinted at him suspiciously. "Yes, by gad, it is true. Where do you come from, young fella? You sound foreign."

Betsy held her breath until Jerome said, "France. I am fleeing Napoleon's tyranny."

"Ah, cannot say I blame you for refusing to live under that blackguard."

Intervening before the man could utter more criticisms of Napoleon, Betsy said, "Sir, would you be so good as to tell us what Revolutionary battles you took part in?"

To her relief, the colonel and Jerome began to discuss military matters.

At Utica, Jerome hired horses and bought provisions for the final leg of their journey, which would take at least ten days. "We should travel in easy stages since you are unaccustomed to riding all day."

"Perhaps at the start, but my stamina may improve," Betsy said, trying to hide her nerves about traveling through wilderness.

Jerome smiled at her. "Do not be anxious, Elisa. We have no need of hurry, and I do not intend to push you. This excursion is meant to restore your health."

To Betsy's surprise, the lands directly west of Utica were heavily settled. They passed farmhouses, fields of wheat and corn, a canal that linked the Mohawk River with a creek, and a reservation that

the Oneida Indians had been granted for siding with the Patriots during the Revolution. The first night, the Bonapartes stayed in an inn
because they failed to find deserted land for camping. Betsy was stiff
from riding all day, so she was grateful to sleep in a bed.

Their second day, the road passed through mixed forests of beech,
maple, hickory, poplar, elm, and oak. Dappled shade fell across the road
most of the day, making for a pleasant ride, and Jerome amused Betsy
by telling her about the tropical plants and birds of the West Indies.

Toward evening, they halted just before a wooden bridge that spanned
a stream cutting across their route. Betsy noticed a rank smell in the
air. Jerome gestured to the right, where an opening in the trees looked
like the beginning of a trail. "I am going to explore that path and search
for a clearing where we can camp." He dismounted, tied his horse to
a sapling beside the road, and headed into the trees.

Betsy pressed her lips together and peered after him until a bend
in the trail took him from sight. Her horse moved restlessly, so Betsy
patted it and murmured, "Whoa."

As the minutes passed, she stared down the road, first in one direction and then the other. The smell was making her ill, and being
alone made her uneasy. The undergrowth beneath the trees was so
thick that it was impossible to tell if anything was hiding there.

When Jerome returned, he said, "There is a clearing. I think someone might have started to build a house here, but they did not progress very far."

He helped Betsy dismount from her sidesaddle, and she walked a
ways to stretch her sore legs. As she glanced down to check where she
was stepping, she saw a long cylindrical object ringed with dark jag-
ged bands lying across the road. Following it with her eyes, she realized it was a snake that had been run over by a wheeled cart; the body
was smashed near the head and the dirt showed traces of blood. Betsy
stepped back, even though she knew it was dead, and then looked for
the snake's tail. It had rattles.

"Jerome, we cannot stay here. There are rattlesnakes."

He came up beside her to stare at it. "*Zut!* So that is the source
of the stink." Putting an arm around her, he squeezed her shoulders.
"The serpent is dead and can do us no harm."

"There may be others. Robert once found a whole nest of copperheads at Springfield."

Jerome looked up at the sky. The sun had sunk behind the treetops, and shadow completely covered the road. "It is too late to go farther. If this region is infested with snakes, the danger will exist wherever we go. We should set up our camp now while there is still light."

Betsy wanted to argue with him, but he grabbed their horses' reins and began leading them down the trail he had discovered. Tears pricked Betsy's eyes as she lifted her skirts and followed him. The trail was barely six inches wide. Ferns, small shrubs, and saplings encroached upon it from either side, and she disliked having them brush against her as she passed.

After a few minutes, they emerged into a small clearing. Betsy halted and looked around. The rocky stream ran along one edge of an open area dotted with stumps. Someone had chopped down several trees and dragged them to the far side of the clearing, which was higher than the ground beside the stream. Betsy could see that the axeman had cleaned the logs by stripping their branches. As she wondered why he had abandoned the site so soon after starting construction, a sense of foreboding settled on her.

Near the center of the clearing was a circle of rocks surrounding a shallow fire pit. Glancing into the woods, Betsy saw several mossy outcroppings of stone. The stench of dead snake was no longer noticeable; instead, she could smell leaf mold and resin.

As Betsy stood pensively, trying to imagine sleeping out of doors, Jerome went to his bags and found his hatchet. Then he removed his coat and began to chop some of the discarded branches for firewood. He told Betsy to gather kindling and tinder. When she started toward the edge of the clearing to look for dried grasses and bits of peeled bark, a movement caught her eye.

She halted and found herself facing a fox that stood just inside the first line of trees. The animal had frozen with its head slightly lowered. A tree blocked part of its body and ferns hid its feet, but Betsy could see its red fur, upright ears, and pointed snout.

"Jerome!" she said in a loud whisper. She turned her head to catch his attention.

He was in the midst of swinging his hatchet. After finishing the stroke, he wiped his forehead with his shirtsleeve. "What?"

Betsy looked back toward the woods, but the fox had gone. "Oh," she said in disappointment. "It left."

"Elisa, what are you talking about?" After leaning his hatchet against a log, he walked toward her.

"I saw a fox over there."

Jerome bent to kiss her. "A pity I did not have my pistols to hand. I could have gotten you a fur collar."

"I am glad you did not. It was beautiful, and foxes do not hurt people, do they?"

"No." Jerome returned to his chopping. As Betsy gathered up twigs and leaves for tinder, she wished she had brought a basket on their journey. Then her mind returned to the fox. She had rarely been so close to a wild creature. The experience had unnerved her at first, but then she had felt a kinship with the animal, which after all was only trying to make its way in the world.

Dusk fell before they finished making camp, and mosquitoes began to bite. Jerome built a large campfire, and its smoke helped drive away the troublesome insects. Then he went down to the stream to fetch water.

As Betsy unpacked the bread and cheese they brought for their supper, she heard a loud half-snarling cry from somewhere in the woods, followed by a terrible, almost human scream. Too frightened to move, she stared into the darkness and waited. After a few moments, she heard something heavy moving in the brush, and she started to tremble. "Jerome?" she called, but her voice was too weak to carry. Betsy pressed both hands against her stomach and swallowed hard.

Then her fear fell away as Jerome stepped into the firelight. "Are you safe?"

"Yes. Oh, Jerome—" She rushed to him and clung to the lapels of his coat. "What was that horrible sound?"

Jerome put his arms around her and patted her back. "Some wild thing catching its prey, I think. Many animals hunt at night."

Betsy began to cry. Hiding her face against his waistcoat, she murmured, "I cannot do this. Why did you insist on camping when there are perfectly good inns where we could stay?"

"Shhh, Elisa. You are tired, and this is all strange to you. The fire will keep wild animals away, and I have my pistols. I will protect you."

She broke away from him and sat on a tree stump a few feet from the fire. "We don't even know what kind of animal made that cry. There could be bears in the woods and—mountain lions. Oh, who knows what lurks out there!"

Jerome squatted before her. "Elisa, you are not listening to me. Everything in life has danger, but I would not risk your safety needlessly. I swear that I will protect you."

His face was in shadow because his back was to the fire, so Betsy could not see his expression, but his tone was annoyed rather than reassuring. Betsy nodded to acknowledge his promise but did not speak. She felt drained of everything but fright.

Wearily, she rose and gathered the food she had dropped when she heard the animal cry. She brushed dirt off the bread, sliced off the end of the cheese that had fallen on the ground, and set their dinner on metal plates. They sat on a log that had been left by the fire pit and began to eat, but Betsy had little appetite.

Because she was so afraid, Jerome combined their bedrolls into one and held her tight. Betsy was certain that she would never sleep, but she soon fell into an exhausted slumber as a way of shutting out the terror.

She woke the next day to the sound of birdsong and the sight of early morning sunlight slanting through leaves overhead. Jerome was snoring softly. She rose, used the latrine he had dug, and then returned to kneel by him. Taking a deep breath of cool air, Betsy felt like shouting in triumph that she had done something she thought impossible. Instead, she shook Jerome. "Wake up, sleepy. Dawn breaks."

He grunted and rolled over with his back to Betsy, but she tickled his side. "We made it through the night, husband, and I am filled with a passion for living this morning. Can you not think of anything better to do than sleep?"

Gazing at her, he wiped the sleepiness from his eyes. "Elisa, you astonish me. You are rarely this lively in the mornings."

She laughed. "I had no conception that it could be so exhilarating to feel paralyzed by fear and overcome it. Is this what surviving a battle is like?"

"In small measure."

Seized by mischief, she snuggled close to Jerome and growled into his neck. "I feel like a lioness."

Jerome rolled her onto her back and pinned her shoulders to the ground, but his eyes were alight with passion, not anger. "You may be a lioness, Elisa, but do not forget who is the lion."

Smiling, Betsy put her arms around his neck. Just before she kissed him, she whispered, "Then let me see if I can make you roar."

AFTER THAT, BETSY no longer requested that they spend the night in an inn, although they did occasionally stop for hot, plain-cooked dinners of fresh venison, quail, or fish if they reached an establishment at a propitious hour. Each night, they exercised caution while preparing their campsite, but although they saw a few more dead snakes on the road and sometimes heard strange noises in the night, Betsy grew accustomed to living outdoors. From learning to carry on despite her fears, she felt a growing confidence.

The country they traveled through was nothing like the wilderness that Betsy's father had predicted. Four days out from Utica, they were still finding bridges and sawmills. As they rode farther west, the region grew more heavily forested. Several times, they passed families in the process of clearing land and, in one case, building a log cabin.

The weather was sweltering that day, so they stopped at the half-built cabin to ask if they could have water from the well. As they drank from a ladle that the husband provided, Jerome inquired about how to erect a log cabin. When he learned that all the process required was a sharp axe and mud, he asked permission to dismount to inspect the building. While the man showed Jerome how to notch the logs to make them fit together, his wife asked if Betsy would rather have fresh milk.

"No, thank you, on a day like today, water is more cooling." Betsy noticed the wife staring avidly at her clothes, as simple as they were. Although the woman was in her late twenties at most, she had dry, brown skin and rough hands. Impulsively, Betsy removed her hat and pulled off the rose-colored ribbon that circled the crown and formed a bow at the side. "This ribbon is not much, but may I offer it in thanks for your hospitality?"

"Oh, ma'am, you should not have ruined your pretty hat."

"I want you to have this."

Hearing the approaching voices of the men, the woman plucked the ribbon from Betsy's outstretched hand, stowed it in her apron pocket, and curtsied.

Jerome mounted his horse and saluted the settlers before riding away. As Betsy brought her horse up alongside his, he said, "How should you like to settle in a place like this?"

She looked at him in astonishment. "Do you know anything about farming?"

"What is there to know? You clear the ground, plant the seeds, harvest the crops. I could build a cabin, and we would be beholden to no one. Napoleon could never touch us here."

Thinking of the loneliness and labor such a life would entail, Betsy wanted to cry. Then as she listened to Jerome rave about how he would hunt and fish and she would make their clothes, she saw that the prospect was not real to him. He was indulging in a romantic fantasy to convince himself there was a way out of the vise tightening upon them.

Betsy decided to play along. "I should have to grow a vegetable garden and make preserves. We always had servants do such things at home."

"You are clever enough to do anything." After a pause, he said, "I would like to see Napoleon's face when he learns that we scorn his empire and its honors. He will regret his high-handedness when he realizes it has driven me away."

Betsy stifled her impulse to sigh. "I am sure he will, Jerome."

On their ninth day out from Utica, they began to hear a low thrumming sound ahead of them. The further they rode, the louder it grew until it was a dull roar, like the distant sound of violent waves crashing on shore. "That must be the falls," Jerome said. "Burr said that you can hear their thunder for twenty-five miles or more."

They did not reach the falls that night or even the next day, although the sound increased continually. Their tenth night out, as Betsy tried to fall asleep, she felt the noise vibrate inside her as a physical presence, and she wondered how anyone ever got used to the roaring.

Early the next day, they reached the Niagara River. Riding on the northeast bank, they passed a place where the river divided to flow around a huge, heavily wooded island. Immediately beyond it, the river was about two miles wide, but the rocky gorge through which it ran quickly narrowed.

The crashing water was deafening. Jerome gestured with his arm and led the way to a high point, where he dismounted. Betsy followed and saw that they were on a promontory overlooking two gigantic waterfalls. The near set of falls featured tons of water plummeting from a wide precipice. The more distant and even wider set of falls was curved like a horseshoe. The waterfalls were much taller than she had imagined; they looked to be more than twice the height of the Presidential Mansion. The cascading water churned and foamed, creating a thick white mist that rose for hundreds of feet.

Jerome led their horses away from the promontory's edge and tied them to a tree in a grove twenty feet away. Returning to Betsy, he slipped his arms around her waist from behind.

The air was filled with a cool spray, and the thunderous sound enveloped them. Mesmerized by the sight of the tremendous stream racing toward the precipice, Betsy felt that it symbolized the way she and Jerome were caught in the onrush of forces beyond their control. As she gazed upstream, she saw a dark shape moving in the water. A young deer struggled in the river, trying frantically to swim to shore, but the forward crush of the water was too powerful to escape. The animal swept over the edge of the falls and disappeared. Horrified, Betsy hid her face against Jerome's chest.

Was that to be their fate? By defying Napoleon, were they flinging themselves over a cataract to their own destruction? For each of the seventeen days of their journey, she had wondered what other course they could choose. They had joked about Jerome becoming a fisherman or a farmer, but neither had been a serious proposal. From early childhood, Jerome had only one end in mind, that of sharing his brother's destiny. Could she deprive her husband of the only life he had ever craved? And what of her own dream of living in Europe and becoming royalty?

Abruptly, Betsy drew down Jerome's head and kissed him. He responded eagerly, and she stroked him through the fabric of his trousers. Jerome moaned and, seizing her hand, led her back into the shelter of the trees. Stopping by a tall oak with a wide trunk, he kissed Betsy again. Then after unbuttoning the front flap of his pants, he raised her skirt, lifted her so that her thighs rested on his hips, and bracing her against the tree, entered her.

The roaring of the water, the insistence of her desire, and the driving energy with which Jerome pushed into her merged into one massive force, and Betsy cried out in exultation as she came to climax. Afterward, she found that a new and steely resolve had taken possession of her. Whether wisely or foolishly, she and Jerome had long since chosen their course. No matter whether they were destined to dash upon the rocks or be swept to safety, it was far too late for them to extricate themselves from the rushing torrent of fate that swept them toward the cataract. She could only pray that they survived.

XIV

In mid-August Jerome and Betsy returned to New York by a northerly route that included a visit to Boston. When they finally reached Greenwich Village forty days after leaving for Niagara, they found Lieutenant Meyronnet living with Dr. Garnier and Le Camus, whom they had left occupying their house. The men were playing whist at the mahogany pedestal table in the drawing room on the evening the Bonapartes arrived home.

Jerome strode over to Meyronnet. "Why did you not sail on the *Didon?*"

"Because the French frigates are still here. The British did not break their blockade for some time, so Captain Brouard decided to wait upon your return to see if you are now willing to obey the emperor's orders."

Posing with one arm held behind his back, Jerome gave Meyronnet his haughtiest stare. "Has Brouard decided to allow Madame Bonaparte to accompany me?"

Meyronnet shot Betsy an uneasy glance. "No."

"Then my resolve has not changed."

"Bonaparte, think before you do anything rash. Captain Brouard asks you to attend a reception aboard ship to discuss the matter."

Jerome thrust out his chin. "There is little point."

Betsy crossed to Jerome and took his arm. "It does no harm to talk to the man. Perhaps a way exists to work this out that you have not considered."

"I will not compromise on the question of leaving you."

"I know that." She gazed into his eyes so he could see her belief.

After a moment, Jerome nodded and turned back to the table where the others had resumed their card game.

Betsy decided to go upstairs and ask her maid Jenny, a girl she had hired in Baltimore, to prepare a bath for her. On her way from the room, she overheard Garnier tell Jerome that, while they were gone, Vice-President Aaron Burr had killed Alexander Hamilton in a duel and then fled to his daughter's home in the South.

"*Merde!*" Jerome exclaimed, a vulgarity he rarely uttered in her hearing. "I was looking forward to meeting him again and telling him about our excursion."

The next day, Betsy worked at checking their food supplies and sending their travel clothes to a laundress. At midday, she found Jerome in the sitting room writing letters. One was an appeal to Napoleon, in which Jerome begged for different orders that would allow him to bring Betsy to France: "Why do you, who claim to uphold public morality, wish to make a virtuous woman suffer the consequences of your anger toward me?"

As Betsy read the letter, tears filled her eyes. She laid it on the drop-down writing surface of the secretary, and Jerome handed her the second letter, written to Minister of the Navy Decrès:

> *I beg you to be so kind as to give my brother the enclosed letter. I explain to him my situation in this country, which daily becomes more cruel, and I urgently ask for orders to leave it. You have yourself been long in this part of the world, and can, best of all people, explain to him how out of place my life is here.*

Betsy did not believe that these entreaties would move the emperor, but later that day, another letter arrived that renewed her hope. In it, Samuel Smith informed them that his acquaintance General John Armstrong Jr. was about to travel to Paris as the new ambassador to France. Smith suggested that they entreat Armstrong to let Betsy sail with his diplomatic party while Jerome sailed aboard the *Didon*.

Jerome instantly wrote the letter.

Because of this new possibility, Jerome decided to attend Brouard's reception after all. He returned from the event in an ebullient mood. "They addressed me as 'Imperial Highness' even though the emperor has not given me that title. I think they believe I must prevail."

Dismayed that his optimism could be restored by such flattery, Betsy held her tongue.

A week later General Armstrong wrote that he would be honored to escort Madame Bonaparte and that she should board his ship in New York Harbor the afternoon of September 4. Accordingly, Betsy packed her trunk, and Jerome made arrangements to give up the house. He would sail on the *Didon* a few days after her departure.

Anxious to be on her way, Betsy arose early on September 4, and they left the house in such good time that they reached the designated landing shortly before noon. However, no ship was moored near that pier. Perplexed, Jerome flagged down a passing boat and asked the crew if they knew where General Armstrong's ship was docked.

"That vessel left early this morning," the skipper called back. "The ambassador took a sudden notion to leave before his scheduled time."

Jerome waved his acknowledgment and returned to Betsy, who stood next to their carriage. "Why would he leave without you?"

"I suspect he reconsidered his position and decided that becoming embroiled in your family quarrel might damage his standing with the French government."

The next day Jerome sent word to Brouard that he would not sail aboard the *Didon,* and Betsy wrote her father that they were returning to Maryland and would stay at the Springfield estate.

IN EARLY OCTOBER, Betsy's brother Joseph rode to Springfield to say that their mother had been delivered of a girl during the night. Both mother and daughter were healthy, and Dorcas had asked to see Betsy and Jerome.

They arrived at the Patterson house late the next afternoon. After hanging her cloak on a peg, Betsy started upstairs, but Jerome lingered in the hall. Gazing at him over the banister, Betsy said, "My mother asked for you too."

He rubbed the back of his neck. "Elisa, I do not belong in a birth chamber. That is the province of women."

"Don't be silly. All signs of the birth will have been cleared away long since."

With a grimace, Jerome followed her upstairs. Betsy knocked lightly on the bedroom door and entered. Seeing that her mother was awake, she said, "How are you?" Leaving Jerome at the door, Betsy crossed the room to kiss her mother's cheek. Then Betsy knelt to look at her new sister, sleeping in a cradle by the bed. The two-day-old infant had a shock of red hair, and she held one fist beside her mouth as if she had dozed off sucking her fingers.

Betsy picked up the baby. "What have you named her?"

"Mary Ann Jeromia."

"Oh." Meeting her mother's eyes, Betsy understood that she had chosen the name to proclaim that Jerome was as much her son as any of the children she had borne.

Jerome drew near. "You would name her for me?"

As Dorcas murmured her assent, Betsy transferred Mary Ann to her husband's arms and showed him how to hold her. Watching him smile into the baby's face, Betsy wondered if she had been wrong to dread having a child. A baby would give Jerome another person to fight for.

THE NECESSITY FOR Jerome and Betsy to travel to France remained, as did the danger that British warships would waylay them. After conferring with his father-in-law, Jerome decided to make secret preparations to travel on a merchant ship leaving from a port they had not yet used. They sent one of Patterson's agents to book passage for "Monsieur and Madame d'Albert" on the *Philadelphia,* soon to leave Port Penn, Delaware, for Cadiz, Spain. Garnier and Le Camus would accompany Jerome, and as her companion, Betsy invited her favorite aunt, Nancy Spear.

After a two-day coach journey, they boarded the ship, which departed on October 24. Because the ship was often used to transport passengers, their quarters were slightly more spacious than those aboard the *Didon,* although the furnishings were basically the same—a bunk, a writing desk and chair, and a washstand bolted to the cabin wall. At

first, the weather was beautiful, cool but clear with brilliant blue skies.
Aunt Nancy proved to be a nervous sailor and remained in her cabin,
but Betsy and Jerome spent most of that first afternoon strolling on
deck enjoying the views of Delaware Bay.

Toward evening, clouds massed over the land to the west, gusts of
westerly wind blew with increasing force, and the temperature dropped.
Betsy saw heightened activity among the crew as they worked to keep
control of the ship, which was listing to port. As rain began to fall, Jerome hurried her below to their cabin.

For hours, the gale lashed the ship, causing it to buck and roll. Betsy lay in the bunk, clinging to its railing to keep from being tossed
about. Jerome sat beside her in the cabin's single chair. Betsy's stomach heaved along with the sea, and she vomited several times into
the washbasin, which Jerome had moved onto the bed beside her. He
did not get sick, in spite of being shut up with a retching wife, but he
looked pale and agitated. Finally, after an hour, he said, "Elisa, do
you feel well enough for me to leave you for a short while? I feel uneasy about Miss Spear."

Betsy felt guilty that, in her distress, she had not thought of her
aunt. "Yes, please go inquire how she is." A wave of nausea rolled over
her again, and she pressed her fist against her mouth. Her diaphragm
ached from the constant heaving.

Jerome made his way out of the cabin, touching the wall as he went
to keep his balance. He was gone for several minutes. When he returned, he said, *"Ta pauvre tante. Elle est plus malade que toi."*

"Oh, dear," Betsy said. If Aunt Nancy was worse than this, she must
feel as though she were at death's door. Betsy tried to push herself
to a sitting position so she could go to the older woman, but the ship
abruptly rose and then descended with a sickening plunge. She lay
back down. "What can we do for her?"

"Nothing, my love. I told her to drink a little water, but she would
not. There is nothing else to do but ride out the storm." He pushed
Betsy's sweat-soaked hair back from her forehead.

After a while, Betsy ceased retching because her muscles were too
exhausted to contract anymore and her stomach had nothing left to
expel. Jerome carried the vomit-filled basin away. Then he carefully

crawled into the bunk and pressed his body to Betsy's back as she lay on her side. His nearness helped her relax, and she fell into a fitful sleep, broken several times during the night by the ship's wild movement.

Toward morning, Betsy awoke and listened to the crashing of the waves pounding the side of the ship. She wondered how long the gale would last. When she shifted her position to lie closer to Jerome, she marveled at how much her abdomen ached from the bout of seasickness. Then the hull of the ship jolted and shuddered. Betsy heard a sharp splintering sound. The ship began to sway like a very slow rocking chair, up and back, up and back.

"Jerome!" He woke quickly, and she told him what had happened.

"*Sainte Mère,* I think we have run aground." He crawled over Betsy, being careful not to press his weight on her, and climbed down from the bunk. When he stood, Betsy realized that the floor of their cabin inclined from the outer hull to the exit. Jerome pushed hard to open their cabin door and left her.

Shoving against the mattress, Betsy struggled to her feet and felt her way along the bunk to reach the washstand bolted to the wall at the end of the cabin. The ewer had been knocked onto its side but prevented from falling by a railing around the stand. The vessel still held a tiny amount of water. Betsy dribbled it into her cupped hand and rubbed it over her face. Then she tried to decide what to do.

The ship was still rocking, and she thought it must be stuck on a sandbar or reef, where pounding waves could batter it. Betsy had heard too many stories of shipwrecks from her father and brothers not to know what to expect. In a storm of this ferocity, the wind and waves could break apart a grounded ship within hours.

Most of their things were in the hold, but their most valuable possessions were stowed in a single wide drawer in the base of their bunk. When Jerome returned, Betsy was leaning against the bunk wearing her cloak and clutching her jewelry casket and the velvet-wrapped sword from Marengo.

"We hit a sandbar. The captain says we cannot launch a boat until the weather subsides."

"Such a plan is suicidal. We must try to get ashore." Betsy stood with difficulty. "We should speak to the captain again."

Grasping the doorframe, Jerome reached for her hand to help her up the sloped floor and out the cabin door. They went next door to Nancy's cabin, and Betsy was shocked to see how pale her aunt looked. "Please, get up. We have to prepare to leave the ship."

"No," Aunt Nancy said. She pressed a handkerchief to her mouth and swallowed hard. "I am sure we are safer on board ship than out in the storm."

"No, Aunt. You must trust my judgment on this." Betsy sent Jerome out of the cabin and then she helped her aunt to dress, a process that took a long time because of the slanted floor and Nancy's weakness. The older woman leaned on Betsy like a child.

Finally, they rejoined Jerome, and the three of them felt their way to the ladder. Betsy went first. As she pulled herself up the ladder rung by rung, while awkwardly keeping the jewelry casket tucked under one arm, she heard a loud cracking overhead. The ship abruptly shifted, and the rocking ceased. Nancy screamed. Betsy gripped the rung tightly until she felt certain that the ship had settled into a stable position. Then she resumed climbing and called down to Jerome to start Aunt Nancy on her way.

Once on deck, they pushed past scurrying sailors as they searched for the captain. Betsy could barely see in the lashing rain. Although it was now mid-morning, the skies were dark grey and filled with turbulent black clouds. Finally, she spotted the captain on the forecastle issuing orders for the crew to cut away the sodden sails to release their weight from the mainmast, which had cracked as it leaned at an angle over the water.

"Captain, I must speak with you!" Betsy called.

He shouted a warning to one of his sailors and then said, "Madam, I am occupied. For your own safety, please return to your cabin."

"No, sir. I insist that you order a boat to be lowered so the passengers can make for the safety of shore."

The officer glared at her. Rain dripped from his hat, giving him an almost comical aspect that did little for his authority. "Do you imagine, madam, that you are in command of this ship?"

Betsy pushed her sodden hood back from her face. "Perhaps I should be since you clearly lack competence. Do not suppose me ignorant of the dangers posed to passengers aboard a grounded ship, sir. I come from a seafaring community."

"Then you should know the risk of trying to row ashore during a gale. You waste my time with this debate, Madame d'Albert."

As he turned away, Betsy cried, "Sir, my name is not d'Albert. It is Madame Bonaparte, sister-in-law to the French emperor. I demand that you send us to safety."

He whirled around. Looking over her shoulder, he said to Jerome, "Is this true?"

"Yes, I am Jerome Bonaparte."

"Damnation." He beckoned to a crew member. "Higgins, prepare to lower the ship's boat. Put four men in it to row the passengers to shore. And send Jurgensen below to gather the others."

The captain strode away, and Betsy approached Higgins. Raising her voice to be heard above the storm, she said, "Before you lower the boat, you must stow these things securely aboard."

"Madam, that is not possible. If I allow you to bring possessions, all the passengers will want to do the same and the boat will swamp."

Betsy fixed Higgins with blazing eyes and held out the wrapped sword. "This saber is an heirloom of one of Napoleon's victories. Do you wish to take responsibility for its loss?"

The sailor's eyes grew wide, and he accepted the sword and casket from her. As they watched the crew hoist the lifeboat and swing it over the side, Jerome moved close to Betsy. "You would make a fearsome empress, Elisa."

When the boat was in the water, the captain approached the huddled group of nine passengers. "With this wind, I dare not use the sling to lower you to the boat. You will have to take it in turns to jump from the gangway."

"I cannot!" Nancy cried.

Seeing her aunt's terror, Betsy put an arm around her. "It will be all right." Then she announced to the others, "I will go first as an example."

As she started toward the side of the ship, Jerome stopped her. "No, Elisa. Your cloak is too cumbersome. You must remove it."

Betsy took it off and handed it to him. Within seconds, the driving rain had plastered her dress to her body. Without hesitation, she moved to the open gangway and, using her hand to shield her eyes from the downpour, looked down. The sea was a dark greenish-grey. Even though the crew was holding onto ropes leading from the ship, the boat was bobbing in the churning waves. Behind her, Jerome shouted, "Leap far out."

Nodding, she took a deep breath, flexed her knees, and jumped. At the same instant, a surge of water caused the boat to buck away. Betsy saw the foam rush up to meet her as she plunged into the cold bay. Her arm hit the side of the boat but could not grasp it, and her head went underwater. As stinging saltwater went up her nose, she started thrashing to regain the surface. The wet skirts of her gown clung to her legs, making it difficult to kick, and Betsy panicked at the thought that she would drown. She felt herself being pulled under, and her lungs started to burn.

Then someone dove nearby, seized her, and pulled her upward. A moment later, they broke the surface, and her rescuer wedged her tightly against the side of his body as he swam. Rain was in Betsy's eyes and her head kept dipping below water so that she had to gulp air whenever her mouth broke the surface. She thought she heard a shout, and a sailor grabbed her under the arms to pull her onto the boat. Once she was seated on one of the wooden benches, she saw the sailor help her rescuer aboard. It was Jerome.

He sat beside her. Betsy was shivering uncontrollably. Jerome put his arms around her, but as he was also sopping wet, his embrace provided little warmth. The howling wind cut through the thin fabric of Betsy's gown, and her hands and feet grew icy cold. It seemed to take an eternity for the other passengers to make it into the boat; most landed in the water and had to be fished out as Betsy had. Only Aunt Nancy avoided going into the bay. The ship's crew took pity on her extreme terror and risked their lives to lean down from the ship and lower her by the arms until the men in the boat could grab her. Once she was settled in the boat, she sat there whimpering and praying.

After everyone was aboard, the crew rowed toward land, but it was slow going because they were heading into the wind. Betsy's shivering grew so violent that her teeth clacked against themselves and would not stop no matter how tightly she clenched her jaw.

Slowly, the day grew brighter and the rain began to ease. When they were about twenty yards from shore, Betsy saw dark shapes huddled together on the beach. "I think people are waiting to meet us."

"No doubt, mum," Higgins said, after checking over his shoulder. "The captain sent up rockets as soon as we hit the sandbar. Those will be sailing folk who live by the water."

Altogether, the journey took nearly two hours because the wind and waves were against them. When the boat finally reached the shallows, a couple of burly men waded into the water to pull it ashore. Then they helped the women from the boat. Betsy's legs were so cramped from cold that, as soon as she put her weight on them, a thousand needles stabbed her. Now that she knew they were safe, she felt faint and weepy, and she turned to find Jerome. However, he was enlisting one of the other men to help him lift the quivering Aunt Nancy from the boat, so Betsy let him be.

Turning back toward land, she scanned the scene. A boy was running up the beach toward a brick house that stood a few hundred yards back from the water. There were no other homes in sight, and Betsy wondered where the people on the beach had come from. As she watched, the boy reached the house and knocked on the door. It opened, and a bearded, middle-aged man came outside, putting on a broad-brimmed hat as he did. He strode toward them with the purposeful gait of a man used to being in charge. He ignored the bedraggled passengers and walked up to Higgins. "Where is the captain?"

"There, sir." The young sailor pointed toward the water, and Betsy looked back at the ship for the first time since she had leaped from it. A second boat was making its way to shore but was still a long distance away.

"I see." The bearded man turned to the passengers. "I'm a pilot, and there is my house. Go make yourselves to home. I will stay here to see that the rest of the crew make it to safety."

The other passengers began to struggle up the beach, but Betsy went first to the boat. After retrieving her jewel casket and Jerome's sword, she too began to trudge up the wet sand.

Jerome and Aunt Nancy were slightly ahead, and they paused to wait for her. They were the last passengers to enter the house. They

found themselves in a warm kitchen that had a massive fieldstone fireplace with an iron oven door in the wall next to it. The room smelled
of roasting poultry. As the group of miserable passengers stood drip-
ping on the stone floor, the pilot's son gave each an earthenware mug
of rum, while the wife passed out towels so they could dry their faces.
Then she led them upstairs to the bedrooms so they could remove their
wet clothes and wrap themselves in blankets. Annoyed by her aunt's
sniveling, Betsy hurriedly stripped off her things and left the room.

Descending the stairs, she realized that, as she had after her first
night camping, she felt intensely alive.

In the kitchen, Betsy saw the pilot's wife at the sideboard carving
a large bird. Next to it was a stoneware crock and a platter heaped
with sliced meat. "Ma'am, I just finished preparing our dinner. Would
you care for some roast goose and applesauce?"

The smell of food made Betsy ravenously hungry, but she hesitated because she knew these people could not be rich. "Are you certain
you have enough?"

"Oh, yes. He was a big bird."

"Then I would gladly accept your offer."

The woman took a stoneware plate from the nearby cupboard, filled
it with a generous portion, and set it on the table. Betsy sat and began to eat with relish. The goose was juicy, the crispy skin was rubbed
with sage, and the chunky applesauce was both sweet and tangy. She
thought it the best meal she had ever tasted. The pilot's wife excused
herself to go out to the springhouse for milk and exited through the door.

Hearing footsteps in the passage, Betsy looked up. She hoped to
see Jerome, but Aunt Nancy entered the room. "Betsy! You should be
down on your knees thanking God for His mercy, not stuffing your
face like a glutton."

Betsy put down her fork and wiped her hands on a napkin. She
found it difficult not to laugh at her aunt's red face. "I mean no disrespect. In my own way, I am thanking God by celebrating how sweet
is the life that He has restored me to."

As she spoke, Jerome entered the kitchen. "I thought I smelled food.
I am famished."

"Sit down, and I will serve you."

As Betsy expected, by the time the storm ended, the *Philadelphia* had completely broken apart, spilling everything from the hold into Delaware Bay. The Bonapartes lost not only their clothes but also Jerome's pocketbook containing his last three thousand dollars. Upon learning that they had rescued Napoleon's brother, the townspeople agreed to house his party, while a boat carrying Jerome's secretary sailed south to the mouth of Delaware Bay. The plan was to voyage down the Atlantic coast to the Chesapeake and then turn north.

To Betsy's surprise, Le Camus did not go to her family in Baltimore but instead landed at Annapolis and traveled overland to Washington to fetch Pichon. The chargé was so shaken when he arrived a few days later that he supplied Jerome with replacement funds even though doing so violated the emperor's orders. As Pichon transported them to Baltimore, he told Jerome that a new French ambassador would be arriving in the United States within the month. "Please, sir, take the frigate *Presidente* back to France. Do not risk another foolhardy passage such as this."

"Must I tell you again that I will do so only if they accept my wife?"

"I cannot authorize such a deviation from the emperor's orders."

"I will talk to the captain," Jerome answered, "and persuade him to do as I wish."

Back in Baltimore at the beginning of November, they moved into the Patterson house to await the *Presidente,* while Le Camus and Garnier took rooms nearby. Betsy and Jerome occupied Betsy's former bedroom, despite the inconvenience of its narrow bed. William Patterson grumbled about the overcrowding, but Betsy was grateful to be home. After the first exhilaration of survival, she realized what a shock her nerves had suffered. She felt unusually tired, and little annoyances made her want to cry.

A week after arriving in Baltimore, Betsy felt nauseated at breakfast. Excusing herself from the table, she barely made it upstairs in time to retch into her chamber pot.

Before leaving the bedroom, Betsy glanced into the mirror and saw vomit spattered on her gown. As she put on fresh clothing, she noticed that her breasts were tender as they often were right before her monthly flux. Perhaps that was what ailed her. What with moving from city to city and living through a shipwreck, she had lost track of her cycle.

Betsy crossed to the small writing table and checked her journal. The last time she bled had been shortly after they arrived at Springfield in mid-September. Her cycle was nearly four weeks late. Laying her hands over her abdomen, she thought, *I am carrying a child.* After living in dread of such a development for so many months, how could she not have known?

It was too soon to get confirmation from a doctor. She would first need to miss another cycle or two. In the meantime, she would keep her suspicions secret from Jerome.

In December, they boarded the *Presidente* at Annapolis, Maryland. To their great surprise, the captain offered no objections to Betsy's presence, and Pichon was so impatient to get Jerome off his hands that he did not challenge the captain's decision.

By then, Betsy had missed two monthly cycles, and she was certain from her other symptoms that she was carrying a baby. She still had not told her husband. Although she had dreaded conceiving a child while their marriage was in doubt, now she wondered if it might not be the way into her brother-in-law's favor. The reason Napoleon had become emperor was to ensure his government's survival by creating a hereditary succession, and if her child was a boy, he would be an additional Bonaparte heir.

The *Presidente* weighed anchor and sailed south down Chesapeake Bay. At Hampton Roads, it turned east to sail into the Atlantic—and found the way blocked by British warships. The captain called Jerome on deck to discuss the matter, and Betsy followed.

Borrowing a spyglass, Jerome scanned the horizon. "What are our chances of running their blockade?"

"This is one of the newest ships in the fleet. She is fast and in excellent condition."

Jerome collapsed the spyglass and returned it to the captain. "And she has forty guns? We are certainly a match for any of the ships arrayed against us."

Terrified that he was looking for an excuse to go into battle as a way of proving himself to his brother, Betsy grabbed Jerome's arm. "We cannot take the risk."

He brushed her off. "Do not involve yourself in this decision."

She pushed herself between the two men. "Please, may I speak with you in private?"

Glancing over her head, Jerome rolled his eyes at the captain. "Excuse us."

He led Betsy over to the side railing. "Elisa, how dare you interrupt my discussion with the captain? Behavior such as this only confirms the general impression that my choice to remain in America was a sign of weakness. Have you not heard that Napoleon has gone so far as to label me effeminate?"

"He says that merely to shame you into doing what he wants."

"Be that as it may, you take too much on yourself when you interfere in matters that are not a woman's business. Besides, you were so brave during the shipwreck. Why can you not display a modicum of courage now?"

Betsy took a deep breath and said, "Because it is not just our two lives we put at risk."

"The crew are fighting men of the French navy. It is their duty to risk their lives."

"Jerome, I do not refer to the crew."

"Then whom? Elisa, I do not understand you."

"Forgive me. I have not said anything yet because I have not received confirmation from the doctor, but—I am certain I am carrying your child."

Jerome's look of annoyance melted away. "A baby? You are going to have a baby?"

When Betsy nodded, he pulled her into his arms and kissed her. She heard catcalls from nearby crew members, but she did not care. Jerome released her, and putting one arm protectively around her shoulders, walked her back to the captain. "Madame Bonaparte is correct. We cannot run such a risk."

"But sir, Ambassador Turreau was adamant that you must go back to France without further delay. When I arrive in Paris, how will I explain your refusal to Minister Decrès?"

Smiling down at Betsy, Jerome said, "Tell him that we dare not endanger the safety of a future imperial prince."

The captain looked from one to the other, and his face registered understanding. "All the more reason for you to make your peace with the emperor. Sir, I beg of you to leave your wife here where her family can care for her and her child, while you sail with us."

"No," Jerome said, reassuming his hauteur. "What you ask is impossible. Kindly have a boat prepared to row us to shore."

✒ XV ✑

ECAUSE it was too late in the year to attempt an Atlantic cross-
ing, Jerome rented a town house in Baltimore for the winter.
He also purchased suites of imported furniture, and sets of
French porcelain and silver.

Betsy asked, "Is all this necessary? Our residence will be temporary."

Looking up from his accounts, Jerome frowned. "Elisa, we must
be seen to live in a manner befitting the imperial family." When she
questioned him further about the expense, he thrust out his chin and
replied that a friend had recently obtained funds for him in Paris.

Since their return, Jerome's temper had grown fitful. Although he
remained affectionate toward Betsy, he was quick to take offense at
perceived slights by others, and he relied more than ever on the pursuit of pleasure to alleviate boredom. That winter they gave party after party.

The Reubells had sailed to France the previous summer, and feeling
lonely without Henriette, Betsy cultivated two other friendships. One
was with Eliza Anderson, a young woman whose father was a Baltimore physician. At nineteen, she had married Henry Anderson, who
later went bankrupt and left town in 1801, abandoning his wife and
baby daughter. Now living in complete dependence on her father, Eliza relished the chance to attend the Bonapartes' elegant parties, and

Betsy enjoyed talking to someone who criticized Baltimore as sharply as she did. Eliza was no beauty—she had a square-jawed face and dull, ash-blonde hair—but she was intelligent, well read, and practical.

The other friendship grew out of Betsy's notoriety as Jerome's wife. To her amusement, she had become an idol to the younger belles of Baltimore, among them Marianne Caton. Three years younger than Betsy, Marianne had just begun to appear in society. She attended the Bonapartes' soirees, called on Betsy in the afternoons, and imitated Betsy's fashions—although somewhat more modestly. To have Charles Carroll's granddaughter emulate her pleased Betsy. When she first entered society, there had been a subtle but very real divide between the daughters of aristocratic planters and the daughters of merchants. Betsy would sometimes hear of balls to which she had not been invited—a practice that stopped as soon as the young men of Baltimore made it plain that they cared more about her beauty and wit than her mercantile origins.

Betsy's one concern about her new friendship was the niggling fear that it might not be safe for Jerome to spend time with Marianne, a stunning dark-haired beauty with melting brown eyes. Marianne had a sweet manner that drew men like honey and an elegant, almost gliding walk. As Betsy's waist began to thicken, she worried that her husband's interest might stray to the appealing younger woman.

Her uneasiness lessened one night when Le Camus remarked that Marianne was the loveliest girl he had seen in America.

"Bah." Jerome poured himself a glass of wine. "Who wants all that sugary goodness? It would be like living with a nun."

"Then she does not attract you?" Betsy asked.

Although she tried to sound casual, Jerome must have perceived her anxiety because he came and stroked her shoulder. *"Non, ma femme.* I greatly prefer your fire to her ice."

That winter, they received several letters from Robert. In October, he wrote that the Paris journals had published a paragraph claiming that reports of Jerome's American marriage were false, that he might have a mistress but could not, as a minor, have a wife. Because any negative report about his family would need Napoleon's permission to be published, Robert sent a warning:

The Consul's determination is now but too plain. It is fortunate Jerome is still in America. He ought to remain there for the present, until his friends have recognized his marriage. If his family are determined on proceeding to extremities, they will possibly, to oblige him to return, curtail his supplies—perhaps withhold them altogether.

That letter arrived in December. A month later, a new letter reported:

I am told, and I have it from such authority as makes it unquestionable, that the other members of the family are very desirous of reconciling the principal. It is not unlikely but they may eventually succeed.

Robert advised remaining quiet and avoiding any actions that might offend Napoleon, but counseled that if Jerome was forced to return to France, he should take Betsy with him.

Characteristically, Jerome took the most optimistic view of the situation, and his hopeful assessment seemed to find corroboration in a warm message from Joseph, his eldest brother.

Since your affections have led you far from your family and from your friends, I feel, for my part, that you cannot renounce them. Tell Mrs. Jerome from me, that as soon as she arrives, and is acknowledged by the chief of the family, she will not find a more affectionate brother than I. I have every reason to believe, after what I have heard of her, that her qualities and character will promote your happiness, and inspire us with an esteem and friendship that I shall be very much pleased to express to her.

Not long after, they received their first communication from Jerome's mother, *Madame Mère,* who sent a warning through a family friend that if they sailed into a French port, Jerome would be arrested and Betsy would be deported. *Madame Mère* suggested that Jerome send his wife to Holland while he returned to France alone to appeal to Napoleon.

"Everyone gives contradictory advice," Betsy said one afternoon after she and Jerome reviewed the correspondence that had arrived over the winter. "How can we possibly decide what to do?"

"I think Robert's counsel is best. We should remain quiet for the time being and allow the tempest of Napoleon's wrath to die down."

What about money? she wondered but dared not ask. Jerome grew angry any time she questioned their finances.

In late February, the newspapers published reports that wounded Jerome's pride. On December 2, 1804, Napoleon had crowned himself emperor and Josephine empress in an elaborate ceremony presided over by the pope at Notre Dame Cathedral. According to the accounts, Napoleon was dressed in a gold-embroidered white satin tunic and a crimson velvet mantle, lined with ermine and embroidered with golden bees, the symbol he had chosen to replace the royal fleur-de-lis. Soon afterward, Joseph and Louis were made imperial princes, while Lucien and Jerome were snubbed because of the emperor's anger over their marriages.

"You can still be made a prince once you and Napoleon have reconciled," Betsy said in response to Jerome's petulant frown.

"Yes, Elisa, I can still become a prince. But I shall never again have the chance to participate in such pageantry. He has denied that to me forever."

And what about me? she wondered. *Did I not have the right to be one of the Bonaparte sisters carrying Josephine's train?*

Folding her hands over her abdomen and feeling the baby kick, Betsy told herself it did not matter. She was now playing for higher stakes than a place at court. Since Josephine had proven unable to give Napoleon a child, one of his brothers would have to provide his heir, and Betsy was gambling that one day the crown might descend to her son.

In March 1805, Patterson offered Jerome and Betsy one of his ships, a slim, new, two-masted schooner called the *Erin.* It was so fast that he was certain it could outrun any warships they might encounter—and because of his experience running ammunition during the Revolutionary War, Betsy felt secure in accepting her father's judgment. Patterson also supplied the ship with provisions and had cabins fitted for the passengers.

Traveling with the Bonapartes would be Jerome's manservant, Betsy's maid Jenny, Dr. Garnier, Alexandre Le Camus, William Patterson Jr., and Betsy's friend Eliza Anderson as her companion.

At the family meeting during which these plans were discussed,

Betsy's mother asked, "Don't you think you should wait until the baby is born?"

Seeing her husband slouch in his chair reminded Betsy of how irritable he had been throughout the winter. She feared that if she caused him to stay longer in Baltimore, he might begin to resent her. "No, we must get to France as soon as possible to heal the breach with the emperor."

Jerome sat up straight and added, "We will have the doctor with us."

Betsy frowned. She had already told her mother that she did not want Garnier to deliver her child. She did not trust him. Ever since Garnier missed their wedding on the pretext of illness, she had suspected him of playing a false part with regard to her. Recently, the doctor had fallen into the habit of reminding Jerome to be careful with his wife because she was prone to hysterics—it made him seem solicitous in Jerome's eyes while at the same time planting the suspicion that Betsy was moody and unreliable. Whenever she protested that she was happy and well, Garnier shook his head and murmured, "See how Madame Bonaparte tries to put on a brave face."

Stymied in her attempt to dissuade Betsy, Dorcas turned to her husband, but Patterson held up a hand. "If they must go, I judge it best that they leave soon, before the British start patrolling for them again."

"Betsy, at least, should stay here."

"Mother, I cannot. Jerome and I must face this together."

Patterson reached over to pat his wife's hand. "My dear, Robert is already in Europe, and I am sending William with Betsy as extra protection. It is known that our family has the friendship of President Jefferson. Napoleon would not dare harm our daughter. The worst that can happen is that he may send her back alone."

"Since that is the case," added Betsy, "we have nothing to lose by my sailing to France and possibly everything to gain."

Dorcas subsided in her chair, and the discussion moved on to practical details.

THEY BOARDED THE ship on Sunday, March 10, and two days later sailed out of Chesapeake Bay. After consulting with Captain Stephenson, they had decided to make for Lisbon, which lay outside Napoleon's empire. As William Patterson had promised, the *Erin* was a swift vessel, and the one time they saw a warship on the horizon, they easily outran it.

During the voyage, seasickness plagued Betsy. The motion of the ship and the smells below deck—tar, mildew, damp canvas, human waste—nauseated her, and she spent many days confined to her bunk with the porthole open to admit fresh air. Jerome, Eliza Anderson, and Betsy's maid also experienced bouts of sickness, but not as severely as Betsy, who attributed the intensity of her reaction to pregnancy.

Spending hours in her bunk alone, unable to sleep because of the creaking hull, the pounding footsteps overhead, and the clanging ship's bell, Betsy rehearsed little speeches to use when she met Napoleon. Jerome had warned her that his brother preferred sweet, submissive women, so she tried to imagine what her mother or Marianne Caton would say. When that exercise grew tiresome, she composed witticisms that might win the emperor's respect despite his reservations.

On days with calm weather, Betsy and Eliza sat on deck enjoying the sun and fresh air. They amused themselves by exchanging gossip about mutual acquaintances, while Jerome, William, Le Camus, and Garnier played whist and backgammon.

Near Europe, they encountered two days of foul weather that triggered another spell of violent seasickness. Betsy could not keep a thing on her stomach and at the end of the second day suffered a prolonged bout of dry heaves. By the time she ceased retching, her diaphragm ached, her throat was raw, and the baby dragged on her body like a boulder. Betsy lay in her bunk as Jerome bathed her face with a damp cloth and dribbled tiny amounts of water between her cracked lips. Finally, she slept.

The next morning when she awoke, Jerome was watching her. "How are you?"

She smiled. "Weary, but so far my stomach feels calm."

He kissed her forehead. "I will fetch breakfast."

About ten minutes later, Eliza entered her cabin with a mug and a plate. "I brought you some tea and bread. Are you well enough to eat?"

Betsy sat up. "I think so. But Jerome said he would bring my breakfast."

"I asked to do so. I need to talk to you alone."

After taking the mug of tea and sipping cautiously, Betsy said, "About what?"

"To warn you to be wary of your husband's companions. I fear they are not your allies."

"Why do you say so?"

Eliza sat on the edge of the bunk and spoke quietly, "Yesterevening I went to ask the doctor if there was anything else to do for your relief. When I reached his cabin, the door was ajar and I heard voices within. Le Camus was complaining that your husband's obstinacy was going to bring down the emperor's wrath on all of them."

"I have never sensed that he favored our marriage."

"He said he had warned Mr. Bonaparte that it was imperative to get out of this entanglement before you found yourself in a family way, and Garnier replied, 'The child is not the problem. The emperor is a man of the world and would surely accommodate his brother's bastard. The problem is Miss Patterson and her insistence on the marriage.'"

Betsy rubbed her forehead. "So after all his professions of concern, even the doctor works against me. I wonder how far their pernicious influence has managed to weaken Jerome's attachment."

"I do not think it has." Eliza stood and picked up a shirt Jerome had dropped on the cabin floor. She folded it and put it in one of the drawers beneath the bunk. Betsy felt embarrassed to have Eliza do such menial things even though she knew her friend was only trying to make the cabin more pleasant for her. Eliza went on, "Le Camus said that he has never known Mr. Bonaparte to be so constant to any woman. He even laughed about growing indolent from lack of his usual employment procuring female companionship."

"What an abominable man."

"Yes, he is devious and given wholly to self-interest." Eliza moved to the writing desk and straightened the untidy papers and quills on its surface. "But you can take heart in knowing that your husband has not wavered in his devotion to you."

"So far. He has yet to be tried in the crucible of Napoleon's wrath." Feeling a slight stomach cramp, Betsy handed her mug to Eliza. "This means if Jerome and I are separated, he will have no one at his side to speak on my behalf."

Eliza looked directly at her. "Except his own heart."
"Yes, there is that. I pray it is enough."

AFTER A VOYAGE lasting only twenty-one days, they reached Lisbon, where they encountered a peculiarity of Portuguese law. Because Portuguese ships customarily took forty days to cross the Atlantic, the port authorities put ships in quarantine for however many days it would take to make their journey last as long. Jerome, however, sent a message to the French chargé asking him to persuade the Portuguese that such laws did not apply to a Bonaparte, and as often happened, the authorities bowed to the power of his name. Jerome, Betsy, and their companions were allowed to go ashore and take rooms in an inn after five days at anchor.

Chargé Louis Barbé Charles Sérurier, a somber, dark-haired man of thirty, called on them and gave Jerome orders from Napoleon, copies of which had been left at every port they might enter. The emperor, who was currently southwest of Milan, commanded his youngest brother to join him without delay. Jerome was to travel by a prescribed route through Spain, southern France, and Italy with specific stops along the way. If he deviated from that route, he would be thrown in prison. Further, the orders specified that if he had dared to bring along the young person to whom he had attached himself, she would be immediately deported.

Although Betsy was not surprised that she was banned, she dreaded what might result from their separation. Would Jerome be strong enough to defy his brother without her?

In spite of his orders, Jerome lingered in Lisbon with Betsy for two days, saying, "Let us take a little time together to see this romantic city."

"All right," Betsy said, even though she was in no mood for sightseeing. Fate had been cruel to arrange events so that, when she finally achieved her dream of arriving in Europe, the order to separate from Jerome had been waiting for her. How could she possibly enjoy a brief holiday in Lisbon when what she really wanted was a lifetime in Paris?

Seeing her glum face, Jerome kissed her forehead. "Let us enjoy this time together, *ma chère petite femme.* I swear to you that our time apart will be short, and then all our troubles will be over."

"I hope so," she said and forced herself to smile.

They left their companions at the inn, and Jerome took Betsy to the Church of San Roche, one of the few buildings to survive the 1755 earthquake and tsunami that destroyed most of Lisbon. The white outer façade was severe with neoclassical windows and two-story-high pilasters. In contrast, the interior was more ornate than any church Betsy had ever seen. The chancel altarpiece, divided into sections by gilded molding and Corinthian columns, featured a painting of Christ surrounded by four niches holding statues of saints.

The church had several side chapels, but the jewel of them all was the chapel of St. John the Baptist. It contained an altar with three superb mosaics depicting the Annunciation, the Baptism of Christ, and Pentecost, each constructed of thousands of tiny tiles, many cut from semi-precious stones such as lapis lazuli, agate, and amethyst. The stunning art filled Betsy with awe. As she gazed at the depiction of the Virgin Mary receiving the archangel Gabriel's announcement, Betsy whispered a prayer for her unborn child. Jerome also must have prayed because she saw him make the sign of the cross before they left the chapel. The gesture surprised her and made her uneasy. Was he asking for divine aid—or forgiveness because he had already decided to abandon her?

The next day, they went to see the aqueduct, built in the mid-1700s to bring water to the perennially parched city. The water channel, supported by stone arches up to 200 feet high, was so solidly constructed that it too had survived the earthquake. Jerome droned on about the importance of water in a dry climate, but Betsy dwelt upon the strength and endurance exemplified by the structure and her uncertainty that her husband possessed enough of those qualities to withstand the tremors of his brother's wrath.

Afterward, Jerome took her shopping in the markets of the Chiado neighborhood, where they bought embroidered tablecloths and sheets edged in lace. At Café Talão, they ate *caldeirada,* a traditional fish and potato stew cooked in olive oil that Jerome said was like the cooking of his native island, except that Corsican fish stew would have been flavored with fennel, not coriander. "Someday I will take you there, and you can see for yourself."

Then they strolled along the street. Betsy loved the local buildings, each painted a pastel color and featuring balconies with delicate ironwork railings. They were so different from the solid red brick edifices of Baltimore that, for the first time, she really felt as though she had arrived on another continent. Jerome led her to a jeweler's shop, where he purchased a topaz necklace and a set of garnet earrings, necklace, and bracelet. On the bracelet's clasp, he asked the jeweler to engrave the French word *fidelité.* That tangible promise to remain faithful brought tears to Betsy's eyes and made her feel ashamed of her nagging doubts.

Before returning to the hotel, Jerome bought a small bouquet of violets from a flower peddler. "These have a special meaning to the Bonapartes," he said, handing Betsy the purple nosegay. "Josephine adores violets, so Napoleon often buys them for her."

Betsy sniffed the blooms, surprised that they were more fragrant than the ones she sometimes picked at home. "I will press these and keep them forever."

When they reached their inn, they received a message from Captain Stephenson. Two French warships had arrived in port and surrounded the *Erin.* Jerome sighed. "I suppose this means I cannot delay my departure any longer."

That night in bed, Betsy felt exhausted by the wild swings of emotion she had experienced since their arrival in Lisbon. Unable to hide her anxiety from her husband any longer, she ran her fingers through his curls. "I cannot help it, Jerome. I am afraid of what may come."

"Do you doubt my love for you?"

"No. I dread the strength of the forces arrayed against us."

"Never fear, I have a plan. Do not be alarmed, no matter what you hear. I may have to tell Napoleon what he requires, but—"

"What are you saying?" Betsy cried, interrupting him. She pushed him away and sat up. "You mean you intend to give me up?"

Undeterred by her sharp tone, Jerome reached over to wipe away the tears that were running down her cheeks. "No, my sweet. Do you remember when your father insisted that I go away with Commander Barney? We pretended for a time to submit to his will, but in our hearts, we remained true to one another. All I am saying is that we should use the same strategy now."

Betsy shook her head vehemently, but Jerome raised his voice to override any protest she might make. "Listen to what I have to say and not to your own fears. Surely, you know how much I love you. For a time, I will act the part of an obedient brother, but in my heart I will remain true to my dear little wife. Once I return to duty and win a great victory, then I will ask to be reconciled with you as my reward."

Betsy sniffed and tried to stop crying. "Do you think that might work?"

"I am certain of it. What Napoleon really cares about is the safety of the empire. If I can help secure that for him, he will not care to whom I am married."

"But does he not want you to make a marriage of alliance?"

"He cannot force me to wed against my will, Elisa."

He eased her back to a prone position and then kissed her breasts and the mound of her stomach. "Yesterday, I asked the Holy Mother to bring me back to you before our son is born."

She sighed. "Are you so certain that it is a boy?"

Looking up, he grinned. "Yes."

When Betsy began to cry again, Jerome murmured, "Shhh, Elisa, all will be well." He moved up to kiss her mouth and then slowly and tenderly made love to her.

Early the next morning, April 9, 1805, William joined Betsy and Jerome in the parlor of their suite. Taking Betsy's hand, Jerome said, "If you should have any difficulty here, sail north to Amsterdam and wait for me there." He turned to William. "You will see that she is settled somewhere safe?"

"Of course."

"Good. Elisa, be assured that I will do everything in my power to soften Napoleon's heart and then come find you as soon as I can. I hope to rejoin you by early June."

Betsy bit her lip, remembering his talk about possibly having to win a battle before Napoleon would relent.

Jerome pulled her close. "Please don't worry. It is bad for you and the child. My job is to win over Napoleon, while yours is to bear a healthy son. Promise me to take care of yourself."

"Yes, I will."

They kissed and he left, having forbidden her to come down and say farewell in the street. Betsy moved to the window and gazed below until she saw Jerome exit the hotel and join Le Camus, who stood holding their horses. They mounted and Jerome waved to her. Then they rode away, and Betsy turned from the window and wept.

The next day, Chargé Sérurier called on Betsy at her inn. She insisted on having William at her side, and she remained standing during the meeting to remind the diplomat that she was carrying Jerome's child.

Keeping his expression neutral, Sérurier said, "The emperor has commanded me to say that you will not be permitted to enter any territory controlled by France or its allies. You must return to America immediately and never use the Bonaparte name."

A hot surge of anger swept over Betsy. "Tell your master that I shall never relinquish a name he has made so famous."

"The emperor's brother is a minor who did not have his family's consent to wed, so your pretended marriage is invalid. However, our emperor is disposed to be generous. If you return to your home, Miss Patterson, and never use the emperor's name, he will give you an annual pension of 60,000 francs."

"Miss Patterson! I do not answer to that name. Tell him that Madame Bonaparte is ambitious and demands her rights as a member of the imperial family."

With that, she turned her back on the chargé and walked to the far side of the room. Behind her, William said, "Sir, I think there is nothing more to discuss."

The sound of clicking heels told Betsy that Sérurier bowed to them. *"Monsieur. Mademoiselle."* Then she heard the shutting of the door.

William came and put an arm around her shoulder. "I think we should leave for Amsterdam."

✍ XVI ✌

CAPTAIN Stephenson decided to stay well clear of the French coast in hopes of keeping the news of their destination from reaching the emperor. On May 8, after a brutally difficult voyage through the north Atlantic, the *Erin* dropped anchor off the southwest coast of Texel, the largest and southernmost barrier island in a chain stretching along the northern coast of the Netherlands and Germany. Because of stormy weather, the passage from Lisbon had taken twenty-six days—five days more than the Atlantic crossing—and the ship's provisions were dangerously low.

Betsy went on deck after William told her that land was in sight. The sky was clear, and looking through a spyglass, she saw a flat island fringed by a wide sandy beach. Further inland, white sheep dotted broad patches of green. Betsy turned the glass toward starboard and saw the channel called the Texel River running between the island and the mainland.

"What now?" she asked Captain Stephenson.

"We must wait for a pilot boat. The Texel River is filled with sandbars, and I cannot hope to negotiate it without a guide."

William asked, "How long will it take?"

"Not long."

The day passed without a boat approaching. They ate a meager supper of two-month-old dried biscuit and salted beef, which Betsy could hardly stomach. She persisted in the attempt only because the child in her womb needed nourishment.

That night, Betsy reread a letter that Jerome had sent back to Lisbon shortly after his departure. After begging her to have confidence in him, he said that the worst thing that could happen would be for them to have to live somewhere outside France, but they would be happy as long as they were together. He gave her instructions for taking care of herself and closed with fervent expressions of love.

After folding the letter, Betsy kissed it and pressed it against her chest. Nearly a month had passed since their separation, and the longing to see Jerome's smile or hear his voice threatened to drive her mad. Her worst times came at night, sleeping alone in her bunk without his warmth beside her. Tucking the letter into her journal, she reminded herself of his promise to return to her between the first and fifteenth of June.

A SECOND DAY PASSED without a pilot boat appearing. On the third day, Captain Stephenson decided to risk taking in the ship without guidance. William, Betsy, and Eliza stood on deck, watching anxiously as seamen in the ship's boat explored the channel and returned with their findings. Then by proceeding cautiously and taking frequent soundings, Stephenson navigated the channel and rounded the island's southern point. As the *Erin* sailed into the Zuiderzee, the passengers gazed north and saw a forest of masts rising above the harbor at Oudeschild farther up the Texel coast. In addition to the ships in port, dozens of vessels of every imaginable size were anchored off shore. Departing ships waited there for favorable winds, while arriving ships waited to be guided into Amsterdam.

Almost immediately, a pilot boat set out from port and came alongside them. After tying his rowboat to the *Erin,* an elderly pilot with a cracked, ruddy face boarded and, taking the wheel, steered them toward the anchoring ground.

As the *Erin* approached, a French ship of the line fired a warning shot ahead of her bow. The boom, followed by the whistling of the ball through air and its splash into the sea, caused Betsy's heart to pound.

Captain Stephenson shouted to the pilot, "Is this customary, man?"

"No, sir, I never seen it to happen before."

Stephenson took the wheel and gave orders to bring the ship to. After it was anchored some way from the harbor, another boat set out toward them.

Once it was close enough, its skipper called to them, "Do you come from Baltimore by way of Lisbon?"

"Yes," Stephenson answered.

"Then you must not come to Texel. It is *verboden!*"

As the boat turned back, the old Dutch pilot slapped his forehead. "*Verdomme! Idioot!*" He snatched the salt-stained cap from his head and wrung it between his hands.

"What is wrong?" Stephenson demanded.

"Three weeks ago, a notice I read describing this ship and forbidding us from guiding her. Now, *Jezus Christus,* I will be hanged unless my age and bad memory they excuse."

His terror caused Betsy such an onrush of panic that she considered ordering the captain to sail to Baltimore at once, even though they had no provisions and her delivery was so close. She turned to William. "Why would Jerome send us here knowing we could not land?"

William shook his head. "He cannot have expected this. Holland and America have treaties guaranteeing the security of each other's vessels in port. Nothing in law justifies this aggression."

"Is the emperor so powerful that he can force neutral nations to attack their friends?" Betsy shivered. Then a more sinister possibility caused her to clutch William's arm. "You cannot think Jerome sent us here on purpose to rid himself of me."

"Do not indulge such thoughts. No one who has seen you together questions Jerome's love. This is Napoleon's doing."

Nodding, Betsy tried to convince herself that he was right. When Captain Stephenson approached, she asked, "Do you think they really mean to sink us if we approach?"

"I do not know and dare not risk it. We shall wait here until tomorrow and see if the authorities make contact."

The old pilot was too terrified to return to town, so he remained aboard the *Erin.* About five o'clock that evening, another rowboat approached them. The skipper called in Dutch to the pilot, who told Captain Stephenson, "Your ship I am to take to a spot they will show."

After the crew hauled up the anchor and set the sails, the pilot steered the *Erin* into a position between the sixty-four-gun ship of the line and a French frigate. Two rowboats began to circle the *Erin* to prevent anyone but the pilot from disembarking.

The next morning dawned grey and windy. Captain Stephenson shouted down to the men rowing around the *Erin* that they were out of supplies, but the guards gave no answer. The wind grew to gale force, and the *Erin* pitched about in the choppy waters. Down in her cabin, Betsy lay in her bunk with her arms cradling her abdomen.

As the gale continued over the next two days, William repeatedly asked to lower a boat and go ashore for supplies, but Stephenson was too afraid of the warships to allow it.

Finally, all that was left of their provisions was a partial cask of scummy water and a handful of weevil-riddled biscuits. When the weather calmed slightly on the third day, William told Betsy, "I have finally convinced Stephenson to let Garnier and me attempt to get away."

An hour later, he returned to her cabin, where Eliza was coaxing Betsy to eat a sour mush she had made by using water to soften the last biscuit. William leaned against the wall. "We lowered the boat without problem, but as soon as we got into it, the gunners aboard the frigate aimed a cannon at us and lighted a taper. We had no choice but to come back."

Betsy lay back on her bunk and curled up on her side. "Thank you for trying."

"What a tyrant Napoleon is!" William pounded the wall behind him in a gesture that reminded Betsy of their father. "Who would have thought that he would go to such lengths to separate you from his brother?"

"I confess I did not think he would be so vindictive."

Later when Betsy was alone, she wondered what punishment Napoleon was inflicting on her husband. Perhaps Jerome was in prison or being tried by a naval tribunal for desertion. She wondered if a princely title was worth this torment and recalled how her father had tried to dissuade her from seeking a noble marriage; he would say her suffering was her own fault. But surely, Jerome deserved to be an equal member of the imperial family. And had he been so irresponsible to marry her? After all, Napoleon had married for love. Betsy cried herself to sleep that night, fearing that she would never see Jerome again.

The next morning the sounds of shouting outside the porthole woke her. Peering out, she saw a man in civilian clothes standing in a rowboat and yelling to someone aboard the *Erin*. Betsy rose, completed her morning ablutions, wrapped a shawl around her swollen figure, and awkwardly made her way up the ladder to the deck. By then, the boat was rowing away.

William rushed up and took both her hands. "That was a messenger from the port commander. When he learned that we are out of provisions and in distress, he promised to report our situation to the Dutch authorities."

"Do you think it will do any good?" she asked, afraid to hope that anyone would be willing to assist people whom Napoleon had singled out for vengeance.

"I feel certain of it. The authorities had no idea this hullabaloo was a malicious attempt to separate a man and wife. Only the French captains knew why we were proscribed."

With the prospect of imminent relief, Betsy felt her strength give way. She swayed, and William grasped her by both arms. "Are you all right? Should I send for the doctor?"

"I am fine, just overwhelmed by the prospect that our ordeal might end soon."

"Let me help you to your cabin."

THE NEXT MORNING a boatload of provisions arrived for them, and later that day Captain Stephenson received orders to sail from the Netherlands as soon as the weather cleared. The *Erin* would not be permitted to land as long as her passengers were aboard.

Betsy, William, Dr. Garnier, and Eliza dined with the captain in his cabin. While the others enjoyed their herring, potatoes, cabbage, and Gouda, Betsy picked at her food, uncertain how much she would be able to keep down. The *Erin* was pitching as the storm still blew.

"I suppose the only thing to do is to head back to Baltimore," William mused.

Garnier vigorously shook his head. "I cannot endorse that suggestion. There is far too much chance of Madame Bonaparte coming to childbed in the midst of the ocean."

Betsy laid her hands upon her abdomen. "God knows I do not want to deliver my child at sea. But where can we go?"

Stephenson refilled his guests' wineglasses. "We shall have to sail to Dover."

"No, it would be certain to enrage the emperor if I sought refuge with his great enemy."

"Besides," William said, reaching over to pat Betsy's arm, "from what we have heard, Napoleon is preparing to invade the southern coast of England. I will not put my sister in the way of such danger."

Captain Stephenson said, "Madame Bonaparte, think about the position you put me in if you choose a more hazardous destination. Your father charged me with your safety, and if I should fail him in this, I might lose command of his vessels."

Eliza shot the captain a disgusted look. "The approaching birth is all that matters. Betsy, how can Napoleon blame you for going to England when he has given you no other choice?"

Closing her eyes and leaning her head on her hand, Betsy tried to shut out the badgering voices. "I wish I knew what Jerome would have me do."

William said, "You know what he would say. His last words to you were that it is your task to bear a healthy son."

"Consider this," Eliza added. "You must get on land as soon as possible. This continual seasickness is debilitating to you and may harm the baby. You need to recover your strength before you deliver."

Betsy looked around the table at her companions and resented them for their bullying. She was convinced that if she gave the British ammunition in their propaganda war against Napoleon, he would never forgive her. To Captain Stephenson, she said, "Is there is no other port we can try? What about Emden or Bremen?"

He made a wide gesture. "Madam, we did not expect that the long arm of the emperor's power could reach to Amsterdam. How can we predict what other ports remain open to us? In your condition, we dare not wander from harbor to harbor."

"But don't you see? The emperor will never receive me if I go to England."

William slapped the table. "How much more anger can he display? He has already had a warship fire upon you, and if we do not leave Texel at the first opportunity, those selfsame ships will gladly send us to the bottom. Your situation cannot possibly get any worse."

"Yes, it can." Betsy's thoughts flew to Jerome. Was he, like her, surrounded by people urging him to do something that violated his every instinct? She wanted to hold out against their persuasion, but unlike Jerome, she had to safeguard their child. "Are all of you in agreement that we have no other course?"

Every other person at the table nodded, so against her better judgment, Betsy consented to the plan.

On May 17, the weather cleared enough to sail, and two days later, they anchored off Dover. As they neared that port, they saw rows of pale canvas army tents encamped on the green heights in preparation for Napoleon's expected invasion.

While William went ashore to obtain permission to land, Betsy and Eliza stood at the ship's railing staring at the white chalk cliffs and the hilltop castle, perched above the port on the eastern height and surrounded by walls that snaked up and down the slopes. "It looks like something from a storybook," Betsy remarked.

Eliza pointed toward the harbor. "Look!"

Turning, Betsy saw two British soldiers walking along a distant quay. Seeing the lobster red uniforms of her husband's enemies made her shiver. "Oh, I feel certain I should not be here."

Eliza put an arm around her. "I know, but there was nothing else we could do."

They watched a fishing boat sail into port circled overhead by squabbling gulls. Then Betsy turned her face to the pale spring sun and tried to absorb its warmth. She had to admit that it felt good to be anchored in a harbor where she ran no risk of being turned away. If only Jerome could be with her—but that was impossible. If he were here, the British would take him hostage.

She reached around to rub her lower back, which ached from the strain of carrying so much weight in front. "Should we go below so you can rest?" Eliza asked.

"No, I have spent far too much time in that stinking cabin."

After more than an hour, Betsy saw a carriage drive onto the pier where the ship's boat was waiting. Her brother and an older man alighted and climbed down into the boat, which then rowed toward the *Erin*. The carriage remained where it was. As Betsy waited for William to reach the ship, she noticed people collecting around the coach. "How odd. Why do you think a crowd is gathering?"

"I cannot imagine. It looks an ordinary enough vehicle."

Eliza went to ask the captain to have their trunks carried up on deck. Then the two women watched as the crowd continued to grow, some shoving to get near the carriage and some gazing toward their ship. Feeling uneasy, Betsy remembered the parties she and Jerome had attended in Washington; people had gathered in the street so they could peer through open windows at Napoleon's brother and his scantily clad wife. "This makes me wary," she told Eliza.

"What do you think may be happening?"

Before Betsy could answer, the boat arrived, and William and a slight, bald man climbed aboard the ship. "This is Mr. Skeffington, our father's agent in Dover. Mr. Skeffington, this is my sister, Madame Bonaparte, and her companion, Mrs. Anderson."

They murmured greetings, and then William said, "Skeffington helped me find a set of rooms in a comfortable inn. Betsy, we will take your trunk with us, and then I will send back for the other trunks and the servants."

To spare Betsy from climbing the ladder again, Eliza went below deck to check that no stray articles remained in their cabins. After she left, Betsy said, "William, I should have spoken earlier, but these last few weeks have been too tumultuous to allow for looking ahead. I do not trust Dr. Garnier or want him to deliver my child. Can you find some pretext to send him away?"

William frowned. "I confess that I also distrust him. He is markedly less respectful toward you when you are absent than he is to your face. But what excuse can we give?"

"Captain Stephenson has to sail back to Amsterdam to deliver part of his cargo. We could say that we must send Garnier to tell Jerome what happened when we tried to land because we dare not commit such a message to the mails."

William smiled ruefully. "Garnier will not like it, but I will convince him to respect our wishes."

"Thank you, that takes a great weight off my mind."

He went below deck. Ignoring Skeffington, Betsy leaned against the railing and watched the seamen load her trunk onto the cargo sling, swing it over the side, and lower it into the boat. A few minutes later, Dr. Garnier approached her. "Madame Bonaparte, I must protest this new plan. Your husband specially charged me with the safe delivery of his child."

Exasperation drove Betsy to the verge of tears. "Dr. Garnier, I must get word to my husband by someone he trusts. Mr. Bonaparte must be told that his brother's anger is so severe that it extends to the use of violence. If indeed, he has not already learned so firsthand." With that reference to Jerome's peril, she began to weep openly.

William bustled up to them. "Doctor, I begged you not to upset my sister. Can you not ease her mind by agreeing to our request?"

"Of course, I—"

Seeing that the sling had returned from the boat, William started to lead Betsy toward it, but she turned back to Garnier. "Please, give Mr. Bonaparte my love and explain why it was necessary for us to come here despite my misgivings. Tell him his child and I live for his return. Nothing else matters. Do you understand me? Nothing."

Dr. Garnier stared at her a moment and then nodded.

Betsy turned away, and William helped her onto the sling. "Hold these ropes tightly. The crew has assured me they will treat you as delicately as a basket of eggs."

The contraption reminded Betsy of the swing her older brothers had rigged for her on a tree at Springfield when she was a girl. At any other time, she might have enjoyed the flying sensation of being suspended over water and lowered into the boat, but in her present condition, the experience left her queasy. After she was settled, she clung to the gunnel and tried not to be sick when the boat rocked as Eliza, William, and Skeffington dropped into it.

Betsy leaned against Eliza and closed her eyes as they were rowed ashore. Once there, she climbed the ladder to the pier with her brother giving her a hand from above. When she was standing on the weather-beaten planking, she was shocked by the size of the waiting crowd. A small contingent of British soldiers stood at attention and pointed their bayonetted rifles over the spectators' heads to keep them away from the carriage.

"My God, William, what is this?"

"When getting the passports, I was required to report your identity and the reason for our journey. It would seem the news has traveled swiftly."

As they walked to the carriage, the mass of people surged forward. Betsy halted, smiled to placate the crowd, and gave what semblance of a curtsy she could with her off-balance figure. A sharp-faced man at the front shouted, "Madame Bonaparte, may I ask you questions?"

Seeing that he held a notebook and pencil, Betsy cried, "No, sir, I beg you." Mr. Skeffington stepped between her and the crowd and handed her into the carriage. Then Eliza and the two men climbed inside.

As William shut the carriage door, a voice from outside shouted, "Never fear, little lady. Our gallant lads will crush Boney for you!"

"How can they possibly think that is what I want?" Betsy murmured.

WILLIAM HAD BOOKED rooms in a historic inn built in the late 1400s. As at the harbor, a crowd loitered in the street to witness their arrival. At the sight of them, Betsy thought back to her girlhood fantasies of being a princess, stepping out of a gilded carriage to be cheered by adoring subjects; the reality of her arrival in England felt like a perversion of that lifelong dream. The faces in this mob displayed no love but only raw inquisitiveness.

Over their heads, Betsy could see that the building was three stories high and made of brick, with the second story overhanging the first story by several feet, and the third story jutting out over the second. The top two floors were whitewashed, and each floor had a pair of mullioned windows.

After insisting that the carriage pull as close to the door as possible, William and Skeffington climbed out first. Betsy heard the Englishman shout in his reedy voice, "Have some decency, and make way for the ladies!" Then William beckoned to her. As she took his hand and alighted, Betsy smiled to appease the avid curiosity in the strange faces surrounding her. William hurried her through a wide black door in the center of a dirty brick wall. Betsy hoped to find relief from the onlookers once she was inside, but people had also gathered in the common room and stood on the stairs leading to the bedchambers.

The innkeeper, a burly man with a broad chest, went up before them, shouting, "Make way! This is not a circus."

As she climbed the stairs, Betsy heard exclamations of sympathy rising from below: *Look how tired the poor mite is and in a family way too. They say French warships chased her out of Holland.* The expressions of concern made her want to weep, but by fixing a tight smile upon her face, she managed to control her emotions until she reached her room.

After Skeffington left them, Betsy, William, and Eliza gathered in the parlor between the bedrooms of the two women. The innkeeper's lad carried up Betsy's trunk, and then William shut the door and leaned against it. "I am sorry, Betsy, that we could not use your incognito."

Betsy shrugged and lowered herself into a chair. "I daresay the truth would have come out anyway. No doubt the British have a spy network, just as Napoleon does." Gazing around the room at the beamed ceiling, smoke-blackened hearth, and heavy oak furniture, she felt as if she had been transported back to the time of Henry VIII and shuddered to think of that wife-murdering monarch. Shifting a cushion behind her to ease her back, she leaned her head against her chair and closed her eyes. A few minutes later, a knock sounded upon their door.

Their visitor was the innkeeper's wife, who brought them a supper of pea soup, roasted chicken, bread, cheese, and ale. "Thank you," Betsy said as the woman laid the table.

Their hostess stepped back to check that everything was in place. She was in her forties with faded ginger hair. Wiping her hands on her apron, she turned to Betsy. "Is it true, ma'am, that you are married to the French emperor's brother?"

Betsy sat up straighter. "Yes. I hope that will not compromise me in your eyes."

"No, ma'am." The woman smiled, showing a gap between her teeth. "No Englishman would blame a lady for her brother-in-law's crimes. Anyway, we look on Americans as being quite our cousins."

Betsy felt tears flood her eyes.

Seeing her distress, the innkeeper's wife said, "Never fear, ma'am. If you have faith, I am sure God will look after you." Then she curt-sied and left the room.

❧ XVII ❧

THE next morning at breakfast, a letter arrived for Betsy. After reading it, she tossed the page down. "Mr. Skeffington begs leave to bring some people to meet me. Lady Augusta Forbes, wife of the officer overseeing the defense of Dover, and General John Hope, half-brother to the Earl of Hopetoun. These English act as though I am come here for their amusement."

Picking up the sheet, William read it for himself. "Do not judge Skeffington so harshly. He also offers to help in any way possible."

Eliza refilled Betsy's cup. "You need not meet these people if you don't wish to."

"You do not know my father. After the money he laid out for this voyage, he will want me to be gracious to his associate."

William cleared his throat. "I do not think he would require such exertions in your present condition. You know how highly he prizes female modesty."

Stung by the reminder that she often failed to meet their father's standards, Betsy grew obstinate. "Perhaps, but I will receive Mr. Skeffington's friends all the same so that no one may rebuke me later."

She rested in bed most of that day, and by evening she felt a lessening of the nervous fatigue that had afflicted her since Texel. The improvement in her spirits proved to be short-lived. The innkeeper sent up the previous day's *London Times* at supper, and seeing William scowl as he had scanned the front page, Betsy demanded to know what it said.

He showed her a paragraph reporting the arrival of the *Erin* and the identities of everyone in their party. It described Betsy's beauty and added that she appeared to be "far advanced in a situation to increase the number of Imperial relatives."

"I feared this would happen," Betsy complained. "Now the emperor will certainly know that I have come to England. Jerome told me he pores over the English papers to keep abreast of what they say about him."

"What else could we do? After the disaster that ensued when Jerome sent us to Amsterdam—"

"How can you blame him?"

William wiped his lips with a napkin before answering, "I do not. I believe him to be as much a victim of Napoleon's machinations as we are."

"I tell you, no good will come of our having fled here!" Betsy pushed on the table to ease herself to a standing position. "I almost wish we had gone to the bottom instead."

Eliza circled the table and hugged Betsy. "You will not feel that way once your child is born. Believe me that once the baby is in your arms, you will be willing to risk everything for him."

The sharp longing in her friend's voice sliced through Betsy's agitation. "Oh, Eliza, how you must miss your daughter. You left her to be with me, and all I seem to do is rage at you."

"Hardly that. Besides, we who love you comprehend that your emotions are in turmoil because of the cruelty you have suffered."

Observing that Eliza had avoided the tender subject of her daughter, Betsy said, "Please forgive my thoughtlessness. I will try to keep in mind all you have sacrificed for me."

THE NEXT DAY's visit deepened Betsy's disquiet about being in England. Lady Augusta and General Hope were polite and claimed to feel concern for her because of the former close association of their two countries. Betsy sensed, however, that beneath their expressions of solicitude, they saw her not as an individual woman whose heart bled for her absent husband, but merely as a symbol that confirmed Napoleon's tyranny.

After they left, Betsy said to Eliza, "You see, I am nothing more than a *cause célèbre* they can use to incite public feeling against the emperor."

"I thought they were kind to offer support in your time of difficulty."

"Ah, but 'we all have sufficient strength to support the misfortunes of others,'" Betsy said, quoting La Rochefoucauld. "It costs them little to murmur, 'You poor abused thing,' particularly when they can exploit my situation for their own ends. I begin to understand why Napoleon hates the English."

William reentered the parlor after escorting their guests downstairs. "Betsy, I fail to understand you. How can you of all people defend the emperor?"

She rested her clasped hands atop her protruding abdomen. "I may disagree with what my brother-in-law has done, and I may despise the way he reduces Jerome to a pawn in his stratagems, but I believe he makes his decisions for reasons of state. None of us can know the immense burden he carries in defending France. Therefore, his actions, though detrimental to me, are more defensible than the insincere flattery of the gentry that called this morning."

Having no wish to argue further, she went to fetch her workbasket. Because she had been so sick during their voyages, she had accomplished very little sewing for her baby. As she exited the parlor, she overheard Eliza say, "Have patience, William. She must defend Napoleon because she still hopes to gain his favor."

"That is a fool's hope. The emperor has already shown his implacable resentment. What could possibly induce him to change his opposition to the marriage?"

"Jerome. If he places the emperor in his debt with some deed of glory, they might still be reunited."

Hiding behind her bedroom door, Betsy heard her brother sigh. "You little know my brother-in-law if you think he has the fortitude to accomplish such a plan."

THE NEXT DAY Betsy had further reason to curse the English papers. On May 21, the *London Times* published another story about her:

> The beautiful wife of Jerome Bonaparte, after being refused admittance into every port in Europe where the French influence degrades and dishonors humanity, has landed, with a part of her family, at Dover, in a state of pregnancy, under the protection of a great and generous people. This interesting lady, who has been the victim of imposture and ambition, will here receive all the rights of hospitality…. The contemptible Jerome was, for form's sake, made a prisoner at Lisbon. His treachery toward this lovely Unfortunate, will procure him an early pardon, and a Highness-ship from the Imperial Swindler his brother.

After reading the article aloud, Betsy slapped the paper on the table. "Now do you see what I mean? Jerome has done nothing to deserve the epithet *contemptible*. And what cause do they have for giving Napoleon the label *Imperial Swindler?*"

"Perhaps the thousands of French troops massed on the other side of the Channel waiting to invade England?" William asked dryly.

"Do you forget that British troops previously violated French soil in an effort to overthrow the republican government established by the Revolution?"

William picked up the silver tongs and dropped three small clumps of sugar in his tea. "What has that to do with the topic under discussion? The day Napoleon became emperor, he ended any hopes of a lasting republic in France."

"He was forced to do that by foreign-sponsored plots to assassinate him!" she cried, frustrated by her brother's refusal to admit that Napoleon had any justification for his actions.

William looked up, his teacup in hand. "Betsy, why are you become the emperor's mouthpiece? You could shout these opinions from the rooftops of London, and it would not alter his refusal to recognize your marriage."

As tears coursed down her face, Betsy inwardly cursed the way her emotions had grown so ungovernable. "Perhaps not, but if I am quoted saying one word against him—whether the attribution is accurate or no—it will destroy my hopes of reuniting with Jerome."

"Then perhaps we should find a less public place for you to await your confinement."

Two DAYS LATER their brother Robert turned up at their inn without advance word.

"Bobby!" Betsy cried when he came through the door. She flung down her sewing and struggled to push herself up from her armchair.

"Little Goose," he said, crossing the room and clasping her hands. Then he smiled. "I had not realized that you had grown into quite such a stuffed goose."

Blushing, Betsy ducked her head.

"Let me order tea," Eliza said, rising. "You will want to hold a family conference."

"I would like you to take part. You know all my deepest concerns."

Eliza nodded and went to tell Betsy's maid Jenny to request tea from the landlady.

Turning back to her brother, Betsy said, "Have you any news of Jerome?"

"Yes, I found letters waiting for you when I reached Amsterdam. And I saw Le Camus."

"Then Jerome is not in prison?"

"No." Robert glanced at William, who was standing beside the table where he had been working on correspondence. Seeing his hesitation, Betsy cried, "Do you have bad news? Has he repudiated me?"

"No, at least I do not believe so. He seems to be playing a double game, espousing the repentance that Napoleon requires, yet secretly hoping to be reconciled with you in time."

"Is that all? Jerome warned me he might adopt that course."

Relieved, Betsy took a seat at the table, while William hastily cleared away his papers, packed them in a satchel, and placed it near the door.

"May I see Jerome's letters?" Betsy asked.

"Of course, forgive me." Robert pulled them from the inner pocket of his coat.

Betsy broke open the seals and scanned the pages hastily. Jerome had written both letters while he was on the road to Milan. She heard her brothers holding a whispered conversation by the fireplace and Eliza returning to the room, but Betsy paid no attention to them as she began to read the letters in earnest. The letter dated April 19 filled a page. In it, Jerome repeated his plan to do anything he could to appease Napoleon. He promised that once he had done his duty, they would withdraw, if necessary, to some "little corner of the world" where they could live in peace. Then he closed by declaring that he had complete confidence in her love and swearing that they would soon be reunited.

Feeling much happier, Betsy turned to the second letter, dated May 3. It was only a few lines but reminded her that Jerome planned to return to her between the first and fifteenth of June. With a spurt of joy, she realized that the first was only a week away.

Betsy pressed the letters to her breast and smiled at her brothers. "Jerome's intentions have not changed. He is doing his duty to the emperor in the hope that all will be well, but if not, Jerome will return to me so that we can retire somewhere beyond the imperial reach."

Robert frowned. "I take it that he had not yet seen the emperor when he wrote those?"

"No, he was still journeying toward Milan."

Gesturing for William to follow, Robert crossed to the table. When they were all seated, Robert said, "I told you that I saw Le Camus. Jerome sent him with a message."

Robert reached into his inner pocket for a wallet and extracted a folded paper. "When they arrived at Milan, the emperor refused to receive Jerome and sent him a formal directive instead. Le Camus would not allow me to keep the emperor's letter, but he did allow me to copy it." He handed it to Betsy.

There are no faults that you have committed which may not be effaced in my eyes by a sincere repentance. Your marriage is null both in a religious and legal point of view. I will never acknowledge it. Write to Miss Patterson to return to the United States; and tell her it is not possible to give things another turn. On condition of her going to America, I will allow her a pension during her life of 60,000 francs per year, provided she does not take the name of my family.

As she reached the end of that directive, Betsy felt the same harrowing shock she had experienced when she hit the cold saltwater after jumping from the shipwreck. "Did Le Camus claim that these were Jerome's instructions to me?"

"He did not go so far as to say that, but I think he wished to convey that impression. However, I do not believe Jerome would dismiss you so callously. I suspect he sent Le Camus to Amsterdam with the sole purpose of making sure we apprehend his difficulties, but the secretary took it upon himself to persuade me that you should relinquish your claims."

"Le Camus is no secretary," Betsy retorted. "He is little more than a panderer."

William huffed as if to rebuke her, but Robert spoke first. "The salient point is that we now know the emperor means to cast doubt on the religious nature of your marriage as well as its standing in civil law. And he objects to your using the Bonaparte name."

"I already knew that from Sérurier, but they cannot prevent me from doing so. Were I to revert to Miss Patterson, my child would be called a bastard. If Napoleon thinks that I would subject his brother's legitimate heir to disgrace for a mere 60,000 francs—what is that, $12,000 a year?—then he has little idea of my mettle."

"I agree that you should not accept the pension while there is hope of reconciliation, nor can you resume your maiden name."

While there is hope of reconciliation? Betsy looked at her brother sharply, wondering if he had reason to doubt that Jerome intended to return to her.

A rapping sound interrupted them, and Eliza rose to open the door. After the landlady laid the tray upon the table and departed, Eliza poured their tea. "So if I understand the discussion aright, you are all agreed to wait for more direct word from Jerome."

"Yes," Betsy answered before either of her brothers. "You know as well as any of us what reason I have not to trust Le Camus."

Raising her eyebrows expressively, Eliza nodded but did not comment, and Betsy let the subject drop. She did not think it would improve her brothers' view of the situation to learn the exact nature of the services Le Camus had rendered Jerome before their marriage.

William then explained their idea to remove to London so Betsy's comings and goings might be less noticed. Approving of the plan, Robert offered to write to James Monroe, the U.S. Minister to the Court of St. James, to ask his advice about neighborhoods.

THEY MOVED TO a hotel in the Mayfair district in late May. As their carriage drove through the main London streets—crowded with closed coaches, open chaises, sedan chairs, horseback riders, and pedestrians—Betsy stared out the window feeling as rustic as the settler's wife she had met on the way to Niagara. During her stay in New York, she had thought it an immense city with its population of 60,000, but London had some 800,000 people, making it so much larger as to be incomprehensible.

The English capital sprawled in all directions. The Pattersons' hired carriage drove for miles past broad green parks with towering trees, stone town houses with classical porticos and ornamental urns on the rooflines; brick churches with stained glass windows and soaring white steeples; and whole blocks of simple two-story structures with businesses below and living quarters above. Most shops had flat signs extending along the wall above their display windows. Two kinds of establishments, however, had old-fashioned hanging signs that dangled into the street. Pawnshops displayed three balls descending from a metal bar, a symbol that dated back to the Renaissance, while each tavern had a colorfully painted signboard with artwork symbolizing its distinctive name—such as the Grapes, the Red Lion, and Ye Olde Cheddar Cheese.

One thing that astonished Betsy was the number of vendors walking the streets and shouting descriptions of their wares. Within one two-minute stretch, she saw a young man carrying a brace of rabbits and calling, "Fresh country coneys"; a woman pushing a heavy cart and crying, "Hot spiced gingerbread, all hot"; and an old man with a bundle of rushes slung across his shoulder singing, "Old chairs to mend, old chairs to mend, if I had money to spend, I would not call, 'Old chairs to mend.'"

Pulling back from the window, Betsy exclaimed, "This city is so lively! And noisy."

Eliza nodded in agreement, but Robert barely looked up from the newspaper he was reading as he said, "Yes, it can be damned annoying."

Betsy sighed at her brother's world-weary reaction. She had already noticed that, after a year traveling about Europe, conducting family business as well as working on her behalf, Robert had acquired an air of sophistication. His wealth of experience stirred Betsy's envy. Were it not for Napoleon's opposition to her marriage, she too could have been familiar enough with European life to remark casually as they passed St. James's Palace, "Rumor has it that King George is having fits of madness."

Never mind, she told herself. *Wait until Napoleon finally accepts me as his sister-in-law.* For the remainder of the drive to their hotel, she amused herself by imagining how her brothers would have to bow to her whenever they came to the French court.

Their hotel was a four-story, brown brick building with white pilasters rising to the cornice that rimmed the flat roof. Much to Betsy's consternation, even in the hurry-scurry of the city, she attracted attention. Reports about her continued to appear in the London journals, and knots of people gathered across the street from the hotel, hoping to glimpse the lovely American victim of Boney's fury. The commotion had caused the recently installed prime minister, William Pitt, to place a guard outside her place of lodging.

At the beginning of June, the newspapers announced that there would be a new type of public entertainment for King George III's June 4 birthday. The trooping of the colors, in which regiments of the British army would display their flags before the monarch, would take place on the Horse Guard Parade Ground near St. James Palace. Robert and Eliza both wanted to see it, but Betsy was afraid she would cause too much disruption if she appeared at such an event. "Please go enjoy yourselves," she said. "I will be fine. I have several weeks to go before my child is due, and Jenny will be here if I need to send for help."

Betsy spent much of that day sitting alone near her hotel window, positioned behind the lace curtain so she would not be visible from the street. All across the skyline, Union Jacks snapped in the breeze, and at noon, church bells tolled across the city. It seemed to Betsy that everyone in the world except her had something purposeful or celebratory to do. Now that she had a few hours alone, she could no longer ignore her inner certainty that June would certainly pass without the reunion Jerome had promised. To be sure, he could not come to her here in England, but she had hoped he would send a message about where she should meet him. Instead, the silence had grown increasingly ominous. To stave off the despondency that threatened to engulf her, Betsy began to sew another gown for her baby.

As the days passed, she came to regard the wooden divisions of her mullioned windows as the bars of a cage. Because of the crowds and her fear of appearing in newspapers, she refused to attend concerts or plays, or even to take carriage rides. Having to forego the cultural attractions she had craved for so long frustrated her, but her situation gave her little choice. She would not be the one to provide more gossip for the British newspapers to use against Napoleon. In consequence, the few times she needed to go out, she wore a veil.

Despite her withdrawal from public view, hardly a day passed without curious aristocrats sending up their cards and requesting permission to call on her. Their visits invariably left Betsy feeling like an exotic animal in a menagerie.

The only visitor who did not make her feel on display was Lady Frances Erskine, a young Pennsylvania woman who had married a British baron. A pretty twenty-four-year-old with large eyes and a fresh complexion, Lady Erskine commiserated with Betsy over her separation from Jerome. In addition, Lady Erskine suggested a reliable doctor who could deliver Betsy's child.

"He is quite abreast of the latest ideas. My mama was shocked when she learned that he persuaded me to nurse my children, but that is what all the best doctors here advise."

"Really!" Betsy exclaimed. "My mother used a wet nurse with all of us."

"Mine too, but think of the filth you might be exposing your child to by entrusting him to some low creature."

Betsy stared at the baby frock she was sewing. Although she would never discuss anything so private, she desperately missed her physical relationship with Jerome. Perhaps, if she nursed his child, it would help restore a sense of an intimate connection with him.

EVEN AFTER SEVERAL weeks, the hullabaloo over Betsy's presence in

London failed to subside. Feeling like a prisoner in her hotel, she asked her brothers to find a place to stay in one of the quieter outlying districts. After again consulting with James Monroe, Robert rented a house in the rural village of Camberwell, located south of the Thames and said to be healthy because of its mineral springs.

They moved in mid June to one of three identical, attached town houses. The buildings were each three windows wide and three stories high with basements and attics. They were constructed of yellow brick with red brick dressing above the mullioned windows, and they each had a black, six-panel door with a decorative fanlight above. Inside the house, the first floor had a parlor, dining room, and kitchen, while each of the upper two stories had four bedrooms.

The fifteenth of June passed without any word from Jerome, and Betsy spent the next day crying. Since coming to England, she had been trying to think of some way to contact her husband, from whom she had heard nothing since the letters Robert brought. She could not write Jerome directly because Napoleon's spy network would certainly intercept any correspondence. Using either Garnier or Le Camus as intermediaries would be useless, and she did not know where Henriette and Jean-Jacques Reubell were because Henriette had ceased to write to her.

Still, Betsy did not cease her efforts. She wrote to several people who might have a chance to deliver a letter surreptitiously. One was Paul Bentalou, a French officer her family had known since he fought in the Revolutionary War. Bentalou had been Robert's interpreter during his meetings with Jerome's brothers Joseph and Lucien—and for providing that assistance, Napoleon had briefly imprisoned him. Despite that, Bentalou remained willing to work on their behalf. Although Betsy feared placing him in further jeopardy, she sent him a sealed letter for Jerome and begged him to use his own judgment to determine whether delivering it was safe.

Betsy sent letters through various channels to Lucien Bonaparte, who was still exiled to Italy as punishment for his own marriage. He did not answer. She also contacted James Monroe's daughter, who was living in Paris and had gone to school with Hortense de Beauharnais, Josephine's daughter from her first marriage. Betsy wrote to

Miss Monroe and, after apologizing for the presumption, asked her to give her old schoolmate a letter to hand privately to Jerome. Since Jerome had often said how close he was to Josephine, Betsy hoped that Hortense—whom Napoleon had pressured into marriage with his unstable brother Louis—would sympathize with her plight. After two weeks, Miss Monroe wrote back that she had left the letter with Hortense but did not know if it had been passed on.

By then, the time for the birth was near. Betsy still believed that her child would one day be recognized as a member of the imperial family, so she decided to proceed as though she were being delivered of a royal heir. In addition to the doctor, she arranged for several women who lived nearby to witness the child's birth.

On July 4, the Pattersons and Eliza Anderson had a quiet Independence Day supper in their rooms, and William and Robert made several toasts to the United States and the revolutionary heroes their family had known. Betsy's back ached and her feet were swollen, so she felt cross and in no mood for displays of American patriotism. However, she held her tongue while the others indulged their nostalgia for their homeland.

Two days later, in the early evening, Betsy's labor started. Eliza went with her into her bedroom and helped her into a loose gown. Robert went to fetch the doctor.

For the first hour or so, Betsy's pains were similar to the cramps she suffered during her monthly flux, and she kept murmuring that she wished Jerome were there, perhaps not in the room with her but somewhere in the house. After a while, her labor pains increased in intensity until each one felt as though a massive force was compressing and twisting her womb, and as she pulled on the knotted sheet that Eliza had tied to the foot of the bed, Betsy screamed and called for her mother. Eventually, she grew too exhausted even to do that. As the contractions grew closer together and harder to endure, Betsy fell into an almost delirious state in which she imagined that Napoleon was inflicting the suffering upon her with his pitiless hatred for her and her child. When the time finally came to push the baby from her body, she felt as though she were trying to expel the emperor himself.

Early in the morning of July 7, she experienced one last agonizing moment of pushing and screaming and tearing of muscles, and then her body freed itself of its burden. Minutes later, a squalling red creature with wet hair was placed upon her chest. "You have a son," the doctor said, and Betsy burst into tears. She stroked the baby's head and whispered, "My little prince." In that instant, she felt a rush of intensely protective love the like of which she had never known, and she laughed from exhilaration.

"What are you going to call him?" Eliza asked.

"Jerome Napoleon Bonaparte. No matter what the emperor says, the world must know who my son is."

❧ XVIII ❧

ONE afternoon a week later, Betsy sat in bed cradling the baby and singing a medieval French song she had learned as a schoolgirl: *"Sur le pont d'Avignon, l'on y danse, l'on y danse. Sur le pont d'Avignon, l'on y danse tout en rond."*

When she finished, baby Jerome yawned, stretched out his arms, and then pulled them in to rest his fists upon his chest. He scrunched his face in a frown that made Betsy laugh. "Oh, you look so fierce. Are you trying to show Uncle Napoleon that you are just as formidable as he is?"

She kissed his forehead and smoothed his fuzzy brown hair. The love she felt for this tiny being had intensified with each passing day, but her joy in motherhood was darkened by sorrow over her separation from Jerome and uncertainty whether he knew of their son's arrival.

"We must take you to meet Papa. He will be so proud to have a son that it will strengthen his resolve to defy the emperor." Betsy tucked the blanket more closely around the baby and imagined a scene in which she presented him to her husband's family, and they all exclaimed in wonder over what a Bonaparte the baby was.

A knock sounded upon her door, and Robert entered. "You wanted to see me?"

"Yes," Betsy said, but she kept her eyes fixed on her son's face. "Look at baby Jerome. Don't you think he looks like Napoleon?"

"I cannot tell. All babies look alike. Is this why you sent for me?"

Betsy met her brother's gaze. "No, but it does have a bearing on what I wish to say. A month has passed since the deadline Jerome set for his return, so I think we must go in search of him. As soon as I am well, I mean to travel to the continent with my son. He bears such a strong resemblance to the Bonapartes that he may soften their hearts in ways I cannot."

Robert carried the chair from Betsy's dressing table, positioned it beside her bed, and sat. "What difference do you suppose it will make to the emperor that your son looks like him? He has not questioned that Jerome is the father."

"I know, but—" Betsy kissed the baby again. "Napoleon does not have a son, and some claim that he is incapable of fathering children. Joseph has only daughters, and Lucien's son was born outside wedlock. That leaves only Louis's two boys to serve as Napoleon's heirs, and—well, rumor has it that Louis might not even be the father."

"You should not lend so much credence to the English journals," Robert said, referring to a recent article that repeated gossip about the Bonapartes' amorous affairs to highlight Napoleon's hypocrisy in rejecting the virtuous daughter of a respected American family. "You have complained often enough about their lies."

"Even so, Louis's boys are young and anything may happen. Napoleon needs my son to strengthen the imperial succession."

Robert stroked the baby's fist. "Betsy, Napoleon would never allow your son to inherit his throne."

"He may think that now, but Jerome has got around his brother's dictates before." The sight of her son opening his mouth and sticking out his tongue distracted Betsy, and her heart filled with wonder over how perfect he was. Smiling at Robert, she said, "Besides, if the baby and I could meet the emperor, we might win him over."

Robert sighed. "What do you propose? You are forbidden to enter any port under French control. Surely you do not imagine that Napoleon has lifted that ban."

"No, but he will not be expecting this move from me. If I adopt an incognito and travel without ceremony—"

"If you were caught trying to enter the country, your ship would be fired upon as it was at Texel, and if you manage to land, you could be thrown in prison like poor Bentalou." Robert leaned toward her with his forearm on one knee. "Think. What would then happen to your child?"

Betsy bit her lip. "Robert, I fear that Jerome may lose heart. There is no one to support him as he tries to uphold our marriage. Both Garnier and Le Camus have proven themselves my enemies, and *Madame Mère* seems unable to defy Napoleon even to please her favorite child. Jerome needs my help to remain firm."

"Is that what you want, a husband who is incapable of playing the part of a man unless you push him to it?"

"I did not say that!" The baby squirmed, and Betsy lowered her voice. "Even if I had, it is not as though I still can choose whether to accept Jerome as my husband. Or do you too doubt the validity of my marriage?"

"No," Robert answered wearily. "Despite certain irregularities attending it, I believe that your marriage is valid before God. But I wish your husband had taken greater care to protect you from legal questions."

"So do I, but we cannot undo the past. The important thing now is my son. Whatever the faults of his father, I must do everything within my power to secure his heritage."

Robert nodded. "I hope you know that, even if I do not fully agree with your plan, you have my unwavering support in anything to benefit young Jerome. Before you do anything rash, allow me to seek James Monroe's counsel. Will you wait?"

"Yes. The doctor will not allow me to travel so soon anyway."

BETSY WENT DOWNSTAIRS eighteen days after her son was born, even though the doctor had prescribed a month of bed rest. The baby was gaining weight and sleeping well, and she was eager to travel. Despite what her brother said, she could not shake the feeling that it was imperative to find Jerome.

Nearly two weeks passed before James Monroe answered Robert's letter, but when he did, he advised Betsy not to go to the continent. He had made inquiries and learned that Jerome had been put in command of five ships and given the mission of sailing to Algiers to rescue 300

Christians who were enslaved there. The squadron had not yet left Genoa, but its departure was said to be imminent. Monroe also cautioned that if Betsy defied the emperor, it might rekindle Napoleon's fury and counteract any exertions that Jerome might be making.

Although bitterly disappointed at being told to wait, Betsy was heartened to receive some concrete news. "This sounds like a worthy mission, does it not?" she asked her brothers. "Surely if Jerome accomplishes this successfully, the emperor must reward him."

Robert and William exchanged a look, and William said, "That does not mean such a reward will be a reunion with you."

Betsy put down the letter, which Robert had given her to read. "Why do you begrudge me what little hope I have?"

"I don't. I simply do not want to see you subjected to further disappointment."

The baby began to cry, so Betsy rose, but before leaving the parlor, she said, "I know you have both given up on Jerome, but I cannot. I remain certain that he loves me, and I believe that no matter how it appears, he is doing everything he can to soften his brother's hostility."

Robert stepped closer and laid a hand on her arm. "We do not doubt Jerome's devotion, but as you have said, he has no one to help him stand firm. I think that even as you continue to hope, you must consider the possibility of returning home without a reconciliation."

Shaking her head vehemently, Betsy said, "I believe the constancy of my faith in Jerome lends him strength even at a distance, and I cannot fail him in the only assistance I have to offer." Then she went upstairs to tend to her son.

AFTER THEY RECEIVED the letter from James Monroe, the great wall of silence surrounding Jerome cracked a tiny bit, allowing snippets of news to leak out over the next few weeks.

On the last day of July, the London journals reported that in June, Jerome had held a reception on board his ship for his sister Elisa and other dignitaries. The report said that due to the exertions of Princess Elisa, Jerome was reconciled to the emperor.

The thought of Jerome indulging in an elegant shipboard banquet only a month after she, at his brother's command, had endured star-

vation aboard a trapped ship caused Betsy to burst into tears. When
Eliza Anderson offered sympathy, Betsy hurried away. No matter what
her feelings, she was determined not to say anything that would express doubt in her husband.

The papers also reported that a battle had taken place between the
British navy and the combined French and Spanish fleets in late July.
As Napoleon's ships were returning from the West Indies, British ships
attacked them off Cape Finisterre, Spain. Although neither side defeated the other, the British claimed a victory because they had thwarted
Napoleon's plan to pull the bulk of their navy away from the English
Channel, leaving it open to the French. Betsy did not know whether
to be glad that the threat of invasion had lessened or worried that the
outcome would worsen Napoleon's temper.

Because their stay in England was lasting longer than anyone anticipated, William needed to leave to attend to their father's business
in other ports. After his departure, Betsy felt abandoned. Even though
William was not her most congenial brother, he had been her protector
during their peril at Texel, and she missed his quiet strength.

In early August, Betsy's determination to stay on the east side of
the Atlantic suffered an unexpected blow. Eliza received a letter in-
forming her that one of her uncles had died and left her a legacy, and
she wanted to return to Baltimore.

"But I cannot live abroad without a companion," Betsy said, looking
up from the piece of soft wool she had spread upon the table to hem
into a blanket. "Can you not wait a little longer?"

Irritation flashed across Eliza's face. "You will hardly be alone. Robert
is here."

"But what if he has to leave on business? I must have someone with me."

Eliza grabbed the top of the chair opposite Betsy so tightly that her
knuckles turned white. "I am not a servant, nor did I agree to such a
lengthy exile from my daughter. When we first embarked upon this
trip, you estimated that I would be in Europe a month or two at most.
I have my own concerns."

Betsy jabbed her needle into the blanket so precipitously that she
pricked the index finger of the hand beneath it. After bringing the
wounded finger to her mouth to suck away the blood, she said, "Believe

me, if I could bring our sojourn in England to an end today, I would do so. I do not like being exiled here any more than you."

"I know, which is why I have supported you in your difficulties. Can you not do the same for me?"

"What would you have me do? You know full well that I am power-less to change my circumstances."

"I want you to admit that you no longer need me as companion."

Betsy stood. "Except for you, I do not have a single friend in Europe. My brothers tire of this muddle and wish to make an end of it. Now you too want to leave me alone in my fight against Napoleon. If that is your wish, then sail back to Baltimore as soon as you can find the money to pay your own passage."

Eliza gasped. Betsy flinched when she saw the stricken expression on her friend's face, but her own feelings were in too much turmoil for her to apologize. She hurried from the parlor up to her bedroom, where she allowed herself to weep.

Betsy remained in her room all afternoon, but as the day passed, she grew increasingly ashamed of her thoughtless words. Yet she also remained hurt that Eliza wanted to abandon her.

In the evening, Robert returned to the house, and a few minutes later, he knocked at Betsy's door. She hastily drew a blanket over her nursing baby and called for him to enter.

He sat on the side of the bed closest to her chair. "Eliza told me of your quarrel."

Betsy nodded. "I responded badly. When she first mentioned the legacy, I was happy to hear of it, but when she spoke of leaving, all I could think was how much I need her here."

"She has been a loyal companion, Betsy."

"I know, and I am grateful." She felt baby Jerome pull away from her nipple, so she peeked under the blanket at him. Then she said, "I just feel so alone, and the forces arrayed against me are so daunting."

"Could you not reach some compromise?"

Betsy shifted the baby to her other breast, taking care to remain covered. "How?"

Robert, who had discreetly glanced away, looked at her again. "I think Eliza might be persuaded to stay if she knew that there would be a definite departure date."

"How can I give her that? I have no idea myself how long I must wait for Jerome."

"No, but if we cannot effect a speedy resolution, then it might be better for you to wait at home rather than to linger here in England."

Betsy bit her lip. "Baltimore is so far away, and it will be much more difficult for Jerome to send for me there."

"But it would have the advantage of removing you from the country Napoleon hates most."

"Yes, there is that." Betsy sighed. "I will go speak to Eliza as soon as I am finished here."

Robert left her. Betsy removed the blanket so she could watch baby Jerome as he nursed. After several minutes, he stopped sucking, released her nipple, and relaxed back in her arms. Gazing down at his contented face, Betsy tried to imagine being separated from him for months the way Eliza had been separated from her daughter. The thought made her breasts ache. She rose carefully, placed her son in his cradle, and tucked a light blanket around him. When she felt certain that he remained asleep, Betsy went downstairs.

As soon as she entered the parlor, Eliza stood to leave. Betsy said hastily, "I am sorry. I responded selfishly earlier, and I regret it."

Eliza turned to face her. "You cannot imagine the humiliation of dependency or the utter gall of having a friend fling the fact of your poverty in your face."

"Forgive me. Truly, I was glad to hear about your legacy, and I regret that my first response was to refer to my inconvenience. You have assisted me greatly these last months."

Eliza's expression softened only a little. "I suppose I can stay until you decide what to do."

"You would be doing me the greatest of favors," Betsy said, grateful that her friend had yielded the point yet irritated that Eliza remained aloof. "I know it must be a hardship to be away from your daughter so long."

At that, Eliza finally relaxed her ramrod-straight posture. "I confess that the last few weeks, having the baby in the house has sharpened my longing for my child."

"I see." Betsy gazed at her friend with new understanding. "So will you stay?"

"A little longer."

In early August, Robert received word from a man named O'Meally, a business associate in France, that Paris was buzzing with the gossip that Jerome was expected back from Algiers within the week.

"Surely, he will get word to me then," Betsy exclaimed. "He will be so close that he must be able to find some discreet messenger."

A few days later, a letter addressed to Mrs. Anderson arrived, but when Eliza opened it, she discovered that it came from Dr. Garnier and was intended for Betsy. She handed it over.

As Betsy read the letter, she grew indignant. Garnier wrote that when he reported what happened at Texel, Jerome had been pained to learn of her suffering but even more upset about her decision to sail to England, which he said had damaged his efforts to win over the emperor.

"Jerome cannot have sent this message! His first concern would be my welfare. He would not blame me for seeking what safety I could."

"Consider who wrote that," Robert said. "You told me that you do not trust the doctor."

"No, I know him to be a villain." As Betsy continued to read further, she discovered that Garnier claimed Jerome wanted her to return to the United States and remain there for twelve to eighteen months while he completed his business on the continent.

For a moment, she found it so difficult to breathe that she had to press one hand against her ribs. Then she said, "He tells me to go home and claims that Jerome will not be able to resolve things for a year or more."

"May I see the letter?" Robert asked.

She passed it across to him and waited with a sense of mounting dread while he read it. Finally, he looked up. "Betsy, I cannot accept that Jerome would adopt such a businesslike tone and not send you a single word of affection."

"Then you do not believe this is what he wants me to do."

"Well—" Robert rubbed his chin. "The advice to return to Baltimore has merit. I have given you the same counsel myself. But the letter does not sound like Jerome."

"Why should it?" Eliza asked, looking up from the novel she was reading. "The doctor no doubt knows of Betsy's dislike, so he would hardly be likely to pass on endearments. I think we should evaluate the letter logically, and by that standard, it offers sound advice."

"You think that only because you wish to go home yourself."

Eliza shrugged. "I do not pretend otherwise, but that does not hamper my ability to see the sense in this proposal. Clearly Jerome has found it difficult to persuade the emperor. To stay here wastes your father's resources and antagonizes Napoleon."

"I cannot leave for Baltimore," Betsy whispered. "Not yet."

On Monday, August 12, Betsy received a letter from what she assumed to be another curiosity seeker. Breaking open the seal, she unfolded the page and was astonished to read that Miss Mary Berry wished to call on her to relay a message from Jerome.

"Listen, Eliza! Miss Berry says that last June, Jerome met a friend of hers, the Marchioness of Donegal, in Genoa. He begged Lady Donegal to bring me a message as soon as she came back to England. She has finally returned but is unable to travel to London at present, so she gave Miss Berry the commission. A few more days, and I will finally hear from Jerome."

Eliza looked up from the letter she was writing. "I hope that the message is all you wish."

"Why do you say that? Do you expect bad news?"

Eliza put her quill into a holder at the side of the ink bottle. "I do not know what the message might contain, and neither do you."

Reviewing Miss Berry's letter, Betsy said, "Jerome would not try so urgently to get word to me if he no longer cared."

"No, almost certainly not. But the question of Jerome's sentiment is not really the issue. The more important point is whether his brother has changed his mind."

Betsy sighed. "I think we can assume that the message would not be sent with such secrecy if Napoleon had yielded."

When Miss Berry called a few days later, she turned out to be a plump, forty-year-old woman about Betsy's height. She wore a grey short-sleeved gown with a lace ruffle around the neck and a grey bonnet with a matching ruffle and white ostrich plume, decidedly feminine attire that Betsy thought was intended to compensate for her plain face.

Miss Berry curtsied. "Madame Bonaparte, I am so happy to make your acquaintance. Lady Donegal was devastated that family matters kept her from town. She sent me in her stead so you could receive your husband's message as soon as possible."

"Thank you," Betsy said, gesturing to one of the twin armchairs while she sat on the sofa beside Eliza. "What did Mr. Bonaparte say?"

The older woman laughed in a coquettish way. "Well, he particularly wanted to convey that his sentiments and intentions toward you are unchanged. He has not been able to write because he is closely watched. Oh, and he also wished you to know that he is in good health and very well liked at Genoa."

"Very well liked," Betsy repeated, wondering why Jerome thought that significant.

"Yes." Miss Berry nodded emphatically. "Lady Donegal said he wishes to make a good impression on his superior officers."

"Oh, I see."

"Lady Donegal also wished me to convey that she has friends in Genoa and would be more than happy to use them to get a message to Mr. Bonaparte."

"Thank you. That is a great comfort to me."

"I would be happy to wait." Miss Berry settled her ample bottom firmly in her chair.

Realizing that her visitor expected her to write immediately, Betsy said, "Thank you for your kindness, Miss Berry, but I believe that my husband is still at sea. Please tell the marchioness that I will avail myself of her kindness soon."

"Certainly." Miss Berry glanced around the room. "I understand from the newspapers that you have recently given birth to a son."

"Yes." Betsy noticed the woman's avid expression. "He is asleep right now."

"Of course." With a show of reluctance, Miss Berry rose. "Then I will take my leave."

"Thank you so much for taking the trouble to call," Betsy said as she walked her visitor into the hall. After saying farewell, she returned to the drawing room. "What a gossipy old spinster. But at least now I know that Jerome is not changed toward me."

"As of six weeks ago," Eliza said without looking up from her sewing.

"That is a cruel thing to say."

"Cruel? I thought it merely accurate." Reaching the end of a row, Eliza knotted off her sewing and snipped the thread. "To own the truth, I find it difficult to be optimistic about your Jerome, but perhaps I should not assume that he will turn out like my Henry."

"I should think not," Betsy said, offended that Eliza would compare Jerome to her runaway husband. "The two cases are not at all alike. Jerome had no choice but to leave me."

"I daresay Henry thought he had no choice either, what with the creditors at his heels."

Stunned at discovering this unexpected vein of bitterness in her friend, Betsy left the room before they started another quarrel.

As summer moved toward autumn, Betsy's resolve eroded. The time that Mr. O'Meally gave for Jerome's stay in Paris elapsed without any communication. As each new day passed without a message, Betsy found it more difficult to believe that her husband was making progress in effecting their reunion. She did not fear that Jerome had ceased to love her, but she realized as never before what a determined adversary Napoleon was. She began to feel like Prometheus, with her torment renewed every day as though the gods had sentenced her to eternal punishment. By the beginning of September, she was flayed raw by repeated disappointment.

Baby Jerome was her sole joy, and she spent hours chattering to him, telling him about his father and spinning tales of what his future would be once he was acknowledged as a prince. The first time he smiled in response to her voice Betsy longed desperately to share the accomplishment with Jerome. Instead, she wrote long letters to Baltimore.

Finally, on the two-month anniversary of her son's birth, Betsy went down to breakfast and announced, "I have changed my mind. It is too lonely here, and I miss our mother. Robert, I would like to go home."

᭬ XIX ᭬

Bᴇᴛsʏ, Robert, and Eliza sailed from England in late September and arrived in Baltimore on November 14. Even though Betsy detested her hometown, she felt relief when the ship docked in the familiar square-shaped harbor with its jutting wooden piers and three-and-four-story warehouses crowding the waterfront. As Robert walked the few blocks to fetch the family coach, Betsy stood on deck holding her son and watching freight wagons and carriages pass on Pratt Street. Irrationally, she hoped to glimpse her father going about his daily business.

She had been standing there a few minutes when Eliza joined her at the railing. Betsy recalled the day—it seemed so long ago now—that the two of them had stood together gazing at England for the first time. "Thank you, Eliza, for all your help these past few months. I do not know how I could have gotten on without you."

Eliza reached over to tuck the baby's blanket more firmly in place to protect him from the chill. "I am sorry for your sake that your voyage did not have a more satisfactory ending."

Betsy sighed. "Yes, I had hoped that—well, you know my hopes as well as anyone. The important thing now is that you will soon be with your daughter again."

An hour later, Robert dropped Betsy and her maid at South Street and then escorted Eliza home. Betsy hesitated before the marble stoop, overwhelmed by a sense that she was returning as a failure. Baltimore society would see her as an abandoned wife, no matter how much she might protest that Jerome intended to come back for her.

Telling herself that lingering in the street would only confirm the impression that she had slunk home in shame, Betsy climbed the steps. The front door opened and her mother stood before her, laughing and crying simultaneously. In the shadowy passageway behind Dorcas lurked the dark figure of Mammy Sue.

"Oh, my child!" Dorcas exclaimed as Betsy entered the hall.

As Jenny closed the door behind her, Betsy held out her dozing baby. "Here is your first grandson, Mother."

"Hello, precious." Dorcas took him in her arms and pushed back the blanket from his face. "He is so big!"

"Yes." Betsy unknotted her ribbons, removed her bonnet, and handed it and her cloak to Jenny. "I cannot account for his vigor because we went for weeks without enough food, but he was a large baby even at birth. I think he must have inherited his uncle's determination to devour the whole world."

Standing back at a respectful distance, Mammy Sue cleared her throat, and Dorcas handed her the baby. The wet nurse clucked at him. "Miss Betsy, I see you only brought back that slip of a maid on the ship. Who has been feeding this child?"

"I am. That is what the doctor recommended."

"Fool doctors don't know anything. You can turn him over to me."

"No!" Betsy cried, determined not to relinquish that special bond with her son. "He is used to my milk, and I do not want to upset him after all he has been through."

Mammy Sue frowned and made to hand the baby back, but Betsy added, "Of course, I need your help with other aspects of his care."

"Yes, ma'am, if you say so." As Mammy Sue carried the still-sleeping baby upstairs, she began to sing a song Betsy recognized from the past.

Betsy took her mother by the arm and walked into the drawing room. There she felt an immediate sense of refuge at sight of her mother's familiar banister-back chair by the fireplace. Before sitting on the sofa, Betsy crossed to the hearth to stare at the portrait of her mother holding her when she was a baby. "I was right. I did not think my son resembled me. He is a Bonaparte through and through."

"He is a handsome boy. Jerome has not seen him?"

Sadness tightened her throat, so Betsy shook her head.

"Have you heard from him since your separation?"

"Only a few messages. His associates would have us believe that it will take a year or more to win the emperor's favor." Betsy gazed at the painting a moment longer and then blurted, "Oh Mother! I try to keep my faith, but sometimes I am so frightened." She turned to Dorcas, who pulled her into an embrace.

WILLIAM PATTERSON ARRIVED home about seven. After curtly welcoming his daughter, he asked, "Where do you propose to live?"

Betsy felt a prickle of anxiety. "I would hope to stay here until I can set up my own establishment, which is what Jerome wishes me to do."

Her father folded his arms across his chest. "Jerome's wishes no longer carry much weight in this family. As for setting up your own establishment, with whose money do you propose to do that?"

Taken aback, Betsy glanced at her mother. Dorcas said, "Mr. Patterson, this is not the time for that discussion. Tonight is Betsy's homecoming."

"As you wish. I expect to see you in my counting house in the morning, Elizabeth."

Betsy swallowed back her annoyance that he would talk to her as though she were still a child. "Yes, sir. I will attend you there after breakfast."

THE NEXT DAY as Betsy sat before her father's desk in his private office, she watched with misgiving as Patterson pulled a sheaf of papers from a drawer. "Do you have any idea how much money this ill-fated marriage of yours has cost me?"

"I know that refitting the *Erin* and supplying the provisions were expensive."

"Two hundred and ninety dollars the food alone cost me." He pulled a paper from the stack and waved it before her. "But that is not the half of it. What about the money you spent during your sojourn in England, drawn upon my accounts? What about the time my two oldest sons frittered away on your concerns rather than attending to business?"

His sons, Betsy noted, rather than her brothers. "I am sorry, Father, to have been a burden to the family, but I had no way of knowing beforehand how the voyage would turn out."

"On the contrary, my girl. We had every reason to suppose that Jerome Bonaparte was a man without honor."

"Father, be fair! He may have committed indiscretions in his youth, but since our marriage, his conduct has been blameless. As for the opposition we encountered, Napoleon was not emperor when we wed, so how could we anticipate his objections?"

"I do not speak of Napoleon." Patterson began to shuffle through the sheaf of papers. "I am referring to your husband's complete lack of self-control."

Betsy dug her nails into her palm. "Did you not hear me say that he has behaved impeccably since our marriage?"

"Impeccably? Did he not lie about his age?" He fixed Betsy with a piercing stare. "And what is worse, he left Baltimore owing hundreds of dollars in debts that I have had to pay to uphold our family's reputation. Look at this!" He pulled out a receipt for $373 that he had paid to a gunsmith and flung it across the desk. "What need had Jerome for a double-barreled gun and a pair of pistols?"

Tossing more receipts her way, he said, "This is his tailor's bill, a sum that would keep any reasonable man in clothing for a lifetime. Here are bills for the blacksmith and stable. Here is a bill for jewelry. Here is a wine merchant's bill. All unpaid, all past due. It has taken me months and cost me several thousand dollars to clean up his profligacy."

Tears filled Betsy's eyes. "According to you, this is the worst of it, not that the emperor casts doubt on my honor and my son's legitimacy, but that my husband cost you money?"

Her father stopped, taken aback by her charge. Then fury consumed him again. "It is all of a piece. A man of honor protects his family's reputation in all things. You chose badly, Elizabeth, and I have had to pay for your foolishness."

"But I had no idea he was running up debts. He told me he had funds."

"You should have realized he was lying."

"How?" She pushed the papers back at him. "You never discuss your financial dealings with Mother. Why would you suppose Jerome was any more forthcoming with me?"

"I do not imagine that he was." Her father collected the scattered receipts and made a great show of putting them back in order—except a single folded page he left upon the desk. "What I do know is that I raised you to live without ostentation, and if you had held to my teachings, none of this would have happened."

"How could I? You always taught me that a wife's duty is to obey her husband, yet now you blame me because I did not compel Jerome to live by your standards."

"No, I blame you for having married him. I knew from the beginning that nothing good could come from this connection, but I let you have your way to keep you from committing scandal. Now do you see that I was right?"

Betsy stood, drawing herself up to her full height, short as it was. "Forgive me, sir, if I dare to hope that you are wrong. For the sake of my son, I must continue to seek a reunion with his father. If Jerome ever returns to us, then rest assured I shall ask him to repay you. Store your receipts meticulously like the exacting businessman you are so that when that day comes, you can make an accurate accounting."

"Never fear, I intend to." Patterson returned the receipts to the drawer and slammed it.

As Betsy turned to leave, her father said, "Elizabeth, there is one more thing." He slid the single folded page across his desk. "This came from Jerome's secretary in September. I did not want to trouble you with it while you were in England, but now that you are home, you should know what it says."

With dread, Betsy resumed her seat and read the letter, skipping through it to find the lines that concerned her most directly.

Your daughter has far removed, if not destroyed forever, the possibility of a reconciliation.... Finding in Holland orders which prohibited her landing on the French territory, she imprudently went to London, instead of going to a neutral port.... The Emperor, in a letter which Mr. Bonaparte received yesterday, expressed to him a strong dissatisfaction.... However, Mr. Bonaparte begs me to assure you that

he will never deviate from the principles of honor and delicacy....
He desires you to rely entirely upon him, and let time obliterate the
first impressions made on the mind of the Emperor.

Betsy felt close to despair as she met her father's eyes. "This is why you think he will never return."

"I do not see how to put any other construction upon it."

She shook her head. "I think Jerome must be under continual harassment, or he never would have commissioned Le Camus to write such a letter. The accusation that I willfully went to London is unjust. Amsterdam was supposed to be a neutral port, yet the French fired upon us there. Afterward, I begged William to sail anywhere but England, but Captain Stephenson feared we would receive the same rude welcome at Emden or Bremen. Garnier was supposed to explain all that to Jerome, but he may have misrepresented my plight."

"On the contrary, I think Jerome knows all too well that you had little choice if you were to preserve the well-being of your child. This letter is a cowardly attempt to blame you rather than own to the fact of Napoleon's tyranny."

Looking down at the letter again, she pointed at one line with her forefinger. "But Le Camus says that Jerome still hopes to win over the emperor."

"That is a fool's hope."

"We do not know that yet."

"Betsy," Patterson said, using her nickname for the first time since her return, "I believe Stephenson was right. You would have been harassed as you were at Texel in any other continental port. Emden is part of Holland, and the French occupy Bremen. Napoleon made sure you would have no place to go except England because he wanted to discredit you in Jerome's eyes."

"But he has not given me up, Father. Two weeks after Le Camus wrote this, Jerome sent a message through an Englishwoman. He is diligently trying to make a good impression so he can bring about our reunion."

Patterson's tone grew sharp again. "The longer you cling to that hope, the more painful it will be once you have to accept that Napoleon has separated you forever."

Betsy lifted her chin. "For the sake of my son and my own honor, I must continue to fight for recognition of our marriage."

Her father pounded his desk. "That marriage was a deal made with a scoundrel. You would do better to accept it as a bad bargain and move on."

"Jerome is not a shipment of spoiled cargo to be deducted from my ledger!"

Patterson shook his head. "Of all my children, you have always been the most stubborn. Have it your own way, but do not expect me to keep bailing you out of your difficulties."

"I would not dream of it, sir," she retorted and took her leave.

HER FIRST SUNDAY back, Betsy walked with her parents to First Presbyterian Church, two blocks from their home. With a membership composed mostly of successful merchants like William Patterson, the Presbyterians had the wealthiest congregation in Baltimore. Their church building was an impressive structure nicknamed the "Two Steeple Church" because it had twin octagonal belfries on either side of a classical temple front.

The reading for that Sunday was from Ecclesiastes: "Cast thy bread upon the waters: for thou shalt find it after many days." Building upon that verse, the Reverend Dr. Inglis gave a long sermon analyzing how God rewards the good that people do, if not in this life, then in the next. As he droned on, building an intricately reasoned argument by quoting ancient philosophers and the Bible with equal ease, Betsy felt like a tightly lidded boiler about to explode. So God always rewarded good deeds, did He? Then why was she suffering for something that was not her fault? What had she ever done to deserve the way Napoleon had treated her?

Betsy and her mother waited on the front steps after the service as Patterson spoke at length to Dr. Inglis about church finances. As Betsy tried to mask her impatience at standing in the cutting November wind, one of the elders' wives approached them. Mrs. Finley was a humorless dowager of about fifty, whom Betsy avoided whenever possible.

"It was a good sermon, do you not agree?" Mrs. Finley asked.

"Oh, yes," Dorcas replied. "Dr. Inglis is such a scholar."

"And what about you, Betsy? Did you not find it edifying?"

Annoyed that the woman had addressed her familiarly as though she were still an unmarried girl, Betsy longed to answer sarcastically. For her mother's sake, she remained polite. "Indeed, it was a prodigious example of the art of preaching."

Mrs. Finley rummaged in her reticule for a handkerchief. "It is a pity that he did not expound a different verse from today's reading: 'Vanity of vanities, sayeth the preacher; all is vanity.' That subject would have been so pertinent."

"How so?"

Looking up, Mrs. Finley said, "Why, I am thinking of your unfortunate marriage, my dear. I was saying to Mr. Finley that your example is the perfect illustration of the maxim *Pride goeth before destruction and a haughty spirit before a fall.*"

Betsy narrowed her eyes but kept her tone as sweet as marzipan. "I can see why that would be a favorite verse of yours. It must afford you much comfort."

Mrs. Finley frowned. "I fail to take your meaning."

"Why, simply that with so little personal merit to take pride in, you need never worry about a fall." As the other woman's mouth fell open, Betsy curtsied. "Good day, madam."

SEVERAL DAYS LATER, Marianne Caton came to call, dressed in an elegant three-quarter-length pelisse of dark green trimmed with brown fur. Beneath the coat, the beautiful seventeen-year-old wore a white dress decorated with an Egyptian motif of lotus flowers. Gazing at the stylish ensemble, Betsy was acutely aware that she had purchased no new clothes for nearly a year.

The friends kissed each other on the cheek, and then Betsy hung her visitor's coat on a peg in the hall while Marianne walked into the drawing room with her slow, gliding gait. She had once explained that, as a child, she trained herself to walk deliberately because she had asthma, and when her attacks occurred, hurried movements only worsened the wheezing.

Betsy followed Marianne into the drawing room and joined her on the sofa. Marianne patted her hand. "I was so sorry to hear of your difficulties in Europe. What do you hear from Mr. Bonaparte?"

"He is still hopeful of changing his brother's mind. He has been doing his part in the war, and if he wins great renown, he will insist on having our marriage recognized."

"What a clever plan!"

Betsy smiled thinly. "I fear that we may not resolve the issue until the war is over, so in the meantime, my son and I will live here."

Lowering her eyes, Marianne toyed with the gold-chain bracelet she always wore on her left arm. "Oh, I do not think I could bear to be separated from my husband so long."

"It is not uncommon during wartime." Betsy looked at her friend quizzically. "But perhaps you are thinking of someone in particular when you express a dread of separation?"

Marianne blushed and shook her head. "No. I have had many eligible suitors, but you must recall what it is like to be courted by men who are nice enough but fail to capture your heart."

"Yes, I remember what that is like."

After a pause, Marianne asked, "How was England? Were you presented at court?"

Shaking her head, Betsy answered, "No, how could I be? My brother-in-law was threatening to invade. I lived very quietly."

"But surely you followed the theatre and fashion?"

Betsy sat back and gazed at the younger woman in disbelief. Marianne had never before struck her as foolish, but the questions she was asking now were exceedingly silly.

"My situation was most irregular," she answered, trying hard to keep her scorn from her voice. "I knew the emperor would be displeased at my going among his enemies, a measure I took only because of the impending birth of my son. The newspapers hounded me, so for most of my time there, I lived as retired a life as possible."

Marianne's face lit up. "How old is your boy?"

"He is four-and-a-half months old and very healthy."

"May I see him? Whenever I visit my uncle and aunt, I love playing with my cousins."

"All right." Instead of ringing for a servant, Betsy went up to the nursery herself. Baby Jerome was awake and amusing himself by sucking his toes, so she lifted him from his cradle. He gurgled with happiness at seeing her.

"What are you doing?" Mammy Sue asked from the other side of the room where she was changing Mary Ann's diaper. "It ain't time to feed that child."

"We have a visitor." Betsy carried him downstairs, murmuring that he was about to meet one of Mama's friends and must show what a little prince he was.

"Here is Jerome Napoleon," she announced, resuming her place on the sofa and holding her son under his arms so he could sit upright on her knee. She bounced him slightly, and he gave a half squealing, half hiccupping laugh.

"He looks like his father," Marianne said, making an exaggerated face to amuse him.

"Yes, he is definitely a little Bonaparte. My bonny Bonaparte boy." The alliteration pleased Betsy.

"What a comfort he must be to you."

"Yes." Betsy rested the baby against her shoulder. He was sucking his fist, and some of his drool ran down her neck, but she did not care. "I must own that I am taken aback by how fiercely I love him. I am no stranger to babies, but the feeling is different when he is your own."

Marianne sighed. "I envy you. It almost seems worth it to accept the first eligible man who makes me an offer so I can start a family."

"Law, you surprise me. A girl's days as a belle are so brief. Do not trade them away for the tedium of child-rearing."

"But you said that you love your son."

"I do. So much that I would fight the emperor himself if it would secure my son's birthright. That does not mean I cannot wish things were different. If Mr. Bonaparte and I had been more deliberate and gained his mother's consent before we married, I would not now be living in exile."

Marianne's brown eyes widened. "You are in your parents' house. How can you refer to this as exile?"

Shaking her head, Betsy said, "My son by rights is an imperial prince, and his place is at court where he can be educated in a manner befitting his rank."

"It sounds strange to hear an American talk of princely rank. My grandfather says that one of the glories of the United States is that we have no titles."

Betsy shrugged as well as she was able with the baby upon her shoulder. "I have never seen much virtue in living in a republic. Ever since I was at Madame Lacomb's school, I have longed to live in Europe. Their traditions have more weight than our raw customs."

"Grandfather does say that Europeans have finer art and music." Marianne fingered her bracelet again and then picked up her gloves from the cushion beside her. "I fear I have stayed too long, but I so enjoy talking with you again. I hope to see you often this winter. My uncle is giving a party at Homewood the end of this month, and I will have him invite you."

The desire to enjoy a bit of uncomplicated pleasure flared up within Betsy, but she firmly doused it. "My husband's absence makes my attendance impossible."

"Nonsense. Bring one of your brothers as escort."

Betsy saw Marianne to the door. As she turned to take the baby back upstairs, Betsy murmured, "Did you like her, little Bo?" She halted on the bottom step, realizing that she had just given him a nickname. "Bo," she repeated and held the word in her mouth as though tasting it. Deciding that it suited the boy, she hummed as she went upstairs.

THE INVITATION ARRIVED the following week, and Betsy decided to attend the party after all. Such an occasion would give her a chance to meet most of Baltimore society at one time and get past any sharp remarks people cared to make. She was also curious to see Homewood, the much-praised mansion that Charles Carroll Jr. had been building since 1801.

After considering Marianne's idea of asking one of her brothers to escort her, Betsy decided that the most suitable choice was Robert. Since his time in Europe, he had acquired more fashionable clothing and polished manners.

Robert agreed, and the night of the dance they drove together to Homewood, located in farmland about three miles north of town. As one concession to her altered circumstances, Betsy wore a chemise beneath her gown so that no one could accuse her of immodesty.

Homewood lived up to its high reputation. Built of red brick, it was an impressive five-part structure: a one-and-a-half story central block and two pavilions linked to the center building by narrow wings. A portico supported by four pillars graced the entrance.

As Betsy ascended the wide marble steps with Robert, she noticed that the entrance incorporated many of the design elements found at her uncle Smith's mansion Montebello, begun two years before Homewood. Both houses had reeded pilasters flanking double front doors, topped by a semicircular fanlight and a cornice carved with a wave design. Betsy smiled in satisfaction that her family, not the Carrolls, should have taken the lead in matters of architectural distinction.

Then she entered the house holding onto Robert's arm. In the front reception hall—whose walls were covered with fashionable and expensive green paint—Charles Carroll Jr. and his wife Harriet greeted their guests. The thirty-year-old Charles had bloodshot blue eyes and a weak mouth, and when he welcomed Betsy, she noticed that his breath smelled of brandy. His wife, standing next to him, was a pretty woman with lustrous brown hair and large brown eyes, but her face wore a strained expression.

Robert and Betsy moved through the receiving line and into the cross hall, where they could glimpse several rooms. The interior of the house was decorated with elegant fanlights, pilasters flanking doorways, and plasterwork medallions on the ceilings. The floors were covered with Belgian carpets, and the very best American craftsmanship furnished the rooms.

Marianne approached them. "I am so glad you decided to come."

After the two young women kissed, Betsy said, "Miss Caton, this is my brother, Robert Patterson. You may not have met recently as he has been in Europe these last two years."

Marianne curtsied, and Robert asked for her a dance, which she granted. As she moved away to greet someone else, Robert murmured, "What a lovely young lady."

"Yes, and from such a prominent family." Betsy laughed and then saw from the flash in Robert's eyes that he was in no mood to be teased. "She is a sweet girl."

"I suppose she is much sought after," he said, tilting his head to watch Marianne pass gracefully through the doorway that led to the back reception hall.

"From what she told me the other day, I believe she has a great many suitors, but—" Pausing, Betsy considered what Marianne had told her in confidence. Finally, she said, "There is no reason why you might not be one of their number."

Robert looked at her quizzically, but she simply smiled.

Once the music began to play, Betsy was pleased to discover that many men clamored to pay attention to her. And because she spent so much time dancing, women had little opportunity to make barbed comments about Jerome's absence.

Betsy found that being at a party after such a long drought reminded her poignantly of her husband. Despite the problems that had attended her marriage, she still found Jerome more desirable than any of her dance partners. To her surprise, the physical proximity to other men made her ache sexually for her husband, the first such desire she had felt since giving birth.

During the supper break, as Betsy spoke to family friend Robert Gilmor, she spotted her brother talking to Marianne. The younger beauty had ducked her head but was gazing up at him through thick eyelashes. *Ah,* Betsy thought, recognizing the classic coquette's glance. *Robert may have more chance with her than he realizes.*

❧ XX ❧

ALTHOUGH Jerome had left the furnishings he bought in storage, Betsy had no money to rent a house. She remained at South Street and moved back into the small bedroom that had been hers before her marriage. As a result, Joseph had to move back into the third-floor chamber he used to share with Edward, which caused both brothers to grumble. Their mother tried to stifle the complaints by explaining that Betsy needed to be near the nursery, but that did not stop the boys from referring to their sister as "the princess." Betsy believed they were encouraged in their disdain by the condescension with which their father treated her, a coldness that did not abate no matter how much she tried to fit into the household.

She remembered Eliza's words: "You cannot imagine the humiliation of dependency." Now that Betsy found herself in the same predicament, she felt ashamed of her earlier lack of sympathy.

Betsy invited her friend to tea in December, and when Eliza arrived, she displayed no lingering resentment over their quarrels in England. Instead, she kissed Betsy's cheek and then, as she removed her gloves and bonnet, said, "Forgive me for not calling earlier. I have been attending to the details of my uncle's estate and making plans for my future."

Taking Eliza's cloak, Betsy noticed that not only were her friend's cheeks pink from the cold, but her eyes sparkled with excitement. "What plans? You seem in such high spirits."

"Wait until we are seated," Eliza answered. They walked together into the drawing room, where they sat on the shield-back chairs at the table near the front windows. As Betsy picked up her mother's fine china teapot, Eliza announced, "I am going to write articles for *The Companion and Weekly Miscellany.* They cannot pay much, but by combining my earnings with my legacy, I may eventually be able to rent a house for my daughter and myself."

Passing Eliza a filled cup and saucer, Betsy asked, "A journal has agreed to publish you even though you are a woman?"

"Well—" Eliza spooned sugar into her tea. "The author will be listed as 'Anonymous.' But it will be a way for me to start using my talents to make a life of purpose and contribution. Perhaps I can build on this and, in time, publish a book of essays or a novel."

Betsy handed her the plate of shortbread. "I did not suspect that you harbored such ambitions."

"I could not tell you until I had proved that I had the requisite talent. When I showed the editor of *The Companion* some essays I wrote, he was very impressed." Eliza laughed and then gave Betsy a brief summary of the essays. She concluded, "I must confess that I sent them to him under my husband's name, so the editor would evaluate the work as though it were written by a man. He wrote back requesting an appointment with Mr. Anderson, and I arrived instead."

"You are fortunate he did not throw you out of his office."

"Oh, Betsy, what would that matter? I would have tried again with someone else. Do you not see? A new age is dawning in which women will claim their place alongside men. You cannot keep half of humanity subservient and hope to make progress! By the time my daughter is grown, I hope that women will be able to manage their own property and perhaps even vote."

"That will never happen," Betsy said, thinking what a difference it would make if she had money of her own. "Men like my father would never allow such a change."

"It is up to women to demand it. Betsy, you are clever. Instead of moping about waiting to hear from Mr. Bonaparte, why don't you do something with your talents? Improve your own lot and the lot of other women."

"Eliza, I cannot. If I am to have any hope of appeasing the emperor, I must not do anything he would judge unseemly."

After taking a bite of shortbread, Eliza asked, "So you still believe that your husband will return for you?"

"Until I hear from his own hand that he has repudiated me, I must continue to hope."

"I know you may not wish to hear this, but I must try to spare you some of the heartache I have endured. Judging from my experience, a man who deserts his wife rarely owns to it in a forthright manner. One of the agonies of our lot is the wearying uncertainty of never knowing absolutely that the scoundrel is gone forever."

Betsy's eyes filled with tears at that accurate summation of her plight, yet she forced herself to say, "Jerome did not leave of his own accord. I cannot believe that he would allow me to suffer such prolonged ambiguity."

"I pray that you are right."

They drank their tea in silence for a minute, and then Betsy said, "You would scarce believe how much baby Jerome has changed the last month. He responds to his name now, and he laughs if I show him his reflection in a mirror."

"I wish I could see him." Eliza stood and brushed crumbs from her skirt. "I am sorry to leave so soon, but I am obliged to finish an essay I promised to give the editor tomorrow."

Disappointed at her hasty departure, Betsy said, "Thank you for coming when you are so occupied."

They walked together to the hall, and Eliza departed. After closing the front door, Betsy leaned against it wearily. For a moment her mind raced with questions about whether it would be possible to use her talents to earn a living. Then Betsy realized that she had spoken the truth. Because of her rank by marriage, she could not be seen to do anything menial or common. She would have to continue to wait upon Jerome and pray that he won her a place at court.

Each morning when Betsy woke up, she faced a day very like the one before with a never-ending schedule of child rearing, domestic obligations, utilitarian needlework, and social calls. Her life was as tedious as if she had never met Jerome—more so, because she could no longer dream of escaping by marriage. Her visits to Washington and New York had only confirmed her opinion that Baltimore was a cultural desert with little to offer a person of intellect. Often as she sat at her dressing table brushing her hair or in the nursery feeding Bo, she drifted into memories of the parties she had attended with Jerome. She spent hours dwelling upon past social triumphs because the memory of more intimate moments stirred her passion and made her irritable.

When Betsy attended parties that winter, she discovered that local attitudes toward her had changed. Now that she was perceived as an abandoned wife, many people saw her as more pitiable than fascinating. Some of the young women who had formerly resented her as their chief competitor for beaux could not resist expressing glee at her downfall. At one ball, a former schoolmate interrupted Betsy as she recounted her experience at Texel. "Napoleon certainly showed you how pathetic your pretensions to rank are."

"On the contrary, the fact that the emperor went to such pains to keep me from the continent proves that he views me as a rival worthy of respect. Not that I would expect you to understand the satisfaction of receiving such a mark of esteem."

After receiving a few such lightning-quick jabs, the young women of Baltimore learned to keep their venom to themselves. Betsy had no doubt, however, that they gloated about her situation behind her back.

For the first few months after her return, no news came from Europe. Because of the difficulties of sailing the Atlantic in winter, Betsy did not expect to hear from Jerome, yet her heart still lurched painfully each time mail arrived or a knock sounded on the door. The second anniversary of her marriage passed without anyone marking the occasion, and Betsy lay awake most of that night crying.

As the weeks passed, she began to imagine terrible things. When she learned of the Battle of Trafalgar, in which the British navy had routed a combined Spanish and French fleet in October 1805, Betsy's fears sharpened. For all she knew, Jerome's ship might have been one of the twenty or so vessels lost, leaving her a widow and her son fatherless.

The only thing that kept her from sinking into a swamp of despair was Bo, who was an even-tempered, healthy baby. By January, he could sit on his own, and he even said *Mama*—a title that made Betsy as proud as if someone had called her *Princess*. Whenever she felt despondent over the silence from Jerome, she would place Bo on her lap and read or sing to him in French, so he would learn his father's language.

The suspicions Betsy formed the night of the Homewood dance turned out to be correct, and Robert began to court Marianne Caton. On one of Marianne's visits to Betsy, she confided that her mother had doubts about the match. "She wants me to marry someone with a plantation."

Recalling the bankruptcy brought about by the disastrous commercial investments of Marianne's father, Betsy could understand Mrs. Caton's concerns, so she said, "My father might be a merchant, but he has invested half of his wealth in property."

"That was prudent," Marianne said lightly and shook Bo's rattle at him.

The conversation lingered with Betsy. She did not want Marianne's family to scorn Robert because of his mercantile background. On the other hand, Betsy was not sure she favored the match. Marianne was sweet-tempered and undemanding, and she kept herself unnaturally calm in an effort to control her asthma. Yet, she spent much of her time talking about clothes, parties, and music, mingled with jarring references to works of Catholic piety such as Pascal's *Pensées*. Robert's two main interests were commerce and horses, and he was not at all religious. Whenever Betsy saw them together, she noticed that her brother barely spoke while Marianne prattled about the latest novel or the last eminent person to visit her grandfather. The dissimilarity between their temperaments troubled Betsy.

The budding romance tried her nerves in another way. Both Marianne and Robert used their time with her to probe for information about each other, and Betsy felt increasingly slighted. Even worse, watching them exchange tender glances and coy smiles was like having grit thrown in the open wound of her loneliness.

In February, shortly after Betsy's twenty-first birthday, Marianne accepted Robert's proposal, and the two families began to negotiate a marriage contract. William Patterson took every opportunity to praise his son's intended: "She comes from a good republican family, and her demeanor is everything a young woman's should be. She is gentle and unassuming, not puffed up about her beauty or unduly ambitious."

Betsy was convinced that such statements were directed at her, and the effusive tributes planted seeds of resentment toward her friend. *No one can be as perfect as Marianne pretends to be. Someday they may find out that a reservoir of vinegar lurks beneath all that sugar.*

Despite such lapses into bitterness, Betsy tried to be glad about the upcoming marriage. At least, she would gain a sister closer to her age than thirteen-year-old Margaret, and if Marianne had a baby right away, Bo would have a cousin to play with.

As SPRING ARRIVED, so did ships with news from Europe, and Betsy learned that Napoleon had won a stunning victory at Austerlitz in Austria on December 2, exactly one year after his coronation. A French army of fewer than 70,000 had smashed a combined force of 90,000 Austrians and Russians. The French victory was so one-sided that Francis I of Austria had been forced to make peace, while the tsar returned to Russia in defeat.

After reading the accounts, Betsy said to her mother, "Another victory like this and perhaps the war will end, and the emperor will no longer feel it necessary to form defensive alliances for France. Perhaps he will allow Jerome to recall me to Europe."

"I hope so, dear," Dorcas said, barely looking up from her sewing.

In April, Betsy received a series of letters that Jerome had written the previous October in Paris. Whether the six-month-old correspondence was delayed by the vagaries of shipping or the interference of Napoleon's secret police, Betsy could not tell, but she was ecstatic to hear from Jerome directly rather than through intermediaries.

The first letter was dated October 4, the day he arrived in Paris: "Life holds nothing for me without you and my son. We, my dear Elisa, will be separated a short time longer, but eventually our misery will end. Be calm, your husband will never abandon you."

In the second letter, dated October 7, Jerome wrote explicit instructions:

*If you go to the United States, I insist, these are my orders, that you
live in your own house; that you keep four horses, and that you live
in a suitable manner, as though I were to arrive at any moment; tell
your father, whom I love as though he were my own, that I should like
it thus, and that I have special reasons for wishing it so.*

Reading that, Betsy felt a pain like a hot poker stabbing her side. She
set the letter aside to show her father, but she knew it would make no
difference. Even though she had been home for five months, he still
found ways nearly every day to remind her of the expense and trouble
she had cost him. He would never agree to set her up in a house just
because Jerome had "special reasons for wishing it so."

In a letter from October 16, Jerome wrote in a more dejected mood:

*You know how much I love Octavius, Jeromia, and the other children;
you can therefore imagine how I shall adore my own son, ill-starred
from the day he was born. He has not even known the gentle embrace
of his unfortunate father. At least, my Elisa, take the greatest care of
him, teach him to love and respect his father and tell him, "Your father
will always prefer you to distinctions, a fortune, and all the glitter of
high rank." I have never had the fatal thought of leaving you, my good
wife, but am acting as an honorable man, a brave and loyal soldier;
I do without my wife, without my son, to fight a war and defend my
country and after I have fulfilled the obligations of a brother of the
Emperor, I shall fulfill those of a father and a husband.*

Even though she knew it made no sense to try to make a nine-month-
old child understand, Betsy immediately carried that letter upstairs and
read it to Bo. To be able to hear the sound of Jerome's own words at
last was like being able to eat the first morsel of pastry after months
of illness in which all she could take was broth.

The following week, shouting in the street below caused Betsy to
rise from the sofa where she sat sewing and look out the window. To
her astonishment, she saw her brother Joseph jump down from the
driver's seat of a wagon and gesture to two workingmen who rode in
back. Joseph hurried in the house and into the drawing room. "Betsy, why did you fail to warn Father that you were expecting a shipment from England?"

"What?"

"Two crates have arrived from the London, and they are directed to you." He pivoted and went outside again.

Heavy footsteps sounded in the hall. The two laborers came through the doorway, set down the wooden containers—one larger than the other—and stood there awkwardly.

Joseph re-entered the room with a crowbar. He handed it to the brawnier of the two men, who pried off the lids with ease. Then the men left.

Seeing fabric in the larger crate, Betsy went to it and saw that it contained several folded garments. On top were two letters addressed to her. The first one was from a Lady Elgin, whom Jerome had asked to convey a box of presents to Betsy in London. "Your husband especially wished me to say that the only pleasure he has known since your separation was the act of selecting the most beautiful gifts for his most beloved wife."

For an instant, Betsy was carried back to the morning after her wedding when Jerome had surprised her with a bedroom full of French fashions. Now, he was repeating the gesture to prove that his love had not diminished.

The other letter, from a Mrs. McKenzie, explained that Lady Elgin had sent the crates to her husband's shipping firm, but by the time they arrived in London, Betsy had already sailed.

As Betsy pulled out the clothes, she saw that Parisian fashions had changed. None of these gowns were sheer. Some were of lined muslin, while others were silk in shades of rose, jonquil, and pearl grey. One was even a deep rich brown. More decoration also seemed to be in vogue. The brown evening gown had a center panel with inserts of cream-colored diamonds, while a muslin gown was embroidered with sunflowers stitched in gilt thread and further embellished with gold sequins.

After Betsy had removed the dresses, she found three hatboxes, each containing an elaborately trimmed bonnet—one of which featured a bunch of silk violets that reminded her of the nosegay Jerome had bought her in Lisbon. The crate also held fine undergarments. "This is an entire wardrobe," she exclaimed to her mother. Excitedly, Betsy hurried to the large gilt-framed mirror that hung on the wall near her father's desk and held up a deep blue gown trimmed in exquisite Valenciennes lace.

As she examined her reflection, Joseph dug through the straw in the smaller crate and pulled out two caskets. "Come see what these contain."

"All right." Betsy draped the blue dress across the sofa back and knelt by him.

The smaller casket was about a foot long, eight inches wide, and eight inches high. Betsy opened it and then sat back on the floor in astonishment. The coffer contained stacks of bright gold coins. As she picked up a handful of coins and let them slip through her fingers, she began to feel breathless.

Joseph picked up two coins that had tumbled to the floor. He counted the stacks in the casket and checked the number of coins in a single stack. "There are a thousand coins."

"How much are they worth?"

"Each one is a little less than a dollar and a half. You probably have about $1,400 here."

"Oh." Betsy tried to calculate what that meant, but she was too flustered.

"Does the other casket have coins too?"

"I don't know," Betsy answered but made no move to open it. After waiting a few seconds, Joseph flung open the lid, revealing that the casket was filled with velvet pouches. He grabbed the top one, pulled open the mouth, and looked inside.

"Jewelry," he said in a tone of disgust

"Jewelry," Betsy repeated as Joseph left the room.

Dorcas approached and carefully lowered herself to sit by her daughter. "Do you want me to help you look through them?"

"All right," Betsy said, but she could not take her eyes off the bright gold. Was there enough money to rent a house? She tried to remember if she had ever heard how much her father charged for his rental properties, but her mind was awhirl.

"Oh, look!" Dorcas took out a choker of fine cameos set in filigree and linked together. A second pouch held a diamond necklace, a third held a square-cut emerald ring, and a fourth held a gold locket engraved with Napoleon's imperial bee. "How stunning."

After glancing inside the fifth pouch, she gave it to Betsy. "You should do this one."

Intrigued, Betsy reached into the velvet bag and pulled out a miniature of Jerome wearing a heavily braided dark blue uniform—and a narrow moustache that reached to the corners of his mouth. "Oh, no! He looks like a pirate!" Betsy dropped the miniature in her lap. "I might not know him when he comes back."

Dorcas gave her a one-armed hug. "Of course you will."

They heard the front door slam, and then William Patterson strode into the room. "Joseph said that the shipment is from Jerome."

"Yes." Betsy placed the miniature on her palm and wondered how it would feel to kiss a mustached Jerome. Then, seeing movement to her side, she glanced up to see her father lift the casket of money.

"This will repay perhaps half the debt your husband owes me."

"Father, you cannot take it." Fighting against her skirts, Betsy scrambled to her feet. "Jerome sent me that money so I can set up my own household."

"Do not be absurd. You would run through this in two months."

"That is not fair. I have never had the chance to prove my ability to manage money. You continually complain about supporting me and Bo, so let us move out."

Patterson tucked the casket more firmly under his arm. "And when this is gone, you will have to move back here and I would again have to pay your expenses."

"Mr. Patterson, please don't be so harsh." Dorcas came to stand beside her daughter. "None of this is Betsy's fault."

"There I disagree with you, madam."

"Never mind, Mother," Betsy said in a low voice. To her father, she said, "You forget that I have furnishings in storage. My only expense will be rent and food, and I can learn to economize. I am sure Jerome intends to send for us before the money runs out."

"That will not happen, Elizabeth. The emperor will never let you live together again. Accept your fate."

"No, sir," she said, lifting her chin. "The most recent letters have restored my hope. Jerome is exerting all his energies to soften Napoleon's anger."

Although her father shook his head, he walked to the table by the front windows and set the casket down. To Betsy's surprise, he began to divide the coins into two portions. "I will give you half. It won't be enough for you to indulge this foolish scheme of setting up your own household, but it will allow you to spend some money on your boy."

"It should all be mine!"

He turned to stare at her. "Do you wish me to repeat the exercise of proving that Jerome owes me far more than this?"

"No, sir," she said, staring at the floor to hide her resentment.

"I expect a little gratitude for the fact that I am allowing you half."

Gratitude. For what is rightfully mine! Betsy knew that if she expressed such thoughts, her father might change his mind, so she pushed down her anger, which felt like swallowing a sizable stone. "Yes, sir. Thank you."

After her father finished dividing the money, he swept his half into the casket and picked it up. Before leaving, he said, "Be grateful that I do not confiscate the pieces of jewelry. If you are absolutely determined to live on your own, I suggest you consider selling them and the other luxuries with which your husband has indulged you. You are not a princess, Elizabeth, and there is no reason for you to live as if you were."

On May 1, 1806, Robert and Marianne were married in Annapolis by Marianne's great-uncle, John Carroll, the bishop who had married Betsy and Jerome. Betsy wore the gold-embroidered gown, glad to have new clothes for the occasion, but her pleasure was short-lived. The ceremony tortured her with memories of her own marriage.

After the wedding feast at the four-story brick house of Marianne's grandfather, Bishop Carroll directed Betsy to a small sitting room attached to the guest chamber, which he occupied. They sat on ladder-back chairs drawn up to a drop-leaf mahogany table. "Madame Bonaparte, I want to speak to you about an important matter. I recently received a communication from His Holiness, Pope Pius VII. It seems the emperor wrote to him requesting an annulment of your marriage."

Betsy could not meet his eyes. "Did he grant the emperor's request?"

"No, he investigated the matter and concluded that he had no grounds to annul the marriage. Since I officiated at the ceremony, he thought it only proper that I should know."

"Oh!" She lifted her head and gazed at him. He had kindly eyes and a normally firm mouth that now curved in a gentle smile. "Thank you, Bishop Carroll. That gives me hope."

As they rose to return to the reception, he said, "I hope that you saw to your son's baptism while you were in England."

Betsy halted, feeling a twinge of guilt. "No, sir, I did not."

"Did you have difficulty finding Catholic clergy to perform the rite?"

"No, I am waiting in hope that he can be baptized in Notre Dame as befits his rank."

Sternness replaced the bishop's genial expression, and he shook his forefinger at her. "Madam, rank has no place in this decision. You imperil your son's soul by not having him baptized."

"But I would like his father to be present at the ceremony."

"Mr. Bonaparte's absence is regrettable, but you must not delay the baptism."

"Yes, sir." Betsy lowered her eyes demurely, yet she remained determined to do as she liked.

✍ XXI ✑.

I N mid-May, a thick letter arrived from Jerome. Before Betsy curled up on the sofa to read it, she handed Bo to her mother, who sat at the drawing room table showing Henry how to write the alphabet. Opening the letter, Betsy saw that Jerome had sent it from French Guiana in northeastern South America.

> *My beloved wife, I have just arrived on the coast of Cayenne and, in spite of my ship being four leagues from the land, I have gone ashore to find an opportunity to get a message to you. Imagine my delight when I looked up the captain of an American schooner to find that he knew you, and had seen you and my son three days before he sailed. I must confess, my Elisa, that this is the first moment of happiness since I left you.*

Betsy's concentration was broken by the sound of crying. Glancing up, she saw Bo struggling against his grandmother's embrace. He called, "Mama!"

She sighed. "Bring him here."

Dorcas carried Bo to Betsy, who set him on her lap and kissed the top of his head. "Be a good boy and let Mama read."

"Mama!" Bo said and crowed with laughter. Betsy scratched his belly with her left hand and went back to reading the letter.

It isn't possible, my dear Elisa, that not one of all my letters has reached you. Any one of them would have removed any apprehension you might have of the fidelity of your good husband. Do you believe, my dear wife, that if I had renounced you I would be in command of one of His Majesty's ships? For an ordinary officer, this commission that I have is good, especially at my age, but for me, who by a single word could have been and could still be anything, what kind of a job is it? Be assured, my good Elisa, that if I had wished to separate myself from you and my son who are the objects of all my affection, I should already have done so, and at the moment that I write you instead of being a subject I should have been a king.

He went on to swear that a crown meant nothing without her, and that after the war, he would rejoin her even if it meant doing without title or fortune. Then he cautioned her:

You must realize, my dear wife, how essential it is that you keep all this in the greatest secrecy, even that you have received a letter from me. Don't tell anyone except your father and your good mother. Don't make yourself unhappy, keep busy with the education of my son; especially make a Frenchman of him, not an American, so that the first words that he speaks will be about his father and his King, that he knows early that the great Napoleon is his uncle and that he is destined to become a prince and a statesman.

"Do you hear that, Bo? Papa wants you to know that you will be a prince. Silly Papa. I tell you that every day."

Betsy folded the pages and tucked them under her skirt so Bo could not grab them and put them in his mouth, which he was liable to do now that he was cutting teeth.

"Was it a good letter?" her mother asked.

Betsy nodded. "Jerome met a captain from Baltimore and learned of our distress, so he went to great lengths to reassure me."

"How much longer do you think it may be before he can send for you?"

Bo whimpered, so Betsy gave him the knuckle of her thumb to rub his sore gums upon. "He writes that we must wait for the war to end, so I fear he has given up the idea of winning a great victory that will change the emperor's mind."

"Perhaps Jerome has realized that the emperor cannot be swayed," Dorcas said as she demonstrated for Henry the correct way to form some of his letters.

"Then why does he not say that our plight is hopeless?"

"Betsy." Dorcas's tone was one of gentle remonstrance. "You know that Jerome is not one to take an unflinching view of circumstances. Have you forgotten that he always describes himself as possessing a nature that lives on hope?"

"I know. But I cannot bear the thought of waiting for peace. France and England have already been at war fourteen years." Bo grew restive, so Betsy bounced him on her knee.

"What else can you do? You cannot go back to Europe until he sends for you, and you cannot live on your own unless he sends you an allowance."

"Even if he did, Father would not let me keep it." Betsy rose and moved the increasingly fussy Bo to rest against her shoulder.

"He would never take more than enough to pay Jerome's debts."

As Betsy rubbed Bo's back, she swayed rhythmically to calm him. "A more loving parent would not take even that. If my son ever lived through such danger as I was in last year, I would embrace him and thank God for his safety rather than harangue him for being a bad investment."

Dorcas rose to face her. "Betsy, your father *was* concerned for your safety. But once you returned home—"

"Whatever fatherly affection he might have felt was consumed by his love for profit."

"You are not being just."

"Just? Is anything that happened to me in the last year just?" In spite of Betsy's efforts to soothe Bo, he began to cry. "And how am I being unfair by observing rightly that Father has expressed more concern for his pocketbook than my wellbeing? He is the one who is unjust, not me." Betsy turned sharply and carried her son from the room.

IN LATE SPRING, news reached Baltimore that Napoleon was remaking the map of Europe. In the wake of his victory at Austerlitz, he wooed several small German states away from their allegiance to Francis I, emperor of Austria and the Holy Roman Empire. Napoleon signed treaties with Bavaria, Württemberg, and Baden, recognizing their full and independent sovereignty. At the same time, he awarded the rulers of Bavaria and Württemberg the status of kings and gave them territory he had taken from Austria.

Then Napoleon made a series of appointments and political marriages that demonstrated to Betsy as nothing else what his plans must be for Jerome. In March 1806, the emperor named his brother Joseph king of Naples. Earlier in the year, Napoleon had arranged for his stepson Eugene de Beauharnais to marry the king of Bavaria's daughter and for his adopted daughter Stephanie de Beauharnais to marry the crown prince of Baden. Napoleon also combined two smaller German states into the Grand Duchy of Berg and Cleèves, which he gave to his brother-in-law Joachim Murat. That act infuriated Betsy more than anything else. Murat might be a great field marshal, but as the son of an innkeeper, his origins were far lower than Betsy's. Why was he good enough to be elevated royalty and not she?

Then Patterson received information from his London associate Mr. James McIlhiny that confirmed Betsy's fears. McIlhiny passed on reports that the previous autumn Napoleon had tried to persuade the widowed Queen of Etruria to marry Jerome, but she spurned the idea, saying she would rather give up her crown.

When Betsy's father read her that passage, her heart quailed but she kept her head high. "Mere gossip. The pope refused to annul our marriage, so Jerome cannot marry again. And just because Napoleon proposes an alliance does not mean that Jerome will acquiesce."

As the news of political marriages trickled in from Europe, the Patterson family finalized an alliance of its own. That summer Betsy's brother John was to marry Polly Nicholas in a ceremony at Mount Warren. Revisiting the plantation where she had been exiled during her broken engagement depressed Betsy. While Senator Nicholas, his wife, Polly, and John greeted the arriving Pattersons in the spacious marble-floored front hall, Betsy hung back, oppressed by memories of having been torn from Jerome, not once now but twice. During the last few weeks, her misery had been eased by the hope she found in Jerome's letters. Now that she was back in this place where she had known such unhappiness, however, the ghost of her old grief came back to haunt her and filled her with such anguish that she wanted to howl. Instead, she nodded, smiled, and said hello as demurely as Polly herself.

As if the reminder of her past wretchedness was not enough, during the three-day visit, the Nicholases and their guests made several remarks to Betsy that contained just enough pity or malice to sting but not enough to justify a sharp retort. When people said, "How sad that your son has never known his father," how could she argue?

Fortunately, the June weather was fine, so whenever the comments about Jerome grew too oppressive, Betsy excused herself to take Bo outdoors. She let him practice walking unassisted on the springy lawn where he could fall without mishap, and she took him to visit the plantation's gardens and animal pens. Bo ate fresh-picked strawberries until his lips turned red, and he clapped at the sight of horses galloping around the paddock. Betsy led him toward the pond to see if any fish were darting to the surface. As they drew near the water, a goose rushed at them with upraised wings and angry honks, causing Bo to squeal and grasp his mother's skirts. When she picked him up, he clung tightly to Betsy's neck and refused to be set back down.

Once they returned to Baltimore, Betsy struggled against an overpowering gloom. When her father, brothers, and sisters went to hear the public speeches on Independence Day, she stayed home and spent the afternoon in her bedroom, ignoring the sounds of celebratory musket fire outside as she reread Jerome's letters.

Three days later, Betsy's parents celebrated her son's first birthday by serving cake and giving Bo a wooden boat, but Betsy felt dejected that nothing came from her husband. She was further distressed when Bo left her side to toddle across the drawing room and lean on his grandfather's knee. Betsy's son wanted a father as any little boy would, and she was afraid that if Jerome did not send for them soon, Bo would look to others to fill that place.

In late July, Betsy received a letter that Jerome had mailed from Martinique. Mary Ann and Bo were upstairs napping, and her mother was teaching five-year-old Henry and four-year-old Octavius at the drawing room table, so Betsy settled on the sofa to read.

*There is one thing that I must admit to you now, my Elisa, but only
between us, that is that three days after your departure from Holland, the general there was given an order to receive you as the wife
of the brother of the Emperor, and that your departure for England
was the only cause of our separation.*

Confused and hurt by the unexpected rebuke, Betsy read the letter
a second time to make sure she had understood it. Then she crossed
to the table where Dorcas was having her two youngest sons count
aloud as she stacked toy blocks in a tower.

"Mother, please read this."

As Dorcas took the sheet of paper, Octavius knocked the tower down.
"Again!"

Dorcas held up one hand and said, "Wait," as she scanned the brief
paragraph. Then she raised troubled eyes to her oldest daughter. "Do
you think this can possibly be true?"

Betsy shook her head. "I don't see how. Robert remained in Holland several days after we left, and the authorities knew who he was
because he had petitioned them while our ship lay under guard. They
said nothing of this to him."

The sound of the little boys shouting as Henry piled up blocks
caused the two women to move away from the table. "Then this makes
no sense."

Betsy took back the page and stared at the bitter words. "Why, after
more than a year, does he reproach me when he knows I had no choice?"

Dorcas shook her head but made no answer, and Betsy felt her hopes
plummet. "It is the emperor's doing. He has finally persuaded Jerome
to blame me for our separation."

"You do not know that." Her mother took her arm. "He may have
written this letter in a dark mood on a day when he felt isolated. That
does not mean he has decided to give you up. It simply means that
even Jerome has moments of despondency."

"Oh, Mother, if he repudiates me, I do not know how I shall go on."

In August, the family moved to Springfield to escape the dangers of
yellow fever in the city. While in the country, Betsy received a letter
from Robert, who was visiting northern cities with Marianne. He wrote

that he had heard that Jerome's squadron was touring the Atlantic off the eastern seaboard, so surely Jerome would find a way to see her.

For days afterward, Betsy was restless with anticipation. Each morning she carefully arranged her hair and put on one of her most attractive gowns. At least once a day, she walked Bo down the driveway, indulging in the fantasy that Jerome would ride up and meet them halfway to the house. She imagined how her husband would kiss her and then lift Bo into the air, exclaiming, "Elisa, he looks exactly like the emperor."

The thought that their long separation might soon be over made her giddy enough to joke and laugh with her younger siblings. After a week, however, Betsy's high spirits palled and she began to fear that Robert's information was yet another false rumor. She still looked up sharply whenever she heard the clatter of hooves or the jingle of a bridle outside, but each time the sound proved to be from normal plantation business.

Finally, a letter arrived:

> *Just a word, my dear and beloved Elisa. I am well and filled with regret at being only 150 leagues from you without having the happiness of seeing you. I embrace you with all my heart. Kiss Napoleon for me and give my compliments to your family.*
> *J. Bonaparte*

Betsy frowned at the instruction to kiss Napoleon until she realized that Jerome must mean their son. As she read the letter a second time, its brevity and cool tone dismayed her.

She went upstairs to where Bo lay napping in the trundle bed that was pulled out from under her four-poster. He lay on his back, sleeping in only a diaper because the heat had given him a rash. His dark blond hair lay upon his forehead in damp spikes, and his sturdy legs were streaked with dirt from the walk they had taken earlier. Betsy sat in an armchair by the window and leaned her head on her hand. That Jerome could be so close and not come to her discouraged Betsy more than anything else that had happened. Either he was under constant surveillance—as he had hinted with his urgings toward secrecy— or he had finally lost heart.

"If only he had braved his brother's displeasure to meet you," she murmured to her child. When she remembered the ardent declarations of love in Jerome's letters, she felt bewildered that he had not seized this opportunity to see his son. Reluctantly, she recalled how during the trip to Niagara, Jerome had spun outlandish tales seemingly to paint himself as a better man than he was. Had all the letters on which she pinned her hopes been only so much bluster?

She stood and gazed down at Bo. "I promise, I will not give up. No matter what your father does, I will never cease trying to obtain your rightful place. You are a prince of the house of Bonaparte, and I will fight for you 'til the day I die."

ALTHOUGH BETSY LIKED being at Springfield where Bo could play outdoors and watch his grandfather's horses, she felt glad when they returned to the South Street house near the harbor. She hoped that perhaps Jerome's ship was still near the coast and he would find a way to visit her when he could evade his brother's spies.

Margaret, George, and Caroline returned to school, while Edward joined Joseph in their father's counting house. At home, Bo learned several new words, one of which wounded Betsy deeply. Mimicking the young uncles and aunt who were his daily companions, he began to call Dorcas *Mother*.

"Do not fret," Dorcas said when she saw Betsy's stricken expression. "No matter what he calls me, you will always be his *Mama*."

"Yes, you are right," Betsy smiled to reassure her mother that she felt no resentment. "But I will not have him misuse the name *Father*. He must reserve that for Jerome."

To Betsy's distress, September and October passed without word from her husband. Each day that the weather was fine, she walked the three-quarters of a mile around the harbor to the south shore. She climbed up Federal Hill and gazed down the Patapsco River, longing to see an approaching French frigate with a curly-haired commander pacing the deck. Betsy continued taking such walks deep into the autumn, but when the rainy, cold weather of November arrived, she stopped tormenting herself with the hope that Jerome would come.

The stomach pains that plagued her whenever she was distraught returned. While she was nursing Bo, Betsy had forced herself to take regular meals, but now that he was weaned, she barely ate. The emptiness in her stomach seemed a fitting companion for the emptiness in her heart, and she embraced the hollowness as the only fit state in which to be. As Betsy lost weight, her mother fussed at her. "You must take care of yourself. Bo needs you to be alert and strong."

Dorcas told the housekeeper to make custards and beef tea that could be easily digested. Seeing her mother's worry, Betsy tried to eat, but every time she took more than a few spoonfuls of food, she felt as guilty as if she had betrayed Jerome by taking another lover.

One morning in late November, Betsy came down to breakfast to find that her father had not gone to the counting house at his usual early hour. Instead he and her mother were sitting together at the end of the dining room table that was Dorcas's usual place, a circumstance that in itself was odd enough to give Betsy a frisson of alarm. The morning newspaper was spread out before them.

As Betsy pulled out her customary chair, her mother looked up with red-rimmed eyes. "What is it?" Betsy asked. "Has something happened?"

"There is a report in the newspaper that concerns you."

A sense of doom swooped down on Betsy. "Is it Jerome? Has he been killed in battle?"

Her father answered, "No, the news concerns your marriage. The emperor has finally had it annulled."

"That is impossible. The pope refused."

"Because the pope did not give him what he wanted, Napoleon used the Ecclesiastical Court at Paris."

Betsy felt dizzy and sat down. "I don't understand. A French ecclesiastical court cannot overrule the pope."

Her father shook his head. "Napoleon must know that this court has no jurisdiction, but he is trying to make it appear that his opposition to your marriage has the sanction of religious authority." He rose, handed Betsy the paper, and pointed out a paragraph he wanted her to read.

The announcement declared that their marriage was invalid because Jerome Bonaparte was a minor who did not have his mother's consent. It went on to say that the clandestine nature of the match led to a presumption that he had been abducted. Further, it charged that the ceremony had been conducted without the presence of an autho-rized priest, and it forbade the parties from ever seeing each other again under penalty of law.

Betsy's mind churned with counterarguments to those claims that she knew to be untrue. "How can they forbid my seeing Jerome?" she asked. "We committed no crime."

As soon as the words left her lips, Betsy understood that a crime was exactly what she stood accused of—or else why the reference to abduction? Napoleon wanted the world to believe that because Jerome was a minor, she and her family had coerced him into marriage.

She gazed up at her father, not bothering to hide her hurt bewil-derment. "This document implies that I was a wanton who preyed on Jerome's innocence, when if anything is the truth, it was the opposite. Why must the emperor spread such calumny?"

"Because he seeks to convince the world that he is acting to protect his family rather than pursuing his ambition," her father answered.

"Protect his family from what?" Again, the truth slapped Betsy in the face. "From me. Napoleon is not content to deprive me of my hus-band. No, he must blacken my reputation too."

Betsy's mother murmured in sympathy, but her father was blunt. "I do not believe he considers you at all except as an obstacle to his designs. If he could accomplish what he wished without causing you further harm, I daresay he would." Patterson pointed at the end of the article. "Notice this declaration that you are both free to provide for yourself as you wish by marriage. That is what the emperor seeks. You must prepare to hear reports of Jerome's second marriage soon."

That bald statement roused Betsy. "No. He loves me."

"Then why has he stopped writing?"

She shook her head. "I do not know. There must be a reason that we cannot discern at this distance. Why would he hold out for a year and a half, only to give in now?"

"Perhaps he is worn out with the struggle," Dorcas said softly.

Although Betsy did not want to admit it, her mother's words lodged themselves in her heart as the truth. She too had worn herself to the bone in the fight to preserve her marriage.

Betsy took a deep breath and lifted her chin in an effort to appear resolute. "No matter what this decree says, the pope ruled that our marriage is valid, so I am going to abide by that opinion. Until I hear otherwise from Jerome, I must assume that he is holding true to me."

"Is his silence not proof that he has yielded to the emperor's demands?"

"No, Father," Betsy answered, although she felt far from sure. "It may only mean that he deems it prudent to lie low for a time. Perhaps spies have reported Jerome's recent communications to me, and Napoleon has increased the pressure on him. If keeping a temporary silence is the only way Jerome can avoid renouncing me, then I will gladly go without a letter."

"Is this what you believe or merely hope?"

She bit her lower lip. "I confess that, until I hear from Jerome, it is more a hope than a certainty. But as we still have no evidence that he will ever consent to give me up, we must act as though we suppose him to be possessed of honor."

As her father took back the newspaper, he said, "Try not to fret yourself. Think about your uncle's party tonight. That will take your mind off this new trouble."

Betsy stared at him in incomprehension. Only after he had left for his business did she recall that Uncle Smith—who was president pro tempore of the Senate now and impressed with being third in line to the presidency—was giving a reception before his annual move to Washington. How could her father think her so frivolous as to be distracted by such an event? If the world accepted this pronouncement denying the validity of her marriage, then society would scorn her as a pitiable figure who lost her honor because of vain ambition. Betsy had stored all her dreams in the hold of a ship sailing for France, but the vessel had sunk on the reef of Napoleon's imperial policies. Now she had very little left with which to build a future.

Rising from the table without eating, Betsy told her mother, "I cannot go tonight. How can I appear in society after receiving such news?"

"This is not a time to be alone. You should be with family."

"No, Mother. I have no heart to make light conversation. Please make my excuses to Aunt Margaret and Uncle Smith."

✑ XXII ✑

IN autumn 1806, William Jr. returned home to marry a Baltimore girl named Nancy Gittings, while Joseph sailed east to oversee the family business concerns in Europe. Betsy was disappointed that William brought no news of her husband. She knew that once December arrived, she was unlikely to receive any letters from Jerome until spring, and the tiny flicker of hope that illuminated her days faded with the dying light of winter. By the time her third wedding anniversary passed, Betsy had begun to wish she could die. She adored her son, but she told herself that Bo was still young enough to forget her if she disappeared from his life.

Betsy longed to confide in someone who would understand her heartache, so she wrote asking Eliza Anderson to call. As they sat together over tea, Eliza told Betsy that not only was she writing articles for the journal, she had also started editing under the assumed name *Beatrice Ironside.* "It is so exhilarating. Do you recall our old complaints about the ignorant young ladies of Baltimore and how little they merit the airs they display? Now, I can publish those criticisms and perhaps better our society."

All Betsy could do was nod; seeing her friend's sense of purpose only deepened her despondency. Eliza added, "Forgive me for prattling about myself when I know you must be dreadfully upset about the annulment. What have you heard from Mr. Bonaparte?"

Betsy set her teacup back in its saucer but stared at it to avoid Eliza's gaze. "I have not heard from him in months. You warned me that this would happen, but I would not listen."

"Have you given up hope?"

"I do not know. If you were to read his letters, you would think he could never abandon me. He even risked his brother's displeasure to send me presents. Then suddenly silence."

"Have you written him?"

Betsy nodded. "I sent letters to the agent he told me to use, but I receive no answer. Eliza, even if he has ceased to love me, how can he give up his son?"

"Men don't feel the same attachment to their children that we do, having borne them in our bodies." Eliza's tone was gentle.

Twisting her napkin into a screw, Betsy glanced at the toys on the floor where Bo and Mary Ann had played that morning. Maybe Eliza was right, but Betsy had seen for herself how much Jerome loved children. Lifting her eyes, she considered the portrait over the mantel. "Perhaps I could have a miniature made of Bo and send it to Jerome. If I cannot convince him to come to our son, then I can send our son's likeness to him."

Eliza set down her cup. "As long as you realize that it may not produce the effect you intend. If the emperor's spies are as active as you say, the portrait may be intercepted."

Betsy nodded to acknowledge the warning, yet in her heart, the dying ember of hope began to glow anew. "Even so, I deem it worth the chance. Our son is the one thing I can offer Jerome that no one else can. It may turn the scales in my balance."

Eliza provided the name of Maximilien Godefroy, a French émigré who was teaching art and architecture in Baltimore. When Betsy contacted him, Godefroy claimed to be too busy for the commission—Betsy later found out that he was an ardent anti-Bonapartist—but he did refer her to a painter of miniatures.

In mid-January, Betsy's family received a letter from Aunt Nancy, who was residing in Washington with the Smiths. She discussed the return of Captain Meriwether Lewis from his two-and-a-half year expedition to the Louisiana Territory and described the Indian artifacts and specimens of western plants and animals the explorer had brought back to Washington. Because the letter contained information of more than usual interest, William Patterson read it aloud at dinner.

After he finished, the family passed the letter around the table. When Edward handed it to Betsy, she made a show of perusing the pages, but she had little interest in the vast western territory. Even so, one sentence captured her attention: "Many dignitaries—both American and European—attended the banquet, and at least seventeen toasts were drunk to the explorers."

European dignitaries. Why had she not thought of that before? If she were in Washington, she could attend receptions where the French ambassador would be present. Perhaps she could gather news of Jerome. Betsy wrote the Smiths to say that she wished to visit them and hoped they could obtain invitations for her to attend events where she could hear diplomatic gossip.

Two days later she and Bo set out for Washington with Edward as their escort. Although William Patterson complained that once again Betsy was dragging one of his sons away from business, Dorcas whispered in her ear, "Never mind. Enjoy yourself."

When they arrived at the Smith residence, Aunt Margaret and Aunt Nancy hugged Betsy and exclaimed over Bo's growth. Then Uncle Smith drew Betsy aside and said that Dolley Madison, acting as Thomas Jefferson's hostess, had invited them to dinner at the President's Mansion. The French ambassador, General Louis Marie Turreau, would be there. Betsy had never met him—in 1804 when he and Pichon were trying to persuade Jerome to return to France, Turreau had refused to be introduced to her. However, for several years he had rented a summer house from her father, so she could claim a connection apart from the Bonapartes.

For the party, Betsy wore a wine-red velvet dress with a low neckline and the garnets Jerome had given her in Lisbon. Before donning the bracelet, she gazed at the word *fidelité* engraved on its clasp and wondered if he really was still faithful to her. Then she kissed the clasp as a way of willing it to be true.

When they arrived at the Presidential Mansion, Betsy noticed that the president had turned the entrance hall into a wilderness museum with mounted animals and Indian artifacts that Lewis and Clark had brought back. Although her aunt and uncle urged Betsy to examine the exhibits, she had little curiosity about them, so she walked on through to the oval drawing room where she greeted President Jefferson. He murmured that he was sorry to see her without her amiable husband and then turned her over to Dolley Madison, who led Betsy to a quiet spot away from the door. Although nearly forty, Mrs. Madison was still remarkably pretty with black hair, dark expressive eyes, and skillfully rouged cheeks. She wore a low-cut gown and a triple-stranded gold necklace.

"General Turreau is not yet arrived, but I will present you to him as soon as he comes," Mrs. Madison said in her soft-spoken voice. "I understand there may be difficulty about introducing you as Madame Bonaparte."

"Alas, yes. The official French view is that no marriage took place and I have no right to the name."

Mrs. Madison squeezed her hands. "Do not worry. I know how to present you without provoking a diplomatic incident."

When General Turreau arrived, his haughty expression sent a shiver of fear down Betsy's spine. She remembered having heard that his troops committed massacres in the Vendée during the French Revolution. Now almost fifty, Turreau had wavy grey hair swept back from a prominent forehead, hooded eyes, and a lower face dominated by a fierce black mustache. His wife, a plain, freckled woman who hung behind him, did not greet anyone.

Mrs. Madison introduced Betsy to the ambassador: "General Turreau, I hear that you know Mr. William Patterson of Baltimore. May I present his daughter Elizabeth?"

He looked down at Betsy for a full five seconds before saying, "Mademoiselle Patterson. Enchanted."

Betsy curtsied. As she rose, she felt her heart pounding and her palms sweating within her kid gloves. All afternoon, she had rehearsed how to entreat him for news of her husband. She hoped her French was up to the task. "*Votre excellence, General Turreau, je vous en prie, pouvez-vous donner moi quelques nouvelles de mon mari? Est-il bien?"*

He replied in icy English, "I know nothing of your marriage and so cannot provide the information you seek."

As he turned from her, Betsy boldly laid a hand on his arm. *"S'il vous plait, monsieur, vous devez savoir que je vous demande au sujet de Monsieur Jerome Bonaparte."*

Turreau brushed her aside. "Mademoiselle, I have no authority to give information about the emperor's family to anyone unconnected with them. Good evening."

His wife flashed Betsy a look of pity before she too walked away. Betsy glanced around and saw that almost everyone in the reception room was busy discussing the exploits of Lewis and Clark. Only Mrs. Madison had witnessed her humiliation. Pressing her lips together, Betsy went to gaze out a window and compose herself before they went in to dinner.

THE NEXT MORNING, Betsy felt so ill that if it had not been for Bo, she would have spent the day in bed. Instead, she rose and cared for her son but made only the briefest replies to her aunts when they asked about her encounter with the ambassador.

In the afternoon, Betsy settled Bo in the center of her four-poster for his nap and lay beside him. As she gazed at the checked linen bed curtains above her, she recalled the devastating night in this very room when she learned that Jerome had given a false age on their marriage license. At the time, she had believed that the worst thing that could happen would be for the irregularity in their relationship to be exposed. Now she wondered if she had missed her chance to avoid a more protracted disgrace. Perhaps she should have denounced Jerome and returned to Baltimore to try to recover from the dishonor. People sometimes remarried after such a misstep. Even Eliza was showing a renewed interest in romance with Maximilien Godefroy.

Then Betsy glanced at her son and brushed back his hair from his forehead. "But how could I wish you had never been born?" Bo was such a handsome, engaging boy. Most of all, he was her little prince, a permanent gift from the man she loved.

As she lay there daydreaming about a misty future in which Napoleon finally sent for her son, a maid knocked softly on the door and entered to say that Dolley Madison had come to call. After taking a moment to smooth the wrinkles from her gown, Betsy went downstairs.

Aunt Nancy sat in the red wingback chair usually claimed by Uncle Smith, while Dolley Madison perched on the gold, scroll-arm sofa. She rose when Betsy entered the drawing room. "My dear Madame Bonaparte, I had to come see you. Have you recovered from General Turreau's rude behavior?"

After glancing at her aunt, whose eyes widened with curiosity, Betsy sat beside Mrs. Madison. "I had little reason to expect anything else. The official representatives of France I have met so far have refused to give even tacit acknowledgment of my claims."

"But surely it is not necessary for their denials to be so brutal."

Twisting the emerald ring that Jerome had sent her, Betsy said, "General Turreau treated me like a beggar. To the French government, perhaps that is all I am."

"You must not think that. Turreau is an odious man with little sympathy for women."

Betsy looked up in surprise. During their few meetings, she had formed the opinion that Dolley Madison liked almost everyone, not in the cloying way that Marianne professed to like people, but with genuine warmth. To hear the older woman disparage Turreau so strongly was shocking. "What do you mean?"

"Well." Tilting her head, Mrs. Madison gave a self-conscious smile. "It has never been my habit to delve into other people's business, but perhaps you should know certain things about the ambassador. You saw his wife. What impression did you form of her?"

"She did not seem a forceful personality."

"In public, no, but she can be quite delightful apart from her husband. She has a pungent sense of humor."

"Really?" Betsy asked, growing interested despite her own misery.

"Truly." Mrs. Madison paused and fingered her gold necklace. Then she said, "She is trapped in a scandalously unhappy marriage. Her husband beats her so brutally that her screams disturb the entire neighborhood. Sometimes, he even has his secretary play the violin to cover her cries."

Betsy shuddered. "How horrible."

"So I think that he might have scorned you simply because of your sex and not because you committed an impropriety in asking about Mr. Bonaparte."

"I see." Betsy considered the possibility. "It could be. My father has said their dealings have always been cordial."

"Then perhaps Mr. Patterson could write to ask him for information."

"Or perhaps my father could come to Washington and meet with Turreau in person. In his own way, he is every bit as daunting as the general."

"That might work." Dolley Madison toyed with her necklace again. "Now may I meet your son? I have one of my own from my first marriage, and I am very partial to little boys."

WHEN BETSY WROTE asking her father to speak to General Turreau on her behalf, he replied that he could visit Washington in March and warned her not to contact Turreau on her own but let him arrange a meeting.

In the meantime, Mrs. Madison continued to invite Betsy to the President's Mansion. Whenever she met Turreau there, Betsy smiled, inquired after his health, and expressed her admiration of the emperor's latest victories. For his part, the ambassador persisted in calling her *Miss Patterson* even though, to everyone else in the capital, she was *Madame Bonaparte.*

Betsy found that her story had excited much interest in scandal-hungry Washington and that many politicians and diplomats, working far from their wives and families, were eager to meet the woman who had so enchanted Napoleon's brother. At parties that winter, she found that if she stood just a few feet in front of a mirror—allowing men to gaze simultaneously at her face, semi-exposed bosom, and bare back—even the most intimidating statesman became almost helpless to turn away. Such triumphs allowed Betsy to feel she was reclaiming some of the power that Napoleon had stolen from her.

On February 6, her aunts gave a supper party for Betsy's twenty-second birthday, and her mother sent her a box of books. The best present of all was having nineteen-month-old Bo—coaxed by his great

aunts—say, "Happy Birday, Mama!" and hug her. His solid, compact
body pressed against hers reminded Betsy that no matter what happened with her marriage, she still had love in her life.

By mid-February, the gossips of Washington had ceased to discuss
Louis and Clark, whose adventures had grown stale through too much
exposure to overheated political air, and now talked about nothing but
the treason charges against the former vice-president, Aaron Burr.
The government claimed that Burr had been raising troops to invade
Mexico and set himself up as ruler—and possibly seize part of the
western territory of the United States.

"He sees himself as another Napoleon and hoped to build an empire
just as the Corsican upstart has," was the common opinion.

Whenever such remarks were made within Betsy's hearing, she re-
futed the comparison. "Burr is eaten alive by ambition, but if you think
the French emperor acts from vainglory, then you misapprehend his
motives. His original purpose was to protect the republic established
by the Revolution, and when the monarchs of Europe persisted in attacking France, he took only what measures were necessary to ensure his country's survival."

Her explanations usually met with scorn: "How can you defend Napoleon after what he has done to you?"

Betsy would shrug away such remarks. "The fact that he is willing
to put the affairs of state above the desires of his brother proves how
important France is to him."

William Patterson came to Washington in mid-March bearing an
invitation to dine with Turreau. During the ride to the ambassador's
house, Patterson said, "Elizabeth, leave the conversation to me. Do
not importune General Turreau for news of Jerome or betray irritation
when he calls you Miss Patterson. A man like that has little patience
with impertinent girls."

Then you are much alike, Betsy thought and turned to gaze out
the window.

When General Turreau received them, his wife was nowhere in
evidence. Betsy could not help but wonder if Madame Turreau was
nursing bruises in another part of the house.

During the first two courses, the men discussed Napoleon's recently instituted Continental System, an attempt to impose a trade embargo on Britain. Betsy chafed under the silence her father had forced upon her. She could not understand why he was letting half the evening go by without raising the question that had brought them there. General Turreau himself finally introduced the topic indirectly. "May I inquire, Mr. Patterson, after the status of Jerome Bonaparte's horses? Are you still keeping them?"

This reference to the carriage horses her father had been stabling for Jerome startled Betsy so much that she blurted, "Why do you ask?"

Her father frowned at her. "General Turreau wrote me after your departure for Lisbon, asking if he could buy the horses. As you know, they are exceptionally fine animals." He turned to their host. "Yes, I have them. I have not received any instructions from Mr. Bonaparte regarding their disposition."

Turreau paused to drink some wine. "You need not wait any longer. I have it on the best authority that his imperial highness, Prince Jerome, will not return to this country."

Betsy gasped. "Prince Jerome? He has been made a prince?"

"Yes, Mademoiselle," Turreau said, turning his hooded gaze upon her.

Nausea swept over Betsy, followed by chills. She knew all too well what conditions Jerome must have met to be elevated to imperial rank. Lowering her eyes, she whispered, "Then he is in Europe now."

"I believe he is fighting in Prussia, Mademoiselle. He supports the emperor in all things, as a good brother should."

Betsy did not answer but instead steeled herself not to cry. In her reticule was the miniature of Bo, which she had considered asking Turreau to send to Jerome. Now she realized that she could not possibly entrust such a treasure to this heartless official.

For the rest of the meal, she remained silent and sipped wine to dull her pain, yet she could not refrain from tormenting herself with remembered phrases from Jerome's letters. How could he have given in after swearing that titles meant nothing without her? She should have known that the more fervent his vows, the less truthful they were.

By the time her father announced they should leave, Betsy had sunk into such a state of misery that all she wanted was to find a dark place where she could weep. She rose, pulled on her gloves, and said good-bye to Turreau without meeting his eyes.

"Mademoiselle Patterson," he said so respectfully that she looked up in surprise. "Allow me to observe that you have handled your loss with unfailing public grace. I intend to inform the emperor of your excellent conduct, and I am sure he would wish me to express his admiration that you have endured your hardships with a soldier's courage. From warriors such as ourselves, there is no higher praise." Turreau bowed over Betsy's hand before escorting her to the door.

As her father handed her into the carriage, Betsy mused over Turreau's compliments. She found it gratifying to have him acknowledge her fortitude, but she would much rather have Jerome back. Still, she wondered if the praise might improve her father's opinion of her.

Patterson settled into the seat opposite. "This puts an end to any possible hope, Elizabeth. Jerome has abandoned you."

Even though she had been telling herself the same thing, Betsy roused herself to refute the assertion. "We do not know that. His plan all along was to win enough glory to compel Napoleon to allow our reunion. Perhaps this new rank means that he has won great renown and is on the verge of achieving that end."

Betsy could not see her father's expression in the dim carriage, but she could hear the anger in his voice. "How can you believe that anything Jerome could do would deflect Napoleon from his plan? The emperor has a will of iron, and Jerome is merely a spoiled, willful boy."

With tears in her eyes, Betsy said, "He has been at war nearly two years. I think we may safely assume that such experiences have matured him."

"Bah! He sends pretty letters and expensive presents instead of taking responsibility for you and your son. In my view, Jerome Bonaparte has not matured one jot."

DISTRAUGHT OVER TURREAU'S news, Betsy returned to Baltimore with her father. Winter passed into spring and spring passed into summer, but still no word arrived from Jerome. The war between Napoleon and the Fourth Coalition continued with an inconclusive battle at Eylau in East Prussia and then a decisive victory against the Russians at Friedland. Betsy searched the papers for any mention of Jerome but never saw his name, and the faintly glowing ember of hope that he might achieve enough glory to command his brother's gratitude died away to cold ash.

One day, William Patterson approached Betsy as she sat reading to Bo. "I have decided to absolve Jerome of his remaining debt."

Astonished, Betsy placed a ribbon as a placeholder in the book. "Thank you, Father. What prompted this generosity?"

"I sold Jerome's horses and carriage, and I am using the furniture and plate he left to stock my house at Cold Stream."

Betsy's gratitude instantly curdled. Moving Bo off her lap, she stood up to confront her father. "You had no right to appropriate either horses or furnishings. Jerome left them so that I could have a household of my own."

"Elizabeth, we have discussed this. You cannot afford your own establishment. You may fight me on this if you like, but any court in the land would uphold my claim."

Too enraged to speak, Betsy stood with clenched fists as her father patted Bo's head and left the room. She felt as helpless as she had the day the warship fired upon her at Texel.

Behind her, Bo crawled to the end of the sofa and grabbed his book from the table. "Story, Mama. Story."

Betsy turned to her son, who was gazing at her with a look of anticipation. She reminded herself that for his sake, even more than her own, she had to find a way to support herself. It would take money to secure the education and future she had in mind for him. "All right." She forced herself to smile. "Mama will read your story."

As news spread of Jerome's new title, the gossips of Baltimore renewed their attacks on Betsy, delighting in the overthrow of her ambitions. Most people did not confront her directly but instead slyly reported what "other people" had said. Some acquaintances, however, could not resist trying to put her in her place. At a garden party in June, as Betsy stood on the lawn eating strawberries and cream with her cousin Smith Nicholas, a young woman named Sally Howard approached them.

Miss Howard interrupted Smith as he expressed regret over Betsy's difficulties. "I do not pity her. She scorned Baltimore as being beneath her. Now she is forced to live here, why should we offer her condolences for being brought down to her proper level?"

The people standing nearby grew silent as they waited for Betsy's retort. She took her time, first handing her empty strawberry bowl to Smith and then smiling at the girl, whose cheeks turned blotchy red in the bright afternoon sun. "Your opinion does not surprise me, Miss Howard. I have always heard that venomous snakes cannot comprehend why birds should wish to soar above the swamp."

By the time July came, Betsy was glad to escape Baltimore and remove to Springfield. Physical exertion seemed to be the only way to quell the exhausting worry that plagued her. To distract herself, she spent hours playing with Bo and Mary Ann under the trees and helping her mother tend the flower gardens. On Bo's birthday, Betsy made her two-year-old son ecstatically happy by mounting the tamest mare on the plantation, holding the child tightly in front of her, and walking the horse around the paddock.

In August, a stranger rode up the long drive to the house and asked to see Madame Bonaparte. When Betsy entered the drawing room, she saw her mother sitting with a man who had dark pockmarked skin, familiar eyes, and one gold earring. He stood, bowed, and said in a Creole accent, "Madame, I am Auguste Le Camus, brother of Prince Jerome's secretary. I am on my way to Europe and was instructed to see if you have any messages for his highness."

"Oh." In her astonishment, Betsy stopped breathing and had to press her hands against her abdomen to expel the air locked within her lungs. "Is my husband well?"

"I have not seen him, Madame. The communication came from my brother."

"Oh," she said again, feeling forlorn after the sudden spike and subsequent plunge of hope. Remembering all the unsent letters in her bedroom, Betsy realized that they were no longer appropriate for a man who had not written her in thirteen months. The anguish of the last year welled up inside her. Then she calmed herself with the thought that she could finally send Jerome the miniature of their son. "Will you wait while I write a letter?"

"Yes, of course. That is why I have come."

She nodded and said, "Mother, would you serve Monsieur Le Camus refreshments? And ask Jenny to bring Bo here. I am sure Prince Jerome would like a first-hand account of his son."

"I will fetch him myself." Dorcas left the room.

Betsy sat at the desk, took out paper, and stared at the blank page. What could she possibly say? Her battered heart longed to make recriminations, but that might alienate Jerome. Minutes passed without bringing clarity. Sharpening a quill as she pondered various openings, Betsy heard her mother reenter the room and introduce Le Camus to Bo as his papa's friend.

"I wide horses," the little boy announced as he stood on the carpet before the visitor.

"Do you? Your papa will be proud to hear that."

Listening to her son chatter easily with this stranger, Betsy felt her own anxieties subside and determination take their place. She would write Jerome a simple, dignified message and trust the image of their son to do the rest.

> *My dearest husband,*
>
> *Congratulations on your elevation to the rank of imperial prince. Your son and I are well. We love you and miss you more than I can say. I beg that you will write to me and tell me your intentions for our future.*

She folded up the letter and sealed it, and then went to join her guest.

AFTER SENDING THE letter and miniature with Le Camus, Betsy warned herself not to expect an answer for several months. The family returned to Baltimore in September, and she kept busy with household chores and teaching her son the names of animals, shapes, and colors.

One morning in late September as Betsy and her mother sewed and the youngest children played, Edward burst into the room. "Joseph has written from France."

When Betsy looked up from her mending, her brother blurted, "Jerome has remarried. Napoleon wed him to Princess Catharine of Württemberg, and together they have been made king and queen of the newly created state of Westphalia."

As Betsy stared at him, the ticking of the mantel clock grew unbearably loud until it sounded like an army marching in her head. In the midst of the tumult, she recalled Jerome saying scornfully, "Do you think I have any interest in marrying a fat, homely princess?"

At the memory, Betsy doubled over her lap and sobbed until her mother came and shook her. "Stop this at once. You are frightening your son."

Betsy lifted her head to look for him. Bo was sitting on the Turkish carpet, sucking his fist and wailing as he watched her with fearful eyes. She pushed herself from her chair, ignoring the sewing that fell to the floor, and knelt by him.

"Shhh, Bo, don't cry. Mama is here, and everything is all right." Betsy pulled him into her arms. "I don't know how, but I promise I will make everything turn out all right."

✒ XXIII ✑

THE night after Betsy learned about Jerome's remarriage, she dreamed that he came to her bearing the sword from Marengo. "Allow me to cut out your heart and take it to Europe. I need a memento of my dear little wife."

She woke crying hysterically. As she tried to regain control of her ragged breathing, her mother entered the room. "I heard you cry out. Are you all right?"

"Yes, Mother. It was only a bad dream."

Over the next few weeks, Betsy's shocked disbelief turned to unwilling acceptance and even, strangely enough, she thought, a grudging relief. All the waiting, uncertainty, and agitation had gone, and in their place came the knowledge that no one was going to rescue her from her dependent position in her father's house. She would have to do that herself.

For a short time, Betsy considered trying to write something for publication. She rejected the idea, however, because Eliza's example demonstrated that opposition plagued any woman who pursued a literary career. Ever since her paper began to publish sarcastic critiques of local culture, invective had rained down on Eliza, and the abuse intensified after she dared to translate and publish a French novel about adultery.

Betsy decided that, even if things had been going smoothly for her friend, writing was not for her. The only story she had that people might buy was the tale of her ill-fated marriage, and she had not yet sunk so low as to profit from being a victim.

She dreaded being an object of pity so much that she refused most invitations that autumn. Instead of going to parties, she stayed home brooding over the past four years and wondering what she could have done differently.

The only good turn of events was that, in September, Robert Gilmor persuaded Gilbert Stuart to give up her portrait at last. When she heard the news, Betsy wrote to Gilmor:

> *Sir—I entreat you to accept my acknowledgments for your successful application to Stuart for the portrait—an act as flattering to me as it is pleasing, and which augments, if possible, the sentiments of regard by which I have ever been actuated toward you. Stuart has hitherto remained inexorable to all our solicitations, and his prompt acquiescence in your demand affords a proof of the estimation in which you are held by this distinguished artist.*

Once the portrait was in her possession, Betsy found herself gazing at it often—even though it pained her to see its expression of bright joy. How had she and Jerome traveled from such happiness to this total ruin?

One evening after Bo was asleep, as Betsy sat on her bed looking through Jerome's letters, her mother came to find her. Standing by one of the posts at the foot of the bed, Dorcas gazed at her daughter with a troubled expression. "I worry about you. It does you no good to keep rereading old correspondence."

Betsy shook her head. "I knew Jerome was weak. I knew he was sometimes lax about the truth. But I never thought he would cease to love me."

Dorcas sat on the bed and removed the box of letters from her daughter's lap. "What makes you think he has?"

"How can you ask? He has married another woman. Even if he does not love his—" Betsy could not bring herself to use the term *wife*. "Even if he still loves me better than this princess, he clearly loves rank more."

"If neither of you cared about rank, you would hardly be in this predicament. You would have made your life here in the United States."

Stabbed by her mother's words, Betsy cried, "So you agree with the gossips that I deserve my fate."

"No, my darling girl. But I think that in your grief, you overlook the most likely explanation for what Jerome did." She picked up a red ribbon that Betsy had taken from the packet of letters. Smoothing the crushed satin, Dorcas said, "I have heard you say time and again that Napoleon acts for reasons of state. Is it not possible he finally convinced Jerome that the survival of France depends on this match?"

"To do so would require only a sufficient promise of luxury."

"That is your bitterness talking. If all Jerome cared about were such things, he would have repudiated you long ago."

Betsy snatched the ribbon from her mother and tied it in knots. "Why could he not write and tell me himself that he was going to marry?"

"Oh, my dear. Some men cannot bear to acknowledge the wounds they inflict, as though to talk of a sin does more hurt than the transgression itself."

"Are you speaking about Jerome now or Father?"

Her mother flushed. "Both, I suppose. And of you, too, and the need to forgive Jerome."

"Forgive him! I cannot."

"It will not be easy, but you must." Dorcas gazed at Betsy with the same look she used to reprimand her young children. "You are wounded now, but you are strong, and you will find a way to carry on for Bo's sake. Jerome has the much harder task. For the rest of his life, he must live with the knowledge that he failed the two people he loved most."

"I hope it burns him like fire."

Dorcas cried, "Do you wish to destroy your son?"

"Of course not."

"Well, then, you have told him every day that he is a Bonaparte prince as though that were the most wonderful thing in the world. If you make him believe his Bonaparte father is a bad man, you will undermine his happiness irreparably."

Lowering her gaze, Betsy pictured her son's bright-eyed, pink-cheeked face. "I do not want Bo to hate Jerome. I hope he might be accepted into his father's family someday." She sighed. "I doubt I can ever forgive Jerome, but I will guard my tongue when I speak of him."

Her mother took her hand. "Try to forgive him, Betsy. I would hate to see my beautiful girl become a bitter woman."

It upset Betsy to think of disappointing her mother, yet she could not imagine getting over her fury at being left behind like a stray dog. Besides, she would need all her hardness to fight for Bo's future. "This is not an instance in which I can meekly turn the other cheek."

Her mother patted her hand and rose. "Perhaps it was too soon for me to say these things. At least, promise me to think over what I have said today."

On November 1, William Patterson turned fifty-five. To celebrate the occasion, Dorcas hosted an open house and invited friends and relatives to call. For a week ahead of time, she and Betsy supervised the cleaning of their home and the preparation of desserts: gingerbread, lemon custard, fruitcake, and the raisin-nut cookies called Maryland rocks.

The family spent Sunday in the drawing room where they could receive visitors. To keep the children occupied, Edward sat on the floor with George, Henry, and Octavius, teaching them to set up wooden soldiers in a battle formation Jerome had taught him years before. As Betsy watched that poignant reminder of her husband, Bo scrambled down from her lap and inched toward his uncles. Edward smiled at him. "Do you want to play too?"

Tucking Bo next to his side, Edward handed him a wooden figure, which Bo clutched with both hands. Edward directed George to adjust one line of soldiers, then told his nephew, "Your papa taught us this. This is how your uncle Napoleon wages war."

Tears flooded Betsy's eyes, and she hurried to the front windows so her son would not see her cry. She leaned her forehead against the cool glass and looked at the dreary November sky above the town houses across the way. The memory came to Betsy, painful in its sweetness, of the November day four years before when she sensed Jerome's presence in the street below even though she had believed him to be in New York. Counting back through time, she realized that they had lived together sixteen months and nearly twice that amount of time had passed since Napoleon separated them. Now that Jerome was a king, would she ever see him again?

Her reverie was broken when her father approached and handed her a glass of Madeira. Raising his own glass to her, he said, "Good health."

Surprised by the gesture, Betsy felt an upsurge of hope that he wanted to start their relationship anew, free of recrimination. As she searched his face, he added, "It is time for you to stop looking to the past and start thinking of your future."

"What future? I am like a fly wrapped in spider's silk and left forgotten on the web," she retorted and took a sip of Madeira; it was the delicate, light golden variety called Rainwater that was favored in Baltimore.

Patterson sighed. "My dearest Betsy, you could have a good life. It only needs for you to cut the cords to the past."

Gazing out at the gloom, Betsy said, "I fail to see how. As you have pointed out often, I have no means of support, so my son and I must live on your charity."

Her father lowered his voice. "Not if you marry again."

Shocked, Betsy turned on him. "I believe they call that bigamy, sir."

Patterson continued speaking softly so that only she could hear. "I know you do not accept the decision of the French court, but you could have your marriage annulled here."

"Why would I do that when I have fought these last four years to get it recognized?"

"So that you can put this unfortunate episode behind you and build a new life. There are men in Baltimore who would be eager to court you if you were free."

"You mean, they would not consider me tainted goods? How generous."

"Your experience with Bonaparte has made you understandably bitter," Patterson said, his voice oily with satisfaction that she was finally disenchanted with Jerome. "It would make me happy to see you settled with a good man who would provide for you and be a steadying influence upon your son. I am fond of the boy and would like to see him raised by a responsible man of upright character. It would be best for all concerned."

Betsy went cold as she realized that her father wanted Bo to grow up to be a solid American merchant like himself. "I do not agree."

Just then they heard the sound of new arrivals in the hall. Patterson gave her a look that said he had not finished with this topic before going to greet his guests.

Betsy turned to gaze at Bo, who sat on Edward's lap watching George and Henry conduct a mock battle between opposing lines of wooden soldiers. As far as she could tell, there was no way to win the contest. George moved a soldier forward and knocked down one of Henry's men, and then Henry retaliated, keeping their forces even. What seemed to give the game zest was that each time one of them struck down an opponent, Bo would giggle, prompting his uncles to use even more flamboyant gestures for their next "kill" to make him laugh harder.

As the last soldier was laid low, Robert and Marianne entered the room followed by Patterson. Betsy's heart clutched with uneasiness as Bo cried out, "Grampa!"

"Oh, look at the little love! Betsy, he has grown so big." Marianne came around the drawing room table to give Betsy a kiss.

"How are you?" Betsy asked, setting her wineglass on the table.

"I am well." Marianne peered into Betsy's face. "How are you? Your cheeks are very red."

Seeing that her father was talking to Robert and William Jr., Betsy gave Marianne a whispered summary of the conversation that had just taken place.

"Oh." Marianne glanced back at her father-in-law, while she fingered her gold bracelet. "I am sure he meant it for the best."

"Hardly," Betsy replied, refilling her wineglass from the decanter and then pouring Madeira for Marianne. "He merely wants to relieve himself of the financial burden that my son and I have become."

"Surely not. But—" Marianne bit her lip. "It occurs to me that if you had accepted the pension the emperor offered, then you would be able to set up your own household."

Betsy's anger at her father overflowed onto this sister-in-law, who was so secure in her possession of a steady husband and generous family. "It came with impossible conditions." Then she caught sight of Bo running across the room and holding up his arms to his grandfather. Patterson smiled, lifted the boy, and held him on his hip.

I have to find a way to move out of here, Betsy told herself.

Tᴇɴ ᴅᴀʏs ʟᴀᴛᴇʀ, Betsy's nine-year-old sister Caroline came home from school with influenza, and the disease spread to all the young children in the house. Betsy moved Bo from the nursery and installed him in her bed. For the next four days, she slept in a nearby chair and nursed her son by bathing his forehead with damp cloths, propping him up when coughing spasms seized him, and coaxing him to swallow spoonfuls of broth. After thirty-six hours, his fever broke, but Betsy would not allow him to get up until she was certain he was fully recovered. Instead, she read to him by the hour to keep him quiet.

In the nursery down the corridor, Dorcas, Mammy Sue, and Margaret nursed the five youngest Pattersons. The sounds of coughing, retching, and feeble complaints filled the second floor of the house. Whenever Betsy and Dorcas passed in the hall, Betsy worried over her mother's fatigue. The lines in Dorcas's face were deeply etched, her skin had taken on the brittle quality of paper, and shadows as dark as bruises lurked beneath her eyes.

Like Bo, the three boys recovered easily, but the girls did not. A persistent cough settled in Caroline's lungs and, after briefly improving, Mary Ann relapsed and grew delirious. Early in the morning of November 17, she died. Instead of wailing as she had when she lost Gussie, Dorcas fell silent. She was a grim figure at her youngest daughter's funeral, refusing to be comforted when older women from church told her that she was fortunate to have so many children still living.

For her part, Betsy thanked God fervently that He had not taken Bo. At the graveside, as she stood listening to the cawing of crows perched on marble headstones, she could not help but reflect on the strange coincidence that Mary Ann Jeromia should leave this world so soon after her namesake had abandoned his family. One by one, even the most tenuous links to Jerome were being torn from her. "Please, God," she whispered, "do not let anything happen to my son."

Iɴ ʟᴀᴛᴇ Nᴏᴠᴇᴍʙᴇʀ, Betsy received a letter from a woman she had never met, a letter that astonished her with its presumption. The writer, Anna Kuhn, had just returned to New York from France, where she had dined with Jerome often:

You, Madam, were no less frequently the topic of our conversation.

He speaks of you as the only woman he ever loved or ever shall love, says he married much against his inclination, which the Emperor his brother cruelly imposed on him, saying you and you only Madam were his lawful wife.

Betsy went upstairs to where her mother was resting in bed. After watching Dorcas sit up and read the letter, Betsy said, "It seems that your supposition about Jerome's motives was right."

"Yes." Her mother gazed at her pensively. "It does not ease your pain, does it?"

"No. Mrs. Kuhn's description makes it evident that Jerome is so busy pitying himself that he gives little thought to our wounds."

Gazing at the miniature of Mary Ann that she had moved to her night table after the funeral, Dorcas said, "Even if he expressed regret in the most loving terms, you would still be alone with your grief."

Betsy hugged her. "I am sorry to burden you with this when you have your own sorrow."

As she pulled away, her mother said, "I am not so distraught that I am insensitive to your suffering. I have been thinking that perhaps you should visit the Smiths again."

"To what purpose? I no longer hope for good news from France."

"A change of scene and society may distract you from your troubled memories."

"I suppose." Betsy picked up the letter. "I do not intend to answer this. I find it very painful to have a stranger approach me on such an intimate topic."

"Perhaps Jerome asked her to send you these assurances," Dorcas said as she rearranged her pillow behind her so she could lean back more comfortably.

"Perhaps, but the only *assurance* I need from the King of Westphalia is the *surety* of a regular income, and he shows no sign of providing that."

"Betsy, does it not soften your heart to know that Jerome was forced into the marriage and that he retains a tender regard for you?"

The reproof in her mother's voice caused Betsy to lay down her cynicism. "It is a small crumb of comfort to learn that he loves me still, but it only makes his betrayal sting all the more. Napoleon understood his brother better than I did. He knew Jerome would capitulate in the end, while I continued to hope that adversity would instill in him a strength of character to justify my faith. I was sadly deceived in him, and I do not know whether to blame him or myself."

Dorcas gave her a sharp look. "You do not blame the emperor?"

Betsy shook her head. "Not for putting the needs of the state above those of a younger brother. Jerome's claim to be coerced has a hollow ring. One need only look at Lucien, who remains true to his wife."

"And yet, Jerome held out for two years."

"Two years, after he promised to be faithful till death." Betsy stood and smoothed her skirt. "Let us not quarrel. I have long known that you are more forgiving than I am, and I honor your merciful nature even when I cannot emulate it. I expect nothing from Jerome now."

Betsy and Bo traveled to Washington in January. Three days after their arrival, Dolley Madison visited Betsy at the Smith home. Betsy received her guest in the drawing room, and after the two women were seated together on the gold sofa, Mrs. Madison said, "I confess, Madame Bonaparte, that I missed your society when you went back to Baltimore, and I hope that during your stay we can renew what promises to be a rewarding friendship."

"Mrs. Madison, you are too kind."

The older woman responded with a demure, close-mouthed smile that Betsy thought must be a legacy of her Quaker childhood, yet her eyes twinkled merrily. "Not at all. I am simply glad to find someone whose companionship is so agreeable."

"Thank you, ma'am. I would be only too pleased to deepen our acquaintance."

Mrs. Madison clapped her hands. "Good, then that is settled. Now tell me all about your son. I am sure he must have grown like a weed since I saw him last."

Not only was Dolley Madison's friendship agreeable to Betsy, so were the parties she attended at the Presidential Mansion and in the homes of the Washington elite. General Turreau, whom she saw often, treated her with new respect even though he continued to call her *Mademoiselle Patterson.* Turreau's own social position was precarious.

He had repudiated his wife and sent her back to France, thus ending the violent relationship that had cast a shadow on his social standing, but people did not forget his reputation for brutality.

Washingtonians were more forgiving toward Betsy. Although the capital remained a rough city, its people had more worldly experience than Baltimoreans, and they viewed her with neither pity nor censure. Instead, as a beautiful, witty young woman with no desire to catch a husband, she was a welcome addition to a society in which the majority of legislators spent the congressional session living in cramped, all-male boarding houses.

Everyone knew Betsy's history and understood that she believed herself to be Jerome Bonaparte's only lawful wife. Still, she exercised more care than she had in years past. Whenever any of the men with whom she danced and dined displayed symptoms of serious regard, she showed them a miniature of Bo and reiterated her vow to dedicate her life to her son.

To further guard her reputation, Betsy avoided any behavior that might imply she was open to easing her loneliness with illicit entanglements. She chatted most often with gentlemen she judged to be safe, such as Samuel Colleton Graves, a young Englishman whose gauche manners revealed him to be a youth learning to negotiate society. At their introduction, Betsy judged that he was someone who would never presume to court her, but who might gain some polish from conversing with a more experienced woman.

The nineteen-year-old Graves had a narrow face with pale skin, small eyes, and a prematurely receding hairline he tried to disguise by brushing his brown hair forward. Although not handsome, he was a devotee of fashion. He wore a long-tailed, hunter green coat, snugly fitted buff trousers, a linen shirt with a stiff collar turned up to his ears, and an elaborately knotted black silk cravat.

He came from a prestigious family—his mother was descended from one of the original proprietors of the Carolinas, and his father, Rear Admiral Richard Graves, came from an English family known for producing admirals—yet young Graves showed none of a naval officer's flair. Rather, he was so awkward that he reminded Betsy of eleven-year-old George, the most diffident of her brothers. Graves jumped whenever he heard loud voices, and in conversation he often paused to clear his throat nervously.

In spite of the maladroit manner that drew attention to his youth, he was well read and had made himself an expert on the history of the English monarchy. Once he discovered that stories of royalty fascinated Betsy, he took every opportunity to show off his knowledge. Betsy encouraged him in this because when Graves was talking about his favorite subject, his self-consciousness fell away.

"Our aristocracy scorns Napoleon as an upstart, but truly, I do not know how the British monarchy can lay claim to more legitimacy than the Bonapartes," he exclaimed one evening. "The line has been broken so many times, resulting in kings with very little claim to the throne. Consider Henry Tudor, descended from an illegitimate grandson of Edward III. Yet he proved to be just what England needed at the time, a strong ruler who could end a century of civil war."

Betsy tapped his arm with her fan. "Is it not dangerous to say such things, Mr. Graves? After all, George III's lineage is more German than English, and some people might interpret your remarks as casting aspersions on your monarch."

Graves blushed to his hairline. "You are right. Thank you for your wise caution."

For his part, Graves was fascinated by the trip Betsy and Jerome had taken to Niagara and astonished by the story of the shipwreck they had survived. When Betsy described the measures Napoleon had taken to keep her from landing in Europe, his face grew red. "Madame Bonaparte, I think you are the bravest woman I have ever known."

In late March, he begged a seat beside her during a dinner at the President's Mansion, yet he spoke little during the first course of leek soup. Betsy knew from Dolley that the young man was leaving Washington soon, so she assumed he was silently composing his farewells. During the meat course, after refusing the butler's offer of wine—Graves had confided in Betsy that he believed the combination of red wine and beef overheated his blood—he turned to her. "Madame Bonaparte, might I call on you at your uncle's house tomorrow?"

Noticing how flushed he was, Betsy said quietly, "Mr. Graves, you know my social position is delicate. I cannot receive gentleman callers."

"But with one of your aunts as chaperon?"

"I am sorry, no. There is nothing you can want to tell me that you could not say here."

The young Englishman shot Betsy a burning look of reproach. "Surely, you would not be so cruel as to pretend ignorance of my feelings."

"Mr. Graves, I had not the smallest idea. You do me honor, but I must remind you that my only thought in life is for my son."

He stared at his plate. After several seconds, Graves cleared his throat and turned to her. "Your refusal is because of your son?" he whispered, "It is not because you think me—foolish?"

"No, you are a respectable, decent young man, and I feel sure you will someday find a woman worthy of you."

"I will never love another." Signaling to the butler, he asked for wine.

AFTER CONGRESS ENDED in March, Betsy and her son returned home. Bo was delighted to be back at South Street with the young uncles who were his playmates and the grandparents he adored. Toward Betsy, however, her father displayed more resentment than ever.

Business troubles soon worsened Patterson's temper. The previous June, the British warship HMS *Leopard* had attacked the U.S. frigate *Chesapeake,* and British officers removed four crew members accused of deserting from the Royal Navy. In response to this violation of U.S. rights, Americans called for war, but President Jefferson instead took the peaceful route of demanding an official apology—which British diplomats declined to give.

Once diplomacy failed, the president persuaded Congress to pass the Embargo Act in December 1807. The act made it illegal for U.S. ships to leave for foreign ports. Although intended to hurt France and Britain economically and force them to stop molesting U.S. ships, the act made it impossible for Americans to export crops, raw materials, or manufactured goods. As a result, Patterson's warehouses held goods that could not be moved, and his ships were trapped in port, where they began to rot as they lay anchored at wharves, exposed to the elements yet not maintained because manning idle vessels was too expensive.

Betsy did her best to help her mother economize by remaking many of her siblings' clothes and helping to oversee the cooking so there would be less waste. Yet she sometimes felt that her father begrudged her every mouthful of food. The atmosphere at home grew even more frosty when a letter from Samuel Graves arrived in mid-May. He could not forget Madame Bonaparte, he wrote, and wondered if he could not do something to win her heart.

Betsy showed the letter to her mother, foolishly overlooking the fact that Dorcas would feel compelled to share the news with her husband.

That evening, William Patterson summoned Betsy to the drawing room after she put Bo to bed. She sat on the sofa, opposite her parents who sat in their usual chairs on either side of the fireplace. Her father asked, "Do you mean to tell me that you had the opportunity to make such an eligible match, and you turned him down?"

"I do not love him, Father."

"Love!" He clenched his right hand, which rested on the arm of his chair. "It is time to consider your future and stop indulging such girlish daydreams."

Betsy felt her anger burn. "I am thinking of the future, sir. My son would never be allowed to claim his Bonaparte heritage if his stepfather were English."

"When will you give up this ridiculous idea that your son will be a prince?" Patterson rose and paced before the hearth. "You have learned nothing from your disastrous marriage. What would you do if I threw you out into the street? I daresay you would lose your scruples about marrying the Englishman fast enough."

Gazing at him coolly, Betsy realized that his bluster did not scare her the way it had when she was a girl. Nothing could be as frightening as being pregnant, starving, and fired upon by one of Napoleon's warships. "I daresay I might, but those scruples would be replaced by new ones. I would never allow my son to see a grandfather who could treat him so cruelly."

"Stop it, both of you," Dorcas said, half rising from her chair and then sinking back down. "Do you not realize that every time you tear at each other, I suffer the most? I love you equally."

Betsy stood, wishing that she were taller to present a more imposing figure. "I am sorry, Mother, to wound you, but I am not a Jerome to be coerced into marriage against my will."

Patterson glared at his daughter. "There is no question of force, Elizabeth, as you well know. Otherwise, I would never have allowed you to marry Jerome against my advice. I ask only that you consider the impact of your decisions upon your family."

"I always do, sir. I consider my son first, then myself, then my family." Betsy told her mother good night and left the room.

BALTIMORE SEEMED DEAD. Because of the embargo, the harbor had few arrivals or departures. Many laborers and sailors were out of work, and churchwomen who called on Dorcas spoke of spreading poverty in the city.

Betsy felt more alone than ever because Eliza was away from town. She and Maximilien Godefroy had decided to marry, but before she could wed again, Eliza needed to obtain a divorce. She was traveling in search of her errant husband to try to gain his agreement.

That summer, Betsy reached the most difficult decision of her life. Shutting herself in her bedroom, she wrote General Turreau. She began by reminding him that she once had every reason to hold the highest expectations for her future. However, the events of the intervening years had made her understand that the needs of the state were greater than those of individuals. Therefore, she yielded to the necessity that separated her forever from the man she loved and whose name she bore with pride. She sought nothing for herself but asked the general to remind the emperor of a child so worthy of his interest. Her son was still young, but soon she would need to train him for his future. Because of her lack of means, she did not know how she would provide him with the education he deserved. The emperor had once been so generous as to offer her a pension. Would he now take an interest in his nephew's future and renew the offer?

After painstakingly translating the letter into French, she sent it to the French minister the day after Bo turned three years old.

XXIV

Gᴇɴᴇʀᴀʟ Turreau responded by asking Betsy to call on him at the summer home he rented from her father. The move was socially risky since Turreau had cast off his wife, so Betsy asked Aunt Nancy to accompany her. In mid-July, they took a carriage to the general's residence, where a servant led them to the drawing room. When Turreau joined them several minutes later, his eyebrows lifted at the sight of Miss Spear. Betsy, however, had not forgotten the court decree that implied she had ensnared Jerome through less-than-virtuous means, and she refused to give the Bonapartes any reason to malign her further.

Betsy and her aunt sat side by side on a sofa, so the diplomat chose a facing chair with claw feet and inlaid bellflowers on the arm supports. "I received your letter, Mademoiselle, and I shall forward your request to the emperor." He toyed with the end of his mustache. "I must warn you that he is busy with affairs of state, so I cannot say how long he will take to reply."

"I understand, *mon général,* but I must ask, if you would be so kind, to convey to his imperial majesty that my situation requires some urgency."

"Urgency? Mademoiselle, your son is but three years old. There can be no urgent need to start his education."

"No, sir, but I have a desperate need to leave my father's house." In a calculated show of emotion, Betsy held a handkerchief to her lips. "The embargo has hurt his business, and he wishes to rid himself of the expense of supporting us."

General Turreau waved her concern away. "These things happen in time of war."

"I understand." Betsy lowered her gaze to prevent Turreau from guessing that she had set a trap for him. "But I must inform you that my father wishes me to remarry and has approved one particular suitor whose father is a British admiral. I have no stomach for this match, but if I continue to lack an income, I might not be able to hold out against my family's pressure. In which case, the emperor's nephew would be raised in Devonshire. As an Englishman."

After a moment's silence, Turreau laughed. "Mademoiselle, have you the audacity to attempt a flanking maneuver against the great Napoleon?"

Betsy shrugged to feign self-deprecation. "I do not understand you, sir."

Turreau brought his two fists together knuckle to knuckle. "When two armies are about to meet, but one lacks the strength to survive a frontal attack, its general often makes a wide sweeping move around the side of his foe to attack a weak spot." With his right hand, he made a curving gesture that bypassed the left fist and hit the wrist instead.

"I see." She gazed at Turreau steadily to show that she was not ashamed of her ploy.

"Is there really an Englishman?"

"Yes, sir. I can produce his letters if you insist."

At that, the diplomat learned forward. "You must not take the child to England. Nothing would be more certain to enrage the emperor."

"I understand, *mon général.* That is why I presumed to use the word *urgency.*"

Turreau smoothed his mustache. "I will do what I can. Now I must ask you some questions. First, it has not escaped my attention that you continue to use the name Bonaparte, which the emperor has expressly forbidden."

"Only because it is the custom in this country. Were I to call myself Miss Patterson, I would be looked upon as a single woman with an illegitimate child. Surely, you must see how disastrous that would be for my son."

Turreau shook his head. "The emperor will be adamant on this point."

"Then he must give me another name to use—or perhaps a title."

"I have heard that you are ambitious."

"After the manner of women, yes. The emperor's rejection of my marriage has cost me everything but my son, so I will fight for him using whatever weapons I have." Realizing that the general would scoff at her true hopes, Betsy decided to dissimulate. "I know my child can never be a prince, but surely as the son of a Bonaparte, he deserves a life of some importance in Europe. All I ask is the means to prepare him for such a future."

"I assure you that his imperial majesty has no desire to harm his brother's son—or that son's mother. But he cannot act in any way that will endanger his state."

She nodded. "I understand, *mon général,* and I honor the emperor for his diligence as a ruler."

Turreau then peppered her with questions: If the emperor gave her a title and an income, would she live in the European town he chose? Would she renounce her U.S. citizenship? Would she swear never to go to England? Would she promise not to marry without the emperor's consent? Would she allow him to take charge of her son once Bo turned seven?

Most of the answers came easily to Betsy since she had long dreamed of living in Europe and truly had no desire to remarry. The question about being separated from Bo frightened her, but she told herself that she would have to send him to school in any case, and surely the emperor would allow her to visit him.

After Turreau finished interrogating her, he said, "I have no authority to put such a scheme in motion, Mademoiselle. I shall have to forward your letter and my own recommendations to Paris."

"Of course." Betsy rose, and Aunt Nancy followed suit. "We will not take up more of your time. Thank you for your assistance in this delicate matter."

Turreau walked them to the front hall, where he studied Betsy in a frankly appraising way. "Mademoiselle, I now understand why we had so much difficulty persuading Prince Jerome to obey orders. You are a more formidable opponent than we realized."

Unable to think of a suitable reply—and uncomfortable under his gaze—Betsy curtsied. Then she and her aunt left.

Once they were in the carriage, Nancy exclaimed, "I believe that old rake fancies you."

Betsy shuddered. "Do not speak of it. The man is an ogre. If I stoop to using honeyed words with him, it is only because I must do so to achieve my ends."

"Are you so sure that the end you seek is the right one?"

Turning to her aunt, Betsy saw that the older woman had pursed her lips, which drew unflattering attention to the lines around her mouth. "I don't wish to quarrel, Aunt. I chose my path long ago, and I do not intend to deviate from it now. I will not see my son deprived of his rights."

Then Betsy fell silent as she tried to calculate how long it might be before Napoleon answered.

Even though Betsy had insisted to Samuel Graves that she could not consider his proposal, he sent another letter to her at Springfield in August. As she carried it into a small back parlor where she could be alone, Betsy was surprised to see that it had been mailed from a place in Massachusetts where she and Jerome stayed on their journey from Niagara to Boston.

She sat on the sofa and dropped the letter unopened on her lap. The name of the village brought back such memories! The inn was one of the quaintest that she and Jerome visited—it had delftware tiles around the fireplace and blue toile bed-hangings—but the sweet décor was not what made it memorable. During that day's stagecoach ride, Jerome had amused the other passengers with stories of their adventures at Niagara, particularly praising Betsy's stamina and courage. She could tell from his ardent glances that he was growing aroused as he spoke, so she was not surprised that the moment they were alone in their room, he kissed her passionately. Jerome was so impatient that he would not wait for her to undress but rather hiked up her gown, bent her over the bed, and entered her from behind. Later, after they dined, he made love to her again, this time with more deliberate attention to her pleasure.

Her eyes filled with tears at the contrast between that wild joy and her present loneliness. How could Jerome have sacrificed a marriage of such passion for one of political expediency? Even after a year, she found his decision incomprehensible.

Betsy sighed, picked up the letter, and broke the seal. Graves explained that he was in New England, and remembering her account of the excursion to Niagara, he had stopped at one of the inns where she stayed and persuaded the landlord to put him in the same room.

Reading that gave Betsy a sense of uneasiness, a feeling that was compounded when she turned to the second page and discovered a love poem in which Graves described tossing and turning all night because his emotions were agitated by sleeping where she had once lain.

Betsy released the letter, which fluttered to the floor. The knowledge that the young Englishman would occupy a bed she had shared with Jerome and then lie awake imagining scenes of love sickened her. Retrieving the letter, she carried it upstairs to lock away with her other correspondence. It would not do for anyone else in her family to read it.

Because Turreau had warned Betsy that Napoleon would be slow to answer, she tried not to feel any hope about each day's post. However, an unexpected letter arrived at the South Street house in late September. Sent by Auguste Le Camus, who was in New York, it enclosed two letters from Jerome, one for Betsy and one for her father.

Betsy handed her father's letter to Dorcas, who sat working with Octavius on his reading. Then Betsy tore open hers. Scanning the page eagerly, she learned to her horror that Jerome was writing, not to beg her forgiveness, but to ask her to give up their son:

> I know in advance, my well-beloved Elisa, what it will cost you to be separated from him, but you will never be so blind to his true interest and your own, as not to consent to his departure. A brilliant destiny is reserved for him. Our son should enjoy all the advantages which his birth and his name give him the right to claim, and you cannot permit him to lose these advantages without ceasing to love him, and without making yourself responsible for his fate.

"No!" Betsy exclaimed. The air went out of the room, and her breath began to come in gasps. The murmur of Octavius reading grew abnormally loud, and Betsy felt her surroundings spin around her. As she struggled against terror, she remembered Eliza saying that her main fear in seeking a divorce was that the courts usually awarded fathers custody of any children.

"Mother! He wants Bo. He intends to take Bo!" Betsy's words tumbled over themselves like stones in a landslide.

Dorcas crossed the room and snatched the letter from Betsy's hand. She skimmed it before saying to Octavius, "Run, get your father. Hurry."

Then she led Betsy to the sofa, where she made her bend over her lap so her head was by her knees. Rubbing her back, Dorcas said, "Shhh, calm yourself. It has not happened yet."

Too desperate to remain still, Betsy sat up and wrung her hands. "Jerome will have the law on his side, so what can I do? If he takes my boy, I will have no reason to live. I swear, I will throw myself in the harbor."

"Don't say that. It is wicked."

"Do you think I care?" Betsy jumped up. "Where is Bo?"

"You know he is taking a nap." Dorcas stood and grasped her by the arm. "You will frighten him if you go up in this hysterical state."

Betsy wrenched herself free, threw herself back on the sofa, and sobbed. As her mother tried to soothe her, William Patterson entered the room.

"What is the meaning of this tumult?"

"Jerome has written Betsy. He wants to raise the boy in Westphalia."

Hearing those words, Betsy froze, her tears halted by a new fear—that, as a man, her father would support Jerome's paternal rights. She watched with dread as her father read his letter from Jerome. During the wait, Dorcas shepherded Octavius from the room.

After he finished, Patterson said, "He claims that Napoleon has consented to this plan, and he urges me to persuade you."

I will take Bo and run away, Betsy thought. *But where can I go? Could Samuel Graves protect us if I married him and went to England?*

As Betsy's thoughts raced, her father swore. "The impudence. He writes that having his son will console him for losing you, Betsy. What of your sorrows? Jerome has attained the rank he always wanted, and now he wants to deprive you of your one comfort."

"Then you do not think his claims outweigh mine?"

Patterson rubbed his brow. "Under the law, a father's claims take precedence. But I cannot imagine that Jerome would leave his kingdom to contest a lawsuit here."

She clasped her hands together. "If the emperor has authorized this plan and submits a formal request to our government—"

"I think it unlikely that Napoleon would exert himself to such an extent to satisfy Jerome. At any rate, our family is not without powerful friends, and I will do what I can to prevent such a thing. I would not wish to see the boy torn from a respectable, honest family to be raised among the dissipations of court."

Instead of comforting Betsy, her father's words reinforced her fear that he intended to turn Bo into a Yankee merchant. Tears pricked her eyes as she realized that she might have to sacrifice her own interests for her son's good. "My deepest desire is for Bo to attain his rights as a Bonaparte prince," she protested. "How can I deprive him of the advantages that are his by birth?"

"What advantage? That of being raised as a puppet king's bastard son?"

"But he *is* a king's son." She stared at her father's purple face and wondered if they would ever understand each other. "If Jerome can give our son his rightful place at court, would it not be selfish for me to put my needs ahead of his?"

Patterson tossed aside his letter. "I *am* talking about your son's needs. What do you think will happen when Jerome's queen gives him a legitimate heir?"

"Bo is his legitimate heir!"

"Not in the eyes of the Bonapartes. When Jerome has a son from this new marriage, he will cast the boy aside just as he did you. And there will be nothing you can do to mitigate his circumstances because they will not let you near him."

Gazing at the Turkish carpet, Betsy had to admit the logic in her father's words. But did they appeal to her because they were what she wanted to hear? She needed to get counsel from someone who understood the political ramifications better than they did.

As Betsy wondered whom to ask, she heard small feet pounding down the stairs. Bo burst into the drawing room and, confronted with

the unexpected sight of his grandfather, shouted, "Grandpa!" He hur-
tled himself onto Patterson's lap. Then, as Bo turned around and wrig-
gled into a comfortable position, he caught sight of his mother's face.

"Mama?" Instantly, anxiety clouded his cheerful countenance. "Are
you crying?"

Betsy forced herself to smile. "It is nothing. I have a headache."

Bo slid down from his grandfather's lap and clambered up on the
sofa. "I can make it better," he said and kissed her forehead, mimicking the gesture she used when he felt unwell.

"Yes, much better." As Betsy pulled Bo into a hug, she met her father's gaze over her son's blond head. In this at least, they were united, even if their ultimate hopes for Bo were at cross-purposes. Neither
of them wanted this precious boy to be taken from them.

In his letter, Le Camus had said that Jerome expected him to take
the child with him when he returned to Europe. Betsy replied that
her son was too young to travel without his mother, and as she was
still barred from France, it was impossible for Bo to make the voyage.

Betsy then attempted several letters to Jerome, beseeching him not
to demand such a sacrifice. In her first draft, she tried to stir the em-
bers of his love by describing her devastation at the thought of losing
their child, her "only happiness" since her separation from him. She
wrote a more formal version in which she appealed to Jerome's vanity by addressing him as "sire" and "your Majesty," but she could not
bear to humble herself to the man she had once teased in bed. In the
end, she sent Jerome no reply at all.

Finally, Betsy wrote to James Monroe, who had been so helpful to
her in England and had recently returned to the United States. She
apologized for intruding upon his time, thanked him for his past counsel, and described her problem. Betsy asserted that her only concern
was for the safety and wellbeing of her child, and she swore that she
would suffer any privation necessary for his best interests.

As she waited for an answer, death again struck her family. In October, William Jr. was working on the docks inspecting the Patterson
ships that were rotting from lack of use. Four days later, he came down
with yellow fever, making him a late victim of the epidemic that had

plagued the Fells Point neighborhood since summer. He died on October 20, leaving his wife Nancy and an infant son. In the days that followed, Betsy did all she could to comfort her mother, but at night when she was alone, she wept as she remembered how William had protected her during the terrible time at Texel.

Two days after the funeral, Betsy found her mother in the nursery gazing at Bo as he napped. When Betsy spoke her name, Dorcas whirled on her with eyes that burned with the madness of grief. "You must not lose your son. Do you hear me?"

"Yes, Mother," Betsy said, gently leading her from the room. "Father and I are doing everything we can."

Finally, three weeks after she wrote to Monroe, Betsy received his reply. The statesman explained that he had followed her history with great sympathy and regret that he had not been able to alleviate her situation: "To the present period your conduct has been distinguished by the utmost degree of prudence and delicacy."

In response to her fears, he pointed out that Napoleon's fame had already suffered because of his treatment of her and that if any calamity should happen to the child in his care, his reputation would be irreparably damaged. Therefore, Monroe assured Betsy that he believed both Jerome and the emperor would do their best to guard the boy's safety.

> *It is not therefore from either of them that I should apprehend any danger to the child. If his situation should expose him to any I should expect it from another quarter. The wife of Jerome, or some of her connections might not see this infant received under the protection of his father with pleasure. She may have children, and he might be thought in their way. Such things often happen in courts.*

Laying down the letter, Betsy immediately thought of King Richard III, rumored to have killed his young nephews to gain the throne of England. Queen Catharine had powerful relatives; her cousin was the Russian tsar. Yes, it was possible that her family might see Bo as a threat to their interests.

If only Napoleon will grant my request for a pension, she thought, *I can keep Bo here where he will be safe from such plots. If I can obtain a good education for him, there will be time enough for him to claim his place at court when he is a man and able to defend himself.*

Near the end of the year, Betsy received another letter from Jerome. Napoleon had told him of her desire for a pension—Betsy rejoiced to learn that the emperor was considering her request—and Jerome was furious that she would seek assistance from his older brother.

Indignantly, Jerome wrote that he had been planning to give Betsy and their son the principality of Schmalkalden, which lay within Westphalia thirty leagues from his capital. She and Bo were to have the titles of princess and prince, and an income of 200,000 francs a year.

> *I was expecting my son, yes, Elisa, and you too, and a noble existence, and one worthy of the objects of my most tender affection, was planned for you and still awaits you. Then, at least, I shall see my son from time to time, and I promise to his mother, to Elisa, to my most loving friend, to leave her son with her until his twelfth year in the principality which I have chosen for him, and that the only sacrifice I ask of her is to let me enjoy a visit from my son once or twice a month.*

After finishing the letter, Betsy felt confused. Could this have been Jerome's intention all along? If so, why had he not said so previously?

Rereading the letter, she saw that Jerome promised her a beautiful home, and she immediately envisioned a small jewel-like palace where she could receive scholars, writers, and aristocrats in her glittering salon. Bo would have the finest tutors and someday inherit his father's throne, and everyone would praise her for how wisely she had raised him.

And Jerome would be only thirty leagues away. Surely there would be times when, to escape the burdens of kingship, he might ride to Schmalkalden to visit the woman who had known him as a carefree youth. Betsy imagined the sound of horses in the courtyard, a stealthy midnight knock at the door, and an intimate supper with too much wine. Then she would be in Jerome's arms again.

As swiftly as the bewitching scenario played out in her mind came the burning heat of shame. They would never be able to keep such assignations secret, and within a short time, all Europe would hear that she had become Jerome's mistress. She knew him too well not to feel certain that he would attempt to seduce her, and she knew herself too, remembering all the times that her passion for him had betrayed her better judgment.

Betsy rose and paced before the hearth as she tried to compose a blistering reply. As she did, her mother entered the room.

"What on earth ails you? You are as restless as a sparrow with a hawk overhead."

"Jerome has written again, and this letter is more insulting than the last." She handed over the page and waited impatiently for her mother to read it.

Moments later, Dorcas looked up. "I do not understand your anger. With this offer, he makes an effort to provide for you and Bo."

"Mother, if you think that, you think wrongly. Jerome's intentions are not nearly so noble. Once I am beholden to him, he will insinuate his way back into my bed."

"My dear, he says nothing to indicate such a desire."

Betsy stared at her mother, astonished that she could be so naïve. "I know Jerome too well not to feel certain what would happen. And once we were intimate again, I would be reduced to the status the emperor always assigned to me, that of a whore."

"Betsy!"

Ignoring her mother's scandalized outcry, Betsy said, "I will not allow him to cheapen me. I was his one true wife and I will not accept any lower rank."

As she spoke, the words she needed to respond to Jerome arranged themselves in her mind. Betsy crossed to her father's desk, took out a sheet of paper, and, without bothering to sit down, wrote.

Sir, I cannot accept your offer of the principality of Schmalkalden. Westphalia is not big enough for two queens. Nor do I feel any remorse at having requested the aid of the emperor. I petitioned his imperial majesty because I would rather be sheltered by an eagle than dangled from the bill of a goose.
Elizabeth

❧ XXV ❧

BETSY realized that her letter to Jerome might end any possibility of receiving assistance from him, but she did not regret sending the stinging rebuke. She had trusted Jerome too long, clinging to his glib assurances for months after all evidence pointed to his defection. While not blind to his weaknesses, she had allowed herself to hope that his love for her and pain at their separation would mature the pleasure-loving boy into a responsible man, just as she had been forced to grow up in ways she never expected.

For Betsy knew she had changed. When she caught sight of herself in a mirror, she no longer saw the girlish charm of the Stuart portrait; she was still a lovely woman, but one with a determined set to her jaw and a hard glitter in her eyes. She had long since ceased to be the romantic young woman who declared that she would rather be married to Jerome Bonaparte for an hour than any other man for a lifetime. That girl, so certain that beauty and cleverness would win her a crown, had learned that the race is not always to the swift, nor the battle to the strong. By marrying into a ruling family, she had subjected herself to inexorable forces that reduced human beings to hostages whose value had little to do with their personal merit. Only someone with the titanic gifts of a Napoleon could subdue such forces and place them under his command.

Yet Betsy was not entirely reconciled to her fate. Even if she could not be a queen, she could fight to make her son a prince. Bo was proving to be a bright, tenderhearted boy, and she did not intend to spoil him as Letizia Bonaparte had indulged Jerome. Betsy would raise him to appreciate his heritage, to gain the best possible education, and to make a suitable marriage to a woman of high birth. If Bo did not inherit his father's throne, she would at least make sure that he found a place among European nobility. The world would see that her son's abilities far outstripped those of his wastrel father, and thus she would show the Bonapartes they were wrong to esteem her so lightly.

Because her mother was despondent over William's death, Betsy delayed her annual trip to Washington. Then in March 1809, General Turreau wrote Betsy asking her to call at the French embassy at her earliest convenience. After assuring herself that her mother was ready to resume running the household, Betsy left for the capital.

Turreau's office had a martial character with swords, pistols, and military flags hanging on every wall. When Betsy and her aunt were seated before Turreau's desk, the general handed Betsy an official communication that the emperor had sent him by way of the Minister of Foreign Affairs, Monsieur de Champagny:

> *I have read Miss Patterson's letter. Reply to Turreau to inform her that I shall receive her child with pleasure, and that I will charge myself with him, if she will send him to France; that, as to herself, whatever she wishes will be granted her; that she can count on my esteem and my desire to be agreeable to her; that when I refused to recognize her, I was led to it by high political considerations; that, apart from that, I am resolved to secure to her son the destiny she may desire.*

Betsy was so overcome by the news that she pressed a hand against her chest and made herself breathe deeply. Could this be the realization of her dreams at last? It hardly seemed possible. After several seconds, she said, "General Turreau, please convey my gratitude to the emperor for his gracious answer."

Then she explained that her son was too young to travel without her. She very much desired to live in Europe, preferably Paris, but was willing to settle wherever the emperor thought best. Betsy also reminded Turreau that to use her maiden name would injure her reputation, as much in Europe as in the United States.

Turreau toyed with his mustache. "Then you would rather receive a title than a large income?"

Sensing a trap, Betsy paused. She took out a perfume-scented handkerchief, dabbed her upper lip, and said carefully, "If I am to have a title, I must have sufficient income to live in a manner befitting my rank."

Turreau nodded. "I think that you should write all these things to the emperor, and I will forward the letter to him. Then we shall have to wait for his reply."

"Oh." Betsy's elation shriveled. "You do not feel authorized to set up a pension for the amount his imperial majesty previously named?"

"No, Mademoiselle. Concerning matters in which the emperor has taken such a personal interest, it is necessary to wait for his explicit orders."

She nodded. "Allow me a few days to compose an appropriate letter."

The next day, Betsy called on Dolley Madison, whose husband had just been inaugurated president. Betsy wanted to provide her friend with the latest news about Dolley's son from her first marriage. Payne Todd was attending a boarding school near Baltimore, and Betsy sometimes visited the boy for her friend. After Dolley gleaned all the details she could about her child, she asked what the Pattersons thought of President Jefferson's decision to repeal the Embargo Act before he left office and replace it with the Non-Intercourse Act that banned exports only to British and French ports.

Betsy toyed with her gloves as she mentally translated her father's caustic response into something suitably tactful. "My father thinks the government should not interfere with trade at all. He says it only hurts American merchants."

Dolley nodded. "Mr. Madison has the power to lift the ban for either Britain or France if they agree to stop harassing our shipping. But he has been in office too brief a time to begin negotiations with either General Turreau or the British minister, the Honorable David Erskine."

Betsy looked up in surprise. "The same David Erskine who married Frances Cadwalader?"

"Yes. Do you know him?"

"I know his wife. She was very kind to me when I was in London. I must write to her."

Frances Erskine responded to Betsy's note by calling on her. Betsy presented her guest to her aunts, who then withdrew from the drawing room so the two young women could become reacquainted. As Betsy poured tea from her aunt's silver tea service, she said, "You must be glad to be back in the United States so that you can see your family again."

Lady Erskine put sugar in her cup and stirred. "I am happy for my sons and daughters to know their American grandparents, but truly, my children find life here rather strange. They are so accustomed to thinking of themselves as English."

Betsy sighed. "I would like to raise my son in Europe—if only I can conclude the necessary arrangements with the emperor." When Lady Erskine tilted her head quizzically, Betsy explained her request for a pension and Napoleon's promise to provide for her and Bo.

Lady Erskine sipped her tea and then set her cup and saucer on the mahogany table between them. "I am astonished. I did not think that he would be so willing to make amends for the harm he has done you."

Her words evoked the memory of their previous conversations in London and the anguish Betsy had felt as she prayed that Jerome would return to her before the birth of their child. She sighed. "Nothing can entirely make amends for that, but the emperor assures me that he did not act from personal hostility but rather because of policy considerations."

Lowering her gaze, Lady Erskine adjusted the ruffle on her three-quarter sleeve. "Perhaps it would be judicious for us to avoid debating the merits of Bonaparte's policies."

"Of course." Betsy passed her the plate of watercress sandwiches and changed the subject, "You will be glad to hear that my son is nearly four years old and very healthy. I don't know if I ever properly thanked you for all you did when I was in England. You were of great help to me during that trying time."

Lady Erskine smiled. "Think nothing of it. I was more than happy to assist you in my own small way."

After her visitor left, Betsy worried that their difference of opinion about Napoleon might have placed a strain on their friendship. The following week, however, Lady Erskine invited Betsy to a small family supper.

When Betsy arrived at the Erskine house, she met Frances Erskine's older brother Thomas and his wife Mary. Thomas Cadwalader had a hawk's nose and eyes that narrowed when he paused to think. Betsy deemed him a cautious man—a good attribute for someone who worked as a lawyer but one that surprised her because Lady Erskine had confided during their earlier acquaintance that Thomas and his wife had been forced to elope because of an unresolved feud between their families.

Perhaps because Mary Cadwalader knew how it felt to face marital opposition, she smiled sympathetically at Betsy. "I am happy to meet you at last, Madame Bonaparte."

"The feeling is mutual, Mrs. Cadwalader," Betsy replied.

Then Lady Erskine presented Betsy to her other guest, a thirty-year-old Englishman named Charles Oakeley, who had just arrived in Washington to be secretary to the British legation. Oakeley had light brown hair, dark eyes, and a long, pointed nose in an otherwise handsome face. His clothes were well tailored but conservative in hue: a high-collared shirt, white cravat, mustard waistcoat, black tailcoat, and buff pantaloons.

Once they were at the table with a first course of oxtail soup before them, Betsy asked, "Have you been in this country before, Mr. Oakeley?"

"No, Madame Bonaparte. I spent the last few years in Munich and Stockholm."

"I fear you will find our summers much hotter than you have ever experienced."

Oakeley laughed. "I am sure the climate here is warmer than northern Europe, but I grew up in Madras, India, and I do not think you can top that climate for heat."

"Really! I have never met anyone who lived in India." Betsy took her last spoonful of soup and rested her spoon on the charger beneath the bowl. "Why was your family there, Mr. Oakeley?"

"My father was the colonial governor."

She sipped her wine. "I do wish you would tell me about it. I have traveled so little."

Oakeley nodded. For the next hour, he described the colonial city where he grew up: the high-walled Fort of St. George on the Bay of Bengal, the white-pillared government house where his father worked, the pyramid-shaped Hindu temples with hundreds of brightly painted idols perched on the outer walls, and lush gardens that produced more fruit than Eden itself: coconuts, mangoes, oranges, pineapples, and plantains. His family's house had large airy rooms with white walls, heavy furniture of tropical wood, and slatted doors that opened to admit the sea air. From their terrace, they enjoyed a sweeping view of the bay, dotted with wooden boats from which dark-skinned men fished by throwing crude spears into the water.

Betsy found Oakeley's stories so fascinating that she forgot to respond with the coolness needed to keep him at bay. By the end of the evening, he was gazing at her with a disturbing mix of admiration and hope.

They saw each other often that spring at the President's Mansion. Under Mrs. Madison's direction, Benjamin Latrobe had transformed the oval drawing room into a blazingly colorful salon that was the talk of Washington. Latrobe had repainted the walls sunflower yellow, highlighted moldings with strips of pink wallpaper printed with white and dark green leaves, hung crimson velvet curtains with gold tassels, and laid a carpet with a red, blue, and gold arabesque pattern. Dolley Madison held open houses every Wednesday in the lavishly decorated room. So many people attended—sometimes as many as 400 in a day—that the regular event became known as Mrs. Madison's "crush or squeeze."

At these receptions, Oakeley made sure Betsy had a chair, fetched her dishes of ice cream, and stood beside her relating stories about other lands. His manner was polished and urbane, and he displayed little vanity, even though Frances Erskine had said he was marked for a brilliant career and would someday be a baronet. The gossips of Washington hinted that he had indulged in a scandalous affair at his last posting, but his behavior toward Betsy remained circumspect. He was a considerate, engaging man who appeared to be smitten with her, yet he refrained from declaring his feelings.

When the time came for Betsy to return to Baltimore at the end of April, she felt regret at leaving such an amiable companion. However, Charles Oakeley had recently begun to pay her pointed compliments, and she feared he was building to a declaration. Resolutely, she packed her trunk and returned with Bo to South Street.

In May, Betsy decided to have Bo baptized as a Catholic. Her parents protested her choice to go outside the Presbyterian Church, but she was adamant. "Catholicism is the religion of kings, and being raised in the Church may help him claim his birthright."

After she finalized arrangements with the priest at St. Peter's Church, she received a note from Bishop Carroll requesting that she wait until he could attend the baptism of the "perhaps future prince." Betsy happily complied and responded by asking him to be Bo's godfather.

Before the event, Dorcas explained the religious significance to the almost-four-year-old boy in terms he could understand, and Betsy instructed him on how to behave during the service. To help him appreciate the gravity of the occasion, Betsy allowed him to be "breeched," to graduate to pantaloons and a jacket from the gowns that young children of both sexes wore. The morning of big event, Betsy brushed his forelock so that it swept upward, dabbed it with pomade to hold it in place, and told him how handsome he looked. Between the influence of the pre-baptismal instruction and the heady honor of wearing his first suit, Bo remained wide-eyed and solemn during the ritual.

That June, President Madison announced that he and David Erskine had reached an agreement that would allow trade with Britain to resume, which gave the Patterson family yet another reason to celebrate. For weeks, Betsy's father and brother Edward worked late hours arranging for their ships to sail with the long-delayed cargoes. With improved business prospects, Patterson grew less grim and even spoke pleasantly to Betsy one day when he came home to find her teaching Bo to count to 100: "He seems to have your aptitude with numbers."

That summer, the newspapers reported that Napoleon was at war on two fronts. To the southwest, he was locked in the Peninsular War in Spain, which had begun the year before as a revolt against French occupation and the imposed kingship of Napoleon's brother Joseph. To the east, Austria—still simmering about the territory it lost after Austerlitz—had attacked French forces in Bavaria. For Betsy, those battles meant that Napoleon was once again too preoccupied to consider her most recent letter.

Eliza, Marianne, and a friend in Philadelphia all told Betsy that rumors were swirling up and down the Atlantic seaboard that the emperor planned to make her a duchess. A year had passed since Betsy first wrote Napoleon, and sometimes she was so impatient for an answer that she walked Bo to the harbor to work off her feverish energy. The little boy loved the waterfront where he could wave to sailors and fishermen, but his mother stared at the ships and thought only of sailing away from the dull provincial town where she was stranded.

In the midst of her frustration, Betsy received a letter from Charles Oakeley saying that he had business in Baltimore and would like to call. Impulsively, she invited him to dinner.

"Who is this man?" her father asked. "Another suitor?"

"Well—" Betsy felt herself blushing. "He is a secretary to the British legation. I met him at the Erskines' home, and we saw each other at parties throughout the spring. He was a very attentive friend."

"Friend?" Patterson's voice curled with skepticism. "Is he a respectable man?"

"Very. His father is a baronet and the former governor of Madras."

"I see." Patterson looked at Betsy musingly.

Her eagerness to see Oakeley surprised Betsy. She enjoyed his company and found him attractive, but he stirred none of the desire she had felt for Jerome. Sometimes she wondered if she was still capable of loving any man. In spite of those doubts, Betsy worked with her mother to treat Oakeley to Maryland specialties such as crab cakes and wild turkey stuffed with oysters.

The day of his visit, Betsy dressed in a gown of azure silk shot with silver. Shortly before Oakeley was supposed to call, she seated herself on the sofa with Bo. When her parents entered the drawing room, Patterson asked, "Why is Bo here instead of in the nursery?"

"Because I think it time for Mr. Oakeley to become acquainted with my son."

A knock sounded upon the front door. The housekeeper showed Charles Oakeley into the drawing room, and Betsy introduced him to her parents. Then she gestured for Bo to stand in front of her. Placing her hands on the boy's shoulders, she said, "This is my son, Jerome Napoleon Bonaparte."

"Hello." Oakeley squatted down to look in the boy's face. "How old are you, Jerome?"

"I am four."

"Ah, that means you are no longer a baby. I come from a very large family, and I have two brothers not much older than you."

"Do you, sir? What are their names?"

Oakeley smiled at Bo's oddly adultlike speech. "Cornwallis and Frederic. Cornwallis was named after a British general."

"I know. My uncles told me he lost the Revolutionary War."

Oakeley laughed. "Yes, but that is not why my brother is named for him. Cornwallis was also the governor-general of India, and my family knew him there."

He rose and patted Bo's head. To Betsy, he said, "You have a delightfully precocious son. You must spend a great deal of time with him."

"Thank you. I believe he has a great destiny, and I am determined to prepare him for it."

Betsy excused herself to take Bo upstairs. When she returned a few minutes later, Oakeley and her father were talking about the recent agreement reached between President Madison and Minister Erskine. The discussion about commerce continued all during dinner, with her father asking many questions about the East India Company.

After dinner, as they sat in the drawing room drinking coffee, the conversation grew more heated. Patterson railed against the British practice of impressment, while Oakeley skillfully avoided expressing an opinion. Betsy finally intervened, "Father, Mr. Oakeley is not authorized to speak upon this matter. Please, do not tax him about it anymore."

Patterson flushed. "Forgive me, sir. I have no wish to be rude to a guest."

Oakeley left them late that evening without having spent a moment alone with Betsy, and she found herself regretting the lost opportunity to talk to him. During the last two months, she had missed him more than she cared to admit.

That night, she lay awake analyzing her feelings. Charles Oakeley was an amiable man with good prospects, and his behavior with Bo had pleased her. If Betsy had never met Jerome, she might consider him an eligible suitor, but to think of marrying him now was absurd. To ally herself with a member of the British diplomatic corps would turn Napoleon against her forever. She might be willing to lose the emperor's favor if only her own future was at stake, but what about her son? He could never inherit a stepfather's title, so he would lose all chance at noble rank if she married Oakeley. She would be destroying her boy's future for the sake of a match that, while a pleasant prospect, promised neither great passion nor exalted status. No, she could not sacrifice her son to gain so little.

Despite having reached that decision, she received Oakeley when he came to Baltimore in two weeks and again ten days after that. By then, Washington was embroiled in a diplomatic crisis. The British foreign secretary in London, George Canning, was furious with the concessions Erskine had made to President Madison, and Canning not only repudiated the agreement but also recalled Erskine to England. On August 9, President Madison once again prohibited trade with Britain.

At first, Betsy assumed that these events would occupy Charles Oakeley and stop his visits to her, but she was wrong. With Minister Erskine gone and his successor not yet arrived, Oakeley began to make the trip from Washington to Baltimore at least once a week.

In late August, her father asked to speak to her privately, so Betsy went next door to his counting house. She sat in front of his desk and, as she waited for him to finish the letter he was writing, picked up the bronze stamp he used to put wax seals on his correspondence. Patterson's seal was simple, just his entwined initials. Betsy wondered if, when the emperor gave her a title, she would be able to use a crest.

After signing his letter and blotting it, Patterson said, "Oakeley wants to make you an offer of marriage and has written to ask my blessing."

"Your blessing?" Betsy could not stop herself from laughing. "Is it the custom now to seek permission from the father of a woman who has already been married?"

"It is when that woman is living as a dependent in her father's house. Oakeley is being respectful. You might learn a lesson from him."

Betsy sobered. "I thought I had made it perfectly plain that I have no wish to remarry."

"You cannot remain single the rest of your life. I would rather see you marry an American, but if you must have a European, Oakeley is better than most. He has made a good start in life and will inherit a title. Does he not offer everything you have always wanted?"

"You cannot be serious. I was married to a prince. How could I stoop to marrying a baronet?"

"Stoop? If anyone is doing the stooping, it is Oakeley. You offer him nothing but a pretty face, which will fade soon enough, and a lively disposition along with the opprobrium of being a cast-off woman and the burden of raising a son who is not his."

Stung, Betsy retorted, "There is no shame in my situation. All the world knows that Jerome's desertion was due to political circumstances, not from any fault he found in me. As for Bo, the emperor will renege on his promises to secure my son's future if I marry an Englishman. How can you urge me to take a step that will ruin your grandson's prospects?"

"And how can you be so foolhardy as to trust anything that madman says?"

"Father, we have never agreed about the Bonapartes, and I daresay we never will. But I expect Napoleon to grant me a pension any day."

Leaning back in his chair, Patterson folded his arms. "I declare, there are times when I think you mad. An honorable man wishes to provide for you and your son, and you would throw that away for the empty promises of the blackguard who caused your troubles."

"Nevertheless, that is my decision. What answer do you plan to send Mr. Oakeley?"

"That he has my blessing but that I cannot vouch for your answer."

She rose. "Fair enough. Now if you will excuse me, I have work to do."

SEVERAL DAYS LATER, Charles Oakeley called on Betsy at her parents' home. She welcomed him into the drawing room and invited him to take her father's wingback chair, while she sat across from him on the sofa.

Instead of settling back in his seat, Oakeley placed his hands on his knees and cleared his throat. Then he rose and paced in front of the fireplace. "Madame Bonaparte, surely you must know what I wish to say. I believe your father informed you that I wrote to him last week."

Gazing at her lap, Betsy said, "I beg you not to speak of it, Mr. Oakeley. Such a discussion may injure us both."

Oakeley ceased pacing, and Betsy raised her eyes just enough to see that he had halted in front of the fireplace with his back to her. She craned her neck to see what had arrested his attention. At first, she thought he was gazing at the portrait of her and her mother but then realized that the angle of his head was wrong. He was staring at the miniature of Jerome that she kept upon the mantel. "Of course," he murmured. "Your heart still belongs to him."

"No!" Betsy exclaimed. Even though she had no desire to give Charles Oakeley false hope, she would not insult him with a lie. "I display that to remind my son that he has a father. It is only for Bo's sake that I can endure looking at it."

Oakeley crossed the room in three strides and sat beside her. He seized her hand. "Oh, Madame Bonaparte. My dear Elizabeth. You will let me call you Elizabeth?"

"No, Mr. Oakeley." She tugged to free herself, but he would not relinquish his grip, so Betsy let their clasped hands lie in her lap. Sitting beside him, she grew self-conscious of her breathing. She could *feel* how close Oakeley's trousered thigh was to hers, protected only by a flimsy gown. The flame of desire began to flicker within her, and a vivid image of Oakeley embracing her seized Betsy's imagination. She wondered whether, if she swayed toward him, he would kiss her. Then she might know if she was able to feel passion again.

Stiffening, she told herself to remain true to her purpose. Betsy forced herself to picture her little boy's face and then swallowed hard. "Mr. Oakeley, I am honored by your attentions, but I have no plans to remarry. I have devoted my life to my son and his future."

"Why should that prevent you from forming a new attachment? I could help you raise your son. We have fine schools in England, and I would provide him with the very best education." He smiled. "And I know how he loves to ride. I would give him a pony and, when he is older, teach him to hunt."

For an instant, Betsy could envision her horse-mad boy riding exuberantly across the English countryside. Then she shook her head. "But what of his future? What about when he reaches manhood? His uncle, the emperor, can award him a title and a place at court. Those are things you cannot offer him, no matter how much affection you come to feel."

Sighing, Oakeley released her hand. "No, I cannot. But are you so very certain that Napoleon will keep his word?"

"He has given me his promise in writing."

Oakeley narrowed his eyes. "My country will never cease to oppose him. If the Fifth Coalition does not defeat him, we will form a sixth and, if necessary, a seventh. The might of the British Empire is committed to defeating Bonaparte, and we will accomplish it in time."

That reminder that Oakeley represented Napoleon's enemies hardened Betsy's resolve. "How could I wish for anything so opposed to my son's interests?"

"Could you not find a new way to define his interests? It is true that when I inherit my father's title, I cannot pass it on to your son, but I will help him any other way I can. I could launch him in a diplomatic career. Or a career in politics if he prefers." Betsy shook her head again, and Oakeley continued in a rush, "There is something else you may not have considered. If we have a son of our own, he will one day be a baronet. Would that not please you?"

Betsy gazed at him in consternation as she contemplated bearing another child and dividing the love she felt for Bo. "I cannot imagine such a thing."

Oakeley knelt before her. "I love you, and I cannot imagine my future without you."

"Please, do not press me any further. I cannot give you the answer you want."

He took her hand and raised it to his lips. "Then do not give me any answer at all. Please, think about everything I have said and see if you cannot change your mind."

After a long moment, Betsy nodded. "I will consider it."

Over the next few weeks, Betsy felt pressed on all sides. Charles Oakeley continued to visit her, and his eyes pled his suit even as he honored her request not to pressure her for an answer.

General Turreau stopped at South Street on his way back to Washington in September and demanded an explanation of the rumors that Betsy planned to marry an Englishman. She explained her predicament and swore that it was not her intention to marry *anyone*.

Turreau frowned. "Are you sure this is not a British plot to gain control of the boy?"

"I do not think so, sir."

"If you are lying, it will do you no good. The emperor will not consider himself bound by any agreement based on falsehood."

She held out her open palms. "I swear to you, *mon général*, I am telling the truth. My father is pressuring me to marry, but this is not what I want."

He stood abruptly. "I will see what I can do."

In mid-September, Aunt Margaret wrote her:

Everyone is gossiping about the poor man. Francis James Jackson, the new minister from Britain, is furious. He ordered Oakeley to return to England with important dispatches, and the secretary balked. You must either accept him or refuse to see him again. He is destroying his career over you.

Betsy turned to her mother. "What am I to do? I turned him down, but he will not accept my answer."

"Then you will have to be rude. You cannot allow this situation to continue."

The following week, a newspaper report drove Charles Oakeley temporarily from Betsy's mind. Earlier that summer Jerome's kingdom had come under attack by the Duke of Brunswick, whose lands Napoleon had seized and annexed to Westphalia. Brunswick sought revenge by leading an army of exiles, dressed in black and wearing the emblem of a death's head, to recapture his duchy. The Black Legion won its first battle and then fought again at Oelper, losing this time to a new contingent of Westphalians. However, the victorious commander failed to pursue the retreating army, allowing it to flee to England.

The general whose incompetence allowed Brunswick to escape was none other than Jean-Jacques Reubell, Jerome's friend who had married Henriette Pascault. According to the report, Jerome had exiled Reubell in disgrace.

Betsy's heart churned with conflicting feelings. Having often wondered if Henriette and her husband were profiting by Jerome's kingship, Betsy took malicious pleasure in learning that Reubell had blundered so badly. However, she still hoped Bo would inherit Jerome's kingdom, so she was distressed to learn that such a bitter foe remained at large.

In October, Turreau wrote that he had sent another letter to France requesting a decision on her behalf. "I number among my duties, Madame, the care of your tranquility and your independence."

Armed with this reassurance, Betsy told Charles Oakeley that she had unequivocally decided against him. "Sir, I must ask you not to importune me further. Such actions on your part will only distress us both."

Oakeley turned very pale. "I will not trouble you again. Please know that my love and esteem remain steadfast, and if you should ever change your mind, you have only to write me and I will come to you from wherever in the world I may be posted." After bowing low over her hand, he left.

❦ XXVI ❧

HAT fall, Betsy decided to refresh her wardrobe. Since she lacked the money for new clothes, she set about remaking the gowns she had. Betsy snipped the lace off the neckline of one gown and used it to trim the sleeves of another; refashioned pleats and flounces that had gone out of style; and bought small quantities of braid, lace, ribbon, and spangles to use as trimmings.

One afternoon when her mother was out and Bo was napping, Betsy sat at the drawing room table designing a floral motif to embroider onto one of her gowns. As she paused to sharpen her pencil with a penny knife, the front door knocker sounded. Betsy sighed. The housekeeper and maids were in the kitchen making preserves, so she would have to answer it.

She rose, brushed pencil shavings from her lap, and went to the door. Henriette Reubell stood upon the stoop. She was heavier than when Betsy saw her last, and her face showed signs of strain, but she wore a fashionable red paisley shawl over a pale yellow gown embroidered with rosebuds.

Betsy stepped back to allow her former friend to enter, and Henriette walked into the drawing room where she sat on the teal sofa. After taking the wingback chair opposite, Betsy asked, "Why are you here? I have not heard a word from you for five years."

Lifting a hand, Henriette smoothed back her hair in a nervous ges-ture Betsy recognized from the past. "Forgive me. When we arrived in France, the emperor chastised Reubell for his role in your mar-riage, and for a while, we feared he might end up in prison like poor Bentalou. I dared not write you, and once we went to Westphalia, I could not think what to say."

Betsy folded her arms beneath her chest. "Yes, how could you ex-plain to your *dear* friend that you had a place at court, knowing what Jerome's kingship had cost me?"

Henriette flushed. "What would you have had me do? Refuse to go when my husband was called to Westphalia? I too am a wife, and my first duty is to Reubell."

"Ah, but I am no longer a wife. Your friends the Bonapartes have seen to that."

"How can you blame me?"

A sharp pain shot through the front of Betsy's skull, and she leaned her forehead on her hand. For an instant, she recalled what a good friend Henriette had once been and how they had shared the ambition to make advantageous marriages. "I am not angry so much as envious. You have been where I wanted to be the last two years. And you still have a husband. I have only my son."

"J'en suis desolée," Henriette said, slipping into her native language to apologize. "Does it not help to have one more friend now that I am returned?"

As Betsy gazed at Henriette's fine clothes, she felt gall rise in her throat. "I do not know. When I think that you have been partaking of the delights of court—"

"Is that what you think?" Henriette lifted her hands with palms up-raised. "That we enjoyed our time in Westphalia?"

"Did you not?"

"At first, but it quickly palled. King Jerome had little interest in gov-ernance and cared only for the pageantry of court. When we arrived in Kassel, he immediately found himself in financial difficulties. He had left France in debt—"

"No surprise there!"

After smiling wryly, Henriette said, "No. He discovered to his chagrin that the Westphalian treasury was empty and the castle in disrepair, yet he was expected to pay tribute to support the French army. He feared that if he raised taxes, it would foment discontent."

Betsy glanced across the room at the table, which held the evidence of her efforts to save money. "Do you mean that Jerome Bonaparte has actually learned to economize?"

Henriette laughed harshly. "No. He went even deeper in debt, ordering uniforms, carriages, luxurious furnishings. You would be shocked by what he has become. He bankrupts his kingdom with his pursuit of pleasure and has lost what self-control he exercised when married to you. He betrays the queen at every turn. Respectable families will not let their daughters attend balls at Kassel for fear that he will seduce them."

Shocked, Betsy raised a hand to quiet Henriette. Examining her heart, she discovered that she still retained enough regard for Jerome to grieve over his shameful behavior. After a moment, Betsy nodded for her guest to continue.

Henriette scooted to the edge of the sofa and, after glancing over her shoulder, said in a low voice, "Once when he was in a good mood, I asked why he did not rule with justice and economy so that he would be remembered as a wise king. The laughter dropped from his face and he answered, 'My brother took from me the only reason I ever had to regulate my conduct. Do not begrudge me my pleasures.'"

"More of his lies," Betsy said. "He seeks to excuse his debauchery by pretending to pine for me, but I know he no longer cares."

After biting her lip, Henriette said, "I think you are wrong. Do you recall the miniatures you gave him? The court painter used them to make a larger portrait of you that the king keeps in his private dressing room. Queen Catharine has never seen it."

Even though Betsy tried to repress the memory of the charming young man she had loved, her mind filled with the image of his laughing eyes and sensuous mouth. She rose and went to the mantel, where she stared at the miniature of him wearing a mustache and braided uniform. "Oh Jerome," she murmured. "Was it worth losing me for such a paltry gain?"

"You have no conception of how colossal Napoleon's rage can be. Much firmer men than Jerome have found it difficult to defy him."

Whirling on her, Betsy demanded, "How can you imply that he is not to blame? For two years, he swore he would never give me up, then he threw me over and for what? To become a figure of ridicule?"

Henriette leaned forward. "Then you don't know what really happened."

Feeling a sudden dread, Betsy pressed her hands against her stomach. "What do you mean?"

"He tried to remain true, but he was surrounded by Napoleon's spies and threatened with imprisonment should he disobey his brother. When he returned from his Atlantic tour, Napoleon presented him with a marriage contract to sign."

"And he signed it."

Henriette shook her head. "No, he refused and joined the army, choosing to risk death rather than betray you. During the Prussia campaign, Jerome was desperate to achieve glory, but fate conspired against him, and the victories went to others. When he returned to France, Napoleon praised him, but everyone knew it was a sham. Even so, Jerome hoped to be allowed to return to you. Instead, the emperor told him that his formal betrothal to Catharine was a *fait accompli.* A proxy had already performed it. If Jerome had refused the marriage then, it would have caused a scandal."

"He has benefited royally from being forced into that marriage," Betsy said as she returned to her chair and sank into it.

"Do you really believe him happier leading a life of dissipation than one of honor with the woman he loves?"

"Why do you tell me this? It was easier when I could hate him."

"Because you need to hear the truth, for your son's sake if nothing else. He needs to know that his father is not entirely devoid of honor."

Betsy slapped the arm of her chair. "Do not presume to tell me how to raise my son. I never abuse Jerome to him."

Henriette shrugged. *"Alors,* I thought you should know the truth. Jerome is too self-indulgent to be a truly good king. But he was a better man with you than he was before your marriage or has been since."

Betsy began to weep. Despite her contempt for Jerome, she took no pleasure in learning that he had sunk so low. Their suffering might have some meaning if he had disciplined himself to become a good king.

Instead, he chose to indulge the most degraded impulses in his nature.

After several moments, she dug her nails into her palm and managed to regain control of her emotions. "You were right to tell me. It confirms that I was wise not to send Bo there."

Henriette nodded. "I think Jerome lives in terror that you will turn his son against him."

Betsy laughed. "After my last letter, I can see why he might think I am filling the boy's ears with venom, but I love my son too much to do that. I still hope he will find a place at court someday."

"Well, Queen Catharine has so far been unable to conceive. Behind her back, everyone in Kassel speculates that your son will inherit Jerome's throne."

"As well he should. He is Jerome's legitimate heir, no matter what Napoleon says."

"If Jerome can retain a kingdom for him to inherit. The Duke of Brunswick's hatred is very fierce, and he means to bring war to Westphalia again."

Betsy shrugged. "If that happens, I am sure the emperor will find some other place for my son. He has promised to assure Bo's future."

"You astonish me." Henriette picked up her shawl from the sofa cushion and draped it over her shoulders. "I would have thought after all that has happened, you would not want anything to do with the Bonapartes ever again."

Betsy waved her words away. "Napoleon dismissed me as expendable because I am American and a woman. Someday I will make him see that he was wrong on both counts."

"You are more indomitable than I." Henriette stood. "Was I right to come?"

"Yes, I am grateful."

They walked arm in arm to the front hall, yet neither suggested seeing each other again and their parting kiss felt like a farewell. As Henriette walked to her carriage, Betsy firmly closed the door.

In December, Turreau invited Betsy to visit him at the embassy. When she and Aunt Nancy were shown into his office, the general was seated at the desk, working on some papers. Betsy noticed that since her last visit, he had added a bronze model cannon to the more utilitarian items on his desk blotter.

After a moment, Turreau looked up. "Mademoiselle Patterson, I have not yet received a reply. The emperor has been engaged in defeating Austria and negotiating the treaty of their surrender. But I am sure it is only these cares that prevent him from attending to your situation, so I have taken it upon myself to use legation funds to start your pension."

"Then you know how much my income will be?"

"No," he said and paused to sign a document. "I think we should work upon the assumption that the original offer remains in effect."

"That seems eminently reasonable." Betsy wondered if he could hear her sarcasm.

"I have authorized you to draw up to $20,000. Here is a letter of credit and a personal note to the bank manager. I hope this will cover your needs until we hear from the emperor. You must not overspend, as I cannot advance you additional money until I receive approval. By doing this much, I have already overstepped my authority."

As she took the all-important documents, Betsy was afraid that her hands would tremble and give away her excitement. She placed the documents in her lap. "Thank you, General Turreau. I am more grateful than I can say."

"There is one other matter we must discuss. I have engaged a French colonel of impeccable reputation to act as your—shall we say, majordomo."

Betsy tilted her head inquisitively. "Why do you imagine I need such a person?"

"His primary duty will be to tutor your son, but he can also help with business matters."

"General Turreau, I am perfectly capable of teaching my son. He is only four and already proficient at both his alphabet and his numbers."

With a condescending smile, Turreau answered, "Yes, but he should learn French from a Frenchman, and I am certain the emperor will want him to be educated in military matters."

"Surely not at such a tender age."

Turreau stroked his mustache. "Mademoiselle, do you not agree that the emperor's nephew will be safer with a military man close to hand?"

"I see," Betsy said, remembering Turreau's earlier fears that the British were plotting to gain control of her son. This "tutor" was meant to act as an unofficial bodyguard—and, no doubt, as a spy who would report Betsy's activities. "Tell me more about this man."

Although it was difficult to tell because of his mustache, Betsy thought that Turreau smiled in self-satisfaction. "His name is Louis de Tousard. He fought in your Revolutionary War and later in Saint-Domingue. More recently, he was the vice-consul in Philadelphia."

Betsy frowned, trying to imagine how the Smiths would feel about having a French officer imposed upon them. Then she realized that she could now afford to set up her own household. "Let me find a place to live, and then I will meet this colonel."

TOUSARD TURNED OUT to be a dignified, sympathetic man of sixty. He had cottony white hair, pale blue eyes, a fleshy nose, and a double chin. His right arm was amputated. When Bo met him, he stared at the empty, folded-up sleeve and asked bluntly, "What happened to you?"

Kneeling before him, Tousard asked, "Do you know about the American Revolution?"

Bo nodded and started to chew his thumbnail, a recently acquired habit Betsy had been trying to break. Tousard gently placed his left palm over Bo's hand. "I can see that I will have to teach you to stand at attention like a soldier."

"I know how, sir." Bo stood up straight with his arms at his sides.

"Good. Now back to my story. I was fighting in the Battle of Rhode Island, approaching a British artillery position to capture the guns, when one of the cannon fired. The shot grazed my arm and shattered the bones. The doctors wanted to treat it, but I had to return to the fighting as soon as possible, so I told them to cut the arm off."

Bo's hazel eyes grew wide. He started to raise his hand to his mouth, but at a frown from Tousard, he returned to attention. "Did it hurt?" he whispered.

"Yes, but there is more than one kind of hurt. I knew that if I had failed to fight with my friends, it would cause a hurt in my heart that would take longer to heal."

Seeing Bo's puzzlement, Betsy wanted to intervene, but then the boy blurted, "Like when someone calls you a coward." His uncles often hurled that taunt during games.

"Right." Tousard braced himself with his left arm and struggled to his feet. To Betsy, he said, "It will be a pleasure to tutor your boy. I have no son, only daughters."

Betsy smiled. "Thank you, Colonel. I want him to learn discipline, as I fear he may take after one who has never shown much self-control."

Raising his eyebrows, Tousard nodded. "I comprehend perfectly, Madame."

Betsy was gratified that he addressed her as *madame* rather than *mademoiselle.* Seeing that Bo was following their conversation, she said quietly, "In English, we have a saying, *Little pitchers have big ears.* Whatever you may know about my past disappointments or about the person with whom I once had an intimate connection, the subject is not to be discussed in front of your charge. The paternal reputation must be preserved."

Tousard bowed his head in acknowledgment. "Yes, Madame."

THAT FEBRUARY BETSY turned twenty-five. She enjoyed herself more that winter than at any time since her separation from Jerome. Having money freed her from the vexing dependency on her father, and having Tousard in her household freed her from the burdensome feeling that she alone was responsible for her son. At parties, she danced and conversed with a new *joie de vivre.* Still, she was careful to state often that she did not wish to remarry, and everyone seemed to take her at her word—perhaps the rampant gossip about Oakeley had taught men in Washington that they would pursue her at their peril.

Turreau finally received a letter saying that Napoleon approved of the decision to start the pension and that he still intended to grant Mademoiselle Patterson a title if she did not marry an Englishman. Betsy received this information with an appropriately sober expression. In her heart, however, she exulted that Oakeley's attentions had roused the emperor at last.

In late winter, Washington society learned the shocking news that Napoleon had divorced Josephine. Earlier, when he was in Austria negotiating the Treaty of Schönbrunn, a rash young German had plotted to stab him, an event that reawakened Napoleon's fear that his empire would not survive his death. He had learned that it was Josephine, not he, who was responsible for their childless state, so he decided he must have a younger wife who could give him a son. In the spring, word came that the emperor had married nineteen-year-old Marie Louise of Austria, thus allying himself with one of France's bitterest enemies.

Although Betsy had less reason to be surprised by the news than anyone, it depressed her. The emperor's willingness to cast aside the woman he adored stirred up painful memories of his ruthlessness in destroying her marriage to Jerome. Telling herself that she had reason to be grateful to Napoleon now, she tried not to dwell on her past unhappiness.

Even so, Betsy's mood crashed to earth. Her pension enabled her to support herself and maintain a suitable position, but she wanted more than that. She wanted to save for Bo's future. Over the years as she mingled in society, she had realized that a lifetime of independent reading was no match for the systematic education that distinguished the people she admired most. Betsy had determined that Bo must become a man of letters like Jefferson and Madison. Such an education would prepare him for a position among the ruling classes—and impart to him the discipline his father lacked.

When she quizzed Tousard, she learned that living in France was more expensive than the United States, so she could not spend all her income now if she wanted to pay for European schooling later. This realization forced Betsy to economize by continuing to remake her wardrobe, washing her own laundry, and hiring a single maid instead of a staff. Because of her own experience of helpless dependency, she had sworn that she would never own a slave.

Betsy soon concluded that she not only needed to cut expenses, but she also must make her money grow. She decided not to ask her father's advice because she feared he would take control of her pension—and also because it would be more gratifying to prove that she could build a fortune without him. To learn sound investment principles, she questioned Aunt Nancy and several gentlemen acquaintances who were experienced at business. At first, the men laughed at the idea of a woman entering the commercial sphere—a reaction that infuriated

Betsy—but she controlled her temper by reminding herself that Bo's fate depended on her success. She hated pretending to be helpless, but whenever she deemed it necessary, she would bat her eyelashes as though fighting back tears and say in a tremulous voice, "But sir, I must take on this task if I am to provide for my poor, fatherless son." Invariably, that performance drew forth helpful recommendations.

Even so, Betsy did not act on all the advice she was offered. She had no intention of indulging in risky speculation of the sort that had bankrupted Marianne's father. Rather, she would take a cautious approach and buy only stocks that looked safe. One company she liked was the Union Manufacturing Company, a textile factory near Baltimore. Because the embargo had choked off imports, industry was developing in the United States, and Betsy reasoned that as the population grew, companies that made necessities were sure to prosper. At first, she bought only a few shares, but when they had grown in value after six months, she bought a few more.

These concerns absorbed her so that 1810 sped by. She and Bo spent the summer at Springfield, but family troubles marred the normally pleasant season. Seventeen-year-old Margaret had been diagnosed with consumption during the winter, and now even in the wholesome country air, her strength failed rapidly. Many afternoons, Betsy sat outside under the trees with her two sisters. Margaret had been studying drawing with Eliza's husband, Maximilien Godefroy, and sometimes Betsy and Caroline sat sketching with her. Increasingly, however, Margaret was too weary to do even that. Their mother tempted her with chicken in aspic, fruit compote, and blancmange, but Margaret continued to waste away.

Even as Betsy fretted over her sister's health, she worried about the possible danger to Bo from living with a consumptive. She thanked God that Colonel Tousard kept him outdoors most of each day learning to ride a pony, an activity the child adored. Tousard also guarded Bo from mishaps. Nine-year-old Henry and seven-year-old Octavius were reckless, and they dared Bo to take risky chances until Tousard told them, "Anyone can ride like a wild Indian. I am teaching him the skills of a soldier in the emperor's cavalry." After that, all three boys followed the colonel's directions.

Betsy returned to Washington that fall but kept in touch with her mother by letter, so she knew that Margaret grew weaker by the month. When Betsy came back to South Street for the holidays, she could see that her sister would not live long. Margaret passed away on January 5, 1811. Dorcas's despair was so deep that she did not leave her room for days, and Betsy began to wonder if she would need to remain in Baltimore indefinitely. After two weeks of mourning, however, her mother told her to return to the capital city. "You have had enough unhappiness. I want you to enjoy yourself now that you can."

Before leaving Baltimore, Betsy asked her brother Robert to look for a small house she could buy, so she and Bo could live independently when they were in town. Her mother was not strong, and Betsy did not want to keep burdening her with two extra people.

A few days after they returned to Washington, Tousard surprised Betsy by coming into her parlor and saying, "General Turreau wishes to be received."

She looked up from her sewing. "The ambassador is here? Surely, he must know I cannot receive him without a chaperon."

"I will remain, Madame, if you wish."

"Thank you, Colonel. Allow me a moment before you show the general in." Betsy rose, folded the gown she was altering, and stored it in her workbasket. Then she sat on the sofa.

As Turreau entered, Betsy saw that he was wearing his best clothes. After bowing to her, he told Tousard, "You may go."

"Please sit down, General. I asked Colonel Tousard to remain. It is not my habit to receive gentlemen callers alone."

Scowling, Turreau sat without argument. Tousard stood silently by the door.

"I have come to tell you that I have been recalled to France. The emperor sent a new ambassador to replace me."

"I see." Betsy's thoughts raced furiously. While Washingtonians would be glad to be rid of the disagreeable man, she wondered if the change would affect her pension.

Turreau crossed his legs and glanced around the room as though curious to know how Betsy lived. He picked up an English porcelain figurine from the table beside his chair—it was a fisherman's wife holding a basket of fish. Jerome had bought it for Betsy years before to remind her of the trip to Niagara and their joking banter of what they might do to escape Napoleon's control. It was one of the few ornaments she had saved when her father confiscated her household things. Turreau looked at the figurine, curled his upper lip in disdain, and set it down.

Then he nodded at Betsy. "Mademoiselle Patterson, you must know the respect I have gained for you by observing your conduct these last several years."

"Thank you, *mon général,* you are very kind."

"Your beauty and other amiable qualities are wasted in this backward country. A brilliant woman like you belongs in Paris."

Blinking in surprise, Betsy wondered why he was saying such things. Had Napoleon decreed that this disagreeable man should escort Bo and her to France? "As you know, that is my dearest desire, but I must wait upon his imperial majesty to grant me permission."

"I am certain that such permission would be forthcoming if he knew that there was no longer any danger of your tempting King Jerome from his current alliance."

"Whatever can you mean? I have severed all connection with King Jerome."

"Yes, but the emperor would feel more certain that you could not be a distraction if you were to become the wife of one of his officers." With a flourish, Turreau placed a hand upon his heart. "I speak of myself, of course. You cannot have failed to notice that the respect I feel for you has deepened into passionate admiration. But I do not ask you to reciprocate those feelings. I speak only of a marriage of convenience so that you may be presented at court where you belong. I have every confidence that once the emperor meets you and sees your admirable qualities, he will elevate you to the rank of duchess."

"Thus making you a duke?"

The general shrugged. "Perhaps."

Appalled at the thought of an alliance with him, Betsy rose to her feet. "What you suggest is completely impossible!"

Turreau stood too but before he could speak, Betsy declared, "After having been married to a man I loved, nothing would induce me to accept such a cold, calculated proposal. I have told you that I am devoted to my son and have no intention of remarrying. However, were I to consider such a step, nothing—not even an order from the emperor—could persuade me to accept you."

Turreau's face grew purple, and he took a threatening step toward her, stopping only at the sound of Tousard clearing his throat. After glaring at Betsy a moment longer, Turreau turned sharply and left. As the outer door slammed, Betsy felt a sudden weakness and sank to the sofa. Colonel Tousard rushed to her side. "Madame, are you all right?"

"Yes, I— Oh, what have I done?"

"You defended yourself with honor and spirit. You behaved exactly as I would want my own daughters to."

"Thank you. But the emperor. Do you think he will be displeased?"

"No, Madame. I have no doubt that this was a plot of Turreau's that the emperor knows nothing about. I am sure you will find soon enough that all is well."

"I hope so." Betsy shuddered as she remembered the stories Dolley Madison had told her about Turreau. She recoiled from the unspeakable thought that this ogre had imagined being married to her and perhaps forcing her to submit to his will. She kicked the workbasket that sat at her feet, upending it and spilling her sewing onto the floor. "What a horrible man. I would rather die than marry him."

XXVII

A WEEK later, Betsy received a letter summoning her and Colonel Tousard to the French embassy. When she saw the signature, her stomach cramped in dread. The new ambassador was Louis Sérurier, the official who had separated her from Jerome in Lisbon.

"Our last meeting did not go well," she told Tousard as they rode together to the appointment. "I responded angrily when he carried out the emperor's orders."

"Madame, he is an experienced diplomat. I am sure he understood your distress."

When they entered the ambassador's office, Betsy saw that it no longer looked like an army headquarters as it had under Turreau. The military paraphernalia had been removed from the walls, which instead featured a portrait of Napoleon and a map of France. On the desk, a brass case holding twin inkwells had replaced Turreau's miniature cannon.

Sérurier looked much the same as he had six years earlier except that his hairline had receded. "Mademoiselle Patterson, we meet again. I trust your son is well?"

"Yes, thank you," Betsy replied, hoping that the query meant the official was not going to be as icy toward her as he had been in Lisbon.

"How old is he now?"

"Five, your excellency. He will be six this summer."

Sérurier nodded and glanced at some papers on the blotter before him. "No doubt you are wondering why I sent for you."

He paused, and Betsy realized that he expected a response. She sat up a little straighter. "No, your excellency. Since you will be my new channel of communication to the emperor, it seems only right that we should become acquainted."

A smile flitted across Sérurier's face, and Betsy felt certain he was thinking of their last, tempestuous conversation. At length, he said, "I hope our dealings will be more pleasant than our first meeting."

Betsy pressed her lips tightly together and then decided to seize this opportunity to demonstrate that she had matured from the headstrong girl he had encountered so many years before. "I am certain they will be. I understand now that you were carrying out your orders, not acting from personal malice. Just as the emperor's actions were dictated by state policy."

He nodded and picked up the cut-crystal stopper to one of the inkwells and rotated it between his fingertips. "I thought you should know that Turreau's recall does not change your arrangement. His imperial majesty has instructed me to continue your pension."

"Thank you. Has he—" Betsy hesitated and clasped her gloved hands together in her lap to keep them from trembling and betraying her eagerness.

"Yes, Mademoiselle?"

"The emperor has promised to grant me a title and arrange for us to live in Europe." She looked at Sérurier inquisitively, but his face betrayed nothing. "Do you know if he has done so?"

Sérurier shook his head. "I regret to say that was not part of my instructions. But I must discharge another matter. I am sorry to deprive you of your aide, but Minister Champagny has decided that Colonel Tousard would serve the empire better by returning to the diplomatic service. Colonel, you have been appointed to the post at New Orleans."

Thinking of Bo's fondness for the colonel, Betsy shot Tousard an anguished glance. His expression remained impassive. To Sérurier, she said, "Will someone be appointed in his place?"

"No, Mademoiselle. If you want your son to have a tutor, you must hire one."

"It was my understanding that General Turreau took on this responsibility less for my son's education than for his protection."

Sérurier put the stopper back in the inkwell. "Minister Champagny believes that the danger is less than Turreau imagined. Please do not alarm yourself, Mademoiselle. The emperor continues to feel the deepest concern for your son." He smiled and folded his hands together on the desk. "Do you have any other questions for me?"

"No, Monsieur."

"Then I believe we have nothing else to discuss." They all rose. Sérurier said, "Colonel Tousard, I will send you copies of your orders by the end of the week."

"Why does he have to leave, Mama?" Bo cried when she told him the news. "I want him to stay. I will study harder."

"Come here." Betsy pulled him onto her lap. Now that he was almost six, he no longer fit there snugly, and when he squirmed as he was doing now, she feared he would slide off. She wrapped her arms around him. "This has nothing to do with you, Bo. You did nothing wrong. Do you remember how I explained why your father cannot be with us?"

He twitched angrily. "You said the emperor needs him to be a king in Europe."

"Exactly. This is a similar case. The emperor has other plans for Colonel Tousard, and we must accept the loss because that is what princes do; they make sacrifices for their people."

Bo struggled against her embrace. "I hate him!"

Betsy bent her head so her cheek was close to his and murmured, "You don't mean that. You love the colonel."

"Not him. My uncle! Napoleon!"

"You must not say that."

"But I do!" He tore free and stood before her with clenched fists. "He makes you cry sometimes. He took my father away and made him marry a new wife. I hate him."

Betsy stared in astonishment. Bo was normally so even-tempered that she had never suspected this subterranean rage. "Darling, rulers sometimes have to do what is right for the country instead of what they want."

"I don't care!" Bo threw himself on the rag rug and started screaming and kicking. Before Betsy could react to the tantrum, Colonel
Tousard entered the room.

"Master Bonaparte, what is the meaning of this?"

Bo immediately pulled himself up to a kneeling position. With tears
streaming down his cheeks and mucus running from his nose, he said,
"I don't want you to go."

"Ah." Tousard sat on a spindle-back chair across from Betsy and
gestured for the boy to stand before him. Pulling out a handkerchief,
he wiped Bo's face. "I do not want to leave you either, but as a soldier,
I must go where my superiors send me."

Betsy held her breath, waiting to see if Bo would reiterate his hatred of Napoleon. Instead he said, "Soldiers have to obey orders."

"Exactly. And so do young princes."

"But—" Bo glanced sideways at his mother. "Grandfather says I am
not really a prince. That is only a game Mama plays to make herself feel better."

Betsy experienced such a surge of anger that her face grew hot. "Jerome Napoleon, who is your father?"

"The king of Westphalia."

"And what is a king's son called?"

"A prince." Bo shuffled his feet uneasily. "But I am not a prince, and
everybody knows it."

She sighed. "Only because the emperor has not decided yet whether to make you a prince or a duke. But he promised to do that soon."

Bo scowled as he struggled to put his thoughts into words. "But we
are Americans, and there is no royalty here."

Certain that he had heard that statement or something very like it
from her father, Betsy snapped, "You are half European. You know that."

"Then will I have to live in Europe?" he asked, and his lower lip
trembled.

Betsy and Tousard exchanged surprised glances. "Someday. Don't
you want to?"

"No, Mama. I would miss Grandfather and Mother and my uncles."

"Oh, Bo." Betsy waved her hand, about to dismiss his fears off-hand-
edly, when the look of apprehension in his hazel eyes stopped her. Be-

cause he was usually such a temperate, conscientious child, she rarely worried that he might be grieving over his lack of a father. Rather, she often told herself he was better without such a poor example as Jerome. Yet, now she wondered if Jerome's absence and the ongoing uncertainty of their position in the Bonaparte family had made Bo unsure of his place in the world. Betsy squatted before him and smiled gently. "Darling, I know you are sad that the colonel must leave, but I promise that no matter what else happens, I will always be with you and love you."

He threw his arms around her neck.

Betsy stroked his hair. "I think it is time for you to go to bed. Go find Sadie and ask her to help you get ready. I will come tuck you in."

Left alone with Tousard, she said, "Thank you for your assistance, Colonel. I have never seen him so distraught."

"He will be fine after a night's sleep. Bo is a good boy."

Nodding, Betsy twisted her emerald ring. "I must confess I think my husband, my son, and I would have all been happier if the emperor had not separated us. But since he did, I must do what I think best for Bo even if he does not understand." She started to leave the room but then turned back. "Colonel, I beg you not to repeat what I said. I try very hard to uphold the emperor's authority."

"Madame, in all the time I have served you, your conduct has been exemplary."

"Thank you." In that moment, Betsy also felt like weeping at the prospect of losing this man who understood her better than her own father did. "We will always think of you as one of our family."

After pausing in the hallway to collect herself, she went upstairs. Bo was already in bed, and a candle was burning in a pewter candlestick on the small chest of drawers. As Betsy bent to kiss him, he murmured sleepily, "Mama, I think you should be a queen."

Betsy smiled and tweaked his nose. "And you should be a king. Good-night, your majesty." She pulled up his covers, blew out the candle, and quietly left. On her way back downstairs, she decided that she would embroider some handkerchiefs with Tousard's initials as a going-away gift.

Since Bo was still young, Betsy determined to save money by teaching him herself for the next year. She also asked Aunt Nancy to move in with her to share expenses.

Robert wrote of a small, two-story house in Baltimore that Betsy could buy from Marianne's grandfather for $9,000. When she expressed surprise at the amount, he wrote back saying, "You are lucky to get it for that price. The rapid growth of the city has created an insatiable demand for suitable housing."

Afraid of losing the opportunity, Betsy sent a down payment by return post and suggested a schedule to pay the balance. Robert had reported that the interior was in poor condition, so she also agreed to the suggestion to have it replastered. Betsy worried over spending so much money, but Bo's comment about his princely status being a "game" had rankled and strengthened her resolve to live apart from her father when they were in Baltimore.

In May, Betsy learned that Empress Marie Louise had given birth to a son in March. Betsy could not help but resent an event that reduced Bo's importance in the emperor's dynastic plans. Her anger also rose because immediately after the birth, Napoleon had named his son Imperial Prince and King of Rome. Clearly, the emperor could award titles quickly when it suited him.

Unhappily, Betsy realized that with an heir to make his empire secure, Napoleon had little reason to consider her and Bo anymore, and she was powerless to force the situation. Even though she still had suitors, she could no longer use the threat of marrying an Englishman to prod the emperor because he would simply stop her income. As the year wasted away, Betsy came to fear that Napoleon's promises would prove as empty as Jerome's.

As 1812 dawned, Washington was also in turmoil. The previous October, at the Battle of Tippecanoe, William Henry Harrison had defeated a confederacy of Indians who opposed settlement of the Northwest Territory. Many Americans suspected that British troops in Canada had incited those tribes, and some people called for an invasion of Canada to drive the British from North America. On the seas, Britain was still blockading continental Europe and preventing American merchantmen from trading with the French Empire, so the non-intercourse regulations remained in effect. Because farmers could not export their crops, prices dropped and incomes suffered. Anger against the British ran high in the agricultural South and West, while merchants in the Northeast wanted to appease Great Britain and restore maritime trade.

In the midst of these tensions, a pair of letters arrived from Jerome in the spring, the first communication in three years. One was addressed to Betsy, the other to their son:

> *My dear Elisa, what a long time it is since I have received any news of you and of my son! In the whole world you could never find a better or a more tender friend than me. I have many things to write to you; but, as I can but fear that this letter may be intercepted, I limit myself to giving you news of myself and asking you for news of you and my son. Be assured that all will be arranged sooner or later. The Emperor is certainly the best, as he is the greatest, of men.*

His words reminded Betsy of their past affection, and she glanced at the miniature of Jerome on the mantel. Then she resolutely put the letter away and called Bo. As he entered the drawing room, she held out the second letter. "Your father has written you."

Bo came close and leaned against her leg. "Can you read it to me?"

Breaking the seal, Betsy unfolded the page and read aloud:

> *My dear son. I hope that this letter will be more lucky than the others which I have written you and which I suppose you have not received. I hope that you will not forget me because I could not do without your affection and I hope that you are always a good and loving son to your mother, who, as the most noble of women, will always set you the best example. I embrace you with all my heart.*

Bo stirred. "Mama, is that really from my own true father?"

"Yes, darling."

Taking the page, Bo frowned at it. "Do you think he really loves me?"

"Of course."

"But he has never met me," Bo whispered.

Betsy knelt before him and smoothed back his hair. "I hope someday you will meet him. But he does not have to meet you to love you. You are part of him just as you are part of me."

Bo nodded in his curiously adult fashion and then started to read the letter for himself. Betsy could see his lips moving as he sounded out the difficult words. When he finished, he handed her back the page. "Should I write Papa?"

"If you wish."

He nodded again. "I will tell him I am going to be seven soon and I like horses and I always do what you tell me. Is that all right, Mama?"

"It sounds very good." She rose and fetched Bo some paper. As he settled at the table, Betsy recalled the stories Henriette had told her. Although Betsy had not wanted to admit it at the time, she now thought Henriette was right. Jerome sounded sad.

NOTICING THAT Bo had become moody after Tousard's departure, Betsy decided that he needed more men in his life—men other than her father. She also wanted him to receive a more systematic education than she could give him, so in the spring, she wrote Bishop Carroll to inquire about enrolling her son at the same boarding school Dolley Madison's son had attended. Being separated from Bo would pain her, but she was determined to do what was best for him.

While she waited for an answer, she spent hours trying to cut expenses and increase her income. Ever since the news that Napoleon had put aside Josephine, Betsy had feared his arbitrary power. Somehow, she had to accumulate enough money to remain independent even if he should cut off her pension.

One afternoon, Betsy pulled up a chair to the round tea table, placed a thick book on the seat, and settled Bo there so he could write comfortably. She gave him a page of addition problems to solve while she went over her accounts. After a few minutes, Bo said, "Mama?"

"Yes?" She did not stop working at her calculations.

"Why are you frowning?"

Betsy looked across at her son and consciously smoothed her forehead. "I was trying to think of ways to save more money."

Bo bit the blunt end of his pencil. "Did the emperor stop your income?"

"No, but I want you to go to school in Europe someday, and that will cost more than I have right now."

"I can go to school here like my uncles."

Betsy laid down her pencil. "Bo, I have explained this. Your grandfather wanted your uncles to go into business, so they did not need a university education. You are quite different. You must be educated in a manner suitable for a prince."

Bo thrust out his lip in a way that reminded Betsy of Jerome in a petulant mood. "But I can go into business too. I can get rich like grandfather and take care of you."

"Oh, dear boy." Betsy went to him and kissed the top of his head. "Your job is to apply yourself to your lessons, not to worry about me."

"But Grandfather says—"

"Bo, you are my son, not his. Please remember that."

"Yes, Mama."

Betsy squeezed his shoulder lightly. "Don't you know that I love you more than anything in the world?"

"Yes, Mama," he answered. Hurt that he did not return the declaration of love, Betsy returned to her seat, picked up her pencil, and added a column of figures. After a moment, Bo blurted, "Mama, I think you are an angel, and I just want to make you happy."

"Then do your arithmetic," Betsy answered, but she smiled warmly at him as she said it. Bo grinned before bending back over his arithmetic problems.

On June 18, 1812, the United States declared war on Great Britain. Supporters called it a Second War for Independence, while critics disparaged it as "Mr. Madison's War."

Almost immediately, Baltimore descended into violence. Most people there favored the war, but one editor named Alexander Hanson published protests. On June 22, a mob destroyed his newspaper office. A month later, Hanson attempted to publish his paper from another building. This time, the resulting violence led to a shooting and the arrest of Hanson and his friends. A mob broke into the jail that evening and beat and tortured several prisoners, including Revolutionary War heroes James Lingan and Light-Horse Harry Lee. Lingan died of his wounds, and Lee suffered permanent injuries, including partial blindness.

The wanton viciousness horrified the rest of the country, and it made Betsy feel justified in her contempt for her hometown. The events had confirmed her belief that a strong monarch like Napoleon was preferable to democracy, in which ignorant mobs held too much sway.

Although tensions had been mounting with Britain for years, the U.S. government had not prepared for war, and the first campaigns of 1812 went badly. An attempted invasion of Canada by General William Hull ended in the capture of his army and the loss of Detroit.

The U.S. Navy was equally unprepared with only about 20 ships when the war began. However, the government authorized privateers to attack British shipping, and in the first four months, Americans seized more than 200 British merchantmen.

When Betsy's brothers gleefully reported such captures, she scoffed, "To the British, such losses are no more than flea bites. You had better hope that Napoleon stays on his throne and the British remain mired in Spain. France is the only thing preventing Great Britain from crushing us."

That fall, after spending weeks debating whether it was wise to be separated from her child in time of war, Betsy enrolled Bo in the boarding school at Mount St. Mary's College in Emmitsburg, Maryland, fifty miles from Baltimore. Bishop Carroll had assured her that the teachers, all priests, would be strict with her son and instill in him the discipline she felt he needed. And Emmitsburg was further inland than Baltimore, so there was less likelihood that it would come under attack. Hardening her resolve, Betsy told herself she was doing what was right for her boy.

Her brother Edward accompanied them, and Betsy was glad of his company when she had to leave Bo. As their coach drove away from the school, her throat tightened so that she felt she was choking on sorrow, and her entire body ached as though she had just gone through a second ordeal of labor. Not even watching Jerome ride away from her in Lisbon had hurt so much as this.

Bo's first letters deepened Betsy's unhappiness. He described how lonely he felt and how much he missed her. Bo was used to rough-and-tumble interaction with his uncles, but he had associated with few boys outside the family. Now he complained that the other students mocked him. They called Napoleon a tyrant and harassed Bo because of his expectations to be a prince.

Betsy was about to fetch him home when she received a letter from the headmaster, Dr. DuBois. He reported that her son had been in a few minor scuffles—but only because he fought back when other boys tripped him or boxed his ears. "It is best for parents not to interfere in these contretemps. Jerome is learning to stand his ground, and this will go far toward achieving your purpose of making a man out of him."

A few days after receiving that communication, Betsy joined President and Mrs. Madison for a private supper. President Madison seemed unusually grave that evening, and over soup, he said, "Forgive me, ladies. This afternoon I received a most troubling dispatch from our forces in the Northwest Territory. As Fort Dearborn was being evacuated in mid-August, a band of Potawatomi attacked and massacred more than fifty people, some of them women and children. I will not trouble you with the distressing details, but they weigh heavily on my mind."

Dolley Madison frowned. "The newspapers are bound to use this report to print more unfair criticisms of you."

Her husband raised his eyebrows as he gazed down the table at her. "Mrs. Madison, my own reputation is the least of my concerns."

Dolley turned a faint pink. She was spared from having to answer as the servants came to clear away the soup bowls.

Once the main course was served, Mr. Madison changed the subject by asking Betsy about her son. She barely touched her roast beef as she spent the next several minutes pouring out her worries about Bo. When she finished, Dolley sighed and fingered her necklace. "My dear, I fear I am not the person to give you advice. My own son Payne continues to be unruly and shows no sign of settling down to a career even though he will reach the age of majority next year."

Mr. Madison gave his wife a tender smile and then said, "Madame Bonaparte, I believe the worst thing you could do would be to rush to remove your son from school. You would undermine his confidence and brand him as a mama's boy. Because of who he is, Bo will encounter jealousies his entire life, and he must learn how to win over his detractors."

Dolley leaned over to pat Betsy's hand. "I think Mr. Madison is right. I was over-indulgent with Payne after his father died, and now I regret it."

Biting her lip, Betsy gazed at her plate. The food had cooled so much that the gravy had formed skin, and the sight spoiled what remained of her appetite. She sighed and reflected that nearly everything in life turned out more disappointing than anticipated. It was true that Dolley's twenty-year-old son had a reputation for drunken mischief. Betsy did not want Bo to turn out like that, but oh, how she missed him. That, she realized, was the heart of the matter. She wanted her little boy by her side and had seized on the trouble at school as an excuse to bring him home.

Reluctantly, Betsy decided to give it more time. Two weeks later, Bo wrote to say that he had not had any recent battles, but he hated having to learn Latin. He pointed out that even though his grandfather had never studied it, he became a millionaire. Betsy knew from teaching Bo that he had inherited her ease with numbers, but that languages vexed him. In her next letter, she repeated that she meant to send him to a European university and that he must do well in all his subjects. Over the next few months, he stopped mentioning fights and reported improving at Latin, and Betsy was glad she had not given in to her impulse to rescue him.

THE WAR WAS not going well. The American forces were repulsed in their efforts to invade Ontario, and New Englanders—who generally opposed the conflict—were reputed to be carrying on a lively trade smuggling with Canada. The war had such mixed support that Betsy wondered whether James Madison would be reelected, but in November, he defeated the Federalist candidate DeWitt Clinton by winning nearly three-fifths of the electoral vote.

The war with Britain was not the only conflict discussed in Washington that autumn. People returning from Europe reported that Napoleon had invaded Russia. The French did not meet with early success. Armies led by Jerome, Marshal Davout, and Eugene de Beauharnais were sent to approach Prince Bagration from different directions, cutting him off from the other Russian forces and destroying his army, but the attack failed through lack of coordination. Most blamed it on

Jerome. The more charitable reports said that his army arrived late because it had bogged down in mud, while others claimed he had dawdled for several days in a pleasant village.

Such stories made Betsy realize what a laughingstock Jerome had become. Travelers brought back tales of his dissolute, extravagant behavior. One scurrilous story concerned the Marble Bath at Kassel, a grand chamber ornamented with marble walls, statues, and carved reliefs surrounding a pool-sized bathtub. It was said that whenever Jerome indulged in a night of strenuous exertions with one of his mistresses, he would bathe in wine to restore his strength.

People often passed on such gossip to Betsy, usually with a malicious gleam in the eye that meant the rumormonger hoped she would respond with one of her stinging insults. Betsy refused to gratify such pot-stirrers.

Despite her pretended indifference, the reports of Jerome's overspending worried her. She believed she was still his only lawful wife, which meant he had the right to control her money. Betsy did not really believe Jerome would deprive her of her carefully accumulated savings, but for the sake of her son's future, she had to protect herself. Therefore, she filed a petition asking the General Assembly of Maryland to grant her a divorce by decree.

As the news of that request raced through the drawing rooms of Washington, Minister Sérurier informed Betsy that according to international protocol, reigning monarchs could not be named in lawsuits. Betsy shrugged and said that she was seeking a divorce from the man she had married in Baltimore, not the European king he became afterward. When Sérurier tried to argue the matter, she gave him the stare she used when Bo was being stubborn. "Monsieur, I did not realize you were the ambassador from Westphalia as well as France."

Her divorce petition emboldened men to court her more aggressively. Jan Willink—the son of a Dutch investor whose land company owned much of western New York—had paid marked attention to Betsy for months. Now, other men tried their luck, including Supreme Court Justice William Johnson Jr., who wrote her maudlin poetry; Henry Lee IV, son of the injured hero Light-Horse Harry Lee; and a married senator who signed his love letters with a false name.

Although Betsy enjoyed flirting with her admirers and proving that she was still an accomplished coquette, none of the suitors tempted her to place herself under the power of a husband. She smiled, laughed, danced, and teased, but whenever anyone grew serious, she reminded him of her solemn resolve not to marry and grew cold until he behaved himself again.

Betsy's divorce became official in January 1813, and when she heard the news, she felt no regret but rather a deep, heartfelt sense of relief. Jerome could now be as foolish as he chose. She and her son were safe from the consequences of his self-indulgence.

✒ XXVIII ✑

BETSY returned to Baltimore in March when Washington emptied at the end of the congressional session. By then, the British navy had blockaded Chesapeake Bay, and the impediment to shipping was further damaging William Patterson's business. Whenever Betsy visited South Street, she found her father in such a bitter mood that she was glad to retire to her own house in the evenings, although she hated leaving her mother to deal on her own with his complaints.

That spring, news reached the United States of the disastrous outcome of Napoleon's Russia campaign. He had begun his invasion the previous June with a force of 600,000 men. During the following months, the French army endured starvation, illness, Cossack raids, a bloody and indecisive battle at Borodino, a month-long stay in deserted Moscow where elusive Russians set fire after fire, and a devastating winter retreat through snow, ice, and temperatures that plunged to 22 degrees below zero. Horses froze to death in droves. When the army staggered out of Russia in mid-December, fewer than 100,000 men remained alive, and most of those were skeletal, frostbitten cripples.

Although the world rejoiced to see the invincible Bonaparte stumble, Betsy did not. The stories stunned her. How could Napoleon have erred so badly in failing to consider that the enemy might not play by his rules? The Russians refused to give battle until they were ready, burned their crops rather than let the French eat, and drew the French further into their vast country with constant retreats—allowing the logistical problems of supply and the unconquerable Russian climate to defeat the invaders.

For Betsy, only two aspects of the news were good. One was that because Jerome had resigned in a pique after losing his command early in the campaign, he sat out most of it in Kassel. Betsy found it exasperating that Jerome's prickly, unjustifiable pride was what saved him, yet she could not help but be glad he had survived. The second piece of good news was that despite the terrible losses, Napoleon held onto his throne, so Betsy's pension continued.

On April 16, a British fleet anchored at the mouth of the Patapsco River, and the residents of Baltimore worried that their city would come under attack. As soon as she heard the news, Betsy arranged to fetch Bo from school and flee to Virginia if the threat became more tangible. She did not trust the British to leave her Bonaparte son alone just because he was a child. Eight days after the fleet appeared, however, it sailed on without battle.

That summer at Springfield, Betsy read newspapers and wrote to friends to keep abreast of events in Europe. Just as Oakeley had predicted, a Sixth Coalition had formed consisting of the United Kingdom, Russia, Sweden, Spain, Portugal, and several German states. The allies no doubt assumed that France was fatally weakened by its losses in Russia. Somehow Napoleon raised another huge army, and during two battles in Germany that May, he drove back combined Prussian and Russian forces.

Then family matters pushed both wars from Betsy's thoughts. Ever since her last pregnancy, Dorcas had suffered shooting pains down her legs, which worsened until she had trouble standing or walking. That summer, a new set of symptoms plagued her. Her back ached, and her face, hands, and feet grew swollen. Once when she and Betsy were alone, Dorcas confided that she was having difficulty passing water, and when it came, it was dark. At Betsy's insistence, her father sent for a doctor, who diagnosed a kidney ailment. The doctor bled Dorcas and told her to take warm baths. Because the bleeding weakened her mother, Betsy instructed the housekeeper to prepare menus with plenty of fresh vegetables to build up Dorcas's strength. Gradually over the next few weeks, the back pain and swelling subsided.

Usually, Bo enjoyed summer more than any other season, but that year he worried about his grandmother. To lift his spirits, Betsy took him riding nearly every afternoon, with Bo on a pony and herself riding sidesaddle on a mare. A few days before his eighth birthday, Betsy went out to the kitchen building to talk to the housekeeper, a black-haired woman in her forties named Nancy Todd. Betsy instructed Mrs. Todd to make Bo's favorite foods for his birthday meal.

On the day itself, Dorcas came downstairs for the feast in spite of her discomfort. As the family sat around the dining table, Betsy was charmed to see her son make his grandmother laugh by repeating jokes he had learned at school.

Once dinner was over, the family retired to the drawing room to watch Bo open his gifts. From his grandparents, he received copies of *Aesop's Fables* and *Robinson Crusoe.* When he opened the latter, he exclaimed, "Oh, Mama, the boys at school told me this is a wonderful adventure. Can we start reading it right away?"

Betsy laughed. "Perhaps at bedtime. Now, thank your grandparents."

Bo jumped up and kissed first his grandmother and then his grandfather, who tousled his sandy hair and said, "You're a good boy." As Bo returned to his pile of gifts, Patterson excused himself and left the room.

Edward had sent Bo a set of ceramic-glazed marbles, Henry and Octavius together gave him a carved wooden horse for his collection, and Caroline had made him a spinning toy called a whirligig, which was a button strung on two pieces of yarn.

Last, Betsy handed Bo her present, an imported English puzzle called Spilsbury's Dissected Maps; this one was a map of Europe that had been affixed to a thin wooden board and then sawn apart along the countries' borders so that each piece represented a different state. Betsy thought reassembling the puzzle would be a fun way for her son to learn the geography of the continent where he would live one day.

As Bo and the other boys started to play with the map, Betsy cautioned, "Be careful not to lose any pieces." Then she glanced at her mother to see if she was enjoying herself.

Dorcas's face was ashen, and she was grasping the arms of her chair.

"Mother, are you all right?" Betsy asked.

"Yes," Dorcas answered, but she sounded out of breath. "Just—tired."

"Do you want to go back to bed?"

When Dorcas nodded, Betsy asked, "I will find Father to help you up the stairs."

"No need." Caroline rose from her seat. "I can take her to bed."

As his grandmother left, Bo's face fell, so Betsy said he could tell the housekeeper to serve the rest of his birthday cake at tea. He eagerly ran from the room, but when he returned minutes later, he was scowling. All evening as he and Octavius played with the map, Bo appeared troubled, but he swore nothing was wrong when Betsy questioned him at bedtime.

Two days later, Dorcas had a prolonged attack of vomiting, so Betsy could not take Bo riding. She gave him permission to go with Octavius but warned her brother to refrain from jumping or racing. In spite of her admonition, the boys were reckless, and Bo fell off his pony and landed on his shoulder. To Betsy's relief, it was only sore, not broken. That night before she tucked Bo in, Betsy had him lie on his uninjured side so she could knead mustard oil into his muscles to reduce the pain.

"Mama?" he began, and Betsy could tell from Bo's tone that he was about to ask something that weighed on his mind. She prepared herself for a query about his grandmother, but instead he asked, "Has Mrs. Todd been feeling poorly?"

"I don't think so. Why?"

"No reason," he mumbled.

"Bo, what is it? Did the housekeeper say something to you?"

He rolled onto his back to gaze at her. "Do you remember when I went out to the kitchen to tell her about my cake? Grandfather was there rubbing her."

Anger swept over Betsy, but she masked her emotion. "Where was he rubbing her?"

Bo bit his lip and said, "Her bubbies. Her dress was open, and she moaned like it hurt."

"Why did you keep this from me?"

"Grandfather said not to tell. He gave me a silver dollar."

Betsy began to pace to keep from venting her fury before her child. She could not believe her father was so callous to his wife's suffering as to seek carnal pleasure with a servant while Dorcas was in so much pain she could hardly walk. And what about the children? Bo had nearly walked in to see his grandfather mounting the woman like a bull on a cow. After nearly a minute, Bo asked plaintively, "Mama, did I do something bad?"

"Not you, dear. Your grandfather."

"But he was just trying to make Mrs. Todd feel better."

She halted to gaze at her son. Was it possible that with so many older uncles, he was still ignorant of such matters? Thinking quickly, she said, "Have you ever seen your grandfather tend the sick? That is not his job. Your grandmother and I can look after Mrs. Todd."

"Oh." His frown melted away, and he relaxed more deeply into his pillow. "Do I have to give Grandfather back his dollar?"

Betsy's immediate impulse was to say yes, but she forced herself to consider the matter. As much as she distrusted her father's influence, there was no denying that Bo adored him, and she did not want to destroy that relationship. She of all people knew how unforgiving her father could be if a child crossed him. "You may have the dollar, but only because you told me the truth. You must not keep secrets from me, Bo."

"Yes, Mama."

Pulling a thin sheet over him, she said, "Now go to sleep."

She kissed his forehead and left the room, but she stopped on the landing to think. Confronting her father about his philandering would reveal that Bo had betrayed his confidence, so she could not do that. She would prefer to have one of her adult brothers handle the situation, but John was in Virginia, Joseph was in Europe, Edward was staying with the Smiths to court his cousin Sidney, and Robert was summering with Marianne's family.

After weighing the possible options, Betsy decided to alert Edward to the affair before she returned to Washington.

IN AUTUMN 1813, news arrived of more fighting in Europe. In June, the British under General Arthur Wellesley, the Marquess of Wellington, won a resounding victory in Spain and caused Joseph Bonaparte to flee the country. The Sixth Coalition also achieved victories in Germany and Bohemia. Everyone was certain that Napoleon's days were numbered.

Betsy resumed her social life in Washington, attending Dolly Madison's open houses, dinners and dances throughout town, and concerts when they were offered. But the game of being the enchanting Madame Bonaparte had grown stale. At parties, Betsy worked hard to be amusing, and she defended Napoleon against his detractors, but she began to feel like an actress repeating the same lines performance after performance. Many men courted her, and the suitors generally fell into two camps—either inexperienced young men who burned with the desire to bed her or men of the world who wanted to win the distinction of conquering the notoriously aloof Madame Bonaparte. As she neared her twenty-ninth birthday, Betsy wondered if she would ever meet a man who loved her for her wit and strength of character as well as her beauty.

Sometimes when she looked in a mirror while dressing, Betsy saw not the reflection of a living woman but that of a beautifully painted porcelain figurine. On the outside she was lovely, but within she felt hollow and scarred with hairline cracks.

Then a new friend helped ease her brittleness—Elbridge Gerry, Madison's second vice president. The sixty-nine-year-old Gerry had signed the Declaration of Independence, attended the Constitutional Convention, and served as a U.S. representative and Massachusetts governor. His friendship with Betsy was intellectual and free of romance; Gerry was devoted to his wife, who remained behind in Massachusetts as an invalid, having lost her health bearing ten children.

Betsy and Gerry often called together on mutual acquaintances, accompanied by Betsy's maid Sadie to safeguard her reputation. As they rode in Gerry's carriage, they debated the relative merits of various political systems. Like Betsy, the vice president did not trust the mob, having once said, "The evils we experience flow from the excess of democracy. The people do not want virtue, but are dupes of pretended patriots." Unlike Betsy, he despised Bonaparte for having abandoned republican government for empire. Gerry thought the ideal system was one in which officials were elected indirectly, and government powers were scrupulously kept in check. Even when they disagreed, Betsy was grateful that he spoke to her as an equal.

That Christmas, when Betsy went to Baltimore, Edward told her privately that he had seen no sign of intimacy between Mrs. Todd and their father. Betsy shrugged. She had more pressing concerns on her mind. Dorcas still tired easily. She was only fifty-two but had the frail appearance and stiff movements of a much older woman. According to Caroline, she frequently spent a day or two in bed with fevers, and Betsy feared that her mother's body was failing her.

Dorcas did not seem to be facing an imminent crisis, however, so at her mother's urging, Betsy returned to Washington before New Year's Day. In early February, she learned that Jerome had lost his kingdom the previous October. The war had gone badly for Napoleon's forces, leading to the loss not only of Westphalia but also of Holland.

When Betsy shared the news with her aunt over supper, Nancy said, "If Jerome has lost his throne, he can divorce that princess and come back to you."

Betsy was so astonished that she dropped her fork. "I would not take him back. He has proven himself unworthy of me."

"But you know he has not forgotten you. Surely you could forgive him and start anew."

Shaking her head, Betsy quoted La Rochefoucauld: "It is impossible to love a second time those whom we have really ceased to love."

She spent a few days trying to decide how to convey the bad news to Bo at school, but then a letter arrived in which her son reported hearing that his dear father had lost his kingdom. Bo did not seem personally upset by the news, yet he worried that she might be depressed because of "the late calamities" that the French had suffered.

Betsy smiled over this proof of her son's affection and took out paper to write to him. The fact that he cared so little about how the "calamities" might affect his own future puzzled her, but then again, she reminded herself that Bo was only eight and had not yet displayed the ambition that had seized her at such an early age. Perhaps it was not in his character. Instead of upbraiding him for his indifference, Betsy wrote that she was fine and then gave a lively account of her latest social engagements, including a humorous story about a man who tried to convert her to an all-vegetable diet.

THREE MONTHS LATER, Betsy stood at the window of her parents' bedroom, staring down at the carriages driving on South Street. A woman in a muslin gown exited the house across the way, and a warm May breeze wafted floral scents through the open window, but those signs of spring seemed like a cruel mockery to Betsy. On the bed behind her, her mother lay dying.

Just days earlier, Betsy had received a letter from Caroline asking her to come at once. Their mother's kidney ailment had returned, and Dorcas was deteriorating rapidly. Betsy hurried to Baltimore to find the house in an uproar. As she climbed the steps to the front door, she could hear angry shouting through the open drawing-room windows. From the recriminations Edward was making, it was clear that he had discovered their father with the housekeeper and forced the old man to turn Nancy Todd out of the house.

"Stop it!" Betsy cried, rushing into the drawing room. "I could hear you from the street. Do you want all of Baltimore to know of this sordid affair?"

Edward turned to her. "I went looking for him because Mother was in distress and found him with his whore. He had dressed her in one of Mother's gowns."

The image revolted Betsy, but she forced it from her mind. Grabbing her brother's arm, she demanded, "Who is with Mother now? Does she know about this?"

Edward squeezed his eyes shut in pain. "I don't know."

"I am going to her," Patterson said and started toward the doorway, but Betsy blocked his way.

"No, sir. I will deal with her."

"Do not try to come between your mother and me."

"I would not dream of it." Betsy allowed contempt to turn her voice as grating as a rusty saw. "Not because you deserve any consideration but because I will not have Mother know how you dishonored her in her last days. I am going up now to say you dismissed Nancy Todd for stealing. And I expect every person in this family to support that story so she can die in peace."

Remembering the scene now, Betsy clenched her fists in rage. Her father had used her mother like a brood mare until she was too sick to receive his attentions, and then he sought other objects for his lust as casually as he would buy a new horse. A married woman had few ways to protect herself from the toll of constant childbearing. By the law of the land, she had to submit to her husband as often as he demanded it even if she had been told that to go through labor again would kill her. According to clergymen, it was God's will for men to have pleasure and women to have pain because Eve had tempted Adam.

Well, Betsy no longer believed that. Jerome might think it was his right as a king to bed every woman in Westphalia, and her father might think it was his prerogative as head of the house to couple with the servants, but the only reason they got away with such behavior was that they had power and women had none. Not every man betrayed his vows—Robert was true to Marianne, and even Jerome had been faithful when he lived with Betsy—but Betsy thought that women inevitably got the worst of marriage.

Hearing her mother moan in her sleep, Betsy turned from the window and returned to her chair at the bedside. Dorcas's whole body was swollen, her breathing was labored, and when awake, she was in terrible pain. Betsy prayed for her mother to find relief and then picked up her sewing. She was altering one of Octavius's old shirts for Bo. As she considered how much to take in the side seams, Dorcas woke up and asked, "How are you, dear?"

"Fine."

"Are you? You do not seem happy."

Betsy pushed a pin into the linen and said, "I am worried about you."

"No need. I am content to die." Dorcas paused to catch her breath. "William and your sisters are waiting for me."

"Oh, Mother." As tears flooded her eyes, Betsy wiped her face with the shirt. "Please try to get well. I cannot bear the thought of losing you."

Her mother gave a deep sigh. Then she plucked at the sheet to pull it closer to her chin. "I wish you would marry again, Betsy. You would not be so alone."

"No, I daresay I would never be alone. I would have a husband to order me about, spend my money, and pester me to satisfy his appetites. Then I would have who knows how many children until my body was ruined." Dorcas flinched, and Betsy repented of her angry words. "Mother, forgive me. I said that only because I am distraught. When I think that you could still be strong and vibrant like Aunt Nancy—"

"And which of your brothers and sisters do you wish had never been born?"

Lowering her gaze, Betsy picked up a stray thread that had fallen onto the bedcovers. "I am not like you. Even as a child, I knew I did not want a large family."

"But darling, it is not natural for a woman to be alone."

"I am not alone. I have Bo."

"You know that I meant a husband."

Betsy blushed. This was an aspect of her life she never discussed, but knowing that her mother's time was running out made honesty seem imperative. "Mother, I have never met another man who inspires me with the passion I had for Jerome. When I think of sharing my bed with someone for whom I have only tepid affection, I feel repugnance."

Her mother sighed. "There was a time that I hoped Charles Oakeley—"

Betsy shook her head. "I admit that I was more drawn to him than any of the others, but in the end, I could not bring myself to do it."

"Are you certain you have not hardened your heart to prevent more hurt?" Dorcas lay a hand on her chest as she struggled to breathe. "If you married a good man whom you like, passion might follow."

Pushing the last pin into the seam, Betsy said, "Who can tell in advance if a man is trustworthy? In my experience, it is impossible."

"Please do not say such bitter things."

Betsy reached out for her mother's hand. "Do not worry about me. I love my son, and fighting for him has become my purpose in life. I can make that be enough."

Dorcas smiled sadly. "Then you will never have a daughter."

As she resumed sewing, Betsy said, "There are many things I will never have. But I am doing what I can to attain that which is possible."

Dorcas Patterson died on May 20, 1814. Betsy was at her side when her breathing stopped. After sitting quietly for several minutes holding her hand, Betsy cut a lock of her mother's faded auburn hair and stowed it in her workbasket until she could put it inside her gold locket. Then she went to tell her father that his wife was gone.

After allowing herself one night of tears, Betsy put her sorrow away until later. With no housekeeper in the Patterson home, someone had to oversee the planning for the after-funeral luncheon, and fifteen-year-old Caroline was too heartbroken to do it. So Betsy spent the next two days making arrangements at South Street and returning to her own house at night.

She asked her father for the painting of herself and her mother that hung above the fireplace, but he said absolutely not, he wanted it to remember his wife. Then he brusquely ordered Betsy to get him tea. In the pantry, she took down her mother's good English china teapot but then set it aside and used the everyday brown-glazed teapot instead. That night, she wrapped the china teapot in a towel and took it home with her.

While Betsy prepared for the funeral, Edward drove to Emmitsburg to fetch her son. Bo was devastated when he arrived. He had believed that "Mother" would get well and could not understand why praying for her during chapel had failed. At the age of eight he thought himself too old to cry, yet he gave way to tears once he and Betsy were alone in their little house.

After he cried himself out, Betsy let him lay his head in her lap while she stroked his hair. Remembering her last conversation with her mother, she realized that Bo would be a grown man and on his own in little more than a decade. Betsy dreaded being alone, but she feared being trapped in marriage to a cruel or disreputable husband even more. Perhaps one day Bo would give her grandchildren, and then her life would have new sources of love.

❧ XXIX ❧

A FEW days after Dorcas's burial, Betsy learned that Napoleon was no longer emperor. The European war had turned against the French—more disastrously than Betsy had realized during the months she was preoccupied with her mother's health. The previous fall at Leipzig, an allied force of more than 320,000 men had attacked a French army of 185,000. Napoleon suffered one of the worst defeats of his career. Nearly 40,000 French soldiers—a number almost equal to the population of Baltimore—were wounded or killed, and the allies captured another 30,000. The allies themselves lost some 55,000 men. Betsy found the numbers horrifying, even more so when she recalled the high losses of the Russia campaign.

The allies soon invaded France itself, and throughout the early months of 1814, a force of nearly half a million closed in on Paris, slowly strangling Napoleon's hope of remaining on the throne. By then he could field barely 30,000 men—and not all of those were adults. The decades of warfare had so thoroughly destroyed France's male population that Napoleon called for teenage boys of fourteen and fifteen to join the army. These conscripts were known as "Marie Louises" after the youthful empress. Betsy realized with dismay that, if the war had continued another few years, Napoleon almost certainly would have sent Bo into battle.

The allies had reached Paris at the end of March 1814. Even though Napoleon was still fighting, the Parisian authorities, led by the former foreign minister Talleyrand, negotiated separately to surrender. In April, Napoleon abdicated, hoping that his crown would pass to his three-year-old son, but the allies restored the monarchy and put a brother of the guillotined Louis XVI on the throne.

The reports left Betsy wondering why she had had to endure so much loneliness and deprivation. The omnipotent titan who had plucked her from her chosen path and flung her back to Baltimore was now toppled like the character of Humpty Dumpty in the book of verses she used to read to Bo. For years, she had believed that she was forced to suffer so he could keep France safe, but now even that morsel of comfort was snatched from her.

For Betsy, the worst of the news was that Napoleon's downfall shattered her hopes for Bo to become a prince. Whenever she looked at her son, who so resembled the emperor, she wondered what his future would hold now that the Bonapartes had fallen from power. Perhaps, she told herself fervently, her son could still become a man of importance if she persevered in her plan of getting him the best education and introducing him to the right people.

A month later, the papers reported that Napoleon was exiled to the Mediterranean island of Elba. Marie Louise and their son had taken refuge in Vienna, where her father dissuaded her from rejoining her husband. The allies gave her a duchy to rule instead. Betsy felt nothing but scorn for the weak-willed young empress, who seemingly had taken a bribe for agreeing to be used as an instrument to punish her husband.

Shaking her head over the report, Betsy folded up the newspaper she had been reading. "Now Napoleon knows how it feels to lose his wife and child. I hope it makes him realize what a bitter thing he did to Jerome."

Bo looked up from the French sentences she had given him to copy. "Mama, if Uncle Napoleon is not emperor anymore, does that mean he cannot give us titles?"

"No, we will not receive titles. I am sorry."

Shrugging, Bo wrote his initials J.N.B. sideways on the margin of his paper. "I like my name the way it is: Jerome Napoleon Bonaparte. It sounds like an important person."

Betsy covered her mouth to hide her amusement. "Does that mean you no longer want me to call you Bo?"

"No, I meant my formal name for when I grow up, not your special name for me."

"Good." She watched him work awhile. "This most likely means my pension will cease. I have saved as much as I can, so I hope we will have enough to live on."

Bo chewed the end of his pencil and then asked, "Can we stay in America?"

"No. I still want you to receive a European education, and I plan to seek advice about the best schools." As she spoke, a happy thought occurred to her. "In fact, Napoleon can no longer prevent me from going to France to investigate matters."

Rising, Bo came to stand by her chair. He put an arm around her and laid his head on her shoulder. "Mama, please do not sail to France. We are at war. What would become of me if your ship were sunk?"

"Don't worry. I will not go until it is safe."

After a moment, Bo murmured, "I wonder what happened to my father."

"I do not know, but I am sure he is all right. Your father has an astonishing way of surviving trouble unscathed. When we go to Europe, you might finally meet him."

"I don't think he wants to meet me. He never answered my letter."

Betsy gave him a one-armed hug. "Sweetheart, a war was going on, and oftentimes the mails get lost. Your father is a very loving man, so I am certain he wants to meet you."

"I hope so." He sighed and trudged back to his chair. "I wish I did not have to study French during my summer holiday."

"A man with an important-sounding name needs to be able to speak French."

Bo looked up and, seeing her smile, laughed. "Mama, sometimes you are very silly."

THAT SUMMER BETSY wrote to her acquaintances requesting letters

of introduction to European society and asking if anyone knew of respectable people planning a journey to Europe with whom she could
travel. On learning her plans, Robert urged her to reconsider. "I understand that the Bonapartes have been banished from France. Might
not this exclusion apply to you?"

"I hardly think so. I was not deemed a member of the imperial family while married to Jerome. Why should I share their punishment
now?" Still, she agreed to find out—a concession that posed a dilemma.
Betsy worried that if she were to write the new royal government asking special permission to visit France, it would convey an unwarrant-
ed degree of self-importance. Instead, she asked Minister Sérurier's
secretary to make discreet inquiries.

By then it was August 1814. The United States was barely holding
its own in the war with Great Britain. America had won a few notable victories—the defeat of the *Guerrière* by the USS *Constitution,* the
capture of a British squadron on Lake Erie by Oliver Hazard Perry—
but for more than a year, the British navy had blockaded the Atlantic
coast and raided communities along Chesapeake Bay at will. Now, Napoleon's defeat had released thousands of battle-hardened veterans to
fight in the Americas, and Baltimore feared that its day of reckoning
was coming. The British had denounced the city as a "nest of pirates"
because it was home to many of the privateers that marauded English
shipping. Despite the widespread fear, few people from the city took up
arms. Earlier that summer, a thirty-nine-year-old Baltimorean, General William Winder, was put in charge of defending a new military
district that comprised Baltimore and Washington. He called for 3,000
Maryland militia, yet only a fraction of that number reported for duty.

On August 16, a lookout stationed near Cape Henry, Virginia, reported that a British fleet of more than twenty vessels had entered
Chesapeake Bay. No one knew whether the target was Washington,
Baltimore, or Annapolis. When William Patterson heard the news
at his Springfield estate, he decided that he and his sons needed to
be in town to look after their property. Betsy also returned to Baltimore because she feared what might happen if invading soldiers found
her alone in the country with only servants and a nine-year-old child.

On the 19th, British soldiers disembarked on the shore of the Patuxent River sixty miles south of Baltimore. The landing indicated an attack on Washington, so additional Maryland militia marched to the capital. On the 22nd, word came that the British fleet had bottled up Commodore Barney's flotilla high up the Patuxent. Barney blew up his ships rather than let them be captured.

It was the hottest August in memory, and tempers frayed under the triple irritants of heat, frustration, and fear. Contradictory rumors circulated through Baltimore all day on the 24th. About ten o'clock that night, a loud knock on her door startled Betsy. A minute later, Sadie entered announcing, "Your brother, madam," followed by Edward.

"Father wants you and Bo at South Street. We think Washington has been taken."

Betsy's heart lurched at the thought of Dolley Madison in danger. Laying aside the shirt she was mending, she rose. "Let me put together a few items of clothing and wake Bo."

She took one of the lighted candles from the mantel, went upstairs with the maid, and found a small valise in her storeroom. Betsy handed it to Sadie and told her to pack for two or three days. "Once you have done that, fetch my jewelry casket."

Then Betsy entered her son's room, put the candlestick on the bedside table, and shook him. He groaned, made a shooing gesture, and curled up on his side. Betsy called his name.

"What?" he muttered, burrowing his face into his pillow.

"Wake up now. We have to go to your grandfather's house."

Slowly, he opened his eyes and squinted at her. "Is it morning?"

"No, darling. There is trouble, and we will be safer there."

Bo sat up. "Are the British coming?"

"Not yet. They are still in Washington, but—" Betsy hesitated, then realized it would be impossible to keep the truth from him. "Grandfather thinks the capital may have fallen."

"Oh." He made no move to get out of bed.

"Please get up and put on your clothes."

"Not until you leave the room, Mama."

Betsy raised her eyebrows at this sign that he was acquiring an adult sense of modesty. "Hurry. If you are not downstairs in five minutes, I will send up your uncle Edward."

When they reached the South Street house half an hour later, it seemed deserted. "Where is everyone?" Betsy asked.

"Watching from the roof of the back building."

"May I go too, Mama?"

"Yes." They walked through to the rear staircase and climbed to the third floor. Then they went to the end of the hall and ascended the ladder to an open trapdoor. Betsy insisted on going first to keep Bo from rushing onto the dark roof, which was flat with a low parapet.

Once on the roof, she moved to where her father and brothers stood near one corner and gazed to the southwest. An angry orange glare lit the horizon. "Merciful heavens! Is that fire?"

Patterson lowered his telescope and handed it to Edward. "Yes. Washington is burning."

Bo crept up beside her and grasped her skirt as he had when he was very little. "Mama, did the British soldiers do that?"

"So it would seem," she said, putting an arm around his shoulder.

"Do you think they shot President Madison?"

"I don't see why they would. They did not shoot Napoleon, and he had been at war with them for twenty years." To her father, she said, "Where is Caroline?"

"In bed. She has had a cold all summer."

Betsy frowned. Her sister had worn herself out during the prolonged stint of nursing their mother, and Betsy feared this "cold" might be the onset of something more serious.

Glancing to where her brothers stood, Betsy saw the telescope being passed from one to the other. Octavius called, "Come on, Bo."

"Mama?"

"Go ahead, but stay back from the edge."

As Bo moved away, Betsy asked her father, "Have they torched the entire city?"

"No, the blaze seems concentrated in three or four spots. Probably the public buildings."

At the thought of the President's Mansion, Betsy felt hatred well up inside her. "Why should the British wreak such destruction? They did not burn Paris when they overthrew Napoleon."

"Reports have come in that they seek retaliation for the burning of

Port Dover, but I think it more than that. They mean to punish us for presuming to claim our independence."

Just like you, she thought bitterly. *You have never forgiven me for not being submissive.*

She walked over to her brothers and asked for the glass. Staring through it, she saw what her father meant about the glow emanating from a few places. As she watched, a tongue of flame leapt toward the sky. Bo crept to her side and wrapped the fabric of her skirt around his fist. Betsy realized that the destruction of the city that was his second home was upsetting him. She longed to hug him, but she refrained from embarrassing him in front of his uncles. "You should go back to bed."

"Not yet, Mama. I want to see what happens."

Even though she knew it was unlikely they would receive any word that night, Betsy gave him permission to remain. After an hour, she went downstairs to make tea and sandwiches. As Betsy found a loaf of bread in the pantry, she heard a door open and close. A moment later, the new housekeeper entered the kitchen. "What are you doing, madam?"

Providence Summers was twenty-four, with blonde hair, a freckled face, and a buxom figure. She was married to a captain who was often away at sea. Although Betsy suspected that her father had bedded the woman, she had decided to ignore the situation since he was now a widower. "The British are burning Washington, and my family are on the roof watching," Betsy said as she sliced the bread. "They want some refreshment, but I did not like to disturb your rest."

"I always hear when someone is in my kitchen."

Laying down the knife, Betsy looked at her. "Your kitchen?"

Providence flushed but did not answer.

"Since you are up, get the cheese and make sandwiches while I brew tea."

Fifteen minutes later, Betsy carried a tray of food to her father and brothers, who ate gratefully. Toward dawn, a violent thunderstorm chased the family inside. As Betsy tucked Bo into bed, he asked, "Are the British going to burn our house?"

"I hope not, but no one can say what will happen in a war."

He frowned. "I wish I had a pistol so I could protect you."

"Heavens, Bo, you are much too young for such things. If things grow dangerous here, we can go to your uncle John in Virginia."

His scowl grew fiercer. "I am not a baby anymore."

"I know, but you are not a man yet either." Betsy stroked his smooth cheek. "Allow me to be your mother a little longer."

That coaxed a grudging smile from him. "You will always be my mama. I will never leave you the way my father did."

His declaration brought tears to Betsy's eyes. "Thank you. Now please try to sleep."

A FEW DAYS LATER, news reached Baltimore that the government had returned to Washington to begin rebuilding. Fire had gutted the President's Mansion, but the soot-blackened stone walls still stood. More importantly, Betsy was relieved to learn that both Mr. and Mrs. Madison were safe. Dolley Madison had even become a national hero because she saved Gilbert Stuart's full-length portrait of George Washington.

Survivors straggled back to Baltimore from Bladensburg, the crossroads town where the British army routed the forces blocking the approach to Washington. The Americans had retreated in a panic that demoralized the entire country. Some men on Baltimore's Committee of Vigilance and Safety proposed capitulating to the British without a fight and negotiating to save as much of the city as possible, but John Eager Howard, a colonel in the Revolutionary War, declared that he had four sons in the army and would not disgrace his country with surrender. His resolve shifted the mood toward defense.

According to the papers, one reason the lines collapsed at Bladensburg was that the troops had been placed too haphazardly to support each other when attacked. If Baltimore was to be saved, someone with military experience needed to oversee its defense. The committee asked Samuel Smith to take charge and obtained the governor's sanction for their choice. That appointment insulted the governor's nephew, General Winder, but Baltimore did not care.

After that, Aunt Nancy often brought the Pattersons war news that she gained from living with the Smiths. One night over supper, she described Samuel Smith's plan to defend the city. The Patapsco River was a tilted Y, with the upper Northwest Branch leading to Baltimore and Ferry Branch leading west. An arrowhead-shaped peninsula called Locust Point separated the two, and at its tip stood star-shaped Fort McHenry. The fort was vulnerable because its artillery had a maximum range of 2,800 yards, while the British bomb ships could hurl mortars half again as far. If ships slipped past the fort up Northwest Branch, they could send boats right into Baltimore Harbor and land troops in the heart of the city. If ships made it up Ferry Branch to Ridgely's Cove, troops could march overland to attack the city from the west. Smith had decided that if the British fleet came, he would sink ships across the entrance to both branches. As Betsy listened to her brothers analyze that plan, she watched her son's rapt face and tried to reassure herself that his safety was in capable hands.

Edward pointed out that another possible line of approach was overland from North Point, the spit of land where the Patapsco River met the bay. By landing there, the British could avoid Fort McHenry and march northwest to Baltimore. But Uncle Smith had thought of that too, Aunt Nancy said. To block that route, he had ordered the creation of fortifications along the ridge of Hampstead Hill east of the city. In the weeks that followed, Baltimore citizens turned out by the hundreds to dig trenches and throw up earthworks along a three-mile line stretching to the water's edge.

Nine-year-old Bo begged his mother to be allowed to dig, but Betsy refused. However, both Octavius and Henry spent time upon the earthworks. They reported that those Baltimoreans who could not fight donated money, bricks, kettles, whiskey, salted fish, and even jars of preserves. The burning of Washington, rather than breaking the American spirit, had fired the entire country with the will to fight. When Samuel Smith put out the call for more militia, volunteers poured in from all directions.

Two weeks of work brought the city's defenses to readiness. To everyone's surprise, the British delayed their attack. Immediately after the fall of Washington, they took Alexandria—which put up no resistance and shamefully handed over ships and great stores of supplies. After a three-day occupation, the British fleet sailed back down the Potomac, anchored off the mouth of the river, and hovered there.

On Sunday, September 11, the prearranged warning of three cannon shots interrupted church services. All afternoon, soldiers reported for duty, while wagons laden with women, children, and household goods streamed from the city, going west on Market Street or north on Charles. Betsy decided it was too dangerous to join the panicked exodus, so she moved back to her father's house where she would have male protectors.

On Monday, the *Telegraph* warned that the British had a new weapon called Congreve rockets, gunpowder-filled iron cylinders tipped with conical warheads holding explosives or incendiary material. They could fly for two miles, but their trajectories were erratic. The article advised Baltimoreans to keep buckets of water at the ready in their homes.

Later that morning, runners brought the news that the British had landed nearly 5,000 marines and soldiers at North Point and were marching toward the city. The American defenders, General John Stricker and 3,000 men, were waiting at a narrow funnel of land between Bear Creek and Bread and Cheese Creek. For hours, the city heard nothing but distant guns. Then about suppertime, wagons bearing the dead and wounded reached Baltimore. Under the relentless pressure of a disciplined advance, Stricker's men had given way—but only after holding off a numerically superior force for two hours. Even in retreat, they did not yield to terror. Instead they fell back to Smith's defenses on Hampstead Hill and took their places on the line.

Meanwhile, British ships approached Fort McHenry—slowly because of the shallow, sandbar-filled river—and discovered that sunken hulks prevented them from taking Northwest Branch. Throughout the day, more ships arrived until a force of sixteen ships and numerous smaller vessels clustered just beyond the fort. That night it started to rain.

About 7:00 AM on September 13, the attack on Fort McHenry began. Despite the storm, Betsy and her family climbed to the roof to stare southeast toward Locust Point. Betsy protected herself with an umbrella, but the men and boys stood exposed to the lashing rain. Patterson used the telescope and reported that the giant 30-foot-by-42-foot flag commissioned by the fort's commander, Major Armistead, flew over the fort.

Even in the heavy weather, Betsy could hear explosions—not as loud as the warning shot fired at Texel but still enough to make her jump. The bombardment turned into a ceaseless onslaught; every few seconds, a British ship fired at the fort. Edward said that in addition to Congreve rockets, the British were hurling mortars. For three hours, the fort's guns answered, but about ten o'clock the American artillery fell silent. Patterson, who held the telescope, said he thought the British ships had moved out of range.

Heading toward the trap door to go inside, Betsy spotted Bo standing with his uncles, and her blood turned cold with a premonition of danger. She cursed herself for not realizing earlier how likely it was that they would come under the power of British invaders. The surname she and her child bore would not endear them to such conquerors.

Betsy called Bo and, when he reached her side, hugged him fiercely. Then she said, "Please go tell Mrs. Summers to make tea."

As soon as he was gone, she approached her father. "Sir, I must speak with you."

He lowered the telescope and glanced at her quizzically.

"I have made a dreadful error. I should have left Baltimore. Please may I have one of your carriages so that Bo and I can escape?"

"Are you mad? A lone woman and child fleeing during an invasion? The horses would be stolen from you, and you would suffer indignities of the worst kind."

"But could you not send Edward or George with me?"

"That is quite impossible. I need them here to protect my property if the army comes."

Betsy tightened the grip on her umbrella handle. "Do you not think it more important to protect your grandson?"

"Why should he be in more danger than the rest of us? Betsy, I know he is your only child, but try to view the situation with a sense of proportion."

He turned back to scan the horizon, but Betsy grasped his arm. "Father, please, listen to me. My son *is* in more danger than anyone else in Baltimore. He is a Bonaparte."

Patterson lowered the glass and snapped his head toward her. Then he growled, "Nonsense, he is a little boy. The British do not make war against children."

"How can you be so certain? Bonaparte is the most hated name in England. Have you never heard of rogue soldiers committing atrocities?"

Her father collapsed the telescope with a sharp click. "You are letting your inflated sense of rank get the best of you. Nothing will happen to you or Bo even if the city falls."

Tears filled Betsy's eyes. "I am not willing to risk his life on your say-so just because you are loath to leave your property without an extra guard."

Patterson glared at Betsy. "Control your waspish tongue. You know I love the boy and would not expose him to harm. He will be safer here under the protection of his male relatives than fleeing upon the open road with his hysterical mother."

Turning sharply, Betsy hurried to the trap door and descended to the third floor, where she ran into an unoccupied room and flung herself on the unmade bed to cry. She had a terrifying vision of Bo being taunted by a room full of soldiers until he responded angrily and was punished for it. All the country knew the story of General Andrew Jackson, the hero of Horseshoe Bend. As a boy courier captured during the Revolutionary War, he had received a saber blow to the face for refusing to clean a British officer's boots.

Hearing footsteps, Betsy sat up and saw Edward in the doorway. He came to sit beside her. "Betsy, I will not let anything happen to Bo. If the British break through our defenses, I will take my horse, put him on the saddle before me, and race out of town."

"Thank you," she said and leaned her head against Edward's shoulder.

Bo found them there a minute later. "What are you doing, Mama?"

Betsy forced a smile. "The rained soaked my clothes, so I came down to change."

"But why are you in here?" He glanced around at the boxes stacked in the bedroom, which had not been used since Joseph left for Europe.

"Oh—" She waved her hand airily. "I have not been in this room for so long, I wanted to see it."

Bo surveyed the room again and shrugged. "May I go up on the roof?"

"Only for a little while. I do not want you to catch cold."

As Bo and Edward climbed the ladder, Betsy descended to the second floor. On her way to her bedroom, she heard violent coughing behind Caroline's door. Betsy knocked and entered the room. To her horror, she saw Caroline leaning over her washbowl and spitting up blood.

"Caro!" Betsy hurried to her sister's side and held her shoulders until the spasm had passed. Then she gently lay Caroline back on her pillow. "How long has this been going on?"

Caroline turned her face away. "I have had the cough for a year or more, but the first time I saw blood was a month ago."

"Why has Father not sent for the doctor?"

"Because he does not know."

Betsy grabbed her sister's shoulders again. "Look at me. Why have you not told him?"

With a sigh, Caroline met Betsy's gaze. "Because it will not do any good. We both saw what happened with Margaret. The doctors know nothing about how to treat consumption."

"Oh, darling." Betsy smoothed damp tendrils from her forehead. Caroline was pale with dark shadows beneath her eyes. When she was healthy, she had the most beautiful skin and hair Betsy had ever seen, and Betsy had looked forward to introducing her to society. Now she feared that Caroline was more likely to leave her for the grave than the altar. "You must try to get well."

Caroline smiled wanly. "I have always admired you, Betsy, but I don't have your strength."

"Much good it has done me."

"It kept you from being crushed by events that would have destroyed me."

Taking her sister's hand, Betsy remembered how Caroline used to trail after her as a very young child. "I refuse to give up on you. When this crisis with the British is passed, I will tell Father the truth about your condition."

Caroline looked away. "If you wish, but I am certain it is too late."

"Nevertheless, we must do what we can." Betsy rose. "Now rest."

She walked into the hall, gently shut the door, and leaned her forehead against the wall. "Lord God, how much sorrow do you expect me to bear?" she whispered.

THE ALL-DAY BOMBARDMENT left Betsy with a pounding headache. As the rain continued into the afternoon, everyone came indoors, but after darkness fell, curiosity drove them back to the roof. Gazing toward the fort, Betsy saw red streaks of light that Edward said were Congreve rockets and orange balls of fire from mortars that exploded short of their target.

"How will we know who wins?" she asked.

"As long as the British continue to bombard the fort, we know it has not surrendered," Patterson said, not bothering to lower the telescope.

Worried about Bo's health, Betsy insisted that he go to bed in spite of his strenuous objections. He was so tired that he fell asleep while Betsy was tucking him in. Leaving him, she climbed to the third floor and found her father and Edward standing at the open front windows of Edward's bedroom where they were listening to the battle.

"How much longer do you think this will go on?"

"I don't know," her father answered. "It is a good sign that the fort has held so long."

Betsy went to her room and, after taking off her gown, climbed into bed. Because she knew that the constant explosions in the distance meant the fort was still being defended, they had grown almost as comforting as the sound of a heartbeat, and she soon fell asleep.

The next morning, a sudden cessation of sound woke her. She jumped from bed and looked out her window, but she could see nothing except that the rain had stopped. Betsy pulled on the gown she had worn the day before and hurried up to the roof where she found her father.

"Why has the bombing stopped? Has the fort fallen?"

Patterson looked at her with a stunned expression. "See for yourself." He handed her the telescope.

Holding it to her eye, Betsy scanned the horizon. Over the fort, snapping in the morning breeze, was a gigantic U.S. flag. Beyond it, she could make out the sails of the British fleet moving down the river toward Chesapeake Bay. Feisty Baltimore had repelled the invaders, and Betsy knew that her son was safe.

⟐ XXX ⟐

JUBILATION at the victory overflowed Baltimore and flooded through the country as people finally had reason to hope that the United States might defeat Great Britain. Giving voice to the joy was a song written by lawyer Francis Scott Key. As an envoy sent aboard a British ship to negotiate the release of a civilian prisoner, Key had been held there during the 25-hour attack, and his verses described a night of watching rockets and bombs pound Fort McHenry, only to have dawn reveal that the "star-spangled banner" still waved. The song became wildly popular. Betsy thought she would go mad listening to Bo sing it upstairs and down in his loudest voice.

Her nerves received a jolt on Sunday, September 18, when Fort McHenry started firing its guns at noon, but Bo ran into the street and learned from a passerby that the shots were a salute to another victory: U.S. forces had turned back a British invasion at Plattsburgh, New York, and a naval force had destroyed the British squadron on Lake Champlain. Reassured, Betsy rode along as a servant drove her son to his school the next day.

Although the country's elation over the victory lasted for months, the Pattersons' joy soon ended. On October 5, fourteen-year-old Henry and twelve-year-old Octavius were racing down South Street when Octavius was thrown from his horse. He hit his head on a cobblestone and died.

Betsy had never seen her father as shaken as he was by the loss of his youngest son. After the doctor had given Patterson laudanum to help him sleep, Betsy sat with Edward and George over a late supper of cold roast beef, cheese, and pickles. "I don't know whether to bring Bo home for the funeral. He has missed so much school."

Eighteen-year-old George, usually the quietest member of the family, spoke up. "They were playmates. You must give Bo the chance to say farewell."

Two days later, the Pattersons gathered at the family burial ground at their Cold Stream estate and watched Octavius's coffin being lowered into the ground. William Patterson stooped beneath his grief, and his face looked ten years older. Betsy stood back slightly from the rest of her family, troubled by her lack of strong emotion. She had never felt a deep affection for Octavius; when he was very young, he had been just another unwanted burden, and in recent years, she had regarded him mainly as someone who too often posed a risk to Bo. Now, however, when she saw Henry and Bo standing hand in hand, weeping beside the open grave, she regretted that she had not been a kinder sister.

More trouble was to come. Soon after the funeral, Caroline began to worsen, and Betsy moved back to South Street to nurse her. She bathed Caroline's face when she was feverish and instructed Providence Summers to prepare nourishing broths and comforting custards, but Caroline grew weaker by the day. Betsy often spent the afternoon reading novels aloud to keep Caro from brooding over her memories of Margaret's decline and the fact that her own deterioration paralleled their sister's journey toward death.

One morning, as Betsy read the newspaper, she learned that Vice-President Gerry had died of heart trouble on November 23. The information came too late for her to attend the funeral in Washington, and the loss of her friend left her forlorn. As Caroline dozed, Betsy shut herself in her bedroom, so she could weep for the courteous old gentleman who had debated her with so much respect for her opinions. Betsy felt her world growing narrower as, one by one, so many of the people who loved her died. Life had never seemed so precarious, not even when she was in danger at sea.

That December, as Betsy still grieved over the loss of her friend,

she received word that the new French government had no objection
to her traveling to Paris. For a while that news lifted her spirits. Then
another friend wrote to say that Princess Catharine had borne Jerome
a son in August. To Betsy's fury, they named the child Jerome Napoleon as if Bo did not exist.

Desperate for a sympathetic ear and unwilling to inflict her anger
on her ailing sister, Betsy called on Eliza Anderson Godefroy.

Eliza's fourteen-year-old daughter, also named Eliza, answered the
door. She hung Betsy's cloak in the hall and then led Betsy into the
drawing room where her mother sat sewing. "I had to come see you!"
Betsy exclaimed. "I have no one to confide in at home."

"Go make tea," Eliza told her daughter, and then she laid aside her
work and nodded at the chair across from her. "Please, sit down."

"I cannot." Too clenched with anger to relax, Betsy pressed her hands
against her stomach and started to pace. "Jerome's fat Catharine has
given him a son, and they named the child Jerome Napoleon. How
could he do it? After all these years of claiming to love Bo, he shows
his true lack of regard. It was not enough for Napoleon to deny us
the family name. No, my son's father has to steal his Christian name
and give it to this pretender."

Eliza rose and, putting an arm around Betsy's shoulder, walked
alongside her. "Surely, you cannot be surprised at your ex-husband's
selfish, careless nature."

Betsy stopped short. "No. For myself, I expect nothing but infamous
treatment from him, but I did not think he would stoop so low as to
wound our son."

Gently, Eliza steered her toward the sofa and sat beside her. "It is
all of a piece. He wants to show the world that he believes this new
son, not yours, to be his legitimate heir."

Betsy snorted. "Neither child has anything but debt to inherit."

"Listen to me carefully. If you can mask your anger over this new
outrage and treat it as some minor peculiarity in the way the Bonaparte
family christens their children, then your son will not be hurt to learn
that his half-brother shares his name. Bo is still young enough to take
his lead from you. Can you regulate your emotions enough to do what
is best for him?"

Betsy blinked in astonishment; she could swear she heard her mother's voice speaking through her friend. After taking a deep breath, she
said, "Yes, I will try."

WORRY SOON DISPLACED what remained of Betsy's anger. Caroline grew
ever weaker, and just before Christmas, she died. As Betsy stood with
her brothers in the bitter wind at the family burial ground, she felt
utterly weary and imagined herself crawling into Caroline's iron-cold
grave, stretching out upon the coffin, and remaining there. Fate had
been cruel to the women of the Patterson family, and Betsy wondered
how long it would be before death tracked her down too. If she were to
die tomorrow, what would she have accomplished? Nothing, it seemed.
Yet, the sight of her son shivering in the December wind reminded
Betsy that she still had vital work to do. She dare not surrender to
melancholy when he needed her to defend his rights.

At dinner the next day, most of the surviving Pattersons were back
at South Street, grouped at one end of the long table with five empty
chairs at the other. As Betsy passed Bo the dish of potatoes, her father said, "How soon can you close up your house?"

"Sir?" she asked in puzzlement.

"Since you are the only female left in the family, I require you to
move back here and see to the running of this household."

Betsy froze, shocked that he could demand such a thing after so
many years of expressing resentment at her presence in his home. After
a moment, she said, "Why? Edward is with the Smiths, so only you,
George, and Henry live here. And you have a competent housekeeper."

"She is not family. Your place is here."

Pressing her lips together, Betsy glanced at Bo, who watched her
with wide-eyed hope. She temporized. "Let me consider the matter."

That night after returning to her own house and putting Bo to bed,
she paced in the parlor. The thought of living with her father maddened her. She was certain he was sleeping with Providence Summers,
and Betsy did not want her son exposed to such immorality. Nor did
she want to subject herself to her father's ceaseless efforts to force
her into a more submissive role.

Weeks earlier, Dolley Madison had written suggesting that Betsy might travel to Europe with Dr. William Eustis, recently appointed the new U.S. ambassador to the Netherlands. Now Betsy wrote to Mrs. Madison, asking her to inquire whether Dr. and Mrs. Eustis would be willing to take her as far as Holland. Once there, she would travel to Paris on her own.

While she waited for an answer, Betsy stalled her father by saying she was not well enough to contemplate a move. Since Caroline's death, she had been despondent, and her chronic stomach problems returned. When she consulted a doctor, he diagnosed her condition as an excess of bile and suggested she take the waters at a health spa to restore her balance of humors.

"I hope to sail to Europe soon," she told the physician. "Is that advisable?"

"Yes, yes, a sea voyage might help, and you could visit one of the spas on the continent."

Believing she now had medical authorization to travel, Betsy was thrilled to hear in mid-January that the Eustises were willing to let her accompany them. They hoped to sail on a vessel belonging to John Jacob Astor, but as they were having trouble getting assurance from the British that the ship would not be attacked, they had not finalized their plans. Dolley Madison said they would forward Betsy the details as they became known.

At the family dinner given to celebrate her thirtieth birthday in February, Betsy announced her intention to travel.

"Have you taken leave of your senses?" Patterson demanded, pausing from carving the roast. "We are still at war, and our ships are not safe from British depredations."

"Dr. Eustis is a diplomat, Father, and he is negotiating with the British admiralty to allow the ship to pass unmolested."

"Even so, it is selfish to undertake such a frivolous journey when I need you here."

Betsy drew herself up straight. "I have two excellent reasons for going. First, my health requires it. Second, I have not been able to obtain reliable information about schools in Europe, so I must find out what is available."

Her father resumed carving the beef with an aggressive sawing that shredded the meat. "More nonsense. Bo will do just as well being educated where he is."

"The priests at St. Mary's are all very good men, but as the United States is yet in its infancy, American institutions are not sufficiently sophisticated to develop my son's intellect. I have been told he possesses such mental superiority that it would be a crime not to give him the best education."

"Bo is a gifted boy," Marianne said in her most placating tone, which would have set Betsy's teeth on edge were her sister-in-law not defending her. "And Betsy has wanted to go to Europe for so long that it would be a shame for her not to seize this chance."

Patterson glared at his daughter-in-law with the rancor he usually reserved for Betsy. "I very much doubt whether the proposed arrangements will come to fruition, so for the time being I will say no more."

Within days, the newspapers published reports that negotiators had signed the Treaty of Ghent on December 24, 1814, agreeing to end the war between the United States and Britain. Betsy took the news as an omen that fate had smiled on her at last, so she made arrangements to depart. She drove to St. Mary's and signed papers giving Dr. Dubois, headmaster at Bo's school, guardianship of her son in her absence. Then she took tea with Bo in the visitors' parlor, which was furnished with a sofa, armchairs, and a small table so that families could visit in more congenial surroundings than the boys' dormitory.

After she informed him of her plans, Bo furrowed his brow. "You will not stay in France forever, will you, Mama? Promise you will return for me."

"Yes, I will return," Betsy said several times, but still he scowled. Having lost his father to the temptations of Europe, he seemed to think it inevitable that his mother would abandon him too. Only after she swore to stay no more than a year did Bo calm down.

Back in Baltimore, Betsy asked Marianne and Edward to write Bo often and act as his parents during holidays. After reviewing her accounts with Aunt Nancy, Betsy put the older woman in charge of her investments with strict instructions to avoid risk. Betsy was very worried about money. Her friend Jonathan Russell, envoy to the court of Sweden, had written that she would need at least $6,000 a year to live in Europe, and her income was scarcely half that.

At the end of March, Betsy set out to meet the Eustises in Boston, taking George as her escort. Because her stomach still troubled her and the roads were bogged with spring mud, they traveled slowly and stopped at several cities along the way. When they reached New York, Betsy found two letters waiting at the hotel. One was from Mrs. Eustis, which Betsy tore open immediately. It said that their sailing was delayed again, so she might as well enjoy herself in New York rather than hurry to Boston. The second was from Bo. Betsy waited until she was in her room to read his letter in privacy.

> *How are you? I am pretty well but my spirits are not very good. Tell me when you start to go to France.... Please send me one of your rings for to remember you if you should get lost in the sea. Do not stay any longer than one year for my sake. You must come for me to go to France with you and no one will do except you and my own Father.*
> *I am yours affectionately, Jerome N. Bonaparte*
>
> *P.S. My dear Mama, I wish you would keep this letter with you all the time you are in France and read it over every month. My dear Mama, I love you very much.*

The letter upset Betsy. How could she bear to part from her sweet boy for a year? She had told herself repeatedly that this separation would not be any worse than having him at Emmitsburg, but now she saw what a self-deception that was. George found her in tears when he returned to the parlor after overseeing the disposition of their trunks.

Wordlessly, Betsy handed him the letter. He read it and said, "The year apart will be hard on him, but someday he will understand that you did this for his sake."

Betsy wiped her eyes. "Yes, you are right."

Since they had time to spend in New York, Betsy sent her card to some acquaintances she had made when she lived there with Jerome. The next day, nearly a dozen invitations arrived.

As Betsy debated which engagements to accept, news was published that threatened her plans. In March, Napoleon had escaped from Elba to France, where he gathered an army and marched on Paris, causing Louis XVIII to flee. The Bonapartes were once again in power.

Soon afterward, Mrs. Eustis wrote Betsy to say that Dr. Eustis thought there would be great impropriety in her traveling to Paris at the present time, particularly with a diplomat. Mrs. Eustis suggested that Betsy defer her visit to Europe until she received permission from France.

Tossing aside the letter, Betsy felt like a pawn, just on the verge of reaching the back row and becoming a queen when a giant hand swept her off the chessboard. Resentment flooded her, and she raged all night before bowing to the necessity of returning home.

Back in Baltimore at the end of May, Betsy considered what to do. Writing to Napoleon to ask him to reconsider her status would be futile; the emperor had more important matters on his mind. More than two months had passed since his return to Paris; almost certainly, his enemies had declared war on him by now. Betsy could wait to see who proved to be victorious, but as she knew all too well, such a conflict might take years.

Betsy's father assumed that she had abandoned all thought of going to Europe, and her brothers refused to listen to her schemes to travel despite Napoleon's return. Only Eliza Godefroy understood that Betsy was suffocating from boredom and sadness, but even she thought Betsy should give up her dream of seeing France and alleviate her unhappiness by exercising her talents. "You don't have to try writing if my example has made you uneasy," Eliza said. "You could institute the custom of holding salons here in Baltimore, or you could take up a worthy cause and try to influence your acquaintances in Washington."

"But that is not the life I want. It would not satisfy." As Betsy walked home from that visit, she felt that she was screaming into the wind, only to have her desperate plea for help blown back in her face before anyone could hear it.

A thunderclap of insight woke Betsy one night. She could still educate Bo in Europe as long as she went to a country outside French control. For years, she had asked people who had been abroad for advice about the best schools, and their suggestions included England, Edinburgh, and Geneva. Now that Napoleon was no longer paying her a pension, he could not forbid her from going to such places.

She rose, lit a candle, and went down the hall to her son's bedroom.

Bo had come home for his summer holiday, and Betsy stood watching him for several minutes. He was such a heavy sleeper that the flickering candle did not disturb him. Now that he was almost ten, his blond hair had darkened to a sandy brown, and he had lost some of his baby fat, so that Betsy could catch glimpses of the man he would become. Her dream had always been for him to be educated in France, but perhaps a school in another European country would serve her purpose just as well.

With the prospect of travel opening up before her again, Betsy felt as though shackles had fallen from her wrists. She vowed not to be a prisoner of her circumstances any longer.

✒ XXXI ✑

Because Napoleon's return had made the name *Bonaparte* too conspicuous, Betsy obtained a passport and booked passage in her maiden name. She sailed for England in June with the Ashleys, a prosperous merchant and his wife to whom friends had introduced her. They reached Liverpool in July and took rooms in a local inn to recover from the voyage before starting the three-day journey to the spa at Cheltenham.

Almost the first thing Betsy learned after her arrival was that the Duke of Wellington had already defeated Napoleon at a place called Waterloo in Belgium. Napoleon was now a British prisoner on the HMS *Bellerophon* in Plymouth Harbor. Betsy briefly wondered if she might journey to meet the great man who had thwarted her destiny yet retained her admiration, but the newspapers reported that Captain Maitland was under strict orders not to let anyone aboard.

While in Liverpool, Betsy wrote to Frances Erskine, who was now living in Surrey. In her reply, Lady Erskine gave Betsy a letter of introduction to a distinguished Irish physician who lived at Cheltenham, Sir Arthur Brooke Falkener, and his wife Anne.

Betsy and the Ashleys set out for the spa town a week after their arrival in England. During the first leg of the trip, they shared a coach with a pleasant old gentleman whose son was an officer under Wellington. The father had read all available accounts of Waterloo and eagerly described the battle to his American companions. Betsy plied the man with questions—so many that she found it difficult to disguise her special interest in the Bonapartes. Finally, unable to restrain her curiosity, she asked, "Was Napoleon's youngest brother in the battle? He visited my city years ago, and I wonder what became of him."

"Do you mean Prince Jerome? Yes, he acquitted himself with distinction, inspiring his men to fight long after all hope was lost."

A wave of unexpected tenderness washed over Betsy. "So he has won military glory at last," she murmured. Then, seeing the old man frown, she shrugged. "Much good may it do him now that his brother has gone down to defeat."

"Well, there's no denying that Boney had genius. As far as I can tell, the rest of his family is a worthless lot who did him no favors."

"Perhaps the emperor's talents have descended to the next generation," Betsy said, thinking of her son. Bo would be pleased to learn that his father had fought well.

The old man snorted. "God help us if they have."

Arriving at Cheltenham, Betsy was pleased by the town's appearance. The main thoroughfare, High Street, was neatly paved, and oil lamps lit the streets in the evening. St. Mary's, located at the center of town, was a picturesque church that dated back to the Middle Ages. It was built in the shape of a cross, with a squat octagonal spire topped by a gilded weathercock. Betsy's first day in town, she noticed an astonishing amount of building taking place, no doubt because of Cheltenham's growing popularity as a resort. One great project under construction was a crescent of connected town houses, built of light stone and fronted by beautiful cast-iron fences. Betsy wished she could rent one of those fashionable residences instead of settling in the same boarding house as Mr. and Mrs. Ashley.

The Ashleys already bored Betsy so much that she had difficult curbing her sarcasm—they were the kind of narrow, commercially minded people she had hoped to leave behind in Baltimore. She could not, however, live on her own in a foreign country. Hoping to make more amiable friends, she sent Lady Erskine's letter of introduction to the Brooke Falkeners.

Lady Brooke Falkener called the next day. She was a slim, elegantly dressed blonde in her late twenties. After greeting Betsy, the English-woman gazed down her nose at the parlor furniture, which had thread-bare upholstery. "Please accept what I am about to say as a friendly caution, Madame Bonaparte. You are a visitor to England and do not know our ways. People of fashion do not stay in boarding houses."

Betsy smiled to show that she did not take offense and then tried to hint at her financial limitations. "Surely it would be viewed as self-important to take larger quarters for just my maid and myself."

"Oh, but there is a sweet little house to let next to ours, and I'm sure Sir Arthur could obtain reasonable terms. Lady Erskine told us your health is delicate, so it would be to your advantage to settle near a physician."

Within a week, Betsy had moved to a two-story town house on High Street, a building just wide enough for a door and single window on the ground floor. It was not as stylish as the houses that she admired in the Royal Crescent but, with neighbors like the Brooke Falkeners, it was far more respectable than her previous lodgings.

Shortly afterward, she consulted with Sir Arthur about her health. The doctor was only in his mid-thirties, but he had many years expe-rience as a physician to his majesty's troops and, just two years earlier, had earned honors by halting the spread of the plague in Malta. Since his retirement from the service, he had been appointed the person-al physician of the Duke of Sussex, George III's youngest son. Betsy had complete confidence in him.

Sir Arthur agreed with Betsy's Baltimore doctor that she suffered from an excess of bile, so he urged her to take full advantage of the spa. Because she disliked the idea of bathing in waters so many others had used, he excused her from using the public bath, but he insisted that she drink mineral water four times a day and take frequent luke-warm baths at home. Betsy followed his prescribed regimen exactly.

After she had been in Cheltenham several weeks, she traveled to Lon-don to see her father's business agent, James McIlhiny. Sitting in his office amid a welter of account books, Betsy explained that her relatives had given her lists of things to purchase in Europe, and she was relying on Mr. McIlhiny to help her with the shipping and transfer of funds.

"Shall I also handle the letters of credit your father provided you?"

"I am afraid you are misinformed, Mr. McIlhiny. My father is not paying for my trip."

He rubbed his chin. "Oh. I gathered from his last letter that he is very concerned about you, so I assumed he was giving you an allowance."

Betsy's heart swelled with emotion. Perhaps her father cared for her more than she knew but because of his stern nature only expressed that love to others. "Pray, what did he say?"

McIlhiny coughed. "He asked me to look after you and keep him informed because you had conceived yourself so ill that you hurried to Europe without the knowledge or approval of your friends."

The words stung like a slap. "Sir, I can assure you that is not the case."

He bowed his head in apology. "Forgive me. I have no wish to offend you."

After smoothing down the fingers of her gloves as a way to calm herself, Betsy said, "I bear you no ill will, Mr. McIlhiny."

McIlhiny rubbed his chin again and then cleared his throat. "Madame Bonaparte, please forgive me if this is presumptuous, but I would like to ask your father to consider making you an allowance. Perhaps he may be moved if I write that it is the custom for gentlemen of his station to provide their unmarried daughters with financial support when they travel."

"You are very kind, sir. I would be grateful for your intervention."

Betsy was so angry with her father that her stomach churned and her head ached during the entire two-day trip back to Cheltenham. The day after her return, she wrote to him:

> *Dear Sir—I perceive with much regret, by your letters respecting me to persons of this country, that you announced to them that I conceived myself ill, and had embarked contrary to the wishes of my friends. I shall answer categorically these two accusations, and answer them without temper. The physicians of England are willing to give a certificate of their opinion that there is an accumulation of bile on my liver, which would have killed me,...had I not gone to sea and tried a change of climate.*

Betsy was gripping her pen so tightly that her hand began to cramp.

She lay down the quill to stretch her fingers and then resumed the letter by saying that those who begrudged her this trip were no friends of hers because true friends would be happy that she now found herself in a society she enjoyed and where she was much appreciated.

> *My misfortune and the declining state of my health have excited more interest here than in my own country, and have been a passport to the favor of the great. My talents and manners are likely to preserve their good opinion. What you have written of me to Europe will have very bad effects. Either people will wonder you should not wish my health restored, and that you should not be pleased at knowing me in the first society, or they will consider me to be a hypocrite and disobedient child, who has bribed medical men to say my life is in danger.*

By then, tears were streaming down her face. The pain of her father's disapproval stung as sharply as it had when she was eight years old, and Betsy searched for words to convince him of the merit that others saw in her.

> *I get on extremely well, and I assure you that altho' you have always taken me for a fool, it is not my character here. In America I appeared more simple than I am, because I was completely out of my element. It was my misfortune, not my fault, that I was born in a country which was not congenial to my desires.*

She went on to describe the excellent living situation she had found with reputable protectors. Then she warned her father to be careful what he wrote about her.

> *I beg... that you will consider the impropriety of writing anything except what will produce a good effect in this country. All my conduct is calculated, but you will undo the effects of my prudence if you write to certain people, who show your letters. Let people think you are proud of me, which indeed you have good reason to be, as I am very prudent and wise.*

Once she had sent the letter to Baltimore, she resolved to put her father out of her mind. Indeed there was much at Cheltenham to distract her as her health improved. The Brooke Falkeners took her to the horse races and dances, where they introduced her to members of the British aristocracy. In late September, Percy Smythe, the Viscount Strangford, brought Betsy an invitation to attend a ball given by the Portuguese ambassador, Count Tonsall, for all the nobility residing in Cheltenham. The evening of the party, Betsy felt queasy, but she did not want to give offense by refusing to attend, so she rose from her bed and dressed in a white chemise beneath a sheer, high-waisted gown with gold metallic braid crisscrossing her bosom and forming a band beneath the short puffed sleeves. For accessories, she added long, white kid gloves and the pearls Jerome had given her for a wedding present. Betsy remained at the party for three hours, talking with spirit and making many titled acquaintances, but when supper was served, she excused herself and left. Before going to bed, however, she recorded in her notebook the names of all the aristocrats she had met whose daughters might be potential brides for Bo.

Betsy did not spend all her time at Cheltenham pursuing amusement. She also sought to increase her knowledge of every kind. In September, she went with the Brooke Falkeners to hear Haydn's oratorio *The Creation* at Gloucester Cathedral. It was a musical retelling of the book of Genesis, performed by three soloists, a chorus, and a large orchestra, and she delighted in the virtuoso performances.

Often during the daytime hours, Betsy and Lady Brooke Falkener attended lectures at the Assembly Hall about such diverse topics as the novels of Miss Jane Austen and the fossilized skeleton of an ancient fishlike creature discovered at Lyme Regis in 1811. The people Betsy met at these meetings were educated, and she reveled in the opportunity to take part in stimulating conversation, including many disquisitions on the recently concluded Congress of Vienna, where representatives of the victorious powers had sought to restore deposed monarchs, redraw the boundaries of Europe, and create a balance of power to preserve the peace. The spa also had several subscription libraries, so Betsy could read to her heart's content. Having access to so many cultural opportunities confirmed her resolve to educate Bo in Europe.

Only two things marred her happiness. She missed her son dreadfully and wished she had a large enough income to have brought him with her. Marianne had written in July that Bo was depressed, but more recent letters said he was resigned to the separation. Betsy wrote him as often as she could afford the postage, recounting lively stories so he might feel part of her life. She also reminded him in every letter that, just as soon as she received permission from the French government, she would travel to France to look for a suitable school for him:

> *Being separated by the Atlantic is as disagreeable to me as it is to you, but I must do what is necessary to secure your future. Reward all my cares for you by studying as hard as you can, so that when I come home I will find that you have proven yourself worthy of the Bonaparte name. I love you, and I shall not rest easy until I can be with you again and look after you myself.*

The second problem was money, as Betsy had known it would be, but she worked hard to keep her conversation witty and amusing so that she would be a much-desired guest—a plan in which she succeeded. Acquaintances invited her to dine so frequently that it kept her expenses in check, and she managed to live just within her means. Even so, she dared to imagine that her father might respond favorably to McIlhiny's suggestion about the allowance, which would give her more freedom. She delayed traveling to Paris until she received an answer.

That possibility was soon dashed like a storm-tossed ship upon rocks. In November, James McIlhiny wrote to say that her father had declared categorically he would never give a penny toward her support as long as she lived abroad.

Betsy felt no real surprise at the answer, but she did berate herself for having been seduced by hope. Shortly afterward, a letter from her father arrived.

> *I am persuaded you are pursuing a wrong course for happiness; but I hope and pray you may soon perceive your mistake, and that you will look to your mother-country as the only place where you can be really respected, for what will the world think of a woman who had recently followed her mother and her last sister to the grave, had quit her father's house, where duty and necessity called for her attentions as the only female of the family left, and thought proper to abandon all to seek for admiration in foreign countries; surely the most charitable construction that can be given to such conduct is to suppose that*

it must proceed in some degree from a state of insanity, for it cannot be supposed that any rational being could act a part so very inconsistent and improper.

The charge of insanity wounded Betsy so deeply that she took to her bed with a severe headache.

Lady Brooke Falkener called the next morning and commented on how ill she looked. Not wanting to reveal the breach with her father, Betsy said, "November never agrees with me. The gloomy weather afflicts me with *tristesse.*"

"Well, this novel I brought will cheer you up. You said how much you enjoyed Lady Morgan's *Wild Irish Girl,* so I feel certain you will want to read her latest, *O'Donnel.* There is nothing like its portrayal of the Irish peasant."

"Thank you, how kind." As Betsy glanced through the pages of the book, she reached a decision. "But I should not borrow this. I think that it is time for me to depart for France."

"Oh, keep it, my dear, and return it to me later."

Arriving in Paris the last week of November, Betsy gazed out the window in rapture as the public coach took her through narrow, winding streets crowded with medieval, sometimes crooked buildings. She had dreamed of this moment for so long. After checking into a hotel recommended by Thomas Jefferson, Betsy sent a note to the American embassy asking if she could call on Ambassador Albert Gallatin, whom she knew from his days as Secretary of the Treasury in Washington.

The Swiss-born Gallatin was then in his fifties. He had a square face, heavy eyebrows, and a bald pate surrounded by a collar-length fringe of hair. At his meeting with Betsy, he gave her helpful advice about suitable neighborhoods and the best way to transmit funds between the United States and Paris. He also invited her to dine with his family. Gallatin's wife Hannah was very kind to Betsy, who became a frequent guest at their table and through them began to make connections in Parisian society.

They introduced her to the writer David Bailie Warden, who helped Betsy find a small apartment for eighty dollars a month. The building had interior stairs that dipped in the center from decades of traffic, water-stained walls, and warped floors, but Betsy did not care because she was in Paris at last. Her suite consisted of two bedrooms, one for herself and one for a maid, and a parlor furnished with fringed, gold velvet draperies, a gold-on-blue damask sofa, and four mahogany fauteuils with blue cushions and winged goddesses carved on the arm supports. On the rare occasions that she dined at home, Betsy had meals sent up from a restaurant in the building next door.

Warden also showed her the sights, including Notre Dame, the tomb of Voltaire in the Pantheon, and Napoleon's unfinished *Arc de Triomph.* As they drove through the city, Betsy's delight in Paris was marred only by the sight of so many British and Russian soldiers encamped in the royal parks. The troops reminded her that, even though she was finally living in her ideal city, she would never experience the glory of the French Empire.

That disappointment faded as Warden introduced Betsy into literary circles. The United States had nothing comparable; the only acclaimed American writer was Washington Irving, whom Betsy had met at Dolley Madison's open houses, but his two books of satiric essays could hardly constitute a national literature. In Paris, Betsy made the acquaintance of several female writers, who eventually became close friends.

One was Madame Germaine de Staël, a woman of nearly fifty with dark hair, a fleshy face, and a slightly buck-toothed smile. She dressed in turbans and shawls of rich Eastern fabrics. During his reign, Napoleon had exiled Madame de Staël from France because her controversial novel *Delphine* explored the subject of women's freedom. Now, she and Betsy commiserated with each other over their unfair treatment by the emperor.

Another literary acquaintance was Reine Philiberte de Varicourt, the Marquise de Villette, adopted daughter of Voltaire. She told Betsy many stories of the great French author, to whom she was still so devoted that she kept his heart in an urn. She also wrote essays under the pet name that Voltaire had given her: *Belle et Bonne.*

At one salon, the hostess introduced Betsy to a tiny woman, even shorter than she was, who had black hair and a charming Irish face with deep-set eyes and a rosebud mouth. "Madame Bonaparte, may I present the novelist Sydney, Lady Morgan."

"Lady Morgan!" Betsy curtsied. "The authoress of *O'Donnel?* I admired that book more than I can tell you."

"You are too kind, Madame Bonaparte." Lady Morgan adjusted her stole, which had slipped off her shoulders when she returned the curtsy. "I have heard of you too, and I am delighted to make your acquaintance. They say that no one in Paris is a more charming conversationalist."

"A minor talent, if that. Nothing like your ability to spin such moving tales."

The two women spent the next hour comparing notes on their favorite novels, and from that day on, Betsy looked for Lady Morgan at every reception she attended. They became fast friends, continuing to correspond after Lady Morgan left Paris.

Before long, *tout le monde* knew that Jerome Bonaparte's former wife had taken up residence in Paris, and the members of high society flocked to her morning receptions, famed for their witty, intellectual discourse. Betsy was delighted to receive the writer François-René de Chateaubriand, whose novel *Atala* had so thrilled her during her the early days of her courtship. The author had dark, wild curls that reminded her of Jerome—ironically, as it turned out, because Chateaubriand was a harsh critic of the former emperor. As a result, Betsy avoided political topics in their conversations and instead questioned him about the romantic journey he had taken from Paris to Jerusalem a few years earlier. Other notable guests at her gatherings included the Prussian explorer Alexander von Humboldt and the renowned Italian sculptor Antonio Canova.

All winter Betsy kept up a public façade of gaiety and charm, but when she was alone at night, her mood darkened as swiftly as if a cold wind off the Atlantic had snuffed out all the candles in a glittering chandelier. At times like that, all she could think of was how much she missed her son. Her only consolation was that she was gradually befriending people of noble blood, contacts she hoped would prove useful when it was time for arrange a match for Bo. She even made an appointment with Albert Gallatin to ask his impression of her growing list of possible brides, and he tactfully indicated which families might not be as financially sound as they appeared. Yet, even the prospect of a noble alliance for her son did not completely ease Betsy's sorrow over their separation.

She also suffered from apprehension that her new acquaintances would discover the precarious state of her finances. The ease with which Napoleon briefly regained power and commanded an ardent following had revealed how little love the French had for the restored monarchy, so the British continued to occupy the capital to allow the king time to consolidate his position. The presence of troops drove up prices in the city so that it was even more expensive to live in Paris than in England.

Betsy made every effort to economize while still maintaining the social position necessary to her purpose. Everyone knew of her father's wealth, so no one suspected the stringent measures she took to survive day to day. She kept her meals as Spartan as possible and heated her rooms only when she expected company. Even though she constantly went to balls and receptions, she bought no new clothing but used her skill as a seamstress to refresh her wardrobe—and did it so expertly that everyone remarked on how beautifully she dressed. Whenever she was invited to an occasion that required presents, Betsy gave a piece of her own needlework. Her gifts were so admired that the recipients never guessed that financial necessity lay behind them, and soon her friends were arguing good-naturedly over which one had received the most charming of her *petits cadeaux*.

In December, the Duke of Wellington invited her to a ball at the English embassy, located in the former home of the Princess Borghese, Jerome's sister Pauline. Betsy knew the exterior of the building. It was a two-story mansion built of the tawny stone so common in Paris with a double Ionic portico and two windows on either side of the entrance. At each end of the central block, a pavilion extended into the front courtyard.

For the occasion, Betsy decided on the same outfit she had worn to the Portuguese ambassador's ball in Cheltenham, with the addition of a small gold tiara set with seed pearls and white topazes, which everyone took for diamonds.

When Betsy arrived at the embassy, she found herself in an entrance hall that featured a grey and white plaid marble floor and, to the right, a sweeping staircase with an exquisite wrought-iron railing. Betsy was presented to Wellington, a tall handsome man of forty-six with dark hair, haughty blue eyes, and an aquiline nose. He was wearing his scarlet dress uniform and, oddly for a ball, boots with spurs. "Your grace." Betsy curtsied.

"Charmed," he answered languidly. "Would you do me the honor of giving me the opening dance?" Without waiting for her answer, he held out his arm.

Amused, Betsy allowed him to escort her into the ball. Wellington was a notorious rake, rumored to go to any length to bed women who had been Napoleon's mistresses, but if he hoped to add her to his list of former Bonaparte lovers, he would be disappointed. Since coming to Paris, Betsy had received confirmation of what she long suspected; the Bonapartes justified Napoleon's treatment of her by claiming she was a trollop who had seduced their baby brother. As a lady, she could not answer such accusations, but she could defend her reputation by maintaining a puritanical chastity.

When they entered the ballroom, a murmur of astonishment swept through the crowd and, as one, the assembly curtsied and bowed. "Extraordinary," Wellington said.

"Do you not usually receive such homage, your grace?"

"Never. Such a reception properly belongs to royalty."

Indeed, Betsy thought. With a shiver of pleasure, she remembered Odette's long-ago prophecy: *You wore a silk gown with a crown on your head. And when you entered a room full of people, they bowed like you were a princess.*

Smiling, she looked around and decided that this was the perfect setting in which to receive such an honor. The ballroom was all white and gold: a square-patterned parquet floor in shades of honey and caramel, cream walls with gilt moldings and applied swags; and gold-framed mirrors that reflected the light from three large crystal chandeliers. Music began to play, and the duke and Betsy took their place at the head of the line of couples.

As they danced, Wellington's spur caught on her hem and tore it. "Oh, me damn spur!" he exclaimed and stopped to make sure that it had not been pulled loose or damaged his boot. Assured that the leather was unharmed, he led Betsy back into the dance without a word of apology for ruining her best garment.

Furious, she danced with a frozen smile and did not even attempt to

make conversation. When the music ended, Wellington looked around
and gestured to a man with an unusually broad face and shrewd eyes.
The gentleman approached, walking with a limp. "Monsieur Talleyrand, allow me to present you to Madame Patterson Bonaparte." After the curt introduction, Wellington walked toward an aide who stood
waiting to speak to him.

Charles Maurice de Talleyrand-Périgord bowed over Betsy's hand.
"I have heard of you from our mutual acquaintance Madame de Staël."

"And all the world has heard of you," Betsy answered, disguising her
scorn with a smile. The wily statesman was such a master of intrigue
that he had not only survived the French Revolution but also served
under every regime that followed it. Ultimately, he had turned against
Napoleon and helped restore the Bourbons, and for that Betsy could
not forgive him. Even though she agreed whole-heartedly with Napoleon's assessment that his former minister was a "turd in a silk stock-
ing," she murmured pleasantries to Talleyrand because he was much
too powerful to risk offending.

Knowing that his lameness precluded him from dancing, Betsy made
her way to a pair of empty gilt chairs and Talleyrand followed. Behind them, Wellington laughed loudly.

After glancing over his shoulder, Talleyrand said, "Knowing that
we were almost certain to meet, his majesty King Louis XVIII asked
me to convey a message to you. He wishes you to know that you are
welcome at court."

Betsy paused in astonishment and bought a few moments by sitting
and arranging her skirts. She could see that her torn hem was dragging badly, but she thought she could salvage the gown by adding a
ruffle. Turning back to Talleyrand, she smiled. "Please convey my
respects to his majesty. I am sensible of the honor he pays me, but I
cannot accept. Having received a pension from Napoleon Bonaparte,
it would be an act of the deepest impropriety for me to enjoy the hospitality of his successor. I have many faults, Monsieur, but ingratitude
has never been one of them."

Although his eyebrows shot up in surprise, Talleyrand said, "Your
discretion does you credit, Madame."

Within moments, a marquis begged to be introduced to Betsy and soon she was back on the dance floor. Buoyed by having been bowed to and flattered by the king's invitation, Betsy was happier than she had been in years. Truly, no matter what her father might think, this was the life she had been intended for all along.

During supper, Wellington approached her. "I have a frightfully amusing story, Madame Patterson Bonaparte. Do you remember how everyone bowed when we entered the ballroom?"

"Yes, of course, your grace. Have you learned the cause?"

"They mistook you for the Princess Borghese. You look awfully alike, don't you know?"

As Betsy realized the cruel joke that fate had played on her, she smiled stiffly. "My former husband used to tell me that I resembled his sister."

The rest of the evening was a torment. By the time she returned to her rooms, her head was bursting from the strain of remaining sociable after such a shock. Standing before her mirror, Betsy stared at herself as she pulled off her long gloves and stripped off her jewels.

"It was all a delusion, my girl," she said. "All the time the prophecy was leading to this moment when you would be forced to admit that your dreams were vanity."

As if she were ten years old again, she recalled the other statement Odette had made, the one she had so long forgotten: *Do not seek how to be high and mighty, seek how to have wisdom.*

"And how do I do that now that I have based my entire life upon a misapprehension?"

Moving to her dressing table, she picked up the miniature of Bo she kept there, and a sweetly intense love for him flooded her. No matter what else went wrong in her life, she could never regret having given birth to her son. He was her purpose for living.

I may not have high rank, but my son was born for something better. I must fight to secure his future. If only I can succeed at that, nothing else will matter.

⚘ XXXII ⚘

On a grey afternoon in October 1817, Betsy walked the deck of the *Maria Theresa,* a ship bound for New York. Even though she wore a woolen cloak with a fur-lined hood, the wind cut through her garments and made her shiver. The sky was filled with dark clouds and a light mist was falling, but the weather was balmy compared to the storms that had dogged the ship since its departure from Le Havre. Uncertain when she would have another chance to escape her cabin, Betsy had gone up for fresh air as soon as the most recent storm abated.

Her traveling companion, who remained below, was Anna Maria Tousard, the widow of Bo's former tutor. During her stay in Paris, Betsy had been delighted to renew her friendship with Tousard and was grieved when the sixty-eight-year-old colonel died. Afterward, Betsy called often upon his widow. Now they were sailing together because Madame Tousard planned to settle in Philadelphia, where her step-daughter lived.

Gazing at the white-capped, greenish-grey waves rolling to the horizon, Betsy found herself wondering what to say to Bo when she saw him again. In spite of her promises, she had remained in Europe more than two years. Eighteen months earlier, depressed after a long winter of being barely able to afford food, Betsy traveled to Le Havre with the intention of sailing home as soon as possible, even though she had not accomplished her goal of visiting schools. During a meeting with Mr. Callaghan, her agent in France, Betsy had just told him, "If any letters arrive for me after my departure, please forward them to my father," when she experienced shortness of breath. Within seconds, her heart was racing, and her body had broken out in a sweat. She had so much difficulty breathing that she feared she would die. Pressing her hand against her chest, she stared at Mr. Callaghan in distress, praying that he would read the appeal for help in her eyes.

He stammered, "M-Madame Bonaparte? What can I do? Do you have smelling salts?" He reached for her reticule, but Betsy shook her head vehemently. A moment later, she sighed as the surge of panic began to subside. As her heartbeat slowed to normal, she felt terribly weak. Mr. Callaghan asked one of his clerks to bring her a cup of strong, very sweet tea, and while she sipped it, he urged her to delay traveling until she could seek medical advice. Once they were certain that the worst of her symptoms had passed, Mr. Callaghan escorted Betsy to her hotel.

Frightened, Betsy returned to Paris where she consulted with the physician husband of her friend Lady Morgan. Sir Charles believed she was again suffering an excess of black bile and prescribed a regimen of hot baths and dietary changes.

By summer 1816, Betsy felt healthy enough to investigate schools for Bo. During her time in Paris, she often met with Albert Gallatin seeking financial advice, and the ambassador strongly recommended the Swiss boarding school he had attended as a boy.

Betsy traveled to Geneva to visit it. Located in a French-speaking part of Switzerland near the border with France, the city stood where the Rhone River exited the stunningly blue Lake Geneva. Mountains surrounded the city on several sides. The climate was cooler than that of Paris, but Betsy found it preferable to sweltering, fever-ridden Baltimore.

The Academy of Geneva, founded in 1559 by John Calvin, was a prestigious school that prepared students for university. Although it originally focused on Protestant theology, the school now taught philosophy, humanities, and science—exactly the rigorous curriculum Betsy wanted for her son. The only problem was that she could not afford the tuition.

Betsy returned to Paris and once again prepared to go home, intending to overhaul her finances based on Gallatin's recommendations. Then, in August, an excruciating toothache confined her to bed for two weeks. After it subsided, her attacks of rapid pulse and panicked breathing returned, with several occurring during the month of September. By then, the Morgans had left for Dublin, and Betsy did not know where to seek medical advice. She went back on the regimen Dr. Morgan had previously advised, and her condition slowly improved.

It had grown so late in the year that any Atlantic crossing would be risky. Worried, Betsy consulted a French physician one of her friends had referred her to, and he advised her not to sail until spring because her tendency to have *mal de mer* in rough seas would undo all the progress she had made toward restoring her health. Betsy wrote Bo to explain her trouble and beg him to forgive her for the delay.

Once winter passed, Betsy decided that it would not make much difference if she postponed her departure a few weeks more. Paris was so beautiful in the springtime, and the lavish blossoming of the city symbolized to her the cultural exuberance she found in Europe. She pursued her social life with a new desperation, born of the desire to stockpile memories of the advantages Baltimore lacked. Betsy went to concerts and the opera, where she heard works by Beethoven and Rossini, and she visited the galleries in the Louvre to gaze on masterpieces only to be found in Europe. In her journal, she kept long lists of the cultural attractions that Bo must see when he finally came to France. When her health permitted, Betsy attended weekly balls, not only to dance but also to engage in the clever repartee Parisians considered *de rigueur.*

In addition, she redoubled her efforts to lay the groundwork for her son's future. Her long-ago conversations with Oakeley had given her the idea of preparing Bo for a diplomatic career, so she used every opportunity to make contacts that he could draw upon as a grown man. Wherever she went, she spoke of her desire for him to be a European, not an American.

Such conversations gave her a sense of purpose, but they also kept her longing for her son uppermost in her mind. By late spring, Betsy missed Bo so much that she spent hours crying over his letters. Her appetite failed and her stomach pains returned, and she wondered if the separation itself was causing her illness. As she wrote to her son at the end of May, she realized that she had dawdled so long she was going to miss his twelfth birthday. Spasms of guilt prostrated her for the rest of the afternoon.

Still she lingered, knowing that once she returned to America it might be years before she came back to Paris—and until she did, boredom and an unslaked thirst for culture would torment her. For Betsy, the dilemma was agonizing: She could stay in Paris and lock away her maternal heart in an iron box or return to Baltimore and similarly lock away her mind. After shilly-shallying for weeks, she realized that if she put off the trip much longer, she would have to stay in Paris a third winter. The next day, she began to put her affairs in order so she could leave.

The goad that finally forced her to book passage was a letter from home, reawakening Betsy's distrust of her father. When Betsy first left for Europe, Marianne had agreed to look after Bo, but her asthma had deteriorated so much that her doctors advised a change of climate. For the past year, Robert, Marianne, and two of her sisters had been in Europe, leaving William Patterson in charge of Bo during his school holidays. Then, in the summer of 1817, Aunt Nancy wrote that Providence Summers had borne Patterson a daughter named Matilda, conceived while the housekeeper's husband was away on a long voyage. According to Aunt Nancy, the only reason Patterson managed to hush up the scandal was that Captain Summers had been lost at sea before he learned of the betrayal.

The unsavory situation reawakened Betsy's fears that her son might develop the same debauched nature as Jerome. How could she teach him the need for honor when his grandfather acted so disgracefully? Ashamed that she had let Bo stay with such an unsuitable guardian for so long, Betsy said good-bye to her friends and sailed for America.

Now, pacing the deck, she fumed over her father's hypocrisy. For two years, she had lived amid the sexual license of Parisian society without a single stain on her reputation, yet her lecherous father continued to berate her for impropriety. He of all people had no right to complain of anything in her character. Patterson was sixty-four years old while Providence was only twenty-seven, five years younger than Betsy herself!

His was not the only family scandal. Since coming to Europe, Marianne had become the Duke of Wellington's favorite, and all of fashionable society believed them to be lovers. Adding zest to the rumors was the fact that Wellington and Marianne had exchanged portraits. Robert maintained that the mutual admiration was innocent, but Betsy did not believe it. She knew Wellington's reputation with women and doubted he would spend months dancing attendance on a virtuous Marianne. Furious that her brother was being cuckolded, Betsy urged him to separate his wife from her lover. Robert, however, grew offended by her meddling, so Betsy washed her hands of the affair, congratulating herself that she had never been taken in by Marianne's angelic demeanor.

It still enraged Betsy that, with such disgraceful goings-on, her father should label her insane because she preferred living in Europe. She suspected that his anger had a much different cause. In every aspect of her life, Betsy defied his most cherished beliefs about women. She was succeeding in a man's sphere, managing money and property on her own. Patterson refused to see that her abilities were the equal of any man's, and Betsy had worn herself out trying to persuade him that she was not so much disobedient as determined to find a manner of life in which she could exercise her talents. He simply would not admit that women had any function other than bearing a dozen children and running the house, the very roles that were anathema to Betsy. She wondered if they would ever bridge the chasm between them.

BECAUSE HER HOUSE was rented to a tenant, Betsy went to South Street when she arrived in Baltimore. Edward was married to their cousin Sydney Smith now, and Henry had moved south temporarily for his health, so the house held only her father, George, and the servants. Even so, Patterson declared that he no longer wished to deal with the "confusion" that attended Betsy's stays. He offered to let her and Bo occupy one of his rental properties.

Betsy's first priority before moving to the new house was to be reunited with her son. The day after her return, she wrote Dr. DuBois asking permission to visit Bo at St. Mary's. After receiving an affirmative reply, she hired a carriage, traveled to Emmitsburg, and presented herself in Dr. DuBois's office the next morning. The office had dark, austere furnishings, but above the fireplace hung an Italian oil painting of a golden-haired Virgin Mary, and behind the headmaster's desk hung an elaborately carved crucifix showing Christ in writhing agony.

Dr. DuBois had thin, greying hair, which he wore short and parted in the middle; the two curves of his hairline mirrored perfectly arched eyebrows. His expression was serene, and he habitually folded his hands over his ample stomach. "Jerome is doing well. He is the top student in his English class, he has progressed to the most advanced level of French, and he shows an exceptional aptitude for mathematics."

"I am grateful to hear that he has applied himself. Does he know that I am here?"

"No." DuBois pursed his lips, and Betsy read in his face that he had not been certain she would keep her word. "I thought it best not to distract Jerome from his work by telling him of your visit beforehand. I will send someone for him."

He stepped out to the antechamber where a young priest worked as his secretary. A moment later, DuBois returned. "Jerome is in Latin class but will be here shortly."

"Thank you." Too agitated to remain seated, Betsy went to the window, hoping to see her son cross the lawn on his way from another building. It felt odd to be back in Maryland with its spread-out towns, rolling hills, and unkempt forests. Even though only two years had passed, she had grown so accustomed to the crooked, tightly packed streets of Paris that her native state seemed alien.

After a few minutes, the door opened and she turned to see an older, brown-haired student enter. "You sent for me, sir?" Betsy realized then that this big boy was her son.

"You have a visitor," Dr. DuBois said with a smile, gesturing in her direction.

"Mama?" Visibly stunned, Bo remained where he was, and Betsy ran her gaze over him eagerly. He had grown several inches taller than she was, and his face was developing the prominent chin of the Bonapartes, but the hazel eyes were still those of her baby.

When he continued to hang back, Betsy said, "You have grown so tall. Are you too great a personage now to come hug your mother?"

He came, and Betsy clasped him tightly, trying to fathom that this husky fellow was her boy, but Bo pulled away too quickly for her to accustom herself to the new feeling of him.

Dr. DuBois said, "Jerome, please show your mother into the visitor's parlor."

"Don't I have to return to class, sir?"

"Not today."

Bo led his mother through the antechamber across a central hall and into a small parlor. Because it was used to entertain families, this room had more frills than the headmaster's office. Betsy took a seat on a gold-striped sofa and patted the cushion next to her, but Bo took the maroon wingback armchair on the other side of the patterned rug.

Betsy sighed. "Are you angry with me, Bo?"

He glanced up, startled by her directness. "No."

"Darling, I know I promised to come home after a year, but I wrote and explained that my health made it impossible."

"I know."

"Then why are you upset with me?"

"I am not," Bo said, but he scowled and would not meet her eyes.

Betsy folded her arms. "I am still your mother, and I can tell when you are angry."

He jumped up and went to stand by the fireplace. Keeping his back to her, he repositioned a marble figurine of the Virgin Mary. "Were you really ill, Mama? Your letters were full of stories about parties, and Grandfather says that people who are truly sick do not have the strength to chase after amusement."

"So has your grandfather become a physician in my absence?"

Bo faced her with a frown.

Betsy said, "It is true that I was not sick every minute, nor did I spend every waking hour confined to bed. But I was prey to debilitating attacks the like of which I hope you never experience. They would come without warning and leave me prostrate for days. I can show you written opinions by the doctors who attended me if you require proof."

The resentment in Bo's face softened. "Please, Mama," he said, but Betsy had not finished.

"I swear to you that the physical suffering I endured, although considerable, was nothing compared to the agony of missing you. If I only had sufficient income to have you with me, I would have sailed home to fetch you no matter what the physicians said."

"But Mama, I don't want to live in Paris."

"You cannot know that. You have never been to Europe, so how can you be certain that the United States is better? European culture is much older and more sophisticated than ours."

He thrust out his chin in a gesture that reminded her of Jerome. "Grandfather says it is a sign of a disordered mind not to be content in one's own country."

"Then why did he come here to make his fortune instead of remaining in Ireland where he was born?"

Bo's mouth dropped open.

"Once and for all, Bo, your grandfather is not qualified to make medical diagnoses, nor is he fit to judge my morals. There are many things about his character you don't know."

He slumped into his chair. "I know about Matilda."

"Indeed. And still you look to your grandfather as the arbiter of my behavior, even after learning what a hypocrite he is."

His head shot up. "He is lonely, Mama. He has been ever since Mother died."

"Really, Bo, I suggest that if you are going to take it upon yourself to judge your elders, then you should not be so naïve. Your grandfather has bedded every housekeeper to come into our employ since I was a girl."

When her son shook his head, Betsy drove the point home. "If you do not believe me—since plainly your grandfather has convinced you that I am a liar—then look to your own memories. What do you think he was doing the time you found him 'rubbing' Mrs. Todd?"

Bo's expression crumpled into that of a hurt little boy, and he stared at the flowering-vine-patterned rug. Betsy waited a full minute, but he said nothing.

In a gentler tone, she said, "I did not want to tell you these things, but I cannot allow him to turn you against me. As I have told you many times, you are my son, not his."

When Bo lifted his head, Betsy saw moisture glistening on his lower lashes, but instead of giving way to tears, he said, "I missed you so much when you did not come home. I know you have given up a great deal for me, and I thought you must be tired of the sacrifice."

"How could you think such a thing?" Betsy crossed the room, knelt before him, and smoothed back the lock of hair that hung upon his forehead. "You are everything in the world to me. I confess that I enjoyed life in Paris, but would you be happier if I had been miserable? I never for an instant stopped wishing you were with me. I love you so entirely that I would gladly sacrifice anything for you. Don't you know that?"

Bo bent down to hug her, and his tears dripped onto her neck. "Mama, forgive me. I am so glad that you have come home. I will live anywhere you want. I will do whatever you want. Please don't leave me again."

Stroking his hair, Betsy murmured, "Dearest boy, I promise that nothing will ever again separate us."

RESIGNING HERSELF TO at least a year's stay in Baltimore, Betsy met with Aunt Nancy to review her finances. One piece of good news was learning that her father had paid Bo's tuition while she was gone and did not want her to reimburse him. Betsy was grateful for her father's unexpected generosity because she would need every dollar to realize her dream of educating Bo in Geneva.

She had come home to find the U.S. economy in a perilous state. The cost of the war had raised federal debt and triggered inflation. Yet the charter for the Bank of the United States had been allowed to expire, so the country had no central institution to manage its economic problems. State-chartered banks issued competing paper currencies, and some issued too many notes, which drove down their value and sent prices still higher. The knowledge that, even though she had not touched her principal, it had lost value during her absence made Betsy once again feel the victim of forces beyond her control.

In normal times, customers could exchange paper money for gold, the standard of value on which the system was based. However, federal borrowing to finance the war depleted the gold reserves, so that practice had stopped. It became impossible to be certain what currency was worth, and inflation galloped unchecked. In 1816, Congress chartered a Second Bank of the United States to regulate state banks, but by the time Betsy returned in November 1817, everyone knew that the national bank was poorly managed and nearly insolvent.

Even so, parts of the economy were booming. During the war, manufacturing gained a foothold in the United States because of the blockade, and industry continued to expand after war's end. To capitalize on that, Betsy's brothers Edward and Joseph had started an iron mill just outside Baltimore.

In addition, demand for American crops soared because the Napoleonic wars had disrupted European farming. Speculators bought up agricultural land, including vast tracts in the Louisiana Territory, causing land prices to double and triple. Banks eagerly loaned the money for such purchases without considering whether the spiraling values would hold once Europe's fields began to produce again.

Gallatin had warned Betsy of the dangerous trends he saw in the economy and advised her on how to protect herself. She spent months re-evaluating her accounts, reinvesting bonds as they matured, and deciding whether to keep each of the stocks she owned. Above all, she avoided the temptation to indulge in risky speculation.

Throughout 1818, she lived quietly and did not even visit Washington. James and Dolley Madison had retired to Virginia after his presidency ended, and Betsy found that her friend's absence diminished her interest in the capital's social life. By remaining at home in the house her father provided rent free—embroidering, writing to European friends, and reading literature such as Byron's poetry—she kept expenses to a minimum and managed to build up her savings. Her happiest hours came when Bo was on holiday from school. She regaled him with stories of Paris and gave him lessons in etiquette and deportment.

"Mama, I feel silly doing this," he complained one afternoon when she made him redo a bow that he had failed to execute with the exact degree of nicety she required.

"Fudge! You will feel far sillier if a beautiful princess refuses your request to dance because you bowed like a clodhopper."

Placing his hands on his hips, Bo stared at her in exasperation. "Why would a princess dance with me? I am just an ordinary American boy."

"You are not. Your uncle was the emperor, and your father was a king."

"But the Bonapartes are no longer in power."

"Even so, they are regarded as princes." Betsy crossed to stand directly before him even though she had to tilt her head to look into his face. "Unfortunately, your father far outspends his income and shows no sign of doing anything for you, so your future will have to depend on your own exertions. You must work hard to achieve distinction, and you must learn how to get along in fashionable society. I intend for you to have a brilliant career in diplomacy or government and one day to make a noble marriage."

He scowled. "What if I meet a girl I like here?"

Determined to crush this defiance before it could take root, Betsy wagged her finger just below his nostrils. "Jerome Napoleon Bonaparte, listen to me and listen well. You have the charge of a great name and must never consider a match that is beneath you. Only in America are people still so foolish as to think love in a cottage a romantic notion. I am sure many an American girl will set her snares for you, so you must stay on guard. What will a hasty match produce but a large brood of children you cannot support? Men in Europe have sense enough not to marry a girl unless she brings a fortune. In your case, she must also equal your rank."

"Mama, that is where I beg to differ. The emperor never gave us titles so I have no rank to match. Why can we not be happy as we are?"

He bent down to give Betsy an exaggerated arched-eyebrow, wide-mouthed look, but she refused to be charmed by his antics. "Because you were born for something better, and the Bonapartes deprived you of your birthright. That is the reason I endure so much trouble and anxiety on your behalf, to win back what should be yours by rights."

Bo sighed and turned away. "All right, Mama. I will do whatever you say."

IN EARLY 1819, the economy ground to a halt, and the United States went into its first national depression. Uncle Smith was one victim of the downturn; his business partner James Buchanan, who was charged with running the firm while Smith served in Congress, had committed fraud to buy risky stocks, and when prices dropped, the firm of Smith & Buchanan went bankrupt. Uncle Smith was cleared of wrongdoing, but he was a ruined man.

In contrast, Betsy remained financially stable because of her cautious approach. During the year leading up the depression, she had managed to increase her principal and, consequently, her income. When the economic crisis occurred, the advice from Gallatin enabled her to keep her money safe. Thus it was possible, in the summer of 1819, for Betsy and Bo to sail to the Netherlands. Betsy's passport was in her maiden name, while Bo's read *Edward Patterson* because his uncle had obtained it for him. Once they disembarked in Amsterdam, they traveled to the French Embassy in The Hague to obtain permission to cross France on the way to Switzerland.

The ambassador, Le Comte du Gouvernet, stared at fourteen-year-old Bo, looked at their passports a second time, and frowned at Betsy. "Madame Patterson, I believe we have a mutual acquaintance in Talleyrand."

Betsy inclined her head. "Yes, Monsieur le Comte."

"Then am I correct in thinking that you once had a—union with Jerome Bonaparte?"

"I was his American wife," she said, drawing herself up and giving the man her most imperious stare.

"Then this young man is his son."

"Yes, sir. He is traveling under the name Patterson because the French government has never recognized our right to the Bonaparte name."

The minister handed back their passports. "I am sorry, Madame, but you cannot enter France. You will have to travel through Germany to reach your destination."

"I do not understand. I was in France two years ago and encountered no difficulties."

"You are not the problem, Madame. Your son bears such a strong resemblance to Napoleon Bonaparte that I cannot permit him to cross the border. His presence might incite demonstrations."

Betsy saw Bo's eyes grow wide, but he knew enough not to speak, which pleased her. Turning back to Le Comte du Gouvernet, she said, "He is just a boy."

"A boy who is sufficiently close to manhood that certain parties may wish to use him to achieve their own ends."

"Then there are factions that still favor the former emperor."

"Unfortunately yes, Madame."

After stowing their passports in her reticule, she rose. "Thank you, Monsieur le Comte, for explaining your prohibition so thoroughly. Good day."

Bo was silent until they were seated in their hired carriage. Turning to his mother, he said, "They are frightened of me, Mama. I did not imagine they even knew of my existence."

With a smug smile, Betsy patted his cheek. "Now do you believe me? You are not just an ordinary American boy. You are a Bonaparte, and in Europe, that means everything."

IN Geneva, Betsy moved into a *pension* and then took her son to be enrolled in school. During their meeting with the headmaster, Bo was surprised to learn that in addition to academic subjects, he would have lessons in drawing, dancing, fencing, and horseback riding. "Are those classes important, Mama?" he whispered when the headmaster left them alone for a moment.

"They are necessary for your success in society."

Betsy had long suspected that Bo applied himself to his studies only to please her and that, if left to his own devices, he could become as indolent as his father. Before leaving, she admonished him, "Never forget that the great name you bear comes with responsibility. I have no estate to leave you, so you must achieve wealth and distinction by your own efforts."

"Yes, Mama."

On her own at the *pension,* Betsy became acquainted with another American guest—the multimillionaire John Jacob Astor, who had come to Geneva to find a school for his youngest daughter. Astor was a short man with dark blond hair, drooping brown eyes, and a large pointed nose. He spoke English with a German accent, and his manners were nearly as rough as the fur trappers who had made his fortune, but Betsy liked him because they shared the traits of ambition, determination, and practicality.

After a few days, Betsy soured on her boarding house. The meals at the *pension* consisted mostly of bread, soup, and potatoes. One afternoon as she strolled with Astor down a cobblestoned street in the old section of the city, she halted before a building of timeworn stone. Beneath a broad rounded arch was a shop window that displayed trays of tempting pastries. Betsy darted inside to buy a cream bun. Returning to Astor with her purchase wrapped in white paper, she said, "These Swiss are too spiritual to suppose that their *pensionnaires* possess a vulgar appetite for meat, vegetables, tarts, or custards."

Astor laughed. "It matters little to me since I leave at the end of this week."

"Well, I for one cannot exist solely on a contemplation of the beautiful mountains, lake, and sunsets the Swiss rave about. I must have more substantial fare."

After Astor left, Betsy moved into an apartment with a sitting room and three bedrooms, one each for herself, Bo, and the maid. The rent was about $60 a month, and for an additional sum, a woman catered her meals. Betsy had selected the apartment because it was within walking distance of the places she frequented—and she could not afford a carriage.

Geneva, long the center of Calvinist orthodoxy, was a sober community without the variety of cultural pursuits that characterized Paris. The town fathers had banned theatre until the 1760s, and even in 1819, plays and operas had to be performed outside the city limits. Dancing after midnight was forbidden. However, the residents were industrious, and Betsy hoped the city's moral atmosphere would be a good influence on her son.

Despite its staid character, Geneva was a popular destination for travelers because of its spectacular alpine scenery. Her first winter there, Betsy was welcomed into the circle of highborn visitors. She met the Polish Princess Caroline Galitzin, who had a country estate at Genthod, located on the lake a few miles north of Geneva. The chateau was a two-story white house with an imposing central block and two side wings, green shutters at the windows, and dormers in the mansard roof. Princess Galitzin and Betsy became such close companions that Betsy had a bedroom in the chateau, which she was allowed to decorate to her own taste.

Betsy also became acquainted with Russian émigrés, such as the Princess Potempkin, and English aristocrats, such as the Duke of Kent's stepson, Prince Carl. Once Betsy became established in Genevan society, she received enough invitations to balls, soirées, and dinners to stave off boredom, and men paid her as many compliments as she had received in her youth. She teased Bo that if she did not have such a big son, people would take her for a woman of twenty-five instead of thirty-five.

Although Bo did well in all his classes, his favorite activity by far was his weekly riding lesson. As spring approached, he begged his mother to buy him a mount. "If I had a horse, I could go riding whenever I wanted and you would not have to pay for lessons."

Looking up from the linen shirt she was sewing for him, Betsy saw Bo standing before her with pleading eyes—and realized with a shock that he was almost the age Jerome had been when he bought the expensive shaving set.

"I see you have inherited your father's false views of economy. Not only would I have to pay for the beast, but I would also have the cost of stabling and feeding him."

Bo paced before her. "What if Grandfather bought the horse? Then you would only have to pay for the upkeep, and I am sure that would be more economical than paying for lessons."

"I am equally sure it would not," she said and continued sewing with tiny, precise stitches. "You would spend your time riding around the country to the neglect of your studies, which would mean the waste of all the money I spend on tuition. No, I would sooner pay for daily lessons than buy you a horse."

"Oh." He stopped short, and a blush covered his cheeks.

Alarmed by his sheepish expression, Betsy demanded, "What have you done? If you have offered to buy someone's horse without my permission, I will void any such deal."

"No, Mama." He bit his lower lip. "I already wrote Grandfather asking for the money."

"Your grandfather is so loath to part with cash that I doubt your plea has a prayer of success, but nevertheless, I shall write and disabuse him of the idea."

Bo slumped into the chair across from her. "But Mama, would it not help me to learn responsibility to have the care of an animal?"

Although she knew she should keep a stern demeanor, Betsy smiled at his persistence. "Maybe when you are older."

As her son rose to leave the room, the sight of his drooping shoulders softened Betsy's heart. "If you truly want an animal, we might get a dog."

Bo whirled around to face her. "Do you mean it?"

She nodded, and he rushed to hug her, nearly causing her to stab herself with her needle. "You are the dearest mama in the whole world!" he exclaimed.

Betsy made inquiries and found a local landowner with a litter of Schweizer Laufhund puppies that were ready to leave their mother. The breed was a lean, muscular hunting dog with long legs, so it would be able to run with Bo when he did go riding. The puppy had an orange-red coat with white legs and snout, and Bo named it *Le Loup,* meaning wolf, even though, as Betsy pointed out, the dog bore little resemblance to its wild cousin.

Because Bo stayed at school during the week, Betsy knew she would have to do the serious training herself. She pretended to be annoyed but secretly felt glad to have the companionship while her son was in classes. During weekend visits, she enjoyed watching Bo roll around the floor with his pup and try to teach the animal tricks.

All that spring, she walked *Le Loup* around Geneva, past the shops in the old town, along the lakefront in fine weather, and through the streets around the Cathedral St. Pierre, a mongrel building with a neo-classical temple façade and two squat towers of contrasting styles. *Le Loup* proved to be a friendly animal that would sit patiently and allow children to pet him as long as they did not pull his long ears. As Betsy and the gangly pup became a familiar sight, the taciturn Genevans began to call out, *"Quel beau chien!"* Betsy would smile and nod, pleased with herself for having chosen a handsome dog for her handsome son.

In March, John Jacob Astor wrote to Betsy from Rome on behalf of Jerome's sister Pauline, the Princess Borghese, whom he had met there. When Pauline learned that Astor had spent time with Betsy at Geneva, she asked him to write and express her desire to see Betsy and her son in Rome. The princess was childless and wanted to leave

Bo a legacy since his father could do nothing for him.

Betsy rejoiced that Jerome's family had finally remembered her son, but she cautioned herself not to expect much. She knew from gossip that the Bonapartes lived as royalty in exile, adopting impressive titles to make up for their lost thrones. Their mother, Letizia, was a shrewd woman who had saved her money. Jerome was penniless and depended on an allowance provided by his father-in-law. Joseph lived in New Jersey on wealth he had smuggled out of Spain after his downfall—rumor claimed he had stolen the crown jewels. Pauline received an income from her husband, from whom she was separated. She was notorious for having numerous affairs and a capricious personality that easily tired of people.

Given that reputation, Betsy decided it would be foolish to upend her son's life to gratify Pauline's whim. Bo was doing well in school, and Betsy feared that if she were to take him to Rome, the Bonapartes' pleasure-loving ways might counteract all her efforts to teach him industry. The specter of his turning out to be like Jerome still haunted her. On the other hand, Betsy did not want to destroy her son's chance to know his father's family and perhaps inherit something.

After a sleepless night, she wrote a letter expressing her appreciation of and gratitude for the princess's interest.

My object in coming to Geneva is to procure for my son the means of education suitable to his rank, which I could not find in America, and to find a simple kind of life which would accord with the destiny I have to offer him. I have taught him to know that I have very little fortune to give him, and that his rank will depend upon his own efforts. Convinced that it is one of the greatest misfortunes to have pretensions without hopes, I have tried to remove from him false ideas of ambition, and to direct him to the cultivation of intellectual pursuits. Without perhaps possessing great talents, he is capable of arriving by his own efforts at an honorable station in society. So far I have nothing to complain of as to his application. My first desire, as it is my first duty, is to give him an especially excellent education suitable to his rank. I have found means of doing so at Geneva. I came for that purpose, and shall stay here to accomplish it. This will not prevent me from making a voyage to Italy a few months hence, for the purpose

*of telling you, Madame, how I am touched by the interest you have
taken in my son, and of expressing to you my gratitude.*

Betsy paused in her writing and decided it would be prudent to drive
the point home that she would not withdraw Bo from school.

*I would at the same time present my son, if I had not decided not to
interrupt his education. Personal merit is the only thing worthy of
his name that I can leave him. This is the reason why a good education is the first desire of my heart....*

*Accept, Madame, the respectful assurance and lively recognitions
with which I have the honor to be your Highness' most humble and
most obedient servant,*
Elizabeth Patterson.

Betsy forwarded the letter to John Jacob Astor, and a month later he replied that he had given it to the princess, who sent a friend to question
him about Betsy's situation. Astor had explained that William Patterson's fortune was tied up in property, and Betsy received no money
from him or her ex-husband. Rather, she was living frugally on what
she had saved from her former pension. Not long afterward, the princess fell ill and made no more overtures, but Astor thought she might
make Bo her heir in time.

In May near the end of Bo's first year at school, Betsy's friend Lady
Morgan came to Geneva from Rome. As Betsy hung up her friend's
bonnet and shawl on a peg in the hall, she noted that Lady Morgan's
gown was fashioned in the latest style, with a lower waistline than
had been popular for some years. Betsy frowned as she wondered how
she could possibly adapt her own high-wasted gowns to this change
in fashion.

Then, as they sat in Betsy's sitting room taking tea, Lady Morgan
said, "I met the Princess Borghese while I was in Rome. She often
spoke of her desire to see you and your boy there, but she would not
pledge herself to doing anything for Bo. She lives in state as though she
were a queen, and her extravagance is boundless. If I were you, my
dear, I would not count on her having any fortune to leave."

Betsy sighed. "She sounds very like my ex-husband."

Lady Morgan leaned forward with a wicked gleam in her eyes. "Most of the family hate the ex-king of Westphalia and his wife. Since their dethronement, they have behaved very coldly to the other Bonapartes. I rather fear that the princess takes an interest in your son merely to put their noses out of joint."

Refilling her friend's teacup, Betsy said, "So we are still pawns to be employed by the Bonapartes in their own games. Even so, I cannot refuse to let the boy know them."

"No, but you do right to postpone the encounter. You would be mad to take the child there now. They all call themselves Majesty and Highness and wait to be returned to power. Your son would adopt the most absurd ideas of his own greatness and be ruined to any useful occupation. The promises of that family are not to be depended on."

"No one in the world knows that better than I." Grimacing, Betsy reached for another tart. "The Bonapartes are all very affectionate in words, but without the least intention of parting with a farthing. No doubt, if they ever see their nephew, they will tell him they love him, take great interest in him, and leave me to pay his expenses. I have been careful not to breathe a syllable of these proposals to him for fear of giving him false hopes."

Lady Morgan patted her hand sympathetically. "I am looking forward to meeting your son at last. I have heard that he is all the rage in Geneva."

Grateful for a fresh topic, Betsy smiled. "People say he has more conversation and better manners than other children his age. Consequently he excites more attention, and I am tormented by the fear of seeing him spoiled by compliments. He is thought very handsome, but I regret that others tell him so, as it is a kind of praise which never made anyone better or happier."

Lady Morgan lifted her cup in salute. "Once again, I think you speak from experience."

Shrugging, Betsy said, "I have had to use my wits rather than my beauty to survive the overthrow of my marriage. I wonder what my life might have been if I had been raised to depend more upon my talents."

"It is never too late to apply yourself."

Betsy shook her head. "All my energies are taken up with seeing that my son makes something of himself. Perhaps when he comes to manhood, I may pursue other endeavors."

The Princess Borghese never answered Betsy's letter, which disappointed but did not surprise Betsy. Economic conditions in Baltimore had taken a downturn, and she feared that her income might shrink, which would make it difficult to keep Bo at school. Therefore, she wrote Jerome and asked him to share the expenses for their son.

He replied with regrets:

> *My fortune is not sufficient to provide for my present family, who must be taken care of by their mother. Elisa, you know my character too well to suppose I ever thought of laying by a fortune; the little I did save, I have been cheated out of by persons I trusted.*

Thinking of his loyalty to scoundrels like Le Camus, Betsy thought, *He always was a poor judge of character.*

Despite these disappointments, fate seemed determined to throw her in the path of the Bonapartes and their kin. The Prince and Princess of Württemberg—Catharine's uncle and aunt—spent a holiday in Geneva, where Betsy met them often. They thought it was a scandal that their niece and Jerome lived lavishly while failing to provide for Betsy's son, and at their request, Betsy brought Bo to meet them. Shortly before they departed, the prince exclaimed to Betsy, "Jerome Bonaparte made a great mistake in deserting such a charming woman as you."

In the spring of Bo's second year at school, Jerome's brother Joseph wrote to offer Betsy the use of his chateau in Switzerland. While grateful, Betsy had to decline because, without a carriage, she could not reside so far from town. Yet, the generous proposal gave her renewed hope that her son might yet be accepted as a legitimate Bonaparte. Madame Tousard, who often met Joseph in society, wrote to say that he seemed disposed to form a relationship with his nephew once Bo returned to the United States. Betsy did not expect Joseph to provide for her son as he had several daughters to settle, but it would help Bo's position to be acknowledged by his uncle.

Among her titled friends, Betsy asked about marriage prospects for Bo. He was not yet sixteen, but she knew that such alliances were often settled in childhood, and she did not want to ruin his chances by neglecting to make inquiries. Her friends listened politely and made suggestions, but to Betsy's frustration, no one offered to negotiate a match.

She repeatedly warned Bo that he was not to make a *mésalliance* and particularly not to marry an American. "I would rather that you never married at all than marry beneath your rank."

"Yes, Mama," he would answer. One day, after Betsy had lectured him at length on the evils of an imprudent marriage, he responded with rare insubordination. "Perhaps my ideas of a suitable marriage do not match yours. You said I could not know I preferred America until I had lived in Europe. Well, I have lived here two years and have dined with many princes and princesses, and I much prefer eating beefsteak with my grandfather on South Street."

"That is because you are young and do not appreciate that the rank into which you were born can open many doors that others may not even approach."

He folded his arms across his chest. "Mama, I am old enough to know what I like. All I want is a quiet life on a country estate where I can raise horses."

The fear that Bo's decisions might render her sacrifices meaningless maddened Betsy. "And where do you propose to get the money? How many times must I tell you that I can leave you no wealth? You will need a lucrative profession to afford the life you covet, so it is only prudent to use the status that is yours by birth as a step toward success."

Bo frowned and remained very still as he considered her words. Finally, he said, "I think I see what you mean."

In May 1821, Betsy heard that Napoleon had died on his lonely island in the South Atlantic. She had never lost her admiration for him, and the realization that they would never meet saddened her immeasurably. The event prompted her to alter her plans. Betsy's original idea had been for Bo to attend the academy for three years and then enroll at Harvard, but in the wake of Napoleon's death, she decided to pull her son from school and spend the winter in Rome. Bo's grandmother Letizia Bonaparte was in her seventies, and Pauline had been ill, so Betsy feared that one of them might die before Bo could make their acquaintance.

Betsy, Bo, and his dog departed for Rome in October 1821, which was very late in the year to cross the Alps. "This will be an adventure," Betsy told her son, "like the excursion I took to Niagara with your father.

You will remember this journey for the rest of your life."

It took six days to travel by coach from Geneva across the Alps to Turin in northwest Italy. The carriage road twisted like a corkscrew to ascend the mountains, and once during the journey, their route was covered by snow that had drifted deeper than the horses' bellies. If it had not been for the help of several local men with shovels, they would have had to turn back.

Near the end of the crossing, an ice storm struck as they traversed a mountain pass in the middle of the night. The road became as slick as glass, and the driver halted the coach in the lee of a rock wall to keep the horses from slipping and carrying them to their doom. Even though leather shades covered the windows, it was bitterly cold in the coach, and Betsy, Bo, and the other passengers—an American couple named the Packards—huddled beneath fur robes that the carriage company had provided. The storm did not subside until shortly before dawn, and Betsy's fingers became so cold that she feared they might snap off like icicles.

They waited until a few hours after daylight to resume their journey in hopes that the road would become less treacherous. By midday, Betsy's throat felt raw, and by nightfall, her head was so congested that she had difficulty breathing. During the week it took the coach to travel from Turin south through Italy, she grew sicker each day, and when they finally reached Rome, she had a deep-seated cough that left her with sore ribs and an aching diaphragm. The Packards offered to put her up in their rented house, which they had reserved ahead of time, and she gratefully accepted. While she recuperated, she sent sixteen-year-old Bo out to find inexpensive rooms they could rent.

After a week, Betsy received a note from the Princess Borghese, who had learned from a mutual acquaintance where they were staying. When Betsy wrote back asking at what hour she should visit, the princess sent her carriage to bring Betsy and Bo to her immediately.

The three-story, sixteenth-century *Palazzo Borghese* had a severe, many-windowed façade and an unusual harpsichord shape, wider at one end than the other with a side wall that bent at an angle partway along its length. As a footman led them through the public rooms toward the princess's private apartments, Betsy saw her son blush at the sight of one sculpture—a full-sized figure of a reclining, bare-breasted Venus. Betsy decided not to mention that the model had been none other than the aunt Bo was about to meet. Instead, she informed him that the artist was Canova, a famous sculptor she had known in Paris. As they walked on, Bo continued to stare at the gilded chandeliers, painted ceilings, tapestries, paintings, and statues that ornamented the rooms. Betsy held back a smile at his awe. He was so proud of his millionaire grandfather that he had never realized how devoid of luxury the Patterson home in Baltimore really was.

When the footman showed them into the anteroom to Pauline's boudoir, Betsy and Bo found the princess lounging on a chaise longue, in a pose very similar to the Canova statue.

Betsy curtsied and introduced her son. Then she examined the face of this woman she was said to resemble. They both had a Grecian nose and slanting eyes, but Pauline's nose was longer and her chin slightly more pointed. The biggest difference, however, was intangible. Betsy found the other woman's expression curiously indifferent for one with such a scandalous reputation.

"I am glad that we meet at last." The princess's voice, while sweet, had a light, artificial quality. With a wave of her hand, she indicated they should take seats, and then she requested that Bo move his chair close beside her.

After he complied, she gazed at him. "Mr. Astor said that you greatly resemble the late emperor. I see that he did not exaggerate."

Bo blushed and lowered his gaze.

Placing one hand behind her head, Pauline leaned back more comfortably against the chaise and regarded her nephew through half-closed eyelids. "Which name do you prefer to use, Jerome or Napoleon?"

"In school, I use Jerome, your highness," Bo answered, and Betsy felt relieved that he had remembered the proper form of address for his royal aunt. Surely, her son's beautiful manners would impress the Bonapartes. He smiled and added, "But my American family call me Bo."

Pauline scrunched up her nose in distaste. "I shall call you Jerome. How do you like to amuse yourself?"

"My favorite activity is horseback riding, your highness,"

"Ah. Perhaps something can be arranged so that you can indulge that pastime during your visit. I believe your Uncle Louis's sons have mounts that you might be allowed to borrow."

The visit lasted for more than an hour, with Pauline asking question after question, nearly all of them superficial. Betsy was glad her son maintained good humor under the inquisition, but she could not help but feel slighted at being so completely ignored.

The next day they were summoned to the palazzo occupied by Letizia Bonaparte, officially called *Madame Mère*. A footman led them to an ornate reception room with marble columns and a painted ceiling, and once again Bo gaped at his surroundings. *Madame Mère* stood waiting for them, still erect despite her years. She was a thin woman dressed in black with an ornate cross hanging on her breast and an elaborate white cap covering her hair. Her dark, hooded eyes bored into Betsy. "So you are the American who nearly ruined my Girolamo," she said, using Jerome's Italian name.

Although tempted to retort angrily, Betsy managed to say, "We believed ours was an honorable marriage, Madame. It was not my fault the emperor had other designs."

"Perhaps not, Madame Patterson. But you cannot deny that it was a hasty, ill-conceived alliance." Shifting her gaze to Bo, she said, "And you claim that this is his son?"

"Look at him closely, Madame. Can you honestly say you doubt it?"

When Letizia Bonaparte stepped within a few inches of Bo to peer into his face, Betsy realized that the old woman was going blind. After a moment, she murmured, "Nabulione," and Betsy knew that she had seen the resemblance to Napoleon. The old woman patted Bo's cheek and gestured for him to sit beside her while Betsy sat on a nearby sofa. Like her daughter the day before, she focused entirely on the boy. "Paolina tells me that you have been attending school in Geneva, my son."

"Yes, Madame."

The old woman frowned and fingered her cross. "It is a Protestant city, is it not?"

"That is its history, Madame, but there are Catholics in Geneva now. My mother has raised me as a Catholic because she knew that was my father's religion."

His grandmother nodded and smiled for the first time. "Do you work hard in school?"

"Yes, Madame." Bo shot an amused glance at Betsy, and she knew he was thinking of her many lectures. "My mother has always impressed upon me the need to be diligent and disciplined."

Madame Mère nodded again. "Your uncle, the emperor, had those traits even as a boy, and they served him well. Are you interested in a military career?"

Bo shook his head. "No, Madame. I do not have any aptitude for it. My mother wishes me to pursue law or diplomacy."

"And what do you wish to do?"

Hesitating, Bo bit his lower lip. His expression grew guarded. "I wish to be a credit to the Bonaparte name."

Madame Mère's younger half-brother Cardinal Fesch entered the room and approached them. He introduced himself and sat beside Betsy. The retired cleric, still dressed in his black cassock and scarlet sash, had pure white hair, a broad face, and an aquiline nose. As Bo continued chatting with his grandmother, the cardinal quietly interviewed Betsy. He was gratified to learn she had brought up her son in the Roman church, and he expressed shock upon hearing that Jerome had contributed nothing to his oldest son's upbringing.

At the end of the visit, *Madame Mère* told Betsy, "I must compliment you on young Jerome Napoleon. He shows unusual aplomb and common sense for such a young man."

Betsy bowed her head in acknowledgement. "I have dedicated my life to him, Madame."

To Bo, *Madame Mère* said, "Come to see me often while you are here, my son. And bring that dog you told me about."

WHILE STAYING IN Rome, Betsy and her son saw most of the Bonaparte family except Joseph and Jerome. Although the Bonapartes teased Bo about his unsophisticated American frankness, they seemed to like him. Betsy, on the other hand, suspected that the family still regarded her as a woman of dubious virtue. While never overtly rude, they frequently omitted to pay her some of the more subtle courtesies considered a lady's due.

Their ostensible hostess, the Princess Borghese, proved to be every bit as erratic as rumor painted her. During the first week of their visit, she professed to be delighted that she and Betsy were so much alike, and she impulsively gave Betsy a richly embroidered ball gown, a pink satin cape, and a bonnet. Several weeks later, without any explanation, Pauline sent a maid to demand the return of the gifts. The incident left Betsy chagrined and worried that she had offended her former sister-in-law, but at their next encounter, Pauline acted as though nothing had happened. Eventually, she returned the items to Betsy, whose pleasure in them was diminished.

Even so, the two women spent hours together. Pauline took Betsy for carriage rides to the ruins of the Forum and Colosseum, asked her to the opera, and extended a standing invitation to her salon, yet often Pauline's manner turned cool. Betsy quickly realized that the princess had latched onto Bo because of long-festering grief at losing her own son years before. Yet no matter how hard Pauline tried to win Bo's loyalty, granting him a clothing allowance of $400 a year and promising him a settlement of $8,000 on his marriage, the princess could not supplant Betsy's place in his heart.

The vagaries of the princess notwithstanding, the visit to Rome proved fruitful. *Madame Mère* shared Napoleon's mania for controlling the clan's matrimonial alliances, and within a month of meeting Bo, she suggested marrying him to Joseph's daughter Charlotte. As Joseph was the only one of Letizia's children to have a fortune, such an alliance would ensure that Bo was provided for despite his father's insolvency. Although Betsy feared Bo would balk at the suggestion, the fact that his cousin lived in the United States dovetailed with his preference for America, so he agreed to consider the match. Betsy herself was keen on the idea. Not only was Charlotte a Bonaparte and an heiress, through her mother she was niece to the Queen of Sweden.

Madame Mère wrote to Joseph urging the marriage, and she persuaded her sons Lucien and Louis to add their support. Only Pauline seemed ambivalent. At length, the family decided to send the boy to the United States to meet his uncle. Betsy wrote her father explaining the proposed match and asking him to make inquiries as to what Joseph Bonaparte might settle on his daughter:

The principal and only thing is to see that Bo will not be left without
any provision if she dies before him, or that he will not be entirely de-
pendent on her as long as she lives. They tell me here, Joseph means
to give a hundred thousand dollars on the marriage. If he does not
secure the whole or any part to her, there is nothing to be said, as the
money becomes her husband's. But if he means to tie it up, I wish at
least fifty thousand to be settled on my son.

Betsy also wrote that if Joseph should not agree to the match, Bo should
attend Harvard as originally planned.

Since Betsy knew her father could handle the marriage negotiations, she decided to remain in Europe for a while. Louis Bonaparte
arranged for Bo to sail from Leghorn in late February, and he hired a
trusted associate to convey his nephew to the port. As Betsy watched
her sixteen-year-old son and his dog climb aboard the coach, tears
filled her eyes so that she could hardly make out Bo's face as he called
good-bye from the window. She told herself that she would enjoy a period of being free from the necessity of constant vigilance over the boy.

The next day, however, Betsy bitterly regretted her decision. She
felt certain she should have gone with him, to watch over his conduct
and see that everything was carried out according to her wishes. She
began to vomit whenever she ate, and her illness kept her in Rome.

Two weeks after Bo left, Betsy received a bill in the mail that compounded her worries about him. She immediately sat down and wrote
him an admonishing letter:

They have sent me a bill for six hundred cigars you took at Leghorn.
For heaven's sake spend as little money as possible, and recollect the
smallness of my income and the many privations it subjects me to....
I shall go to America if you think there is the least necessity for it. Let
me know everything about my finances. Do read as much as you can,
and improve in every way. I ask you to reward my cares and anxieties
about you, by advancing your own interests and happiness. I am very
uneasy about you, and almost blame myself for not going with you to
take care of you, and shall never forgive myself if you meet any ac-
cident by being alone.

Betsy's agitation increased when she learned that her ex-husband and his wife had come to Rome. Jerome visited Pauline and harangued her about the impropriety of having invited Betsy and Bo to meet the family. Word reached Betsy of the quarrel—and of the duplicity of the princess, who claimed that Betsy had come uninvited and forced her company upon them.

The possibility of an encounter with Jerome made Betsy eager to leave the city. When she learned that the Packards planned to travel to Geneva by way of Florence, she decided to accompany them.

IN THE PALATINE Gallery of the Pitti Palace in Florence, Betsy stepped forward to examine *La Donna Velata* by Raphael. The young woman in the portrait had a round face with dark eyes and dark hair pulled back from a center part. She wore an elaborate dress with cascading folds of material, a choker of oval stones, and a headdress that fell past her shoulders. She was a lovely girl with evenly arched eyebrows, a straight nose, full lips, and a rounded chin.

"I think she looks like you," whispered Mrs. Packard.

Betsy analyzed the comparison objectively. "No, my face is thinner, and we have different coloring. And of course, I am middle-aged, not blooming with youth as she is."

"But you have not lost your beauty. Why else would Massot want to paint your portrait when you return to Geneva?"

Betsy patted the other woman's arm. "You flatter me, trying to lift my spirits because you know I miss my son."

Smiling wistfully at the memory of Bo, Betsy moved toward another painting, then paused as she saw a couple standing about ten feet away. Normally, she would have paid them no attention, but the man was staring at her. Glancing into his face, Betsy was reminded of her son. Then she felt her smile freeze and slide away.

The man was her former husband. She had not seen Jerome in seventeen years, but she could not mistake the dark eyes that used to caress her or the sensuous mouth that had loved to laugh. He was not laughing today. Instead, he looked mortified. His chin—a double chin, she noted spitefully—was sinking into his throat as though he were a turtle withdrawing into its shell. Betsy also noticed that his hairline had receded, so that the black curls she used to play with during lovemaking no longer tumbled riotously onto his forehead. He had brushed his hair forward and pomaded it in place in a vain effort to disguise his growing baldness.

Jerome's companion, who was clinging to his arm, looked from him to Betsy and back again. She was a pasty dumpling of a woman, which meant that she must be his fat wife Catharine rather than one of his mistresses. Giving the pair a mocking smile, Betsy flung the edges of her cape back over her shoulders to show Jerome that she had retained her perfect figure even at the age of thirty-seven.

Unexpectedly, the noise in the gallery faded as Jerome's eyes locked on hers. For a moment, the years of bitterness fell away, and Betsy was eighteen again, pronouncing her vows of fidelity to the man she had loved so passionately that she married him despite her father's protests. Standing across from him in this palatial hall—with its marble floor, ornate gilt moldings, and brilliantly painted ceiling—reminded Betsy of the dream she and Jerome had once shared of being the most dashing couple at Napoleon's court. How young and naïve they had been. Searching his face, she tried to transmit the message, *Have you ever stopped loving me?* An instant later, she could have sworn that, like the faintest vibration of a butterfly's wings, came the return assurance, *Non, ma chère Elisa.*

Then Jerome turned to leave. As he and Catharine walked away, Betsy heard him say in a cracked voice, "That was my American wife."

Catharine grasped his arm more tightly and leaned close to whisper a reply as they exited the gallery. The familiar intimacy of the gesture stabbed at Betsy.

Shaken to the core, she turned to her companion. "I am feeling unwell. Do you mind if we take our leave?"

"Of course not. Are you faint?"

No, Betsy thought, *but I cannot breathe the same air as Jerome Bonaparte.* Instead of admitting the truth, she answered, "I am having an attack of acute *ennui.* I think it is time for me to leave Florence."

❧ XXXIV ❧

THE shock of encountering Jerome upset Betsy's nerves so greatly that when she returned to Geneva, she suffered from periodic nausea for a month. Her distress grew so oppressive that she wrote to Lady Morgan to unburden herself:

My dear Lady Morgan,

It is with a heavy heart that I report myself to be tormented by great affliction of the nervous system. You will scarce believe what took place during my sojourn in Florence. While touring the gallery at the Pitti Palace, whom should I encounter but the ex K. of W! He is greatly changed since the days of our youth, and I do assure you, not for the better. His infamous manner of living has completely destroyed his figure and his looks. His character was already corrupted beyond redemption.

You possess such good sense that I feel certain you can comprehend better than anyone else of my acquaintance how little I wanted to see that man again. If ever anyone was misnamed, it is he; I always think of him as J. Malaparte now.

My spirits are sadly depressed when I contemplate how little he has suffered for his misdeeds. I have long known the justice of La Rochefoucauld's maxim that "The world oftener rewards the appearance of merit than merit itself." Seeing the K. of W. impressed upon me an even more dispiriting truth. Scoundrels may go about the world carelessly doing harm with little consequence to themselves, while those who try to live honorably must struggle merely to survive. Nothing ever turns out as we desire. But thus it has ever been, and I must adapt to my fate or be broken by it.

Remember me to Sir Charles and pray give him my love. Adieu, dear Lady Morgan. Do not forget me. Write me sometimes and send such petits mots de sagesse *as may comfort me and dispel this bitter ennui.*

Betsy sighed as she signed the letter with a flourish and then sealed it. Even more galling to her than encountering Jerome had been seeing Catharine. If that brief glimpse had been any indication, the princess still viewed her husband of fifteen years with tender regard, and Betsy had been offended that such a vapid, unaccomplished woman had taken her place as the wife who could cling to his arm and solicitously inquire about his mood. It made little difference that Jerome was an unfaithful lout who almost certainly would have made Betsy miserable. When Catharine looked at him, her eyes glowed, and Betsy felt the princess had no right to be so happy.

After brooding for days, Betsy resolved to put the past behind her. Once she felt well enough, she traveled to Paris to enliven her spirits. The Gallatins gave her a standing invitation to dine with them every day, and Betsy also frequently visited the Marquise de Villette, whose reminiscences of Voltaire made her glad to be back in literary society.

That spring, Jerome astonished Betsy by sending her $1,200 for Bo's expenses and promising to make the sum an annual allowance. Cynically, she inferred that either the Prince of Württemberg or Cardinal Fesch had shamed him into taking responsibility. Knowing Jerome as she did, Betsy did not suppose that his resolve would hold for very long, so she decided to keep her expenditures exactly the same as if he had sent nothing.

Early in the summer, Betsy received letters from both her father and Bo. The visit to New Jersey had taken place, and Bo got along well with Joseph and his daughter Charlotte, but nothing had been said about a match between the cousins. Later, when Bo wrote to propose a second visit, he was told that his uncle was traveling. Both Patterson and

Bo concluded that Joseph Bonaparte had decided to marry his daughter to someone else.

In response, Betsy wrote to her father: "There is nothing that can, or ever will, surprise me in that family. The only way is to act and feel exactly as if they said and promised nothing."

Even so, she was not sorry she had taken the trouble to make Bo acquainted with the Bonapartes. To be acknowledged by them could only help his standing in society and further his chances to make an alliance with some noble house.

Paris was still too expensive a city for her, so Betsy returned to Geneva for the winter and resumed her place in its society. Patterson wrote her there that since the proposed marriage had fallen through, he had complied with Betsy's wishes of continuing her son's education. Bo lacked enough Greek to meet Harvard's enrollment requirements, so he was living in Lancaster, Massachusetts, with a clergyman tutor. Betsy learned with regret that *Le Loup* had not been allowed to accompany Bo and wrote her father asking him to take special care of the dog. If she had known that the animal would be left in Baltimore, she would have kept it as her companion.

That winter, her father sent heartbreaking news. In October, Robert had caught cholera and died within a few days. Remembering their childhood when they had called each other Bobby and Goose, Betsy felt bereft in spite of their estrangement over the Wellington affair. Even learning that Marianne had risked her own life to nurse Robert during his illness did not lessen Betsy's animosity toward her sister-in-law.

She also received word that her friend, the Marquise de Villette, had died. Those two deaths, together with her own recent ailments, convinced Betsy to make a will. She believed firmly that parents should never leave property away from their children, so she made Bo her sole heir.

Betsy missed her son terribly and frequently regretted that she had not gone home with him. In the evenings, she had little opportunity to be lonely—she went to a ball or party every night—but during the day, she thought of Bo often and worried that he would lose his industrious habits without her supervision.

Despite her fears, Bo applied himself to his studies, passed the examination, and was admitted to Harvard in February 1823. Yet, even though Betsy knew he was doing well, she felt increasingly sad about their separation. She began to think of sailing for home to be near him and wrote to Lady Morgan:

I love him so entirely that perhaps seeing him may render my feeling less disagreeable. I hate the séjour of America, and the climate destroys the little health which has been left me; but any inconveniences are more supportable than being separated from one's children.

Before she could make up her mind, she received a report from Aunt Nancy that Bo had spent $2,150 in his first fifteen months after returning to the United States. Shocked, Betsy wrote him three letters in a week and another to her father declaring that her income was not sufficient to cover extravagance and Bo must live on $1,100 a year. She had received a second payment of $1,200 from Jerome, but his finances were still too precarious for her to count on his annual support—especially since he now had three children with Catharine as well as the guardianship of his late sister Elisa's daughters.

In 1824, financial concerns made it imperative for Betsy to return to the United States. In July she sailed to New York, arriving there in late August. Bo, whom she had written about her plans, met her at her hotel the following day.

After hugging her son and laughing over how much he had grown—he was now nearly a foot taller than she was—Betsy sat on the sofa and patted the cushion next to her. "Did you have any difficulty obtaining leave from your classes to come meet me?"

"No." He sat down after sweeping back the tails of his coat. "The fact is, Mama, that I have been suspended for three months."

"How many times have I told you that you must be far more circumspect in your behavior than other young men?"

Bo thrust out his Bonaparte chin. "Mama, have the goodness not to reproach me until you hear all the facts."

Betsy raised her eyebrows skeptically but folded her hands in her lap and listened.

He rose and paced as though pleading a case before a jury. "There are several clubs authorized by the college that have libraries annexed to them. One of the ones I belong to had a meeting on July 29th to choose a librarian, and after that business, the members stayed to drink punch. This club has assembled regularly two or three times a term for the space of fifty years and has always had something to eat or drink afterward. No one has ever before been punished for the practice, and I can assure you I was astonished when the president said I was suspended."

"You might have known they would disapprove of young men drinking. You are meant to be studying, not consuming punch."

Bo stopped before her and held out his hands, palm upward. "I ask you, Mama, how can prudence teach a man how to avoid that which has never happened before?"

Of all that Bo said in his own defense, the phrase that smote Betsy's heart was hearing him refer to himself as a man. Her hand flew up to her mouth as she realized that her nineteen-year-old boy was now the exact age Jerome had been when they married. How strange it was to think that she and her husband had viewed themselves as adults when they were so young.

Pulling herself back to the present, she said, "Do you really mean to say that what you did was customary and the college's decision completely arbitrary?"

"Yes, I swear it. Surely you are not so severe as to blame me for receiving an unjust punishment."

"No, I am not so unreasonable as that." She patted the cushion again, and as he sat beside her, Betsy felt her anger shift to the college president. "I will go to Cambridge and lodge a protest. Perhaps the president will overturn the suspension."

Bo blanched and shook his head. "Mama, please, do not entertain thoughts of doing so. I am not a child and do not need my mother to fight my battles."

Smiling, Betsy patted his cheek. "You will always be my child, but I will not go to the college if doing so would embarrass you. Will you spend the three months in Baltimore?"

"No, I am not allowed to go home. I am living quietly in Lancaster and improving myself by doing general reading."

"Oh." Betsy looked down at her lap. "I suppose that means that I will not be allowed to stay near you."

Bo hesitated. "They did not say anything to forbid visits." Then he impulsively pulled her into a hug. "Oh, Mama, I have missed you. I do wish you would stay."

They had an enjoyable three months together discussing what Bo was reading and taking a few short trips. In late November, when Bo returned to Harvard, Betsy looked for rooms to rent near the college in Cambridge. After her second day of searching, she returned to the hotel to find a note asking her to meet with the college president, Dr. Kirkland.

Fearing that Bo was in trouble again, she went to the administration building right away. She was shown in to see the president, a ruddy-faced bald man with a bulbous nose. After greeting her, Dr. Kirkland said, "It has come to my attention that you are looking for rooms to let in Cambridge."

"Yes, sir," she answered, wondering if he had something to recommend.

"I am sorry to say this so bluntly, but we do not approve of the boys' mothers living in town. One of our goals is to assist our young men in reaching full maturity, so—"

"You need to separate them from their mothers." Rising and adjusting her skirt, she said, "Very well, Dr. Kirkland. I will abide by your rules."

He walked her to his office door. "Madame Bonaparte, I hope I have not offended you."

"No. While I might claim extenuating circumstances, as my son and I have had more separations than is normal for a boy his age, I fully comprehend that you cannot make an exception for us or all the mothers would be asking you to bend the rule."

"Thank you for understanding." He opened the door. "Please accept my assurance that, despite the recent need for discipline, Jerome is doing well. We are pleased with his attention to his studies, and he shows a remarkable head for metaphysics, perhaps our most difficult subject."

"Thank you," Betsy said and left him.

WILLIAM PATTERSON TOLD his daughter that he did not want her to live at the South Street, and hurt, Betsy retorted that she had no intention of settling in Baltimore at all. Over the next few months, she did what was necessary to secure her financial stability and shore up her income, which was now about $5,000 annually. Then she returned to Europe in 1825.

Although she expected to stay there only a year, Betsy found once again that she enjoyed Europe too much to leave. She spent an extended period in Florence, which became her favorite city. Ferdinand III, the grand duke of Tuscany, showed Betsy marked attention whenever she attended his balls. He had the long face typical of the Hapsburgs, a high forehead, and light-blue eyes. Ferdinand was sixteen years her senior and had recently married a very young and pretty second wife, but that did not prevent him from whispering blandishments in Betsy's ear whenever they danced together. It became a kind of game between them, a mockery of seduction that neither one took seriously.

Betsy also dined at least three times a week with her close friend Count Nikolai Nikitich Demidov, the Russian ambassador to the duke's court. Demidov, who had a stout figure, a round fleshy face, and hooded eyes, had inherited one of the largest fortunes in Russia from his industrialist father. Unlike William Patterson, he did not care about wealth for its own sake but rather used his money to amass an extensive art collection and to finance the establishment of hospitals and schools in Tuscany. Betsy considered him a man of great natural sense and one of the most good-natured people she had ever known.

She was at her happiest whenever she lived in Florence. Unfortunately, the cool rainy winters in the city did not agree with her, so she often traveled to Geneva or the spa at Aix le Bains in France to recover her health.

In 1826, Bo graduated from Harvard, with the plan of studying law. Before settling to that task, he sailed to Europe so he could finally meet Jerome. Although Betsy had been proved right, and her ex-husband had ceased his support payments after two years, he had expressed a wish to know his son. Betsy wrote her father on the subject:

> *I think that it is perhaps a duty to let Jerome know his father, that he may never reproach himself at any future period, at all events. I should not like to take upon myself the responsibility of refusing my consent to such a proceeding, being desirous to fulfill to the extent of my power my duties as a parent.*

Bo met her in Switzerland, and they traveled to Florence, where they stayed for three weeks so Betsy could introduce him to her friends and perhaps excite some interest in a noble match for him. She also made inquiries among the ambassadors she knew, particularly Demidov, about a possible diplomatic career for Bo. All who met him thought he showed an aptitude for the life.

Then, because Betsy had no wish to see her ex-husband ever again, Bo traveled by himself to Rome to visit his Bonaparte relatives. The plan was for the two of them to return to the United States the following spring so Bo could commence his law studies with Betsy living nearby.

While in Rome, Bo wrote Betsy that Pauline, who died of stomach cancer the year before, had left him $4,000. Jerome was not in Rome because he feared his wife's relatives might feel that, by acknowledging his eldest son, he was casting doubt on his second family's legitimacy. So at the end of October, Bo traveled to meet his father at a secluded country estate near Camerino, Italy, where they would be out of the public eye. He remained there two months. Then in January, when it became apparent that Catharine's relatives made no objection to Bo's visit, the entire family traveled to Rome.

Bo wrote Betsy that his father and stepmother treated him kindly, and he enjoyed meeting his half-siblings, Jerome Napoleon, Mathilde, and Napoleon Joseph (nicknamed Plon-Plon). He did say, however, that his father and Catharine's way of life was very hard to get used to after the long hours of study he had been keeping. They rose late, breakfasted at noon, did not take their last meal of the day until eleven or twelve at night, and went to bed two hours later. All they did was sit around and gossip, and Bo found it impossible to read. He estimated that his father spent three times his income, and Bo worried that if he stayed with them too long, he would get used to a way of life he could not afford.

In early March, Bo rejoined his mother in Florence. As they sat together over breakfast the morning after his arrival, he said, "I am glad I took this opportunity to get to know my father. He was very affectionate and tried to persuade me to stay with him, but their mode of living and thinking is so entirely different from my habits that I cannot accustom myself to it. I have always known that America is the only country for me."

Betsy set down her coffee cup with a clink. "Really, I wish you would not discount all of Europe simply because you do not find your father's way of living congenial. I manage to live economically and still gain admittance to the first circles of European society."

"Mama, I don't care about the first circles of Europe. I am too much attached to the government, customs, and manners of America to be happy anywhere else."

"If you are to be a diplomat, you must adapt to all manner of society."

He frowned at the mention of a diplomatic career. "At any rate, I must go home and study the law before I can embark on a profession. Shall I book passage for us?"

"Do we have to go just yet?"

Bo chose a hard roll from the breadbasket, tore it in half, and began to butter it. "I thought you had agreed that we would sail for home in the spring."

"So we shall, but spring has just begun and will run for three months more. Surely after having stayed five months with your father, you can spend a few weeks humoring me."

"If you wish. But I must sail home by summer so I can begin my studies in the fall."

They spent the next three months attending balls and parties, with Bo riding in the mornings on a horse he borrowed from a cousin. At the end of May, he knocked on the door of Betsy's boudoir and, after she gave him permission to enter, came to stand behind her as she styled her hair. Gazing at her in the mirror, he said, "Mama, I mean to sail by the end of June. Do you intend to come too, or has your partiality for Europe entirely overcome your affection for me?"

Betsy set down her brush and twisted around to look at him directly. "What a cruel thing to ask! After all the economies I practiced and the diligence I exercised on your behalf, how can you begrudge me a time of freedom and amusement now that you are a grown man? Yes, I have a partiality for Europe. I am only surprised that you should wonder at my resembling every woman who has left America. I never heard of one who wanted to return after she got away."

Folding his arms across his chest, Bo said, "Then what are we to do? I fear I am frittering away my life here. I am now of an age when I must think of doing something that will enable me to support myself."

"I know. It is time for you to settle to a career." Even as Betsy said that, the thought of returning to Baltimore made her feel as though she were being sent to an exile every bit as barren as Napoleon's imprisonment on St. Helena. Her shoulders slumped.

"Oh, Mama." Bo stepped forward and kissed the top of her hair. "I know it will not be much fun for you to sit embroidering while I slave over my law books. Perhaps you should stay in Europe one more year while I pursue my studies."

Lifting her head, Betsy shot him a saucy look. "Are you sure you would be happy if I did? I would not have you think I prefer Grand Duke Ferdinand to my own son."

To her relief, Bo laughed. He chucked her under the chin as though she were a girl. "I do believe the grand duke has turned your head, Mama, but I know you quite well enough to feel secure of your affections. Stay in Florence and enjoy your much-deserved year of amusement. But don't let any of these rogues talk you into becoming his mistress. My fencing is not proficient enough to fight a duel in your defense."

"Impertinent child." She turned back to her dressing table. "As if an old woman like me is still in want of protection."

After Bo left Europe, Betsy consoled herself for his absence by telling herself that she could do more to secure his future on the continent than she could in Baltimore. To that end, she continued to make inquiries about both a noble marriage and a diplomatic post.

She began to receive letters from her father complaining that Bo showed little inclination for the law and an increasing tendency toward indolence. Betsy wrote her son reminding him of the necessity of working to achieve prominence, but she remained in Europe rather than hurrying home to chastise him. She felt confident that her father was already riding the young man hard.

The next year, Betsy's plan to return to Baltimore fell through. She was delayed in the early summer by the need to go to Paris and see to her European investments. By the time her business was complete, the only ship available at Le Havre was a rickety old vessel she would not risk taking, while traveling to an alternate port would make it too late in the year to sail. Knowing that Bo was still tied up with his studies, Betsy felt little regret about stretching her extra year in Europe into two. Then almost effortlessly, she found that another year had passed, and by late summer 1829 she had decided to add a third year to her sojourn.

On November 3, 1829, Betsy received a letter from her father announcing that twenty-four-year-old Bo had become engaged to Susan May Williams, a seventeen-year-old Baltimore girl whose late father had left her a large fortune. Mrs. Williams was not eager to see her daughter marry so young, but Patterson had offered to give the couple several valuable pieces of property and a cash gift of $50,000, so the mother agreed to the match.

Betsy wrote back furiously, repeating all her old arguments against an American marriage. In the weeks that followed, she talked at length upon the subject with her friends, and finally after a month, she wrote what she believed to be a more temperate letter:

> *I tried to give my son all my ideas and tastes, and, in the first weeks after hearing that he meant to marry an American woman, I was in despair. I think that I did my duty in trying to elevate his ideas above marrying in America, and you well know that I left nothing undone to effect this. I have considered now that it is unreasonable to expect him to place his happiness in the only things which can make me happy.... He has neither my pride, my ambition, nor my love of good company; therefore I no longer oppose his marriage.... As the woman has money, I shall not forbid a marriage which I never would have advised.*

While waiting for further word, Betsy learned through mutual acquaintances that Bo had written to his father and his Bonaparte relatives to announce his upcoming marriage as early as September. At first, she told herself that his letter to her must have been lost. Perhaps he had been mistaken about her itinerary and sent the news to the wrong city.

Then she received two letters from home, not from Bo as she had every right to expect, but from Edward and her father. Only then did she learn the full extent of the deception that had been practiced upon her. The wedding had already taken place; indeed, it occurred on the very day she received the original letter from her father announcing a "possible engagement." With his grandfather's collusion, her son had deliberately excluded her from this event in his life.

Betsy screamed when she realized what they had done and then sobbed for days. Princess Galitzin consoled her by reminding her of what she had already written home, that she could not force her son to desire the same things from life that she wanted.

"You don't understand! They have treated me as if I were a maniac or a wretch convicted of an infamous crime. Look at this copy of the letter I wrote after I learned of the engagement. I said I would accept the marriage. But how can I forgive treachery and deceit?"

After the initial storm of grief, Betsy took a hard look at her son's character and realized that she had been pushing him to fulfill her own dreams and had refused to listen when he said he had little taste for them. Bo's choice of an American wife and an American life was truly not surprising, but Betsy had thought more highly of their relationship than to imagine he could act in such a mean, dishonest fashion as to marry behind her back. Bitterly, she reflected that for all of her husband's faults, at least Jerome had been man enough to write his family to plead for their marriage.

Betsy found it impossible to write to Bo, who still had not sent her a line. Every time she tried to describe her hurt, she suffered a headache and nausea for days. Eventually, she calmed herself enough to write again to her father:

I have no right to oppose his living in the way he likes best. It is possible that your judgment and his are better than mine. I hope that they are. I tried to give him the ideas suitable to his rank in life; having failed in that, there remains only to let him choose his own course. A parent cannot make a silk purse of a sow's ear; and you found that you could never make a sow's ear of a silk purse.... When I first heard that my son could condescend to marry any one in Baltimore, I nearly went mad. Every one told me that it was quite impossible for me to make him like myself, and that, if he could endure the mode of life and the people in America, it was better to let him follow his own course than to break off a marriage where there was some money to be got.

In spite of her deep hurt, Betsy decided not to disinherit her son, which would violate her principles of how parents should act. Even so, her feelings about her duty to Bo changed. Now that he had married into money, she no longer felt obligated to sacrifice her own comfort for his, so she cut off his monthly allowance. She increased her spending to make use of her full income and gave up any thought of returning home.

The following spring, five months after his marriage, Bo wrote to her about some business having to do with her Baltimore property, and thus, at least a formal level of communication was restored between them. To Betsy's chagrin, her son never apologized or explained the clandestine manner of his marriage, so she kept their correspondence as brief and businesslike as possible.

During one of her extended stays with her friend Princess Galitzin, Betsy complained, "He is just like his father. My ex-husband was never able to acknowledge that he chose to betray his solemn vows to me. My sainted mother once told me that men often have difficulty owning up to the hurt they inflict upon those they love, but I find it hard to excuse such thoughtlessness."

"My dear." Princess Galitzin laid a hand upon Betsy's, which was resting on the tea table between them. "You are not listening to your better nature. You yourself told me that your son has never possessed your ambition nor your drive."

"No, he has not. Do you mean to say that excuses his weakness?"

Sitting back in her chair, the princess shook her head. She picked up the teapot and refreshed Betsy's cup. "No, but I think I can understand the situation from your son's point of view. Remember that I know young Jerome. I have often seen you together, and I am convinced that he loves you deeply. He has spent his entire life trying to please you, but I believe he hated the very thought of the life you had chosen for him."

"Then why did he not tell me so instead of shutting me out like a stranger?"

Prince Galitzin smiled at her fondly. "You are rather a force of nature when you set your heart upon something, you know."

Betsy frowned and dropped extra sugar in her tea to sweeten the bitter conversation. "So you are saying that it is my fault because he knew I would have trampled upon his expressed wishes. In short, you blame me for my son's disloyalty."

"No, my dear, I do not. I am asking you to see your son as he is. He could not endure the course you set for him, yet he could not bear to confront you and witness the pain of your disappointment. So he took the child's way out of acting without your knowledge."

Tears pooled in Betsy's eyes as she remembered all the times that her little boy had sworn he would take care of her and ease her difficulties. In her heart, she wanted desperately to believe that Bo still loved her. Was it possible that his fear of her temper could have led him to commit such a dishonorable act?

She sighed. "You may be right, but I need more time to recover from this blow. I cannot endure seeing my son again. As long as he refuses to apologize, I don't know if I ever shall."

The princess nodded and did not look surprised. "You will know when you are ready to reconcile. Keep your heart open, and it will tell you."

Betsy knew that her mother would have offered much the same advice, but that knowledge did little to salve her lacerated feelings. Bo had wounded her as deeply as ever her father or husband did. Not even when she learned a year after the marriage that Susan May had given her a grandson did Betsy's attitude soften. She was still enjoying herself in Europe, and she honestly did not care if she ever saw Baltimore again.

✍ EPILOGUE ✐.
JUNE 1870

S TANDING alone in the Bonaparte room of her son's Baltimore
mansion, Betsy sighed as she gazed at the miniature of her ex-
husband. "Oh, Jerome. Our son is dying. How I wish I did not
have to face this alone."

She glanced from the miniature in her hand to her favorite photograph of Bo, the one that showed his remarkable resemblance to Napoleon. Ever since Louis-Napoleon Bonaparte had restored the French
empire, Betsy's dearest ambition had been to see Bo or one of his sons
become emperor of France should the line of Napoleon III fail. Now
it seemed that her son, who had throat cancer at the age of sixty-five,
would die before his cousin.

So much loss. At her advanced age, Betsy had outlived her parents,
her ex-husband, and most of her siblings. If Bo should die too, how
would she summon the strength to go on?

When I see him, she thought, *I must make sure he knows that my love
for him has never wavered. If he must die, I want him to go in peace.*

"You can come up now," a man's voice broke into her thoughts.

Betsy turned to see Jerome standing in the doorway, as handsome
as ever with his dark hair and eyes. Gasping, she dropped the miniature and heard the glass break.

Then her nineteen-year-old grandson Charles stepped toward her.

"Grandmama? Are you all right?"

Placing one hand on her chest, Betsy exhaled and leaned against the table. "For a moment, you reminded me so much of your grandfather, I thought he had come back to life."

"I'm sorry I startled you. It was not my intention."

"That is quite all right." She held out her hand, and Charley came close so she could take his arm. "I was lost in my memories, you see."

"You always said that Jerome Jr. favored Grandpapa more than I do," he replied, referring to his much-older brother. "Are you sure you feel up to this after having such a fright?"

"Do not condescend to me. You may think I am a silly old woman, but I am a tougher bird than you imagine. I have something I must say to your father before it is too late."

"All right, Grandmama. But take the stairs slowly, OK?"

"Yes, yes, if you insist."

As they moved toward the doorway, Betsy glanced back and saw the miniature lying on the floor amid fragments of glass. "Your grandfather."

"Don't worry. I will take care of that later."

Turning her back on the shattered image of her husband, Betsy crossed the hall and then slowly ascended the staircase. She kept one hand on the banister and the other tucked into Charley's arm. As she climbed, she remembered how her father had used Bo's wedding to take revenge for the trouble her marriage caused him.

He could not have devised a more perfect way to express the resentment he had nursed for twenty-five years. It must have given him great satisfaction to usurp her role as parent so completely that he was able to convince Bo to shut her out of that event. At the time, Betsy thought that having taken his vengeance, her father would let her live in peace. But she had been wrong to assume that William Patterson's rancor could be appeased by a single act of retribution.

As she and Charley reached the second-floor landing, the old feeling of being choked by outrage seized Betsy, and she had trouble catching her breath.

"Grandmama, are you all right? Do you need a doctor?"

"No, no. Just let me rest a moment."

He led her to a sofa that sat against a wall not far from the top of the stairs. After easing her onto the seat, he leaned down with his hands braced on his knees. "Grandmama, truly, you look very distressed."

Betsy forced herself to smile. "All that afflicts me are bitter memories. If you would fetch me some water, I will rest a minute before I go in to see your father."

"Of course, but—are you sure you are well enough to be left alone?"

Gazing into her grandson's face, so very like his mother's, Betsy thought, *How young he is and how little he knows of the decades of loneliness I have had to endure.*

"You will be gone only a minute. I believe I shall survive."

As Charley walked away, glancing back over his shoulder, Betsy returned to her memories. After learning of her son's marriage, she had remained in Europe five more years, traveling among her favorite places and taking part in the social life she loved so well.

She had even had a last chance at love. In Florence, Betsy formed a friendship with a Russian diplomat named Prince Alexander Gorchakov. He was in his early thirties, thirteen years her junior, and had wavy dark brown hair, a full mustache, and a goatee—not as dashing as Jerome had been but handsome in his own way. With other women of their acquaintance, he flirted, but with Betsy he discussed politics and world events. For her part, she relished the stimulation of debate; no other man except Elbridge Gerry had ever treated her as an intellectual equal. However, after several years of correspondence and intimate conversations whenever they found themselves in the same city, the prince made it clear that he wanted more from Betsy than a meeting of the minds, and she—knowing that his noble family would never accept his marriage to a commoner or a woman past childbearing age—broke off the relationship rather than become his mistress. In the decades since, she had followed Gorchakov's career with tender admiration and pride. He had become one of the most influential men in Russia.

Finally, nearing the age of fifty, Betsy grew tired of wandering the cities of Europe. Her father wrote warning her of a pending financial crisis in the United States, so she used that excuse to return home and finally meet her daughter-in-law and four-year-old grandson. She found Jerome Jr. adorable and regretted having neglected him so long.

Although Betsy did her best to be cordial, Susan May never forgave her for her initial opposition to the marriage. It saddened Betsy that she was not welcome to live in her son's house, but she knew that trying to convince the young woman that the criticism had never been personal was a futile task. After all, she herself had never yielded to her mother's urging to forgive Jerome. Instead of continuing to try to win over her daughter-in-law, Betsy contented herself with being a doting grandmother to Jerome Jr. and much later to Charley, born twenty-one years after his brother. Her relationship with her son eventually grew warm again, although they never completely restored their old closeness.

In 1835, a year after she returned, William Patterson inflicted on Betsy one last grievous injury. When he died, his will revealed that he had deprived her of an equal share of his estate. He left stocks to his sons, his grandchildren, and even his illegitimate daughter Matilda, but not to Betsy. Nor did he bequeath her any money. All that he gave her were a few properties, including the house where she was born. Patterson also denied Betsy her equal share of her mother's settlement from Grandfather Spear, in defiance of Dorcas's wishes. More wounding, though, than the scant inheritance were the words Patterson wrote in his will:

> *The conduct of my daughter Betsy has through life been so disobedient that in no instance has she ever consulted my opinions or feelings; indeed, she has caused me more anxiety and trouble than all my other children put together, and her folly and misconduct have occasioned me a train of expense that first and last has cost me much money. Under such circumstances it would not be reasonable, just, or proper that she should inherit and participate in an equal proportion with my other children in an equal division of my estate.*

If Patterson's final intention on earth was to crush his daughter's spirit and force her at last into the broken submissiveness he thought appropriate for women, he nearly succeeded. He left instructions for his will to be published in the newspaper so that all of Baltimore would read his condemnation of Betsy. She was mortified.

Betsy was not the only person on whom William Patterson played a cruel joke at the end. He left $100 to Aunt Nancy, who by then was in financial difficulties, but only on the condition that she give up attending the sessions of Congress, a pastime he had never considered proper for a lady. Even more maliciously, he bequeathed a case of brandy to John, who was a drunkard. Yet knowing that others had been mocked in her father's will did little to alleviate Betsy's humiliation.

After the initial shock, Betsy mustered enough of her old spirit to fight back. She still had her marriage contract of 1803 in which her father had stipulated that he would leave her an equal share of his estate. She and her son consulted lawyers, including Roger B. Taney, who only a year later became the chief justice of the Supreme Court.

The lawyers found the will so extraordinary that they doubted Patterson's sanity, but they could not prove he was out of his right mind. As they explained to Betsy and her son, the legal situation was complicated. Although Patterson left no money to Betsy, he did leave a bequest to Bo—which, though sizable, was not as large as what he would have inherited through his mother if she had received her equal share. If Betsy succeeded in using the marriage contract to break the will, she would receive a larger inheritance, but Bo would lose his portion because the estate would be divided equally among Patterson's children.

Betsy's legal inquiries delayed the settlement of the estate, and the family reacted furiously. John, Joseph, Edward, and Henry lined up against her and tried to amass evidence that she deserved their father's censure. They searched Patterson's papers and took away his copy of the marriage contract, hoping that Betsy had lost hers. They gathered up the letters their father had received from Betsy and paid Aunt Nancy for the letters Betsy had sent her, so they could use their sister's correspondence against her. As a result of these schemes, Betsy's relationships with her aunt and four brothers were irrevocably broken.

Only George found the will unjust. He disagreed so strongly with the decision to exclude Betsy from sharing their mother's money that he signed over his portion to her. She wrote him her thanks and tried to enlist his support in the lawsuit, but when she realized that he did not want to become embroiled in his siblings' conflict, she did not push him.

The nastiness even affected Bo. Although he never confronted his mother directly, his correspondence to her lost its warmth as though he blamed her for being so imprudent as to lose his inheritance. Sadly, she noted that he never called her "dearest mama" anymore.

Finally, exhausted by the acrimony, Betsy gave up the lawsuit. She contented herself with the city properties her father left her and continued to live off the income from the investments she had tended so carefully since 1810.

The irony was that over time, her urban property grew in value more dramatically than the stock or country estates her brothers had inherited, so her estate was now worth well over a million dollars. In the end, her father benefitted her far more than he had intended. But nothing could heal the knowledge that William Patterson had deliberately held her up to public derision. Betsy became almost a recluse, living in a boarding house, pouring over the mementoes of her past, and taking pride in her grandsons, but rarely traveling or receiving guests. She took little interest in the affairs of the United States, and not even the cataclysm of the Civil War and its destructive effect on Maryland stirred her from indifference.

In the 1840s, Betsy did receive one foreign visitor who brought her some consolation. Marshal Henri-Gatien Bertrand, who had been with Napoleon in exile, came to Baltimore to say that Napoleon had admired her talents to the end and regretted the shadow he had thrown upon her life. The former emperor was grateful that she always praised him, saying, "Those I have wronged have forgiven me; those I have loaded with kindness have forsaken me."

Sighing at the memory, Betsy glanced up to see Charley coming down the hallway, holding a glass of water. "How are you now?" he asked.

"I am well. It was merely an attack of an old pain, but it has passed."

She drank the water and then rose. Taking Charley's arm, she allowed him to lead her down the corridor as slowly as he thought prudent. As they walked, she thought of her older grandson, who bore an uncanny resemblance to his grandfather Jerome and had inherited the military interests of his great-uncle Napoleon. He was serving as a colonel in the French Army. "It is a pity Jerome Jr. cannot be here."

"Grandmama, he cannot leave France right now. They say tension is brewing with Prussia."

"Yes, yes, I know." She refrained from reminding him that she had been following French politics since decades before his birth. "But surely, as cousin to the emperor, Jerome could take leave during a family crisis."

"Papa forbade us to send him a wire. He believes he will recover."

She stopped and tilted her head to look up at him. "Do you think he will?"

Charley shook his head gravely and opened the master-bedroom door.

Bo was lying in the massive mahogany four-poster with his wife sitting beside him, one hand laid upon his chest. As Betsy entered, Susan May stood. "I will leave you alone."

"No need, my dear," Betsy said. "I have nothing to say to my son that you cannot hear."

Charley carried the chair from his mother's dressing table to the side of the bed and helped Betsy into it. Then he and Susan May withdrew to a far corner.

"Mama," Bo said in a harsh whisper that hurt Betsy's heart. She grasped his hand. They gazed at each other a long moment and then he whispered, "Forgive me."

"Oh, my dear boy. I forgave you long ago."

For an instant, his eyes shifted to his wife across the room and then he refocused on Betsy's face. "Understand—don't—regret my choice."

"Nor should you," Betsy said firmly, speaking loudly enough for her daughter-in-law to hear. "Susan May has been an excellent wife and mother."

Bo winced, whether from emotional or physical pain Betsy could not tell. Then he spoke again in the same agonized whisper, "Sorry—excluded you."

"I blame that on your grandfather," Betsy said, unable to restrain her anger even though she knew how much Bo had loved her father. "That bad old man wanted to pay me back for marrying against his wishes."

Shaking his head, Bo whispered, "No. My cowardice."

"Don't think of it anymore."

Despite her reassurance, Bo retained a troubled expression. After a moment, he released a shuddering sigh. "Are you sorry—married Father?"

"How could I be when he gave me such a fine son as you? You have always been my shining prince."

Closing his eyes, Bo grew so still that Betsy thought he had fallen asleep. After a minute, though, he shook his head. "No. Denied me."

Betsy patted his hand, knowing exactly what he meant. After Bo's cousin Louis-Napoleon, the son of Louis Bonaparte and Hortense, became Emperor Napoleon III, he had restored Bo's French citizenship and made it legal for him to use the Bonaparte name in France. Bo had not, however, been included in the imperial line of succession, so he and Betsy had filed suit in the French courts after Jerome died. In spite of all the documentation they were able to produce—the original marriage contract, the love letters from Jerome to Betsy, and years of correspondence from the Bonapartes greeting Bo as dear son, grandson, brother, nephew, and cousin—the ruling went against them.

"Never mind that now. We did our best. Refusing to make you an heir was their mistake, which they will regret eternally if Plon-Plon ever becomes emperor." In spite of his pain, Bo smiled at the disparaging nickname for his universally disliked half-brother. "Besides, I hope that Jerome Jr.'s obvious worth and service to France may eventually induce the imperial family to reverse their decision in his favor."

Shaking his head, Bo said, "You never change."

"I set my feet upon a certain course the day I met your father, and I have never deviated from it."

Sighing, Bo closed his eyes. Knowing that this might very well be their last meeting, Betsy wanted to sit with him for hours, but she could tell from the shadows beneath his eyes and the lines etched by his mouth that he was exhausted. Reluctantly, she rose. "I will let you rest."

Bo stirred and met her gaze. "I love you, dearest Mama."

"I love you too, my boy."

Betsy smoothed back his hair, taking some slight comfort in the fact that he still wore the upswept hairstyle she had given him as a boy, and then she kissed his forehead in a gesture of farewell. As Charley led her from the bed, her daughter-in-law stepped in front of her. Although Susan May's face held no warmth, she whispered, "Thank you," and Betsy felt they had made peace at last.

Out in the hall, Betsy gave way to tears and Charley held her close.

"Don't cry, Grandmama. Papa loves you."

Pulling away, Betsy nodded and wiped her eyes. "Thank you for try-ing to comfort your poor old grandmother. You are exceptionally adult for your years. At your age, your grandfather thought of nothing but amusement."

"You and Grandpapa must have made quite a pair." Charley tucked her hand in his arm again. "I wish I could have seen you when you were young and taking society by storm."

"We were as thoughtless and vain as peacocks." Thinking of her son lying on his deathbed, Betsy reflected how strange it was that, with herself and Jerome as parents, Bo should have turned out to be such an unambitious man. He had wanted nothing more than a quiet life on his country estate, raising his sons and breeding his horses. "A pair of peacocks who somehow gave birth to a house sparrow."

"Father is a good fellow, and he is proud of being a Bonaparte even if he did not want to live in Europe." Charley's voice cracked. "I am going to miss him dreadfully."

Pressing herself tightly against his arm, Betsy murmured, "We will miss him together."

Charley drove her to Mrs. Jenkins's boarding house and helped her up to her rooms, where he settled her into the rocking chair he had given her on her last birthday. Then Betsy asked him to drag the trunk that held her most precious mementos so that it stood next to her. She did not open it right away.

Remembering a long ago ball in Florence when Gorchakov had watched with thinly masked jealously while she danced with the French writer Lamartine, Betsy murmured, "Once I had everything but money. Now money is all I have left."

"Grandmama, that isn't true." Charley squatted before her and took her hands. "You have Jerome Jr. and you have me. We will always love you."

"Thank you, my boy," she murmured, grateful for the reassurance and yet not entirely satisfied. How could she tell this nineteen-year-old boy, who knew her only as a grandmother, that she had always longed for more than a merely domestic existence?

Charley rose. "Shall I come back tomorrow to fetch you for an-other visit?"

Betsy shook her head. "No, your father and I have said what we needed to say to one another. To see him again would only upset us both needlessly."

"If you say so, Grandmama. But I shall look in on you just the same."

After he left, Betsy opened her trunk. On the very top, wrapped in tissue paper, was the dress in which she had been married. Directly beneath it lay Jerome's purple wedding coat. Fingering the plush velvet, she thought back to the first time she danced with him and the way her necklace had caught on his uniform. "Do you see, *chère mademoiselle?*" he had whispered. "Fate has brought us together, and we are destined never to part."

Betsy closed her eyes, and almost immediately, her imagination carried her to another place, to Napoleonic France at the height of the emperor's power. In her vision, she was still young and beautiful, and her husband was at her side. Together they crossed the parquet floor of an imposing reception room decorated with red draperies, neoclassical paintings, and gilt moldings. Crowds of courtiers watched their progress, but she and Jerome kept their gaze fixed straight ahead on a gilded throne with a round back that held a uniformed man who, although of no great physical height, towered over all of Europe by virtue of his genius. When they reached the dais on which he sat, his grey eyes drilled into Betsy. Jerome introduced her, and she made a deep curtsy. Napoleon rose and, taking her by the hand, raised her up and kissed her on each cheek.

THE AMBITIOUS MADAME
BONAPARTE

✍ ACKNOWLEDGMENTS ✍

I wish to thank the Maryland Historical Society for preserving the Elizabeth Patterson Bonaparte papers and for giving me permission to quote from them. I am grateful to the staff of Homewood House Museum on the campus of Johns Hopkins University in Baltimore and to the guides at Fort McHenry for historic information that helped shape this novel.

My intrepid team of readers made many helpful suggestions. My gratitude goes to Ginni Davis, Susan Eisenhammer, Kate Elledge, Steve Hillis, Deb Modde, Lise Nauman, and Erika Nicketakis. I also want to thank Sid Allen-Simpson, Rich Elliot, Richard Halstead, and Chris Johnson for useful and timely advice. Kathryn Ariano provided an invaluable service as my Baltimore-based research assistant.

I owe very special thanks to the wonderful people at Amika Press: to Jay Amberg for giving me a chance to bring this story to completion, to John Manos for insightful editorial suggestions, and to Sarah Koz for creative design work.

Last but not least, I want to thank my husband, Michael Chatlien, for being a reader, critic, cheerleader, and travel companion on the journey of discovery that was this novel.

✑ BIBLIOGRAPHY ✑

Biographies of Betsy, Jerome, and Bo

Atteridge, A. Hilliard. *Napoleon's Brothers.* London: Methuen & Co, 1909.

Bourguignon-Frasseto, Claude. *Betsy Bonaparte: The Belle of Baltimore.* 1988. Baltimore: Maryland Historical Society, 2003.

Burn, Helen Jean. *Betsy Bonaparte.* Baltimore: Maryland Historical Society, 2010.

Didier, Eugene L. "An American Bonaparte." *The International Review.* Volume 11. July 1881.

Didier, Eugene L. *The Life and Letters of Madame Bonaparte.* New York: Scribner's, 1879.

Lewis, Charlene M. Boyer. *Elizabeth Patterson Bonaparte: An American Aristocrat in the Early Republic.* Philadelphia: U of Pennsylvania P, 2012

Mitchell, S. *A Family Lawsuit: The Story of Elisabeth Patterson and Jérôme Bonaparte.* New York: Farrar, Straus, & Cudahy, 1958.

Saffell, W.T.R. *The Bonaparte-Patterson Marriage in 1803 and the Secret Correspondence on the Subject Never Before Made Public.* Philadelphia: privately published, 1873.

Sergeant, Philip W. *The Burlesque Napoleon.* London: T. Werner Laurie, 1905.

Histories, Memoirs, and Other Resources

Adams, Henry. *History of the United States in 1800.* Library of America, Book 31. New York: Library of America, 1986.

Arthur, Catherine Rogers and Cindy Kelly. *Homewood House.* Baltimore: Johns Hopkins UP, 2004.

Beirne, Francis. F. *The Amiable Baltimoreans.* 1951. Baltimore: Johns Hopkins UP, 1984.

Callcott, Margaret Law, editor. *Mistress of Riversdale: The Plantation Letters of Rosalie Stier Calvert 1795–1821.* Baltimore: Johns Hopkins UP, 1991.

Childs, Frances Sergeant. *French Refugee Life in the United States 1790–1800: An American Chapter of the French Revolution.* Baltimore: Johns Hopkins P, 1940.

Côté, Richard N. *Strength and Honor: The Life of Dolley Madison.* Mount Pleasant, SC: Corinthian, 2005.

Cronin, Vincent. *Napoleon.* 1971. London: Harpercollins, 1994.

Dungan, Nicholas. *Gallatin: America's Swiss Founding Father.* New York: New York UP, 2010.

Gallatin, James. *The Diary of James Gallatin, Secretary to Albert Gallatin: A Great Peace Maker: 1813–1827.* New York: Scribners, 1916.

Hayward, Mary Ellen and Frank R. Shivers, Jr. *The Architecture of Baltimore: An Illustrated History.* Baltimore: Johns Hopkins UP, 2004.

La Rochefoucauld, Francois Duc de. Translated by J.W. Willis Bund and J. Hain Friswell. *Reflections; or Sentences and Moral Maxims.* London: Simpson Low, Son, and Marston, 1871.

Lay, K. Edward. *The Architecture of Jefferson Country: Charlottesville and Albemarle County, Virginia.* Richmond: UP of Virginia, 2000.

LeFever, Gregory. "Men's Pocketbooks." *Early American Life.* December 2007.

Lord, Walter. *The Dawn's Early Light.* 1972. Baltimore: Johns Hopkins UP, 1994.

Maude, John. *Visit to the Falls of Niagara in 1800.* London: Longman, Rees, Orme, Brown, & Green, 1800.

Monroe, James. *The Writings of James Monroe, Volume V, 1807-1816.* Edited by Stanislaus Murray Hamilton. New York: Putnam, 1901.

Morgan, Sydney. *Lady Morgan's Memoirs: Autobiography, Diaries, and Correspondence.* London: Allen & Co., 1862.

Parton, James. *Daughters of Genius.* Philadelphia: Hubbard Brothers. 1886.

Perkins, Mary Mendenhall. "The Marble Bath of Jerome Napoleon." *Art and Achaeology.* Volume 12. July 1921

Rath, Molly. "You Never Know What Will Turn up Among the Collectibles at the Maryland Historical Society." *Baltimore Sun.* November 20, 1994.

Reynolds, William. *A Brief History of the First Presbyterian Church of Baltimore.* Baltimore: Session of the First Presbyterian Church, 1913.

Wake, Jehanne. *Sisters of Fortune: America's Caton Sisters at Home and Abroad.* New York: Touchstone, 2010.

Wass, Ann Buermann and Michelle Webb Fandrich. *Clothing Through American History: The Federal Era Through Antebellum, 1786–1860.* Santa Barbara, CA: Greenwood, 2010.

XX

Jerome Bonaparte to Elizabeth Patterson Bonaparte. Letters of October 4, 1805; October 7, 1805; October 16, 1805. Elizabeth Patterson Bonaparte Papers. MS 143. H. Furlong Baldwin Library. Maryland Historical Society. [Hereinafter, MdHS]

XXI

Jerome Bonaparte to Elizabeth Patterson Bonaparte. Letters of May 23, 1806; June 20, 1806; July 17, 1806. Elizabeth Patterson Bonaparte Papers. MS 143. MdHS.

XXIII

Elizabeth Patterson Bonaparte to Robert Gilmor, Jr. September 30, 1807. Didier. 40.

Anna Kuhn to Elizabeth Patterson Bonaparte. November 24, 1807. Elizabeth Patterson Bonaparte Papers. MS 142. MdHS.

XXIV

Jerome Bonaparte to Elizabeth Patterson Bonaparte. Letters of May 15, 1808; November 22, 1808. Elizabeth Patterson Bonaparte Papers. MS 143. MdHS.

James Monroe to Elizabeth Patterson Bonaparte. *The Writings of James Monroe, Volume V, 1807–1816.* Edited by Stanislaus Murray Hamilton. New York: Putnam, 1901.

XXV

Napoleon Bonaparte to M. de Champagny. In *The Living Age.* Volume 215. Boston: The Living Age Company. 1897.

XXVII

Jerome Bonaparte to Elizabeth Patterson Bonaparte, February 20, 1812. Sergeant. 111–112.

Jerome Bonaparte to Jerome Napoleon Bonaparte. February 20, 1812. Elizabeth Patterson Bonaparte Papers. MS 143. MdHS.

XXX

Jerome Napoleon Bonaparte to Elizabeth Patterson Bonaparte. March 30, 1815. Elizabeth Patterson Bonaparte Papers. MS 144. MdHS.

XXXI

Elizabeth Patterson Bonaparte to William Patterson. September 2, 1815. Didier. 42–45.

William Patterson to Elizabeth Patterson Bonaparte. November 16, 1815. Didier. 50–51.

XXXIII

Elizabeth Patterson Bonaparte to Pauline Bonaparte. March 25, 1820. Didier. 59–60.

Elizabeth Patterson Bonaparte to William Patterson. January 29–30, 1822. Didier. 90.

Elizabeth Patterson Bonaparte to Jerome Napoleon Bonaparte. March 8, 1821. Didier. 96.

XXXIV

Elizabeth Patterson Bonaparte to Lady Morgan, beginning, "I love him so entirely...." Didier. 118.

Elizabeth Patterson Bonaparte to William Patterson. February 21, 1826. Didier. 176–177.

Elizabeth Patterson Bonaparte to William Patterson. December 4, 1829. Didier. 219.

Elizabeth Patterson Bonaparte to William Patterson. December 21, 1829. Didier. 221.

EPILOGUE

Last Will and Testament of William Patterson. In James Parton. *Daughters of Genius.* Philadelphia: Hubbard Brothers. 1886. 515–516.

1   Had you ever heard of any of these people before reading this book? Were you surprised to learn that there were American Bonapartes?

2   What role does Odette's prophecy play in the story? Do you think Betsy would have made the same choices if she hadn't received it?

3   What was Betsy's view of her mother's life? How did her view of Dorcas's circumstances shape her own decisions?

4   Betsy often says that fate brought her and Jerome together. Do you agree, or was that viewpoint just an excuse for her decisions?

5   How did you feel about Jerome's character? Did your feelings about him change over the course of the book?

6   If Betsy had been reunited with Jerome, do you think they would have had a happy marriage? What do you think would have happened, and why?

7   For most of the story, Betsy is torn between the desire to win her father's approval and the desire to break free of his domination. What events reveal this inner conflict?

8   What do you think was Betsy's main reason—spoken or unspoken—for never marrying again?

9   What were Betsy's strengths and weaknesses as a mother?

10   Why did Bo exclude Betsy from his marriage? How did you feel about the way he handled it?

11   Was Betsy as cruel to Susan May as Napoleon was to Betsy? Explain.

12   Betsy's friend Eliza urges her to use her talents to achieve a meaningful life. In what ways did Betsy use her talents, and in what ways did she fail to do so? Did her failures stem more from her character or from society's limits on women?

13   Whom do you blame most for the disappointments in Betsy's life: Jerome, Napoleon, William Patterson, or Betsy herself?

14   Several times, Betsy says she does not intend to deviate from the course she set for her life, yet at times, she asks herself, "What could I have done differently?" If she were to ask you that question, how would you answer?

✐ ABOUT THE AUTHOR ✑

RUTH HULL CHATLIEN has been a writer and editor of educational materials for twenty-five years. Her speciality is U.S. and world history. She
is the author of *Modern American Indian Leaders* and has published
several short stories and poems in literary magazines. *The Ambitious
Madame Bonaparte* is her first published novel.

She lives in northeastern Illinois with her husband, Michael, and a
very pampered dog named Smokey. When she's not writing, she can usually be found gardening, knitting, drawing, painting, or watching football.

✑ THE TYPE ✑.

The Ambitious Madame Bonaparte is set in Ronaldson, one of the first truly unique American text typefaces. It dates back to 1884, when expert punchcutter Alexander Kay designed and cut it for the MacKellar, Smiths & Jordan type foundry in Philadelphia, which later became the main branch of American Type Founders.

Ronaldson is famous for its clarity and legibility, as well as its pronounced and confident capitals. Shortly after its release, it became the best-selling and most-read text typeface of the nineteenth century, and continued as such until the early 1920s.

Work on the Ronaldson family of digital fonts began May 2006 and finished February 2008. Lovingly redrawn by Rebecca Alaccari and Patrick Griffin of Canada Type, this American beauty couldn't have been brought back to life without the help of Simone Chisena, Stephen O. Saxe, Philippe Chaurize, and Rebecca Davis. Amika Press is proud to utilize it for the first time in this book.

11107170R00272

Made in the USA
San Bernardino, CA
07 May 2014